CROSSROADS OF DESIRE

Rachel—She and Jed Gill played together as children—until the act of love made them man and woman. But Rachel vanished from Jed's life in a night of Indian attack, and he did not want even to imagine what had happened to her.

Redbud—A beautiful Indian girl on the very brink of womanhood, and the sister of the brave who made Jed his blood brother. She was forbidden to Jed—but was as irresistible to him as he was to her.

In a struggle that swept Colonial America from the settlements of New England to the battlements of Quebec, the fate of the continent hung in perilous balance. In captivity to an Indian tribe, torn between this new life and his old, Jed Gill was at a crossroads of his own. . . .

THE BLOODBORN

Americans at War #1

Great Reading from SIGNET

☐ **MUSIC FOR CHAMELEONS by Truman Capote.**
(#E9934—$3.50)*
☐ **FORGOTTEN IMPULSES by Todd Walton.** (#E9802—$2.75)*
☐ **FEELING GOOD by David D. Burns, M.D.** (#E9804—$3.95)
☐ **SUMMER GIRL by Caroline Crane.** (#E9806—$2.50)*
☐ **CHILDMARE by A. G. Scott.** (#E9807—$2.25)†
☐ **RETURN TO SENDER by Sandy Hutson.** (#E9808—$2.50)*
☐ **TWO FOR THE PRICE OF ONE by Tony Kenrick.**
(#E9809—$2.50)*
☐ **BITTERSWEET by Susan Strasberg.** (#E9760—$3.50)*
☐ **GLITTER AND ASH by Dennis Smith.** (#E9761—$2.95)*
☐ **THE EDUCATION OF DON JUAN by Robin Hardy.**
(#E9764—$3.50)*
☐ **LADYCAT by Nancy Greenwald.** (#E9762—$2.75)*
☐ **HAWK OF MAY by Gillian Bradshaw.** (#E9765—$2.75)*
☐ **GAMEMAKER by David Cohter.** (#E9766—$2.50)*
☐ **CUBAN DEATH-LIFT (3rd in the MacMorgan series) by Randy Striker.**
(#J9768—$1.95)*
☐ **"DEAR ONCE" by Zelda Popkin.** (#E9769—$2.50)
☐ **THE OTHER ANNE FLETCHER by Susanne Jaffe.**
(#E9805—$2.75)

* Price slightly higher in Canada
† Not available in Canada

Buy them at your local bookstore or use this convenient coupon for ordering.

THE NEW AMERICAN LIBRARY, INC.,
P.O. Box 999, Bergenfield, New Jersey 07621

Please send me the SIGNET BOOKS I have checked above. I am enclosing
$_____ (please add 50¢ to this order to cover postage and handling).
Send check or money order—no cash or C.O.D.'s. Prices and numbers are
subject to change without notice.

Name _____

Address _____

City_____ State_____ Zip Code_____
Allow 4-6 weeks for delivery.
This offer is subject to withdrawal without notice.

THE BLOODBORN

(Americans at War #1)

By
Robert Leckie

A SIGNET BOOK
NEW AMERICAN LIBRARY
TIMES MIRROR

To my brother-in-law,
Dr. Louis L. Salerno,
for his many kindnesses
to my parents

Author's Note

This novel contains numerous historical personages lesser known than, say, George Washington or the Marquis de Montcalm. To identify them for the reader, an alphabetical listing of all real characters has been provided at the end of the book.

Part I

King William's War

1

Although the village of Schenectady lay under a thick mantle of snow, and a cold biting wind howled around and inside its white-plastered wooden palisade, the council room was stiflingly hot. About fifty Dutch householders who had crowded into the chamber upon the invitation of Magistrate Clarke had quickly thrown off their blanket coats. Yet, they were perspiring, the warmth of their bodies and the blast of heat flowing from an oak-log fire in a huge fireplace in the center of the side wall combining to make the room almost suffocating. Magistrate Clarke, seated at the table in front of them, had done little to cool them off when he announced that England was again at war with France.

"Py Godt," a red-faced, bald-headed, sweating householder shouted, rising to his feet, "King Villiam's var iss King Villiam's var—nod mine!"

Cries of approval arose from the Dutch. They stomped their feet and knocked their pipes against their benches.

"He iss right!" one of them yelled. "Peter Vrabel iss right! Vy should ve fight the Vrench?"

Jonathan Clarke stared sourly through the blue pipe smoke at the sturdy, stolid men seated before him. Twenty-six years! he thought wryly—the colony of New York has been English

3

since 1664, and these damn Dutchmen still act as though it belongs to Holland.

"Good householders," he said patiently, "King William is your sovereign. You must fight his enemies."

Vrabel waved his pipe excitedly. "You mean ve iss going to invade Ganada?"

Clarke shook his head. "No. I mean the French are coming here. The Mohawks have informed Albany that a war party has set out from Montreal. Canadians and Indians. Maybe three hundred of them."

The magistrate had expected his words to produce a shocked silence. Instead, he was momentarily stunned by an outburst of mocking laughter.

"Here?" Vrabel repeated, shouting above the outcry. "*Schenectady?* Dis leedle blace? Vat for dey vant here ven dey can gapture Albany? Den dey can go down der Hudson und take New York!" He grimaced and shook his round bald head in open contempt.

"Hey, Peter," one of the householders cried, "maybe dey vants your vife"—and the laughter began again.

Clarke waited for it to subside. He was a man of courage, steadfastly loyal to the English government in Albany. He knew that these stubborn villagers resented this. Only a year before, he had outfaced them when they sided with the rebel Jacob Leisler, even after they had threatened to kill him. He wondered if Vrabel and his friends weren't being stubborn just to pay him back for supporting the Albany convention. When the council room had become quiet again, he stared hard at Vrabel and said: "They aren't strong enough to take Albany, and they're certainly not strong enough to capture it and then attack New York. But they are strong enough to massacre all of you." He paused dramatically. "Yourselves, your women, and your children . . ." Clarke turned to the tall young officer of Connecticut militia seated next to him. "How many men do you have, Lieutenant Gill?"

Benjamin Gill started. His mind had been upon his wife, pregnant with their first child. Her time was near and he was wondering if he should set off that night for Albany to fetch Dr. Redmond. "N-nine, Sir," he replied, stuttering slightly in embarrassment. Clarke swung on Vrabel and the other Dutchmen, who were eyeing him dubiously. "Do you see?" he pleaded. "Nine men and one officer—to stop three hundred bloodthirsty Canadians and Indians. Can't you see you're in mortal danger?"

They shook their heads doggedly, and Vrabel spoke for all of them when he muttered, "Dey von't come here. Ve is so far away from zivilization dey don't even know ve iss alive."

"My God, men!" Clarke cried, his voice rising in dismay. "You must arm yourselves! Prepare for the worst! It could come any moment. Even tonight!" There was no reply, and Clarke began to plead with them. "Won't you at least close your gates and post sentinels?"

Again they shook their heads. "Dey von't come here," Vrabel repeated, pointing toward the door and the wind whistling outside. "Dere iss anudder storm becomink. Dere is already too much snow. Dey vould die in der forest."

Murmurs of assent followed Vrabel's words. Some of the householders began reaching for their coats. Clarke got to his feet, his gray eyes cold with suppressed rage. "All right, then," he said bitterly, "let the blood of your own be on your own heads."

Their faces sullen, scowling at the magistrate's words, the Dutchmen got to their feet. They knocked out their clay pipes, grinding the smoldering tobacco into the beaten earthen floor. One of them broke up the fire. Then, putting on their coats, grumbling, they followed Vrabel out the door.

Clarke watched them go, sighing wearily. He pulled out a large brass pocket watch and said, "I've got to be going if I'm going to be in Albany before dark."

Lieutenant Gill glanced up eagerly, but then his face darkened. "Don't you think it's too late?" he said. "Not at all," Clarke replied. "It's only fifteen miles, and my horse knows the way." Lieutenant Gill's face flushed hopefully again. "Oh, Sir," he cried, "would you be kind enough to stop in at Dr. Redmond's? My . . . my wife is near her time. It . . . it may be tomorrow . . ."

"Certainly," Clarke said, putting a reassuring hand on the flustered young man's shoulder. "I'll see him first thing." He drew on his greatcoat and put on a round beaver hat. Snatching a musket leaning against the table, he made for the door. "I hope it's a boy," he said with a grin, and went outside to mount his gently neighing horse.

Clarke nodded at the group of householders as he trotted past the open Mohawk Gate. They bobbed their heads stiffly in reply, watching him descend slowly to the meadow before beginning to canter. Two small boys engaged in building snowmen to either side of the gate finished their work by pushing charred wood coals into the faces to make eyes and noses. Then they stuck turkey feathers into the heads for bonnets. Laughing, they began to pelt each other with snowballs.

Peter Vrabel swung around and strode toward the snowmen. "Sentinels!" he exclaimed resentfully. He seized two lengths of sapling from a pile of kindling lying against the palisade and thrust them down the sides of the snowmen. "Now ve iss armed, *Mynheer* Magistrate," he snapped contemptuously. "Dere's your sentinels!"

Benjamin Gill did not smile when he saw the snow sentinels. "Damn dumb Dutchmen," he muttered aloud angrily. "Do they think Frontenac is joking?" Gill had heard from Magistrate Clarke that morning that the Count Frontenac, the mortal enemy of the English in northeastern America, had returned to Canada as its governor and military commander. "He'll do everything he can to hurt us," Clarke had said, and then, vehemently, "and to help that goddamn garlicky mouser of a Louis the Fourteenth put Shitty Jimmy Stuart back on the English throne." The news had alarmed Gill, and now, turning up the collar of his greatcoat against the wind and beginning to stride rapidly toward the widow Oostdyck's cabin, where his wife, Abigail, lived, he decided not to tell Abby about it.

Abigail Gill looked up in surprise from her knitting when her husband entered, stomping the snow from his boots. "I thought you were going to the blockhouse." "I am," he said, "but I thought I'd look in on you first." He gazed with concern at his wife's drawn mouth and noticed that her protruding stomach beneath the homespun dress seemed lower. She nodded, and he tried to smile. "Don't worry, hon, I think we'll have the doctor here tomorrow—if the storm lets up." Her eyes brightened, and he said: "The magistrate said he'd tell Doc Redmond."

"Oh, Benjy, that's wonderful! Mrs. Oostdyck just stepped out to fetch Mrs. Zuke, but now I won't need her. I'll feel so much safer with a doctor than a midwife." She glanced at the stove and moved as though to go there. "How about some corn mush, Benjy? Mrs. Oostdyck just boiled a new batch."

"Too early," Lieutenant Gill said, putting up the collar of his greatcoat again. "I'll be back in an hour for supper. Then I'll drop in on you later in the evening." He bent over her and kissed her on the cheek. "Almost finished?" he said, pointing to the knitting. She held up the little woolen shirt in her lap. "Pretty roomy," Benjamin said. "What if it's a girl?" Abigail shook her head. "I know it's going to be a boy." Gill frowned, thinking again of Frontenac and the war party. "I wish I'd made you stay back in Albany like I should have."

"I know, but the Mohawk woods are so beautiful in the fall. Besides, we never expected it this soon. You said yourself I could go back home the end of October. It's really Dr. Redmond's fault."

"Well, you stay off your feet," Benjamin said, turning to go out the door. Walking to the blockhouse, he noticed that the snow was falling thicker and the wind was rising. Who'd be crazy enough to try anything on a night like this? he thought. But Vrabel was right. Much as he distrusted that pop-eyed troublemaker, the French would hit Albany. Who wants a little good-for-nothing village like Schenectady?

It was warm inside the blockhouse. Blue-and-orange flame leaped high from a roaring fire. Gill saw with approval that the four fireports were manned, and that the remaining five militiamen were busy scouring their muskets and making shot. "Double the issue of ammunition tonight," he said to his sergeant. "Albany says the French have a war party out."

The sergeant laughed aloud. "In this weather? My Jesus, sir, you couldn't even find Boston in snow like this."

"Maybe so. But I still want an all-night watch. Three men to a watch, four on and four off."

"Yes, Sir."

Gill nodded and clumped on the stairs to the tiny room that served as his office and sleeping quarters. That night, as he lay fully clothed on his straw pallet beneath his worn military blanket, he wondered why he was so warm—until he realized that the men on watch were keeping the fire going. Before he dropped off to sleep he thought again of Frontenac. But even in his best days that old warhorse wouldn't try a night like this. And Clarke had said the count was at least seventy.

Louis de Buade, the Count de Frontenac, was indeed in his

seventieth year, but still so full of fire and zeal that King Louis XIV of France did not hesitate in sending for him, once he had decided to begin what history was to call the War of the Grand Alliance.

"We shall soon be at war with William of England," the king said.

Frontenac bowed graciously. As usual, the diminutive count with the aristocratic features and piercing eyes was beautifully dressed. He wore a honey-colored waistcoat with pale blue facings on the lapels, white silk breeches, a white shirt with blue ruffles and white high-heel shoes. His powdered wig was also white. The king, though richly clothed in brocaded brown, perhaps to match his long brown wig, seemed drab in contrast. Yet, this was Louis, the Sun King, an absolute monarch since his youth; and his glance was not only piercing but also imperious—the dark brown eyes above the long nose flashing as he spoke.

"*King* William," he repeated in disdain. "How does he dare! He is but a prince. A usurper. A pederast and a Protestant. A patricide, if you will. His own father-in-law, and he steals his crown." Louis coughed, and Frontenac detected a faint odor of garlic issuing from the throne. "Well, Frontenac, we shall remove him and put my Catholic friend James back where he belongs."

Frontenac bowed again. "Indeed, Sire."

"This is why we are sending you back to Canada. And it is our pleasure that you should know that all the charges made against you are without foundation." The king motioned to a secretary standing near, who handed him a roll of parchment. "You will return to Canada and execute this plan which we have approved."

Frontenac took the proffered document with a bow. "It is again an honor to serve you, most gracious Majesty. I shall do as you desire," he continued with his customary confidence. "Your command I take as the command of God in heaven."

The king nodded in approval, and Frontenac withdrew.

Studying the king's plan as he journeyed by coach to the port of Rochelle, Frontenac saw at once that, if successful, it would make Louis the virtual master of the New World. Under it, Frontenac was to organize a force of about sixteen hundred men to sail down the lake-and-river chain from

Montreal to capture Albany. Then he was to advance down the Hudson to attack New York City from the landward side while French warships invested the port from the harbor. With the English defeated, the feared and hated Iroquois, deprived of English arms and aid, would be at the mercy of the French. Louis would then possess a warm-water port to give him year-round access to Canada; the English colonies would be cut in two and New England left naked to future conquest; and the lucrative fur trade with the western Indians would become a French monopoly.

Thus, the audacious old count sailed for Quebec full of enthusiasm; but when he arrived below the city on the cliff nearly three months later, even his valiant heart was dejected. Contrary winds had wrecked the plan. It was late fall, and the iron Canadian winter was barely a month away. No time even to organize the expedition, let alone to undertake it, before the lake-and-river chain became frozen and impassable to large bodies of men. Moreover, the Iroquois had just massacred the inhabitants of the town of Lichine, and Frontenac found the colony fearful and in despair. Still determined to serve his sovereign, he organized three war parties: one at Quebec to harry Maine, another at Three Rivers to ravage the borders of New Hampshire, and a third at Montreal to seize Albany. The Montreal party was to leave first, and Frontenac summoned the commander, Jacques Le Moyne de Sainte-Helene, to his presence.

"We need a victory," the count said. Again, he was immaculately clad, a symphony in lace and silk of white and green. "The colony is in despair," he continued. "The people are discouraged. We need to punish the English to raise their spirits." Sainte-Helene nodded silently, the buckskin shirt and leggings which he wore contrasting with Frontenac's finery. It was as though two worlds—the New France of the trackless forests and uncharted streams, and the Old France of the minuet and the *philosophe*—were confronting one another. "When you have taken Albany, Monsieur, you will hold the town until the spring, when I shall come to join you to take New York City."

"Yes, your Excellency," Sainte-Helene replied, bowing—but not quickly enough to prevent the shrewd old count from detecting the look of apprehension in his eyes.

"You do not like it, Monsieur?" Frontenac asked sharply.

"It is a pretty plan, Excellency, but . . ."

"But what?"

"The Great Mohawk of the Saut has told me that his relations among the Iroquois say that Albany is very strong. Two hundred soldiers. Many of them English regulars." He shrugged. "You know that I am not afraid, Excellency, but with less than three hundred men . . . against a fortified town . . . in the dead of winter . . ." He paused, drawing himself erect. "We shall probably be starving by the time we get there, but if it is your wish . . ."

Frontenac lifted his hand in irritation, the lace cuff flapping. "I understand," he snapped, rising from his desk and going to a captured map of New York hanging on the wall. "This place," he said, putting his finger on the map. "It is in English. How do you pronounce it?"

"Schenectady," Sainte-Helene answered, coming to his side. "But it is *un tout petit morceau*. A tiny place."

"But it is something," the count said musingly, his dark eyes thoughtful. "And we must have something." He returned to his desk and sat down. "Monsieur, if you find Albany too strong, or if your march is too exhausting, you will make a hell of this place." Sainte-Helene bowed silently. "And tell the Great Mohawk that the Onontio will pay five dollars for every English scalp his braves bring back to Montreal."

"And my *coureurs de bois*, Excellency?" Sainte-Helene asked with a faint smile. "My bushrangers?"

Frontenac grimaced. "They are no different from the savages, eh, Monsieur? Very well. Their scalps, too. *Six* dollars." Frontenac shuddered. "It is *filthy*, this border war," he muttered savagely. "I have served my king with honor since I was sixteen. And now, in my gray hairs, I have become his butcher." He glanced up irritably at Sainte-Helene, and the lace at his cuff again flapped limply as he lifted his hand in dismissal.

Sainte-Helene had 210 men, of whom 96 were Indians. Most of these were converted Iroquois from the two mission villages of Saut St. Louis and the Mountain of Montreal. The rest were Hurons, Abnaki, and the other Canadian Indians.

They had painted themselves for the warpath. Their faces were hideous with vermilion, blue, or ocher stripes, horizontal bars, or waves. Some had smeared their faces jet black with red rings around their eyes like gaudy owls, others were red with black rings. One man had painted his entire shaven head black, for he was in mourning for his father, a high sachem of the Caughnawagas. All wore blue or red blankets belted at the waist. At their head strode the Great Mohawk, chief of the Saut St. Louis.

The rest of the party consisted of Canadians, almost all, except for the handful of officers drawn from the *noblesse, coureurs de bois*—those mutinous and undisciplined but brave and hardy bushfighters. Like their leaders, they wore buckskin underneath their blanket coats. Each had his hood drawn over his head, his musket grasped in his mittened hand, a hatchet, a knife, a tobacco pouch and a bullet pouch at his belt, a pack on his back, and his precious pipe slung around his neck in a leather case.

Together the red men and the white men crossed the frozen St. Lawrence on snowshoes, dragging their provisions behind them on Indian sledges. Proceeding single file through a snow-blanketed forest, they reached the frozen River Richelieu, advancing down it and down the frozen Lake Champlain. A snowstorm struck and they pitched camp. They cut saplings and roofed them with bark and huddled together beneath them, their jaws working and teeth grinding on the pemmican in their mouths.

The Great Mohawk came to where Sainte-Helene sat squatting in his lean-to. "Where does the great Onontio send us, my brother?"

"Albany!" Sainte-Helene said, filling his pipe and lighting it.

"Albany!" the Indian repeated in dismay. "How long is it since the French grew so bold? There are two hundred soldiers there."

"We have as many."

"But they have walls to stop our bullets, and we have only our shirts to stop theirs."

Sainte-Helene nodded in assent, puffing thoughtfully on his pipe. "We will speak of it again, my brother," he said, and the Great Mohawk left him, shaking his head dubiously.

In the morning, the weather broke and they resumed the march. It became warmer. The ground thawed. They waded knee-deep through melted snow, floundering in icy swamps or sinking through the rotten ice of the rivers. It took three times as long to pull their sledges through the mud and slush. By the time they reached the Hudson, they had been marching thirteen days and their provisions were all but exhausted. They stopped at a point where two trails diverged, one to Albany, the other to Schenectady, and the Great Mohawk again confronted Sainte-Helen.

"My braves are cold and hungry," he complained. "Which way, my brother?"

Sainte-Helene's Canadians were also frozen and starving, half-dead with fatigue, and he had already made up his mind. He pointed north to Schenectady, and the chief grunted in approval. "We will take easy scalps," he said.

Yet, it took nine more days to march about forty miles, so slow and painful had their progress been. Then the weather changed again and the snowstorm that had raged around Schenectady engulfed them. The storm was like a white sorceress. It came pelting at them in flakes as big as shillings, and then, changing, swirled about them in gusts of tiny pellets, blinding them as they stumbled over rocks or snaked around boulders. Sometimes it fell straight down upon them in a sheeted rain, or came billowing and smoking through the forest, beating at their faces to penetrate their hoods, and then, melting on their necks, to go trickling cold on their bodies beneath their shirts. About them in the hollows, the sheltered trees stood sheathed in white, but upon the ridges the oaks and elms and beeches were blown a bare wet black and gray. On the twenty-third day after they had left Montreal, they reached the Mohawk River. They stumbled across it. An hour before midnight, they peered through the snow and saw before them the snow-plastered palisades of Schenectady.

Immediately Sainte-Helene gave the order: "No fires. We will attack in three hours, when they are all surely asleep."

Hungry as wolves, they lay down shivering in the snow.

One of the Sainte-Helene's officers knelt beside him and whispered, "The *coureurs* are mutinous, Sir. They say they can't wait any longer. They haven't eaten for three days and their shirts are frozen to their bodies." Sainte-Helene sat bolt erect, and the officer concluded: "If you don't attack at once, Sir, they say they'll go in and surrender."

"Very well," Sainte-Helene said, putting his hand inside his shirt to draw out a small silver whistle on a cord which he let dangle on his chest. "We will attack at once."

Peter Vrabel was still awake. The next day would mark his fiftieth birthday and he and his young wife, Lana, were preparing for the festivities. Lana had been so busy all day that she had neglected to tie her long blond hair into its customary neat bun at the back of her head and had allowed it to hang down her back in a golden shower. At nine, she shooed their four children to bed in the loft and began to bake a *verjaardags taart,* or birthday cake, with precious chocolate and sugar brought from Albany.

Abigail Gill, in the cabin twenty yards away, was also awake, but in agony. Her time had come. The pains had begun shortly after Benjamin had finished supper and returned to the blockhouse. Twenty minutes apart . . . fifteen . . . ten . . . She began to scream, just as Mrs. Oostdyck burst into the cabin with the corpulent Mrs. Zuke behind her. Both women rushed to the stove, where the pots of water were boiling over. "Benjy!" Abby screamed. "Oh, someone please get Benjy!" The two women ignored her. What could a man do?

The attackers had changed their snowshoes for moccasins or bear-paw shoes. They slipped silently inside the Mohawk Gate, glancing with momentary curiosity at the snow sentinels to either side. They peeled off, Indians left, Canadians right, stealing around the cabins until they had the settlement completely surrounded. All the buildings were dark except two alongside each other. Sainte-Helene held his whistle in his hand, awaiting the arrival of the officer whom he had sent to close the Albany Gate to cut off escape. When he did not come, the French commander concluded that he must have lost his way in the storm—and he put his whistle to his lips and blew.

Peter Vrabel had just dipped his finger into the cake batter to sample it when he heard the whistle and then the war whoops. His eyes bulging in terror, he ran for his musket over the fireplace. But it was too late. The door crashed open and the Indian with the blackened head rushed in, brandishing his tomahawk and yelling hideously. Lana Vrabel shrank back against the wall, covering her eyes in horror. The Indian seized Vrabel by the shoulder, spun him around, and sank his tomahawk deep inside his forehead between the eyes. Vrabel opened his mouth to scream but sank soundlessly to his knees. The Indian wrenched his tomahawk free, pulling Vrabel forward on his face, where he lay with his toes drumming a tattoo on the earthen floor. Kneeling on the dying man's back, the Indian drew his scalping knife. He twisted Vrabel's head around so that he could insert the point in the gaping wound, after which he made an incision around and below the scalp. He reached for a handful of hair to yank the scalp free and found only Vrabel's smooth bald pate. The Indian yelled in anger. He tried to dig his fingernails under the incision to pull a handhold free. But he could not. Infuriated, he knelt beside the body and began gnawing the skin with his teeth. But he still was unable to tear the scalp from Vrabel's head. When he realized that even if he were successful a hairless scalp was worthless, he sprang to his feet screaming in frustration, whirling his tomahawk around his head while he advanced remorselessly, step by step, upon Vrabel's cowering wife.

He struck her repeatedly in the face. Blood spurted upon him in streams. He laughed, dipping his free fingers in it and sucking on them. At last he struck the death blow—straight into the forehead.

Other Indians poured into the room, and he bent quickly to take the woman's scalp, holding it up triumphantly with the golden hairs swirling around his elbow, shaking it at them tauntingly. Two of them made to rush past him to the ladder leading to the loft. But he was quicker. He clambered nimbly aloft, disappearing from sight. The other two followed. Childish screams filled the cabin. Then there was silence. The Indian with the black-painted head scrambled down the ladder, grinning, brandishing two more blond scalps. The others followed, each with a red-haired scalp. Putting them in their belts, the three of them raked the wood fire onto the floor, piled the table and chairs on top of it, and dragged the bed on top of them. Soon the tip of the flames had reached the ceiling. The Indians ran out the door. But the black-headed one ran back in. He stopped to seize Lana Vrabel's bowl of batter which had fallen to the floor. He scooped a fingerful into his mouth and grimaced in delight. Grinning, he swept the chocolate into his mouth by the handful. Then he licked the bowl clean and threw it contemptuously on the fire.

The other lighted cabin was Mrs. Oostdyck's. Three *coureurs* battered down its door. They found Abigail Gill lying screaming on her bed and the two older women on their knees with their clasped hands outstretched in supplication. "Blease," Mrs. Oostdyck cried in terror, "blease for the luff of Godt . . ." One of the *coureurs* who understood English laughed roughly. "For the luff of Christ," she went on, and the *coureur* lifted his hatchet.

"What would these heretic carrion know about *le bon Sauveur?*" he sneered, killing and scalping her within a few seconds. Mrs. Zuke had already mercifully fainted, and she, too, was quickly tomahawked and scalped. Abigail Gill had also lost consciousness. Scenting the opportunity for rape, the three Canadians came to her side. When they saw her condition, they were disgusted. For spite, they dragged her off the bed and outside into the storm and the light of the burning Vrabel cabin. Here, the first *coureur* pulled her erect, killed her and scalped her, and threw her body savagely to the ground. He lifted his hatchet to plunge it into the child within her, but his blow was deflected by an enraged Sainte-Helene. "We do not make war upon the unborn," the French commander snarled, seizing the man by the arm. The man swore and pulled himself free. "Is *monsieur le commandant* telling me that nits will not be lice?" he sneered. Sainte-Helene blanched and took a step toward him, only wheeling, when he heard a volley of musketry, to run through the swirling snow toward the blockhouse, where Benjamin Gill and his militia were holding out.

But the snowstorm obscured their targets. Peering through the gunports, they saw only the wind-whipped whiteness—until they heard the sound of logs being heaped against the blockhouse wall. "Oh, my Jesus," a young private whimpered, "they're going to set fire to the fort." He fell on his knees and began to pray. The sergeant knocked him to the ground and kicked him. "A fire in this storm?" he shouted, pulling the youth erect. "You stupid yellow little bug-tick, that's just what they want you to think." He turned to Lieutenant Gill. "It's a trick, Sir. They want us to try to make a break for it." Gill nodded, running his lips over his tongue. He had heard the women screaming. *Abby, my Abby . . . the baby . . . oh, God, no . . . no, God, no . . .*

A heavy thud on the door chilled their hearts. Sainte-Helene had ordered a large oak cut for a battering ram. *Thud . . . Thud . . . Thud . . . Crash!* Splinters flew. The door buckled and the head of the ram came through it. It was withdrawn, clearing a hole through which Benjamin Gill could see an Indian with his entire head painted black. He fired his pistol and the man fell. A *coureur* aimed his musket at Gill and fired. The lieutenant fell, shot through the eye. Neither he nor his men were alive when they were scalped.

Outside, Sainte-Helene put his whistle to his lips to blow, when he heard the sound of hoofbeats coming out the Albany Gate. A Canadian ran forward, knelt in the snow to bring his musket to his shoulder and fire. In the flickering light of the burning cabins, the rider was seen to waver in the saddle. But he rode on and out of sight.

Sainte-Helene blew his whistle. "He's headed for Albany," he cried to his officers. "We'll march at dawn. Round up the prisoners. We want only the healthy ones who can survive the march." He stopped, aware of the *coureur* whom he had insulted staring at him with contempt. "And what, *monsieur le commandant,* shall we do with the others?" he inquired in a purring voice. "The little ones," he began, "the old, the—" "Enough!" Sainte-Helene cried sternly. "If you bait me one more time, I will have you bound to a stake and left for the Iroquois in the morning." Turning his back disdainfully, the French commander called to an officer: "Le Ber, round up all the horses. Have all the plunder piled at the Mohawk Gate. Then set fire to the houses. When all is ready, we will eat."

Before dawn had come, the village of Schenectady was alight with the flames of about fifty burning cabins. Only one was spared, because a French officer lay wounded in it. He could not be moved. To guarantee his safety, Sainte-Helene ordered that the old men, women, and children unfit to make the march be set free unharmed. His decision enraged the Indians and disgusted the *coureurs de bois,* but he refused to change it.

By noon, Schenectady was a pile of ashes and charred logs. Sainte-Helene blew his whistle. His troops, gorged on the food and drink they had found in the cabins, arose and fastened their snowshoes to their feet. Thirty or more captured horses began dragging the sledges laden with loot. The same number of imprisoned men and youths staggered after them, bent under their own loads, prodded by the knives of their captors. Behind them came the main body. Within ten minutes' time the war party from Montreal had vanished into the snow-covered forest.

It was not until dusk that a party of horsemen from Albany, led by Magistrate Clarke and accompanied by some Mohawks, reached Schenectady. Clarke cantered slowly into the smoking town, grimly remembering how he had left it the day before. He dismounted, going silently from body to mutilated body of some sixty Dutch men, women, and children, trying to identify them. After him came Dr. Redmond. Clarke stopped beside a murdered and scalped young woman. He did not recognize her, but he guessed from her pregnant condition that it was Lieutenant Gill's wife. Clarke shuddered. He remembered his parting words: "Let the blood of your own be on your own heads"; and yet, he could no longer blame them for their stubbornness. He could only feel sad, a deep, empty, aching sadness—until, when the savagery of the massacre and the wanton destruction of an innocent village had sunk in upon him in all its brutality, this was supplanted by a foaming rage which seized his whole being and made his body shake.

"You filthy idolaters!" he shrieked, shaking his fist toward Canada. "You cow—" A piece of blood-spattered parchment had blown against his ankle, and he stooped to seize it. He unfolded it and read: "To the Sieur de Sainte-Helene . . ." It was Frontenac's written instructions to his commander. Clarke crumpled it in his fist. "Sainte-Helene, you cowardly murderer," he screamed into the wind, "I know you now. Sainte-Helene, a name that will stink in hell! I will kill you, Sainte-Helene, all of—"

Magistrate Clarke paused, incredulous. He could not believe what he had heard. But Dr. Redmond knew what it was. Both men turned. There, between the sprawling, outthrust legs of Abigail Gill, lying in a pool of blood and afterbirth, its naked body smeared red, its tiny fists dug into its eyes, and its little rosebud mouth wide open and wailing, was a live baby boy.

2

The coach swung into Boston Common with a clatter, the wheels spraying mud to either side, raising angry cries from a crowd gathered about a tall, powerfully built man who seemed to be haranguing them.

"Slow down, you mother's mistake!" one of them called to the driver, flicking a clot of mud from his face.

"Slow down, hell!" another shouted. "Stop! Rein in your horses, you up there. They're making so damn much noise we can't hear what Sir William is saying."

Grinning, the driver brought the coach to a halt, reining in his horses so hard that they reared back on their hind legs. Inside the coach, Jonathan Clarke chuckled. He patted the breathing bundle of blue on his lap and said: "Well, Jeddy, old cock, here we are in Boston." A footman opened the door and Clarke stepped out, holding his bundle gingerly. He surveyed the crowd, which had begun to cheer the orator.

"Port Royal, that's the ticket!" some of them cried. "We'll pay those Frenchies back."

"Let's burn that damn pirate's nest!"

"Remember Salmon Falls!" someone cried; and another: "Remember, Falmouth, too!"

"I'm from New York," yelled a third. "Let's not forget

Schenectady!" The crowd roared approval, and when someone cried: "Three cheers for Sir William!" it broke into wild "Hurrahs!" only falling silent when the speaker renewed his harangue.

Jonathan Clarke stroked his newly grown black beard approvingly. Evidently, he thought, Count Frontenac's war parties have backfired on him. Boston, it appears, is going to hit back. Then he started, staring incredulously at the tall orator. "Sir *William*," he breathed aloud. "If it isn't Sir William Phips!" He moved as though to join the crowd, but then, remembering the precious parcel in his arms, he turned away—just as a magnificent coach-and-four came thundering up behind him. The coachman braked, showering Clarke with mud, and swerved his white horses. But Clarke still had to jump to avoid being run over. "You fool!" he shouted up to the coachman, shaking his fist. In an instant the coach was past him, but not before Clarke had glimpsed the occupant, a young woman with beautiful chestnut hair and green eyes. Her startled face was pressed to the window and her full mouth was parted in dismay. Still fuming, Jonathan Clarke strode down a side lane, brushing the mud from his clothing. "Damn these people!" he cursed angrily. "Don't any of them know how to handle horses?" He stopped in front of a small, weather-beaten house with the name "Cowlett" burned into a wooden board nailed to the gate. He passed through the gate and rapped the polished brass knocker affixed to a heavy door of lacquered teak. In a moment it was opened by a plump woman in her late thirties. Her jet-black hair was piled high on her head and her flushed face suggested that she had come directly from her stove.

"Jonathan!" she exclaimed in delight, moving as though to embrace him, until she saw the bundle in his arms. "What have you got there?" she asked, puzzled.

He grinned, shoving it toward her. "Be very, very careful," he said. She took it, her arms sagging momentarily under the unexpected weight. Her eyes widened. "It's . . . it's *alive!*" She plucked back the blanket. "It's a *baby!* Oh, look at that dear little rosebud mouth." She all but ran to the settee in her little parlor and sat down. "Thomas," she called up the stairs, "my brother Jonathan is here." She drew back the blanket breathlessly, her adoring eyes on the child's face.

"Whose . . . whose is it, Jonathan?" she asked shyly. "I

mean, it isn't yours? You never wrote that you were married."

"I'm not, Aggie," he replied with a grin. "I'll tell you all about Jed in a minute. It's a boy, you know. But first, how about a spot of tea and maybe even a biscuit? The food on that packet from New York City was so wretched I couldn't eat it."

Agatha Cowlett put the baby aside. "Of course! I've got some lovely tea. And sugar! A ship arrived from the West Indies yesterday, with sugar and rum and tea. You're just in time."

"Aye, he is that," Thomas Cowlett said, his wooden shoes clumping on the narrow stairway from the second floor. He took his pipe from his mouth with his left hand and extended his right. "You're looking fit, Jonathan," he said, grasping his brother-in-law's hand. "Although I must say that beard makes you look a little like the devil." Clarke unclasped quickly, rubbing his hand with a rueful grin. "Never shake hands with a shipwright," he said wryly, and Cowlett laughed. His rough, seamed face sobered when he caught sight of the baby on the settee. "What's this you've brought us?"

Over tea laced with rum, Jonathan Clarke related the hideous circumstances of Jedediah Gill's birth. When he had finished, his sister was weeping and his brother-in-law's ruddy face was white with anger. "The scum!" he muttered. "They did even worse at Salmon Falls. The Indians took the babies and little ones from their mothers and brained them against the trees. They said they didn't want them to cry out on the march and give them away." He struck his hands together savagely and cried: "I tell you, Agatha, I'm going to 'list for Port Royal."

"You are not!" Agatha retorted hotly. "You're too old and you know nothing about soldiering."

"I'm only thirty-eight," Cowlett protested. "And what's so great about shooting off a musket?"

"Well, there's a little more to war than that, Tom," Clarke said gently; and then, thoughtfully: "You know, I just might like to go myself."

"But why didn't you 'list with the New York army, Jonathan?" his sister asked. "The one that's going to Montreal? As a magistrate, I should think they'd make you a colonel or at least a major."

"So they know about that out here already?"

"Of course. There's almost as much gossip about Montreal as there is about Port Royal. But why did you come here instead?"

"Well, first, Aggie, I had to do something about Jeddy. He has no living relatives, and a bachelor like me couldn't take care of him." He paused, cautiously eyeing his brother-in-law somberly sipping his tea, and his sister, watching him expectantly, her dark eyes dancing as though she had guessed what he was about to say. "I know you and Tom have been dying to have a baby all these years. I . . . I thought if you couldn't have one of your own, maybe you'd take care of J—"

Agatha Cowlett jumped erect with shining eyes. She ran to the settee where Jed had begun to cry. She seized him and pressed him to her breast, crooning softly. The child fell silent. Agatha glanced at her brother reproachfully. "You could at least have mentioned him in your letter. Then we'd have been all ready for him." She stared sharply at her husband, who was quietly filling his pipe. "Are you just going to sit there and smoke?" she snapped. "You can't see that a baby needs a cradle?" He got slowly to his feet, grinning sheepishly. "And you'd better stop off at Tryon's farm on your way back from the lumber mill. We'll be needing fresh milk every day." Cowlett scratched his head with the stem of his pipe. "Don't take long to make a mother, do it, Jon?" he murmured to his brother-in-law. Agatha ignored him, kissing the child in her arms gently and patting him on the head. "How old is he, Jonathan?"

"Going on six weeks."

"And you took him on a *sea* voyage?" She was aghast. "I wonder if he can see yet?" she said, holding her hand in front of Jeddy's face and moving it back and forth. "Guess not. What color was his mother's hair?"

"Black, I think . . . and his father's was kind of a reddish blonde."

"He's going to be handsome, Jonathan, I know he is. Look how his hair curls. He's going to be blond, too." She gasped and put a finger on the child's forehead. "Jon! He has a scar!" Clarke nodded. "Dr. Redmond reckoned he'd been hit the tiniest glancing blow by a hatchet. That's what opened the womb, you know." Agatha shuddered. "Here. You hold him for a spell. I've got to finish my baking." He took the child and followed her into a tiny kitchen with a fireplace into which a soot-blackened pot on a movable arm had been fastened. Shining copper pots and pans hung above an iron stove. "We're going to have fresh beef for dinner, Jon," Agatha said proudly. "Tom's had it hanging out back in the springhouse for a week. I've just finished larding the sliced squash, and this morning I baked some apples in maple sugar." She turned toward him from the stove. "And Tom's got a bottle of sack he's been keeping since we got your letter."

Clarke grinned. "You always were a great cook, Aggie," he said, resisting the temptation to add that her plump figure proved it. "And a good housekeeper, too. His eyes roved approvingly over the clean, neat kitchen. The baby began to cry again. "Oh, give him to me," Agatha said, wiping her hands clean on her apron and taking Jed fondly to her bosom again. "Now, what else made you leave New York?"

"Leisler," her brother replied succinctly. "That no-good *Heiniekoplatz* got himself elected acting governor after Nicholson cleared out. You know, he never forgave me for opposing him in Albany and Schenectady." He narrowed his lips bitterly. "That's why we never got the troops we needed upriver. Anyway, he had no use for me, so I cleared out."

"You're . . . you're not a magistrate anymore?" she asked falteringly, her lips beginning to quiver.

"I guess not," he said, laughing. "Oh, come on, Aggie—no sense crying over spilt milk. Just you wait, I'll give you something else to brag about. Right here in Baston," he said, mimicking the local accent. "You see, Sir William Phips is an old friend of mine. I served under him in the Caribbean. And as soon as I sleep off this beautiful dinner of yours, sister dear, I'm going to pay him a call."

Jonathan Clarke was a little awed as he walked down the Green Lane in North Boston where Sir William lived. The houses were certainly imposing. There weren't many houses like them in New York, and certainly not in Albany. Some of them were three stories high or had stained glass above the door. All the doors were either of teak or mahogany, and the knockers were heavy brass figureheads: gargoyles or lions or mermaids. Jonathan had heard that Philadelphia had some fancy streets like this, but he doubted that any of them could match the Green Lane. Coming to Sir William's residence, Clarke stopped short. It was the finest house on the street! It was painted a pale green, like the seawater that foams off a ship's stern, and had a wing to either side. Beautiful glass lamps stood by the windows. Jonathan was almost afraid to go up the steps and knock, but he braced himself and went up the walk.

A servant in a sea-green coat with gold frogging opened the door. Clarke introduced himself, handing him his card, and the servant glided away. Now, where have I seen that livery before? Clarke wondered. Of course! That damned coachman on the coach-and-four. Once again Clarke saw the beautiful startled face pressed against the window.

"Sir William will see you in the drawing room," the servant said, returning. Clarke followed him into a large room dazzling with gilded mirrors, a chandelier, swept-back curtains of broacaded gold and fine chairs with sea-green backs and seats. Sir William had just risen from a chair opposite a young woman. Clarke gaped in astonishment. It was the girl he had seen in the coach!

"Well, well, if it ain't my old first mate," Sir William cried in his booming voice. "Allow me to introduce my ward, Miss Martha St. John," he said, turning to motion the girl forward. She, too, gaped. "Oh, sir," she burst out. "I'm so sorry. I hope we didn't hurt—"

"Not at all," Clarke said, bowing. "Johathan Clarke at your service, madam."

Phips glanced from one to the other, first in surprise, then with suspicion. "You . . . ?" He paused warily. "You know each other?"

"Oh, no, Uncle William. But yesterday as we were coming to carry you home . . . Well, you know Adam . . . once he gets up on the box . . ."

"Come, come, girl," Phips said testily. "Get to the point."

"Well, we almost ran this gentleman over. Really, Mr. Clarke," she rushed on, flushing, "I really must apologize for Adam."

"Not at all," Clarke repeated gallantly, bowing again. "It is a pleasure to make your acquaintance, Miss St. John."

Coloring faintly, Martha St. John nodded and left the room. Clarke turned toward Sir William, confusedly aware of the warmth in his own cheeks. Phips was studying him shrewdly. But then his jovial manner returned and he clapped Jonathan on the back. "Last time I seen you, Clarke, was five years ago in London."

"Yes, sir . . . and I had some golden guineas in my coffers, then—thanks to you."

Phips chuckled again. "Nobody in England believed that I'd find that Spanish galleon, and sometimes I doubted it myself. But I done found it, and it made our fortunes. Made me a knight, too," he continued, looking around him proudly.

"You deserve everything you've got, Sir William," Clarke said eagerly. "And if it hadn't been for you . . ."

"You mean the mutiny?"

"I do indeed! D'ye know, sir, every time I tell that story, people laugh at me. They can't believe that a single man beat down an armed mutiny just using his fists."

Phips smiled in pleasure, balling his huge fist and examining it proudly. "There ain't many men who can face down William Phips," he murmured. "Of course, you know I was a plowboy before I went to sea."

"I know, sir. By Jesus, Sir William, you're a self-made man if there ever was one! And you did get your fine house on the Green Lane, just like you always told me you would."

Phips flushed again with pleasure. "Thank you, Clarke. They's some fancy fellows around here likes to snicker about the way I talk. Well, let 'em, by God! I'm proud of what I come from. My mother had twenty-six children, by Jesus, and I were the first—and if that ain't sturdy stock, Clarke, there ain't no sech thing. A shepherd and a plowboy, too. Didn't learn neither to read nor write till I were twenty-one. Let 'em laugh!" he cried, clapping his huge hands together. "Ain't any of 'em can shear a sheep or plow a furrow like I can . . . and I've still got more money'n they do." He laughed and clapped his hands again. "All right, Clarke, what brings you to the land of the bean and the cod?"

Clarke retold the story of Schenectady, and Phips scowled. "D'ye know, Clarke, I've heard so many of these stories I've sort of worn out my anger. But, they'll pay!" he exclaimed grimly, his rough features hardening. "It won't be long, either, Clarke. We're sailing against Port Royal next week."

"I heard. In fact, that's why I'm here."

Phips stared at him in delight. "You mean you'd like to come along."

"Indeed I do."

"Done!" Sir William cried, clapping his hands together. "I've seen you in tight spots, Clarke, and I don't mind saying I'll rest easier with you aboard." He paused thoughtfully. "Maybe I can wangle a commission out of Governor Bradstreet and the Council," he mused. But then he shook his head. "Not them skinflints," he muttered. "You'd think every bean and bullet I put on board my fleet came right out of their backsides. No, Clarke, you'll sail as my personal aide. And I'll pay you out of my own pocket." He turned to a sideboard to seize a decanter and pour two glasses of sherry. "To the destruction of the French," he said, handing one to Clarke.

They both drank, and Clarke raised his glass. "To their death!" he said savagely.

Since sunup the people of the neighboring towns had been pouring over Boston Neck into the city to see the "army" off for Nova Scotia. They came on foot, on horseback, or in carts. Children skipped and ran ahead or to the side of the hurrying crowd or darted in and out of it. Many women carried parcels of food, and there were bottles of rum or stone jugs of beer in the carts, for they intended to make a day of it.

All Boston, it seemed, was also on its way to the wharf where Sir William's fleet of seven small ships was moored. The throng swelled until there was scarcely standing space left. Young men and boys climbed onto the roofs and chimneys of the shops and taverns fronting the harbor. There was a great cry as the Massachusetts "army"—about five hundred militia divided into five companies—marched down to the ships behind squealing pipes and rattling drums.

Jonathan Clarke could hear the commotion clearly as he stood at the door of the Cowletts' home to say good-bye. "Take good care of Jeddy, Aggie," he said, kissing the child in his arms on the forehead and returning him to his sister. "And remember," he said seriously, "if anything happens to me, all that I own is his." Agatha Cowlett nodded, her lip beginning to tremble. "Nah, nah, Aggie, none of that," her brother said soothingly. "And listen," he went on, taking in both of them, Agatha and her husband standing soberly beside her, "if something does happen, as soon as he begins to understand, I want you to tell him every night just how he was born. *Every night,*" he repeated fiercely. "I want him to hear every night just what the French and their Indians did to his parents. Sainte-Helene," he whispered, his glittering eyes fastening on the baby in his sister's arms. "That is his name, the name of the devil's twin. Don't forget it, Aggie— *Sainte-Helene.*"

Agatha Cowlett stared at her brother in disbelieving horror. "Jonathan, are you mad? That's sinful. I can't turn a child's head like that. 'Vengeance is mine, saith the Lord.' Do you want him to grow up thirsting for revenge?"

"Yes!" Clarke hissed. "I do want him to grow up thirsting for revenge. Why do you think I gave him a name like Jedediah? Because I want him to be like an avenging king of the Hebrews, a scourge of God riding out of the Old Testament. Do you hear me, Aggie?"

Agatha Cowlett nodded her head silently. Her brother's venomous savagery had all but stunned her. She could only hold tightly to the baby and nod. Jonathan Clarke kissed her gently on the cheek. "Don't worry, Aggie," he said lightly, "I'm going to take good care nothing happens to me. C'mon, Tom," he said to his brother-in-law, "I can hear the bugles blowing them aboard."

Tom Cowlett stooped and swung Clarke's sea bag onto his shoulder. Clarke seized his pack and musket, blew his sister another farewell kiss, and the two men strode down the alley to the wharf. Jonathan was surprised to see that Sir William had brought his ward with him. She stood demurely alongside her tall guardian. She wore a modest dress of green silk which brought out the auburn glints in her chestnut hair and the green of her eyes. She also carried a green-and-white parasol, although it was a day of bright sunshine. Phips wore a general's uniform. His black tricornered hat with white lace on the brim accentuated his height, and his broad shoulders and chest did much to distract from the paunch swelling against his red-and-blue coat. A ceremonial sword dangled from his left hip.

Aware of Sir William's eyes on him, Jonathan bowed stiffly to Martha St. John, and she nodded gravely in reply. Phips's searching glance went from one to the other. Oh, my Jesus,

Clarke thought suddenly: damned if I don't think the old devil has designs on her himself. But then the fifes and drums began to play "Peas upon a Trencher," and as the militiamen began filing up the gangplank, a great cheer arose from the crowd. Before noon, on the outgoing tide, the army of Massachusetts set sail for Nova Scotia and Port Royal.

Two weeks later the little fleet stood off Port Royal, halfway up the west coast of the Nova Scotian peninsula. It had been a glorious voyage. Spring had broken and a golden sun danced brightly on the waves, making glittering points of light, like a huge coat of mail, when the wind riffled the surface of the sea. Many of the militiamen became seasick, but other than that, it was an uneventful trip—one that Jonathan Clarke enjoyed hugely because he was pleased to get his sea legs back, and because, with so much free time, he could sit idly on the stern of Sir William's flagship with the breeze bathing his face and his mind's eye almost always full of the face of Martha St. John. On May 11, 1690, the fleet sailed through the harbor's narrow entrance and began unloading troops.

The bands played gay military marches as the militia began rowing themselves ashore. Standing on the quarterdeck with Sir William, Clarke focused his eyeglass anxiously on the ramparts of the fort. At any moment he expected to see puffs of smoke and hear cannonballs go howling into the English boats. Surprisingly, none came.

"They're afraid of us, eh, Clarke?" Sir William crowed jubilantly. "I knew they wouldn't fight—not when they know they have to deal with armed Englishmen instead of women and children." Clarke nodded silently, still keeping a watchful eye on the fort. It remained quiet. Within an hour, all the troops were ashore and a beachhead was established. Now the empty boats returned to ferry supplies and cannon ashore.

"Well, Clarke," Sir William boomed, "we might as well go ashore ourselves to begin the game." He made for the landward gunwales, clambering awkwardly over to go down a Jacob's ladder. Clarke followed him, jumping after him into a waiting boat. Sir William had bent his sword in the process, and he shook his huge fist at the coxswain. "You there, you damn landlubber, I can tell you don't come from Marble-head."

"Nantasket," the man replied sullenly, and Phips shouted into the wind: "You think I couldn't tell?"

Once ashore, the two men proceeded to the English camp alongside Allen's River which lay between them and the fort. At once Phips gave orders for scouts and foragers to be sent into the surrounding territory. With Clarke beside him he climbed a small hill. Both men trained their glasses on the silent fort. "Seems damn awful quiet," Phips grumbled. "D'ye reckon it's a trick?" Clarke shook his head, slowly scanning the fort with his glasses. "Not at all, Sir. If you ask me, the fort's practically falling apart."

"You don't say!" Phips exclaimed eagerly. "I didn't really notice. But of course, your eyes are younger than mine."

"The ramparts are crumbling. I can see soldiers in full view, and they look pretty ragged to me. Their flag is torn and faded like a dishrag. I can't even make out the golden lilies. Some of the cannon are sagging through the gunports." Clarke put down his glasses. "A piece of cake, Sir," he said, grinning.

Sir William's emotions were torn between delight at his good fortune and doubt that it could be true. Phips studied the fort again. "It can't be that easy," he muttered. "Tomorrow I think we'll cross the river and start digging approaches. Work my guns into range . . ."

"You don't need to, Sir! I'll lay my life on it. All you need to do to take that fort is beat a parley. I wouldn't waste a man or a ball on it."

Phips straightened. "Done!" he cried, clapping his hands. "Clarke, take a drummer boy and ride forward under a white flag. You can tell Governor Meneval that my terms will be generous."

Grinning, Clarke sprinted down the hill, swinging aboard one of the horses just brought ashore while a drummer vaulted onto the horse's rump behind him. They forded the river and trotted to within a hundred yards of the fort, where they dismounted. Clarke took off his white shirt and wrapped it around his musket, holding it aloft and waving it while the drummer marched in front of him beating a parley. Within minutes the gates were opened and two French officers in white uniforms came toward him on foot.

Without a word, they escorted Clarke into the fort. Jonathan was amazed that they had not blindfolded him so that he could not study the fort's defenses, but when he saw the starving faces and worn uniforms of the handful of soldiers within it, he realized at once that Meneval was anxious to haul down his flag.

"I cannot hope to defend Port Royal, Monsieur," the governor said to him in his quarters five minutes later. "Not with seventy sick and hungry soldiers against five hundred. Nor can I, with no hope of victory, expose an innocent population to your cannon." Meneval bowed his white-whigged head. "Therefore, Monsieur, I will surrender—provided your general will grant my men full honors of war and respect the life and property of my people."

Clarke bowed graciously. "I will convey your terms to Sir William," he said, and withdrew. Half an hour later a delighted Sir William Phips accepted the terms. Next morning, with shouldered arms, drums beating, and flags flying, the French soldiers marched out of the fort, saluting Sir William as they passed him en route to a waiting ship, after which the militia marched in. Though victorious, they were unhappy, and already grumbling.

"Sorry terms they be," they muttered.

"Where be the plunder promised us?"

"Be Sir William a Frenchman?"

Undeterred by the disaffection of his troops, Sir William held a ball for Governor Meneval, his officers, and the ladies of the fort. Phips played the role of gracious conqueror so well that the charmed Governor Meneval next day entrusted all his money, his silver plate, his and his wife's finest clothing, and even his pistols to him for safekeeping. He also had his chef prepare a fine luncheon for Phips and himself. They were just sitting down to it when an English officer rushed in crying, "General Phips, the men have just found a French cache in the woods."

"What? What's this?" exclaimed Sir William, throwing down his napkin and glaring at Meneval.

"Yes, Sir! Golden louis, silver plate, and all manner of merchandise. Much of it belongs to King Louis, but there's a lot of the local merchants' stuff, too."

"*King* Louis, indeed!" Phips snorted. "It belongs to us! All of it!"

"My dear Sir William," Governor Meneval demurred with trembling lips. "What are you saying? You gave me your word you would respect our property."

"Not after this damned trick!" Phips shouted, pushing back his chair and jumping to his feet. "I hereby renounce the terms of our agreement—and with good and sufficient cause. Lieutenant Wilcox," he said to the officer, "you will inform Colonel Riley that I want him to disarm those ruffians in French uniforms and put them in irons. They ain't going back to France to kill more Englishmen for that blood-drinking king of theirs. They're going to Boston! Then I want him to take two companies to go through the town and seize everything in the possession of the merchants. No looting, mind you—and no violence. Pack it all into hogsheads to be loaded aboard ship. And have the colonel muster the army and tell the men they'll get their fair share when we get home." Saluting, the officer turned to go, but Phips restrained him. "One other thing: Chaplain Roberts may do as he wishes with their church."

"Oh, no!" Meneval cried in horror. "That is sacrilege, Monsieur! Your word, Sir William . . . your sacred word!"

"Word, indeed," Phips snorted in contempt. "Why, you sly little trickster, who are you to talk of honor?"

Meneval lifted his hands entreatingly. "Sir William, I swear to you I know nothing of this cache. If it exists—and I can scarcely believe that it does—I know nothing of it, nor did I authorize it."

Phips glared at him. "You ain't insinuating that this is a trick on my part, an excuse for voiding the terms?"

"No, no, not at all," Meneval stammered; and then, again lifting his hands: "Sir William, what of me? What of my fortune? What of my money, my silver, my pistols, all that I possess I entrusted to you this very morning?"

"Forfeit!" Phips snapped.

"Sir William!" Meneval cried in anguish.

"Shut up!" Phips boomed. "Shut up, I tell you, or I'll have you and your wife thrown in irons too."

Drawing himself up with dignity, Governor Meneval arose and left the room. Sir William Phips clapped his hands together gleefully. He grinned, did a little two-step, downed a glass of wine set at his untouched plate, and went outside to take personal charge of the plundering.

Jonathan Clarke had gone into the little Catholic church out of curiosity. Like any other Englishman of New England, he detested and abhorred the Church of Rome. But his was an inquiring mind and he had never seen a Catholic church before. So he went in. He walked slowly down the aisle with an unconscious reverence, gazing with contempt at the little stained-glass windows portraying biblical events. He stopped at the white wooden altar rail to study the little white marble altar flanked by brass candlesticks and plaster statues of the saints. "Idolaters," he muttered under his breath. He stared uncomprehendingly at the scene carved in marble beneath the altar, unaware that it was a reproduction of Michelangelo's *Last Supper*. Then, pleased that he had dueled with the devil himself and not been corrupted, he went back the way he had come.

Blinking in the sunlight, Clarke saw a squad of militia led by Chaplain Roberts approaching. The men carried axes and saws and sledgehammers. Chaplain Roberts, grim-faced, grasped his own hatchet. "There she is, the Whore of Babylon!" the chaplain shouted. He pointed to the cross rising from the steeple. "Abomination of abominations!" he cried, shaking his hatchet at it. "Cut it down!" Within a few minutes, four of the men with axes had scrambled onto the roof. Their blades rang as they bit into the wood. In another two minutes the heavy cross had crashed to the ground. "Say a prayer, men, before you go into this unholy place, lest you be contaminated." The militia nodded, casting their eyes heavenward in supplication. Then they went inside.

Clarke followed them, trying to conceal his dismay. Desecrating a church, he told himself, was not nearly to be compared to what happened at Schenectady, but still, he thought with misgivings, it is no way to make war. A crash and tinkling of glass burst into his consciousness, and he saw that the men with sledgehammers were knocking out the stained-glass windows. Others with axes were at work smashing the statues. Chaplain Roberts sang the Doxology while he chopped briskly away at the altar. Next the carving of the *Last Supper* was battered into shards, the pews were chopped up, and nothing was left entire except the candlesticks, appropriated by the chaplain, and a ruby-red-glass lantern suspended above the sanctuary on a brass chain. Unknown to the

New Englanders, it contained a consecrated host, which the Catholic French believed to be the presence of Christ upon the altar.

"That's mine!" a brawny militiaman yelled, jumping up to pull it down. He opened the lamp and carelessly flicked the wafer onto the floor. "Aye, lads," he chortled, swinging it back and forth, "just the thing for Guy Fawkes Day." He began to whistle a Morris dance, swaying to the tune, swinging the lamp back and forth and singing softly:

> From Peter's devil-dome
> We'll hang the Pope of Rome . . .

Jonathan Clarke turned and left the church in disgust.

Outside he saw teams of horses pulling wagons, loaded with hogsheads filled with plunder, down to the harbor. Waiting boats carried the barrels out to the ships. Clarke was surprised. He thought that Sir William had prohibited plundering, and he mentioned it to him that night as they ate in the dining cabin of his flagship.

"They tried to trick us," Sir William mumbled, chewing his food and averting his eyes. He pushed his empty plate away and reached for the Stilton cheese. Munching cheese and sipping wine, he explained why he had renounced the terms. Clarke listened intently. The cache did not seem to him such an outrageous trick, nor even a violation of the agreement. After all, the money and merchandise belonged to the French. They had hidden it for fear it would be taken from them. What was so treacherous about that? But he said nothing, and Sir William, anxious to change the subject lest the matter of Meneval's possessions come under discussion, occupied himself cutting more cheese and pouring more wine.

"Uncommonly good Stilton, Clarke," he said. "The claret's excellent, too. How them rogues from Nantucket do do themselves fine." He pushed the captain's decanter toward Clarke. "Have some more, my man. You won't regret it." Sir William filled and refilled the decanter from the cask on the sideboard. He was getting drunk.

"Nice bit of work, eh, Clarke?" he crowed, slurring his words slightly. "Port Royal for King William, without the loss of a drop of blood. Not even a ball wasted." He hiccuped and hastily put a hand to his mouth. Jonathan noticed wine stains on his lace shirt. "I'm for the peerage, Clarke, no doubt of it. No more plain Sir William. Phips of Port Royal and Nova Scotia," he babbled proudly. "*Count* William . . . maybe even Marquish. M'lord Phips, eh, Clarke?" He giggled. His eyes gleamed, and he staggered to his feet to seize a jewel case on the sideboard. Opening it, he held up a string of flawless matched pearls which once had graced the neck of Madame Meneval. "How's that, Clarke, eh? How's that for a wedding present?"

"Wedding present, Sir?"

Phips smirked, returning the necklace to the box and staggering back to his seat. He winked. "Yeah, my good man, wedding preshent."

"Who's the lucky lady, sir?"

Phips ogled him in astonishment, as though the question were a supererogation. "Why, Martha, of course. Martha St. John."

Jonathan Clarke stared in disbelief at the tipsy middle-aged man in front of him until he realized that he was telling the truth. He is fifty, if he's a day, Jonathan thought with suppressed anger, and he is coarse and bloated and conceited. And this uncouth old rooster is planning to ravish that beautiful young . . . ?

"Martha'll come of age next week," Phips lisped on. "No longer my ward. How can she reshist, Clarke? William the Conqueror. Phipsh of Port Royal and Nova Scoshia. . . . She'll be rich, Clarke, a countess . . . maybe even a marqhisha . . . how can she reshist?"

3

Sir William Phips and his army were welcomed as conquering heroes when they returned to Boston.

Harbor guns were fired in salute when the masts of their ships first became visible, and soon the throng gathering on the wharves heard the faint, hollow booming of Phips's guns firing in reply. A few hours later the ships were safely moored, and the militia began filing ashore while bands played and the crowd cheered. Sir William came down the gangplank last, and there arose such a roar that Parson Increase Mather later wrote in his diary, "The Lord Himself must have heard it in Heaven."

Sir William was delighted to see Governor Bradstreet and his Council standing on the wharf. Bradstreet stood leaning on a cane, his thin white hair blown awry in the breeze. His chain of office hung around his neck, the badge resting on the breast of his black coat, just below his stiff white collar. Both the governor and his councilmen wore high-crowned, high-buckled black hats with wide brims. Bradstreet had just celebrated his ninetieth birthday, but his voice was strong when he took Phips's hand and said, "Done like a true Englishman, Sir William. You are a credit to the Crown. The entire colony is in your debt." Phips bowed graciously, and the governor pointed to his ships. "You've brought something home?"

"Indeed, Sir. We ain't calculated it yet, Governor, but it should be worth close to five thousand guineas."

"Excellent," Bradstreet said, his faded eyes gleaming, a faint mist of saliva spraying from his toothless mouth. "We'll be needing it for the expedition against Quebec."

"Quebec, Sir?"

"Yes, damme," the old man replied, angrily shaking his cane northward. "It's the only way to protect our borders. After we take Quebec, the rest of Canada will wither away, and then the only language spoken on either side of the border will be English."

"So they've finally seen the light in London?"

"Well . . . er, no, Phips. We asked King William for help, but he said he was too busy with the Irish war. England can't spare a gun or a man. But who needs 'em?" he burst out excitedly, spraying saliva again. "Massachusetts can do it on her own. After all, Phips, we are English. And didn't you just prove that there isn't an Englishman alive who isn't worth a dozen Frenchmen? I admit that we're short of funds, but that's why what you've brought home ought to help us buy what we need."

Sir William frowned. "I . . . I promised the men—"

"They'll get their fair share," the governor said testily.

"And there are . . . ah, a few personal trophies of my own . . ."

"Keep 'em. But the colony will convert the bulk of the plunder into money to hire ships."

Sir William nodded. "And the troops?"

"They've been drilling on the common for two weeks. Upwards of fifteen hundred of 'em. With your troops, we'll have two thousand men." Governor Bradstreet's eyes were rueful as he looked out to sea. "They didn't all 'list like we thought they would," he muttered. "We had to use press gangs here and there."

Sir William coughed. "And who is to lead the expedition?"

The governor spun around to face Sir William. "Who else but you, Phips?" he asked, smiling a toothless smile. "Who else but the conqueror of Port Royal?"

Sir William Phips bowed. "My dear Governor," he murmured, "I am overwhelmed."

"Victory?" Jonathan Clarke snorted in contempt, pouring more rum into his tea. He had just finished his sister's meal of roast suckling pig, as well as another of Tom Cowlett's bottles of sack. Beside him, little Jedediah Gill slept peacefully in the cradle made for him by his foster father. "What victory?" Clarke repeated, fingering his shirt sleeve. "Port Royal was taken with my white shirt and a pair of drumsticks."

"Pshaw, Jon," his brother-in-law scoffed good-humoredly. "You can't mean that."

"But I do," Clarke said grimly, going on to explain how Meneval had surrendered.

"Oh, my Jesus," Cowlett groaned, pulling noisily on his pipe. "And all them milishy tellin' the girls how they took the fort by storm. A body can hardly believe men of English stock would pretend like that."

Clarke laughed. "Well, they do. And I guess when you've got a pretty lass on your knee, it's hard to resist the temptation to play the hero."

"Men!" Agatha Cowlett snorted. "Play actors, every one of them." Tom Cowlett grinned and winked at Clarke. "Did Aggie tell you I tried to 'list, Jon?" Agatha snorted again and shook her knitting needle at her husband. "I tell you again, Tom Cowlett, if you try to go off to war, I'll shoot you dead, first. You with a wife and baby to feed."

Both men chuckled, and Cowlett said, "What d'ye think of them fellers drilling on the Common, Jon?"

"Not much. A bunch of mechanics, clerks, and plowboys. Half of 'em have two left feet, and the other half never saw a musket before."

"Guess so. Governor Bradstreet sure did a lot of pressin'. I heard tell the town of Gloucester lost two-thirds of its men. Parson Emerson tried to stop 'em, but they just put 'em on wagons and brought 'em here."

"Who's their commander, Tom?" Clarke asked, idly stirring more rum into his tea. "That stocky fellow with the moon face?"

"John Walley," Tom answered proudly. "Major John Walley. Successful farmer out Barnstable way. John and me grew up together."

"Farmer, eh? What's he know about soldiering?"

"John Walley ain't missed a muster for nigh on to twenty year," Tom Cowlett said heatedly. "His father fit in King Philip's War."

"Musters, eh?" Clarke repeated, laughing. "I've seen enough musters, Tom. In New York, here, and in New Jersey, too. All the same. Plenty of rum, not much discipline, a practice volley or two—and with the girls be handy."

"They'll lick the French, Jon—just you wait and see. Englishmen like John Walley are no cowards."

"Oh, I know that. But bravery just isn't enough. Raw courage can't conquer well-aimed cannon, Tom." Jonathan Clarke started in his chair, and his hand flew quickly to his beard. It had just occurred to him that he had passed an entire day without once thinking of Martha St. John. But tomorrow, he thought eagerly, I'll be seeing her.

Jonathan did see Martha, but she did not speak to him. She came hurrying out of Sir William's chambers just as Jonathan approached behind the liveried servant. Her face was flushed a deep red and she was biting her lip. She seemed highly agitated, and the moment she caught sight of Jonathan she lowered her eyes and rushed silently past him. Jonathan looked after her in dismay, but then, seeing the servant holding the door open, he went quickly inside.

Sir William also seemed agitated. He strode back and forth behind his desk, a quill pen in his ink-stained fingers. "Confound it!" he muttered savagely. "Who would have thought it?" When he saw Clarke enter, he compressed his lips and sat down.

"Congratulations, Sir William!" Clarke said, trying to sound cheerful. "I've just heard the great news."

"Thank you, Clarke," Phips said absently, his mind obviously elsewhere. "It's quite an honor, yes."

"May I venture to say, Sir," Clarke began shyly, "that it may turn out to be Phips of Quebec *and* Port Royal?"

"Quite so, Clarke, quite so," Phips boomed, recovering his hearty manner.

"Boston is certainly up in arms, Sir. I've never seen a town so excited. Bands playing, soldiers drilling, blacksmiths clanging away. Even the churches are breathing fire. The governor's proclaimed a Day of Repentance for Sunday."

"Yes," Sir William said a trifle sourly. "Parson Mather is

certainly in his element these days. He said grace at the victory banquet last night. It was half an hour before we could break bread."

Clarke grinned. "Glad I'm a Church of Englander, Sir. These Puritan parsons sure do have iron lungs and fireproof throats. I hear Mather and his son, Cotton, have got a couple of fire-eating sermons ready for Sunday meeting."

Sir William nodded. "They'll roast a peck of papists, Clarke. They'll burn Quebec to the ground in hellfire. Sulfur and brimstone all the way." He sighed. "I wish I could plead sick . . . but I don't dare." He put aside the quill in his hand. "I've just finished an appeal to the king for arms and ammunition. We need them badly. Even with what we brought back from Port Royal, the colony's treasury is absolutely empty."

"But, Sir—won't that delay the expedition?"

"Not too long—if the fair winds hold up. One way or the other, we should hear by mid-July. Plenty of time to sail up the St. Lawrence." He frowned. "That reminds me, Clarke— we need a pilot. I'd hate to try those winds and shoals without a pilot. You've got to find someone who knows the St. Lawrence." He clapped his hands together dolefully. "We ain't got enough warships, either. Four was all I could scrape up. Got one beauty, though. The *Six Friends*. West India trade. Forty-four guns. It'll do for my flagship. But I need more ships, Clarke. Traders and fishermen. I'm counting on you to hire at least a dozen more."

Clarke nodded. "I'll do my best, Sir. But do you think it's wise to *hire* ships? Their owners and their captains might not want to risk them under Quebec's guns. After all, they are their livelihood."

"Nonsense!" Phips boomed. "They're Englishmen, ain't they? All I'll need to do is holler, 'God save King William!' and they'll sail them scows of theirs right up to the mouths of them French cannon." He shook his head. "Frankly, Clarke, I'm surprised to hear you talking that way." He winked slyly. "Kind of fergit you were a New York man." Jonathan turned scarlet and Phips chuckled heartily. "Never mind, Clarke—I know the color of your kidney. And for God's sake, find me a pilot, will you?"

Jonathan's efforts to find a pilot proved fruitless. He rode up and down the coast, stopping at all the ports from Cape Cod to Nantasket—even sailing down to Nantucket. But he found no one who knew the St. Lawrence. His failure also made his attempts to hire transport ships more difficult. Many of the sea captains or owners shied away when they learned the fleet would sail blindly up the great northern river. "It's *my* ship, Clarke," one Nantasket merchant explained. "If it sinks, will the colony pay me for it?" Eventually, however, Clarke hired a dozen more small vessels, thereby expanding the invasion fleet to thirty-eight ships. Each time he acquired one, he hastened to the Green Lane to report—and for an opportunity to speak to Martha St. John.

But he never saw her, even though he lingered in the halls and corridors or prowled them softly for a glimpse of her. At length he decided to spy on the house. Whenever he was free, he rode to the Green Lane and tied his horse behind a huge spreading elm tree across the street. One Tuesday he was thrilled to see the gates open and Martha drive out in a little white gig drawn by a beautifully groomed black horse. He could see a hamper on the floor beside her and guessed that she was going picnicking. Martha stopped the gig at the end of the lane, waiting until another girl her age came out carrying a violin case. They drove off together. Jonathan followed at a discreet distance. Three or four miles outside of town, the gig came to a hillside dotted with grazing cows. It turned through a gate leading to a mill beside a millrace and a waterfall, stopping there. Jonathan walked his horse closer. Soon he heard voices chattering gaily, and then the sound of a violin. Dismounting, he crept toward a hill overlooking the mill, from which he could see Martha solemnly dancing a solo minuet while her friend played the fiddle. Jonathan smiled softly, left the hill, and rode back to town.

Two Tuesdays later, Martha drove the gig out the gate again, clattered down the street, and stopped. When no one came out, she went up the walk, returning a few minutes later alone. She made as though to turn her little carriage around, but then, apparently changing her mind, she clucked to the black horse and rode out to the mill again. She was just attempting to lift out the hamper when Jonathan cantered inside the gate.

"Lord in heaven, if it isn't Miss St. John," he exclaimed in a transparent attempt to seem surprised. "Here, let me help you with that hamper."

"No, thanks," Martha said coldly, tossing her chestnut hair. "I can do it myself."

"But it's heavy," Jonathan said, dismounting and coming toward her.

Martha swung on him with blazing green eyes. "Why did you follow me here, Mr. Clarke?"

"But I just happened by."

"You did not! I saw you sneaking around that hill there last Tuesday—and the Tuesday before that." She glared at him scornfully. "You can't be much of an Indian fighter to let a couple of girls catch you out like that."

Jonathan grinned sheepishly. "Aw, I . . . I just wanted to talk to you."

"What makes you think I want to talk to you?"

"You did once," Clarke said, tethering his horse to a tree and lifting the hamper onto a table beneath it.

"That was because Uncle William introduced me to you. I couldn't very well snub you, could I? . . . And what are you doing with my hamper?"

"Just curious," he replied, lifting the lid. "You've sure been snubbing me ever since. I've been to see Sir William at least two times a week for a month now, and I haven't seen a speck of you."

Martha blushed. "Why . . . why should you care?"

He put down the lid and came to her. "Because I love you," he said simply.

"How dare you!" Martha cried angrily. "You . . . you impertinent scoundrel! If I were to report you to Sir William, he'd have you horse-whipped!"

"Probably," Jonathan said easily, and then, taking a shot in the dark: "Have you given him your answer yet?"

Martha gasped, putting her hand to her mouth. She sank down on a bench, the color draining from her face. "What . . . what are you trying to say, Mr. Clarke?" she stammered.

"Jonathan," Clarke replied. "Call me Jonathan. And you, Martha, know exactly what I'm saying. Sir William has asked you to marry him."

Her green eyes blazed up again. "How do you know?" she cried hotly.

"He told me. On the way back from Port Royal. He was a

little tipsy. He said he expected to be elevated to the peerage and that you couldn't resist him."

"He did say that?" Martha murmured; and then, angry again: "It's none of your business!"

"But it is, Mar—"

"Stop calling me Martha!"

"I will not. I love you, Martha, and I want you to marry *me*."

"You fool! Sir William is the most powerful man in Boston."

"Apparently not powerful enough to win your hand. At least, not yet."

Martha lifted her head proudly. "I told him I would give him my answer before he leaves for Quebec."

Now it was Clarke who was indignant. "You're *considering* him? That puffed-up old fraud? Why, he's old enough to be your grandfather."

"Stop saying such horrid things!" Martha screamed, covering her ears with her hands. "I won't listen! I won't let you talk like that! Sir William is the sweetest, kindest, most gentle man I've ever known. Nothing like you—you . . . you blackguard!" Martha began to cry. Holding up her skirts and sobbing, she ran to the gig. Clarke pursued her relentlessly. "Very pretty." He sneered. "Sweetest, kindest, gentlest, eh? Has it ever occurred to you why? Because he was waiting, that's why! Biding his time. Sure, he gave you everything you wanted. Spoiled you rotten. But were you ever left alone in a room with any male under sixty? Did you ever go to a ball for young people? To a fish fry? A sugaring? Anyplace where you might meet a young man?" Martha stared at him in horror. She had stopped sobbing, but her full breasts still rose and fell. Jonathan fought back a desire to seize her by the waist and press her to him. Seeming to read his mind, she shrank from him. "Don't touch me," she whispered. Clarke bowed and walked toward his horse. While untying it, he heard the wheels of the gig rattling and looked up to see Martha St. John driving back to Boston. Her figure seemed waiflike and forlorn as she sat huddled on the box, and Clarke wondered if she were weeping again.

Two weeks later, on August 9, 1690, the fleet set sail for Quebec. King William had again said no—not a cannon or a cartridge—and Phips had decided to put to sea immediately before any more time was lost.

Once again the wharves were black with people and full of the sound of bands and marching feet. Jonathan Clarke had again said his farewells to the Cowletts and little Jeddy, but this time he did not share the mood of exaltation which had seized the crowd and the soldiery. Success at Quebec, he thought bitterly, could mean the hand of Martha St. John for Sir William Phips. And yet, he had not forgotten Schenectady. He still burned to destroy the French, still hoped that he might find Sainte-Helene among the defenders of the city and avenge Jeddy's murdered parents.

Clarke saw Sir William standing on the wharf in his general's uniform, surrounded by the governor and Council. Martha was a few feet away by herself, wearing the green dress she had worn the day they sailed for Port Royal. Jonathan wondered dully if she had given herself to Phips. He made as though to pass her, and to his surprise felt her hand on his arm. She smiled at him gently. "I've been thinking about what you said, Jonathan," she whispered, "and I haven't given him my answer yet." Jonathan's mouth flew open, but Martha put a finger to her lips, glancing anxiously toward Sir William. She pressed a small white envelope into Jonathan's hand and walked quickly away.

Jonathan's heart was beating wildly. He turned to cast one more glance at Martha, standing quietly apart from Sir William's group, and then ran to the flagship's gangplank, where he stopped to open the envelope. It contained a lock of chestnut hair. Jonathan pressed it rapturously between his thumb and forefinger, seduced by its softness as though it were her very flesh. He put it to his nose to inhale its fragrance. Then, replacing it in its envelope and placing it in his breast pocket, he ran up the gangplank with a wild yell. At the top, he turned to raise his fist in a gesture of victory.

"Now, what the devil's got into him?" Sir William Phips mumbled to Governor Bradstreet, pointing toward Clarke. "The way he's carrying on, you'd think *his* name was Phips."

4

At the end of July, alarmed by reports of Iroquois war parties burning and butchering French settlements on the upper St. Lawrence, Count Frontenac sailed upriver to Montreal. At once he stationed detachments of regulars in stockade forts among the endangered parishes, detailing troops to guard the settlers while they worked in the fields. Satisfied that the settlements were safe, he prepared to return to Quebec, until an agitated Sainte-Helene burst into his chambers crying, "Monsieur le Comte, the lake is covered with war canoes!"

"*Mon Dieu*," Frontenac swore, bringing his fist down hard upon his desk. "Iroquois! Iroquois and the accursed English. At once, Sainte-Helene—sound the warning cannon! Have the soldiery fall back on the town. Bring in the habitants. Drive in the cattle. Send a dispatch boat downriver to warn Quebec."

Soon the roar of cannon reverberated along the banks of the mighty stream. Men and women, alarm and fright etched deep in their faces, rushed from the fields to their cabins. Carts were yoked to oxen and quickly filled with possessions on top of which the smaller children quietly climbed. Older children helped their parents round up the cattle and drive them ahead of the carts. Babes in arms were clasped anxiously to the bosoms of mothers riding on the box. Slowly, in a long snaking line, crawling beneath a cloud of dust uncoiling above them, the inhabitants of the upper river toiled toward the open gates of Montreal. To either side of them, files of French soldiers in white uniforms marched to the vivacious beat of drums and the gay squeal of pipes.

"Eh, *bien,* we are ready," Frontenac said a few hours later to Sainte-Helene.

"Ready, yes, Excellency, but not for battle," Sainte-Helene replied, smiling. "It is a false alarm. The war canoes are not of the Iroquois. It is the Indians of the lakes, come to trade again."

Frontenac beamed. "*Ma foi,* they have come to us? They have not traded here since I left Canada eight years ago."

"Your war parties have had the desired effect, Monsieur. Our little affair at Schenectady has frightened the lake Indians. They have abandoned the English. They are afraid of the Iroquois. The Ottawas and the Hurons ate an Iroquois this summer and broke the treaty with the Five Nations." Sainte-Helene also beamed. "Now the tribes of the lakes are coming to us. There are two hundred war canoes, Excellency, filled with beaver skins."

Next day the canoes came down the rapids and landed near the town. Five hundred painted and greased Indians—Hurons, Ottawas, Cree, Ojibwa, Pottawatomi, and Nipissings—came ashore laden with furs to set up a market. Next day more canoes filled with French traders and more furs shot the boiling waters. Frontenac watched the colorful unfolding of the Indian market with unconcealed joy. "*Ma foi,*" he breathed to Sainte-Helene, "I have never seen so many skins. A hundred thousand crowns yesterday—fifty thousand today. The colony has never been so rich. Now, what will those scoundrels in Versailles say of Frontenac, eh, Sainte-Heleñe? What of Bishop Laval, him and his rascally councillors?" Almost capering for joy, the little count, resplendent in violet silk and lace, swung aboard a white horse and cantered slowly toward a ring of about eighty chiefs and sachems, all in war paint and war bonnets, seated smoking around a council fire. Behind him came his officers, like himself peruked and bewigged, powdered and perfumed, in silks and satins of the rainbow, buckles and sword hilts gleaming, their groomed and high-stepping mounts snorting and shaking their manes.

"Ho, ho, ho," the Indian chiefs chanted as the French dismounted and took their places in the council ring. A Huron chief arose to speak, addressing Frontenac: "With all our hearts, we welcome the great Onontio back to the land of our fathers. We are glad, for the Onontio is a great warrior. We will fight with him to put his foot on the neck of the perfidious English. We ask our father to destroy the Iroquois, too, for they are a ravenous dog who is biting everyone. Onontio must not fight the English only, but the Iroquois, too. If this is not done, my father and I shall both perish." The Huron chief sat down to deep-throated cries of, "Ho, ho, ho," and Frontenac arose.

"I am pleased to see that you have accepted the protection I have always offered you. You know that once before I tamed the Iroquois dog and tied him up. But when I returned to France, he behaved worse than ever. Now he shall feel my power. So shall the English. I am strong enough to kill the English, destroy the Iroquois, and ruin you, if you fail in your duty to me. The Iroquois have killed and captured you in time of peace. Do to them as they would like to do to you, do to the English as they would like to do to you, but hold fast to your true father, who will never abandon you. Will you let the English rum that has killed you in your wigwams lure you into the kettles of the Iroquois? Is not my brandy better, which has never killed you, but always made you strong?"

Shouts of approval followed Frontenac's speech, succeeded by yells of delight when the aged Frenchman seized a tomahawk and began to dance the war dance. "Wah! Wah! Wah!" he yelled, striking his mouth with his fingertips, brandishing the hatchet over his head, and leaping and spinning while his violet coattails went flying. Soon most of his officers had joined him, and then the Indians arose and mingled among them, and the Indian market was transformed into a wildly whooping and gyrating amalgam of the savage and the civilized, the skin-clad and the silken.

Then came a solemn war feast. A pair of oxen and six large dogs were chopped into pieces and boiled in kettles full of prunes. Kegs of wine and casks of tobacco were opened. Frontenac wisely refrained from issuing brandy, for he did not wish his allies to drink themselves into the customary killing rage and destroy each other. As a final gift, he gave them a captured Iroquois to devour. "Come, my children," he called, "let us roast an Iroquois."

Shouting frenziedly, the Indians ran to seize a naked captive who had been led forward with a rope around his neck. They planted a stake and tied him to it, with enough rope so that he could move back and forth as though on a dog run. They fired charges of powder into his skin, laughing hideously as the unfortunate man ran back and forth upon his tether. Soon there was not an inch of his naked body not black with powder burns, but because he had begun to scream and plead in a manner unbecoming a warrior, his disgusted tormentors shot him dead and cut him up and threw the dripping pieces into the cooking kettles.

Frontenac, meanwhile, had departed—fearful that he might be asked to share their grisly delicacy. He returned to Montreal to receive a report from an Abnaki Indian who said his tribe had captured an Englishwoman near Portsmouth. She told them that a great fleet had sailed from Boston for Quebec. At once the count embarked in a small sailing ship. It sprang a leak and began to sink. Exasperated, Frontenac returned to Montreal, where he boarded a canoe and sailed downriver, ordering Sainte-Helene to follow him with two hundred men. It began to rain. An autumnal torrent pelted the French war chief, plastering his violet silk against his skin, but he pressed on. Next day he met another canoe coming from Quebec with the report that the English fleet had been sighted above Tadoussac, three days' sail from Quebec. Frontenac sent a messenger back to Montreal instructing the governor to gather all the forces at his disposal and descend immediately to Quebec. The count hurried on, huddled in the bow of the canoe, his old bones aching, his teeth chattering. Four days after he left Montreal, he arrived at Quebec. A throng of townspeople and soldiers, priests and nuns, even the detested Bishop Laval, greeted him with cheers and music as he alighted on the strand of the Lower Town. Waving their hats and hailing him as their deliverer, they followed the old man as he strode up the steep incline of Mountain Street to the Upper Town and went immediately to inspect the defenses he had ordered to be built.

"*Imprenable!*" he murmured proudly to Sainte-Helene at

his side. "Impregnable! See," he said, standing on the cliff above the St. Lawrence and pointing to the broad Basin of Quebec, wide as a sea harbor, below them. "We are safe on two sides. A goat cannot climb these cliffs, Monsieur, and certainly not an English soldier with pack and musket and underneath our fire. The St. Charles protects our left flank. Only our rear lies open, Sainte-Helene, and I have secured it with barricades, ditches and towers of stone."

"What of the Lower Town, Excellency?"

"They may have it. They cannot climb the cliffs. They will be in the open for us to destroy them at our leisure." Frontenac smiled confidently. "Let them come, Monsieur."

Throughout the night, while Count Frontenac lay sleepless in the Château St. Louis, men came flocking into the city from the surrounding parishes. Militia, regulars, *coureurs de bois*, they trooped along St. Louis Street, singing and whooping—warming the heart of their commander in his room above them. With the soldiers from Montreal, he thought jubilantly, I shall have close to three thousand men. He went to sleep unaware that his sentinels on the Saut au Matelot had already sighted the slow-moving lights of ships sailing slowly upriver. In the morning, Louis de Buade, the Count Frontenac, beheld the sails of his enemy.

Sir William's long delay at Boston, waiting for the help that never came, had cost him invaluable time. The voyage to the St. Lawrence had taken weeks; other weeks were wasted groping up the unknown river without a pilot. Once he had cleared Tadoussac, Sir William cast anchor and spent nearly three weeks holding councils of war and drawing up regulations for his army. All this, Jonathan Clarke thought glumly, should have been done between Boston and the St. Lawrence. Aloud, he urged speed upon Sir William.

"It is already October, Sir," he warned, "and the river could very well freeze before the end of November. If it does, we'll be lost."

"Nonsense, Clarke," Phips boomed. "Nothing to worry about at all. My prisoners say Quebec is in bad shape. Frontenac's away in Montreal. Their cannon are dismounted and they've got barely two hundred soldiers against our two thousand. Come, come, Clarke—you've seen how them French knuckled under in Nova Scotia. Do you think these Canadians are any different?"

A fusillade of shots rang out from the Canadian shore. Phips jumped erect and rushed from his cabin to the quarterdeck, followed by Clarke. Both put their glasses to their eyes. They saw a flotilla of small boats sent to seize provisions and fresh water turn about and come speeding toward the *Six Friends*, the sun glinting on the blades of their oars flashing in and out of the water. The boats drew alongside. Clarke gasped and Sir William frowned. Fully half of the men in each boat were dead or wounded. The hulls of the boats were holed and their gunwales splintered. Clarke heard the groans of the wounded and ground his teeth.

Phips seized a speaking trumpet and called to the helmsman in the boat below him. "You, there—what happened?"

"Ambush!" the man shouted, holding his broken left arm with his right hand. "They hid in the bushes. Just as we touched shore, they opened fire. Had a goddamn priest leading 'em. Cape and cassock, by Jesus—I saw the bloody hellion. *'Maut les Protestants!'* they kept hollering. Damn the Protestants."

Phips's face blanched and he wheeled silently to return to his cabin. Clarke stayed at the rail, watching the able men helping the wounded climb painfully up the Jacob's ladder. Looks like the Canadians are different, he thought bitterly, glancing quickly upriver when he heard another volley of musketry. Once again he saw English boats sent to plunder the Canadian shore turning to flee for the safety of the fleet. They're whittling us, by God! he thought. By the time we reach Quebec, we might not have an army. *If* we reach Quebec.

At last, on October 16, seventy-one days after leaving Boston, the fleet sailed through the shredding mists of dawn into the Basin of Quebec. Phips and Clarke stood again on the quarterdeck. They had already been impressed by the roar of the Montmorency cataract tumbling into the Montmorency River on their right. Now they stared in awe at the enormous expanse of the basin, at the warlike city on the rocks above them, its ranks of cannon with their ominously gaping mouths, its fluttering flags and church spires framed against the faint silhouette of the Laurentian Mountains in the distance. Through their uptilted glasses they could see the

Château St. Louis perched boldly on the edge of the cliff, and the white flag of France with its golden Bourbon lilies flaunting defiance to the invaders. It was a full minute before either man spoke.

"Well, well," Sir William said fussily, "it looks a little tougher than Port Royal, I'll admit that. But we'll crack it, Clarke. Them Frenchies just ain't got the heart to stand up to Englishmen." He strode to his cabin, returning with the surrender demand he had written out the night before. Clarke took it with a silent nod, descending the Jacob's ladder to a waiting boat. Midway between the *Six Friends* and the shore, he was met by four French canoes. Taken into one of them, he was immediately blindfolded by a bandage covering half his face. When he stepped ashore, he was seized roughly by the arms and drawn every which way. He bumped into walls and clambered over hogsheads placed in his path. Giggling women shoved him or spun him around, crying, "Colin Maillard! Blind man's buff." At length he realized that he was ascending a series of staircases and then walking down a long hall. Suddenly he was in a room filled with voices, which fell silent upon his entrance. The blindfold was removed. Blinking, he found himself in a huge chamber under large, glittering chandeliers. Before him stood Count Frontenac, dressed in the white uniform of a French general, surrounded by his officers, all of them also elegant in gold and silver lace. For a moment Jonathan felt self-conscious, inferior, in his homespun breeches and plain blue sailor's jacket. But he quickly recovered his composure. Staring coolly into Frontenac's eyes, he handed him Sir William's summons. The count handed it to an interpreter, who read:

Sir William Phips, Knight, General and Commander-in-chief in and over their Majesties' Forces of New England, by Sea and Land, to Count Frontenac, Lieutenant General and Governor for the French King at Canada; or, in his absence, to his Deputy, or him or them in chief command at Quebec:

The war between the crowns of England and France doth not only sufficiently warrant, but the destruction made by the French and Indians, under your command and encouragement, upon the persons and estates of their Majesties' subjects of New England, without provocation on their part, hath put them under the necessity of this expedition for their own security and satisfaction. And although the cruelties and barbarities used against them by the French and Indians might, upon the present opportunity, prompt unto a severe revenge, yet, being desirous to avoid all inhumane and unchristianlike actions, and to prevent shedding of blood as much as may be,

I, the aforesaid William Phips, Knight, do hereby, in the name and in the behalf of their most excellent Majesties, William and Mary, King and Queen of England, Scotland, France, and Ireland, Defenders of the Faith, and by order of their said Majesties' government of the Massachusetts colony in New England, demand a present surrender of your forts and castles, undemolished, and the King's and other stores, unembezzled, with a seasonable delivery of all captives; together with a surrender of all your persons and estates to my dispose: upon the doing whereof, you may expect mercy from me, as a Christian, according to what shall be found for their Majesties' service and the subjects' security. Which, if you refuse forthwith to do, I am come provided, and am resolved, by the help of God, in whom I trust, by force of arms to revenge all wrongs and injuries offered, and bring you under subjection to the Crown of England, and, when too late, make you wish you had accepted of the favor tendered.

Your answer positive in an hour returned by your own trumpet, with the return of mine, is required upon the peril that will ensue.

Cries of indignation arose from the French officers. Clarke heard a tall, hawk-nosed man shout angrily. "Insolent rebel! Does he think we are cowards? It is an insult, Excellency, for which we ought to hang this pirate's lackey!"

"Monsieur Sainte-Helene," Frontenac murmured, "we fight a barbaric war, but we are not barbarians. We do not kill mess—"

"*Sainte-Helene?*"

Clarke's snarled and hissing query cut across Frontenac's voice like a whip. "You are Sainte-Helene? You are the butcher of Schenectady?"

"I am Sainte-Helene, yes," the Frenchman replied, his hand falling on his sword hilt. "Your second question, Monsieur, I did not seem to hear."

"I was in Schenectady the day you left," Clarke rushed on with glittering eyes and trembling voice. "I saw the butchery. The scalped heads with the brains falling out. Not even pregnancy was a defense against your devils."

Angry cries arose again, but Sainte-Helene lifted a restraining hand. "And were you also in Lachine or La Prairie the day your Iroquois left? There, too, the brains were strewn among the snow. And the burned Frenchmen tied to stakes, eh, Monsieur? The lips cut off . . . the finger ends bitten off . . ." Sainte-Helene's lips curled in contempt. "You Anglo-Saxons are indeed angels, Monsieur. You excite your ghouls against us, but you do not march with them. You do not bloody your own hands. No, you lift them in horror when you have heard what they have done. You English angels are above such conduct, eh, Monsieur?" Shouts of approval followed Sainte-Helene's words. Even Frontenac nodded. But he contained himself and said to Clarke:

"Tell your general that I do not recognize King William, and that the Prince of Orange, who so styles himself, is a usurper who has violated the laws of blood in attempting to dethrone his father-in-law. I know no king of England but King James. Your general ought not to be surprised at the hostilities which he says that the French have carried on in the colony of Massachusetts. Since King Louis, my master, has taken the King of England under his protection, and is about to replace him on the throne by force of arms, he might have expected that his majesty would order me to make war on a people who have rebelled against their lawful prince." Turning with a smile to the officers around him, Frontenac continued: "Even if your general had offered me conditions a little more gracious, does he suppose that these brave gentlemen would give their consent, and advise me to trust a man who broke his agreement with the governor of Port Royal, or a rebel who has failed in his duty to his king?"

Clarke bit his lip listening to the wrathful murmurs of assent among the French officers. He was shaken by the fervor of Frontenac's reply and dismayed that he would have to recount it in person to Sir William. "Will you give me your reply in writing, General Frontenac?" he asked.

"No," the count said, shaking his head grimly. "I will answer your general only by the mouths of my cannon, that he may learn that a man like me is not to be summoned after this fashion. Let him do his best, and I will do mine." He nodded to the young ensign who had escorted Clarke into the room, the blindfold was again placed over Jonathan's face, and he was taken back the way he had come.

"Called me a rebel and a pirate, eh?" Sir William Phips muttered angrily. "Well, we'll see who'll dingle-dangle from whose yardarm tomorrow." He turned to the officers assembled in his cabin. "Tide's turned," he said. "We'll have to wait until morning. But let me go over the plan again. You, Major," he said to John Walley, his second-in-command, "will take twelve hundred men and land at Beauport below the St. Charles. You will cross the river at the ford there. Meanwhile, you, Clarke, will lead the small ships of the fleet up the St. Charles as far as the ford. You'll keep the enemy in check with your guns while bringing food, ammunition and entrenching tools to Walley's men. After you and Walley cross the St. Charles, you'll attack Quebec in the rear. And then," he continued with obvious satisfaction, "*I* will cannonade Quebec from the front." He clapped his hands together in pleasure. "We'll crack that French nut wide open."

Major John Walley sat grim-faced in the stern of one of the longboats being rowed slowly downriver toward Beauport on the port side. Although there had been high winds the day before, postponing the attack another day, the St. Lawrence was now calm and the great basin lay like an oval of blue glass under the sun. John Walley trailed his hand in the water, surprised at its coldness. Almost freezing, by Jesus, he thought—we've got to get this over in a day or two or we're done for. Lifting his glasses, he studied the approaching Beauport shore, and was reassured by no sign of the French. The boats slowly passed the mouth of the St. Charles in line. "Seth," Major Walley called to the young bugler seated admiships, "blow the attack." The bugler lifted his instrument to his lips and blew lustily. The notes pealed and reverberated across the water, followed by a solid beat of drums, and the vessel swung to port and headed shoreward, the oarsmen plying their blades faster and faster, urged on by the cries of

Walley's twelve hundred English colonials. Their commander watched the maneuver with approval. He had only rehearsed a landing once, back in Nantasket, and it had been a perfection of confusion. This one, the real thing under the eye of the enemy, was well-nigh flawless, Walley thought.

So did Jonathan Clarke, watching through glasses while moving from ship to ship in a cockboat. To Jonathan, Walley's men looked like swarms of black ants as they leaped into the shallow water and plodded through the mud onto the drier footing of the strand. He was pleased to hear no sound of gunfire. He was not pleased, however, with the treatment given him by the small ship captains. To a man, they had refused to sail up the St. Charles to help Walley's force cross the ford. Jonathan's face was black when he came aboard the *Six Friends* to report to Sir William.

"They won't move," he said. "They say they signed on for transport, not fighting."

Phips struck his hands together forcefully. "The scoundrels!" he exclaimed, rushing to the rail. "Look at them—they're pulling foot! The cowards! I ought to wipe their noses with bow shots."

It was true. The hired traders and fishermen had set their sails and were slowly retreating below the St. Charles. The *Six Friends* and the three other large ships were left by themselves on the lower edge of the basin, still safely out of range of Frontenac's guns. To Jonathan's surprise, Phips gave the order to sail in closer and signaled to the other trio to follow.

"Is this wise, Sir?" he asked, nervously studying Quebec's ranked cannon. "They've got some twenty-four-pounders up there. And if I'm not mistaken, they've got more of the same in the Lower Town."

"Nothing to be afraid of," Phips sniffed. "They won't shoot. Besides, I've got to be in position to support Walley."

"But he isn't across the river yet!"

Phips did not hear him. He was intent upon a puff of smoke rising above Quebec. A few seconds later the two men heard the report of a cannon shot. A geyser of water rose into the air off the port quarter facing the city.

"They've opened fire!" Phips bellowed, wheeling on the drummer standing beside him. "General quarters!"

At once the sharp, staccato beat of the naval call to arms

rang out aboard the *Six Friends*, and then from her three companions.

"Clear the decks for action!" Phips roared, and the sails of the bombardment fleet came tumbling down while seamen swarmed up the masts to furl and bind them. The sound of running feet was everywhere, followed by the rumble of iron wheels as the gunners rolled their cannon into the gunports. They crouched there, blowing on their slow matches—waiting for the order to fire. Jonathan Clarke was stunned.

"My God, Sir William—you're not going to bombard the town?"

"Indeed I am! What d'ye think I came here for?"

"But, sir—Walley isn't over the river yet! And we don't have that much ammunition."

"Enough to smash them unclean sons of Satan. I cain't wait, Clarke. Besides, you heard what they called me."

Jonathan stared at Sir William in incredulous dismay. The premature bombardment would ruin all hope of success, he realized. Even if Sir William did succeed in silencing Frontenac's guns, Walley's force was still on the wrong side of the St. Charles and there was no hope of ever ascending those rocky heights above them. And there would be no more ammunition for the artillery. Jonathan Clarke wanted to shout these truths into Sir William's ear, to persuade him to adhere to his own plan—to sail out of range until some means could be found of crossing the St. Charles and *then* to resume the cannonade.

But it was too late, he realized hopelessly, listening to the sound of cannonballs wailing overhead, watching Sir William striding up and down the quarterdeck in exultation. There was a crash above him. Warning cries arose on all sides, and Jonathan looked up to see a furled spar plunging toward him. He sidestepped and it hit the rail with a loud snapping sound, pitching over the side and narrowly missing Sir William. A French ball screamed toward the *Six Friends*, carrying off the head of the drummer boy standing beside Sir William, and splattering Phips with the boy's brains. "My, my," Phips murmured, brushing the grisly strings from his face. "I never realized the child was so brainy. You, there," he called to a steward, "bring me an orange to freshen my mouth."

He's a *fool!* Jonathan thought fiercely, watching in disgust while Sir William calmly peeled the orange and began sucking on it. He may be brave, but he's a complete, utter and incredible ass! A cry of pain arose from one of the guns. A seaman staggered out of the smoke, clutching his stomach and screaming—trying to contain the blood and intestines squirming through his fingers. He sank to the deck. Jonathan seized the slow match from his hand and ran into the smoking cockpit. He plunged it into the touch-hole of an eighteen-pounder. The cannon roared and belched orange flame, rolling backward so quickly in recoil it tore the foot from an unwary sailor. Vaguely Jonathan heard him scream, busying himself again at the gunport as his cannon's smoking mouth was swabbed, a charge of powder rammed home, and a ball shoved down the barrel. Once more Jonathan applied the match.

"BA . . . LOOM!"

Now the artillery duel was truly joined. Reeling out of the roar and smoke of the gunport, Jonathan Clarke staggered to the rail, gasping, digging at his smoke-watered eyes with his knuckles. He leaned over the side to escape a cloud of black gunsmoke drifting low over the ship. All around him he heard a continuous roar, as though the basin were an iron bowl and the sound of the battle went crashing and reverberating around it, rolling back redoubled from the rock of Quebec and the chain of mountains behind it. Straightening, Jonathan saw that the French in the Upper Town had hung a tapestry of the Holy Family from the cathedral spire. Phips saw it, too.

"Shoot it down!" he bellowed to his gunners. "It's the flag of the fiend! Shoot it down, I tell you!"

Broadside after broadside thundered out from the *Six Friends,* causing the ship to buckle and roll. Jonathan eagerly trained his glasses on the cathedral. But the balls screaming out over the basin fell harmlessly off the stone walls of the building. Some of them failed to get that far, striking the cliffsides and falling back on the Lower Town, spent. At once Jonathan realized that Sir William, to save powder, had ordered the guns undercharged. He also knew that, for the same reason, the fishermen and merchant seamen manning the fleet's guns had had almost no practice in firing their pieces. It's a fiasco, he thought glumly, catching at the rail after a French ball struck the hull beneath him with a splintering smash.

Gradually, with the approach of darkness, the roar of battle subsided. A breeze riffled the surface of the basin, and the English on their battered ships could hear bells pealing and the faint sound of chanting on the rock above them.

"It's the bishop and his pack of priests," Sir William snorted in contempt. "They're claiming a miracle for that foul flag of theirs."

Miracle! Jonathan Clarke thought in disgust. The miracle would have been if we had hit it! Turning toward the scuttle butt to rinse his dried-out mouth and clean his powder-blackened face, he heard the sound of musketry below the St. Charles.

Major Walley had formed his men in companies along the Beauport strand. With drums beating and amid cries of "God save King William!" they marched in a ragged line up the rising ground toward the river ford behind a line of thickets. Among the trees, unknown to the English, were three hundred sharpshooters Frontenac had ordered across the ford under the command of Sainte-Helene. They opened a galling fire on the approaching English.

Some of Walley's men began to fall. The major saw his little bugler go down with kicking legs, a ball in his brain. The rest of his troops broke in disorder.

"Form, men . . . form!" Walley roared.

The English recovered and formed a line, more ragged than before.

"Charge!" Walley yelled, and they swept forward into another volley of musketry. But few fell, for the French fire was high. "*Soldats,* lower your aim!" Sainte-Helene cried. His order came too late, and the disorderly but still onrushing English came under a second high volley into the thickets. Again crying, "God save King William!" and stabbing at the French with bayonets, they drove the enemy back toward the river. Now Sainte-Helene's men began to fight in the Indian fashion they knew so well, leaping from tree to tree, dodging among the rocks and bushes to fire at the exposed English. After night fell, they withdrew across the ford, wading the icy water waist-deep with their muskets held over their heads.

Walley immediately posted sentinels and encamped for the night. Although embittered at the failure of Clarke to appear with the covering force of ships, he was nevertheless relieved to find that his losses were not so great as he had imagined: only four dead and sixty wounded. Throughout the bitter-cold night he could hear the groans of the wounded and the coughing of those already down with smallpox and pneumonia. All of them were hungry, having had nothing but a biscuit apiece to eat all day. Walley could not sleep. There was a strange clattering in his ears which he mistook for katydids, until he realized that it was too cold for insects and that the sound was the chattering of teeth—including his own.

At dawn the New Englanders brushed the ice from their clothing and arose, beating their hands together. A sentinel escorted Jonathan Clarke into the camp. "Sir William is anxious to know your situation," Jonathan explained.

"Couldn't be worse," Walley grunted.

"D'you think you can make a dash of it across the ford? Sir William thinks you can still take Quebec in the rear."

Walley shook his round head. "Take Quebec, eh?" he repeated grimly. "With a half-barrel of gunpowder and a biscuit a man? That's what he landed us with. Where's your covering fleet, anyway, Clarke?"

Jonathan pointed downriver. "Gone. They said they weren't paid to fight."

"The scum!" Walley fell silent, stroking his stubble of beard. "I think I'd better pull foot."

Jonathan nodded. "I don't blame you. But you'd better speak to Sir William first. I've got a boat on the beach."

The two men walked back to the Beauport shore, reaching it just as Frontenac's first shot of the day plunged down from the rock to break a film of ice an inch thick that had formed on the river. Clarke and Walley watched the renewal of the artillery duel. Once again, the light and undercharged cannon of the English were no match for the French. Phips's ships were being systematically smashed. One of the French balls shattered the flagstaff of the *Six Friends,* and the Cross of St. George fluttered down onto the river. Canadians in a birch canoe paddled out on the basin to seize it and bring it back to the Lower Town in triumph.

Clarke ground his teeth. "A ship's a fool to fight a fort," he growled. Walley nodded, pointing grimly to the English ships. "They're floating wrecks. They'll have to cut and run."

Even as he spoke, one of the four warships upped anchor

and began moving downstream on the tide. The *Six Friends* soon followed. But with her rigging in tatters, her mainmast cut in two, her cabin a shambles, and her hull full of holes and leaking, she had to be cut from her moorings, only able to drift on the tide. Within a few minutes the other pair also retired.

Watching the battered and listing English drifting slowly out of range, hearing the ringing of bells and beating of drums on the rock above him, Jonathan Clarke felt like weeping. "It's all over," he said bitterly.

A volley of shots rang out behind them. "Not yet," Walley cried, turning to run toward the St. Charles. Clarke followed, drawing a pistol from his belt. Reaching the thicket topping the rising ground, they found Walley's men engaged in a hand-to-hand struggle with Sainte-Helene's sharpshooters, who had recrossed the ford.

"*Vive le roi!*" the French shouted.

"God save King William!" roared the English.

Jonathan Clarke stood still, his nostrils dilated, his heart beating. He had seen Sainte-Helene crouched behind an elm tree, aiming his musket at Walley, beside him. Jonathan aimed his pistol and fired. Sainte-Helene gave a cry of pain. The ball had grazed the back of his hand and made him miss his shot. "Sainte-Helene!" Jonathan Clarke cried above the yells and explosions of battle. "I've come for you, you devil!" The Frenchman came slowly erect, taking careful aim at Clarke. He fired. The shot knocked Jonathan's pistol from his hand. Sainte-Helene bent to reload his musket, and Clarke drew his cutlass and charged.

Jonathan's first blow struck the musket held by Sainte-Helene at port arms with a loud, ringing clang. The Frenchman grinned, baring his white teeth. "You are strong, Monsieur." He paused. "But I am quick," and he hurled the musket butt-first at Jonathan's face. It struck the surprised Clarke on the side of his forehead, knocking him down. At once Sainte-Helene drew his tomahawk and swung.

Clarke parried the blow on his cutlass. The blades clashed. Clarke struggled erect, supporting himself with one hand while holding his cutlass outthrust. Sainte-Helene backed warily off, his tomahawk held beside his ear. He threw it. Clarke ducked, and the hatchet buried itself in a white birch tree behind him. Now Clarke advanced with a gloating grin. "You will kill no more unborn babies, Sainte-Helene," he crooned.

Backing away, glancing wildly around the battlefield for a fallen weapon, the Frenchman halted. A look of dawning comprehension came over his face. "So that is it, Monsieur?" he said softly. "You think it was I who killed the pregnant woman in Schenectady?" "Who else?" Clarke snarled, lifting his cutlass. "You or your men. What's the difference?"

Sainte-Helene paused. He had noticed a body sprawled beside him, a hand holding a cocked pistol. "It was not I," he replied, gently dislodging the pistol with his toe. "But it was I who deflected the blow against her womb. Tell me," he asked, slowly bending his knees, "did the baby live?"

"It did, and it does!" Jonathan yelled, tightening his grip on the cutlass. "But you won't!" He brought it down just as the Frenchman stooped to seize the pistol. The blade bit deep into Sainte-Helene's neck. He sprawled backward with a long, trailing scream. Clarke lifted the cutlass for another blow, but slowly lowered it when he saw that the Frenchman was dying.

"You have killed me," Sainte-Helene gasped, his eyes beginning to turn upward in their sockets. He gave a cry of pain and bit his lip. *"Mon ami,* I . . . go . . . . to meet . . . *le bon Sauveur.* . . . Around . . . my neck . . ." Blood gushed from his mouth.

Clarke bent to open his buckskin shirt, pulling out a rosary. He lifted the beads over Sainte-Helene's head and gave them to him. The Frenchman took them reverently in his trembling hands. He raised the crucifix to his lips to begin the sign of the cross and opened his mouth to pray. But the sound that came out was the death rattle.

Jonathan Clarke could not understand why his eyes were hot with tears. The exultation which he had felt when he struck the death blow had been only passing. He had avenged Jeddy's parents. But he had killed a brave man. Absently his finger strayed to the gash on his forehead. He brought it away thick with warm blood, which he wiped on his breeches. Sheathing his cutlass with a low, scraping sound, he turned and walked wearily toward the evacuation boats arriving on the Beauport shore.

5

One after another, sometimes months apart, the ships of Sir William Phips's defeated attacking force limped into Boston harbor. It was not until February that the last of them arrived, and Governor Bradstreet could calculate that what he had described as " the awful frown of God" had cost Massachusetts close to half its soldiers and four of its ships. More men had died of smallpox, exposure, shipwreck, and pneumonia than of French gunfire; yet, they were dead and the church bells of the colony tolled a doleful dirge.

Throughout the winter, the Parsons Mather, father and son, reproached their flocks for the sins that had called down the wrath of heaven upon the colony. "Do penance!" they thundered from their pulpits. "Do penance, for the face of the Lord is full of wrath." The Mathers also inveighed against the Puritans' custom of celebrating Thanksgiving and Christmas by consuming flesh meat, recommending instead that they don sackcloth and ashes on those feast days and dine on bread and water. "It is for these thy lusts and selfish indulgences that the God of Battles has punished us."

Indeed, the holidays that did ensue upon the defeat at Quebec were probably the most somber in Massachusetts history. For Jonathan Clarke they were a trying time as well,

60

for he had returned to Boston certain that Sir William Phips intended to make him the scapegoat for the disaster. The day after they had set sail from the Island of Orleans, behind which the fleet had lain a week for repairs, Sir William showed his displeasure by barring Clarke from his dining cabin, supping instead with Major Walley. Each night, as he sipped his postprandial port, Sir William placed more and more of the blame on Jonathan's head. "I tell you, Walley, I told that bungler we couldn't risk having *hired* ships. We had to have captains who would fight!"

"That's a lie!" an angry voice out on deck shouted, and the door swung open to admit Jonathan, his eyes black, his forehead whitening around the deep red scab. "It was *I* who told *you* that."

"Callin' me a liar, Clarke?"

"No," Jonathan shot back, his face flushed. "I just want Major Walley to know the truth."

Phips brought his glass smashing down on the table. "Careful, Clarke," he growled, his long face reddening. "You know who commands here, eh? One more word out of you, and I'll have you in the fo'c'sle. By God," he rushed on, working himself up, "I'll put you in irons—I'll have you keelhauled, God damn your eyes!"

"Easy, Sir William," Walley said softly, carefully brushing the broken glass into a little pile. "Clarke here was just defending himself. I don't think it would set well with Massachusetts men if they heard he was in irons for speaking his mind."

"Confound it, Walley—you ain't taking his part, are you?"

The major shook his round head, and Phips arose, avoiding Jonathan's eyes, going to the sideboard to obtain a fresh glass. As his back was turned, Walley's eyes fell significantly on the open door, and Clarke slipped outside.

Back in Boston, he saw almost nothing of Sir William, who was now seldom seen in public. Each day he rode from his home to his waterfront office in a closed carriage. Nor did Jonathan see Martha St. John. Because of the season, she no longer drove her little gig out to the picnic site, and she also had dropped the custom of riding each evening in the coach-and-four to carry Sir William home. One day Jonathan slipped through the open gates into Sir William's stable. He was surprised to find Martha's gig gone, along with the black stallion.

"What happened to them?" he asked the groom.

"Sold," the man grunted.

From behind him, Jonathan heard a prim voice ask reprovingly: "What are you doing here, Mr. Clarke?" Turning, he confronted Samuel, Sir William's chief servant. "I . . . I'm in the market for a horse," Jonathan stammered. "I remembered that black stallion . . ."

"Mr. Clarke," the servant said stiffly, "Sir William has informed me that you are no longer welcome here. Please leave."

Jonathan turned to go, but then, swinging around on the startled servant, he barked: "Where's Martha?"

"Why . . . why, that's none of your business."

"Yes, it is. Where is she? Is he holding her here against her will? A prisoner?"

Samuel was shocked. "How dare you speak so of Sir William!" he cried. "Why, if I was him, I'd have you put in the stocks. But I'll tell him what you said, Mr. Clarke," he said with grim satisfaction. "And you can count on it, you'll be hearing from the constable."

Clarke shrugged, studying Samuel with distaste. For a moment he thought of seizing him by the gold frogs on his coat and tossing him on the pile of horse manure the groom had swept into a corner. Instead, he turned and left the stable.

Walking back to the Cowletts', Jonathan's worries about Martha St. John gradually gave way to his concern for his own deteriorating affairs. Most of his share in the prize money recovered from the Spanish galleon was gone. He needed gainful employment. The rebel governor, Jacob Leisler, had been hung in New York, of course, and he might now return to Albany to recover his office of magistrate. But Jonathan liked Massachusetts. He enjoyed living with the Cowletts and he did not want to leave little Jeddy. In the first few weeks following his return, Jonathan had thought of going to sea again. But no one would have him, and it soon became obvious that if the vessel Jonathan wished to ship aboard was not owned by Sir William Phips, it was the property of some other merchant obligated to or in fear of him.

"Why don't you open a school, Jon?" Tom Cowlett said

that night before dinner. "You're an educated man, leastways you speak English as good as anybody."

"I did have a couple years at King's College. But where?"

"Here!" Tom said triumphantly. "Shucks, Jon—I could make you the desks in a day or two." He began to fill his pipe proudly. "Tom Cowlett, you put that pipe away," Agatha called from the kitchen. "Dinner'll be ready in two minutes." Studying his pipe ruefully, Cowlett returned it to his pocket. He sniffed the aroma drifting in from the kitchen, his eyes twinkling mischievously.

"Too small, Tom," Clarke said. "I appreciate the offer, but the schoolboys would only get in Aggie's way. And Jeddy might get hurt." He paused, his gray eyes thoughtful. "But it's not a bad id—"

Agatha Cowlett had come in from the kitchen, triumphantly holding a roast turkey on a platter.

"*Turkey!*" Clarke exclaimed. "But, Aggie, Thanksgiving isn't until next week."

"It's Thursday, isn't it?" Agatha shot back with pretended crossness. "Besides, I'm sick of being told we got licked at Quebec because of my sins. Sackcloth and ashes, indeed! And now they say we can't eat meat Thanksgiving or Christmas. Well," she said, defiantly thrusting a fork into the succulent brown roast, "I paid for this bird with the king's good money, and I'm eating it!" She sharpened her carving knife with a vigorous rasp of steel on steel and expertly separated the legs from the body. "Maybe next year," she said, smiling down at her foster son lying in his crib, "there'll be a drumstick for Jeddy." The child laughed, watching her intently with round blue eyes, his head a mass of blonde curls.

"He's sure growing fast," Jonathan said, watching his sister slap a thick juicy slice of white breast on his plate. "By God, Aggie, I think that next year he will be big enough to eat a drumstick." He helped himself to fried squash and sweet potatoes. "Mmmm," he said, chewing with great relish. "If this is penance, Aggie, it must be a great thing to be a sinner." He grinned impishly. "Are you really going to eat bread and water next Thursday?"

Agatha sniffed in disdain. "If I do, there'll be maple syrup on my bread and cider in my water glass. The idea! Life over here is hard enough as it is, without trying to turn us all into a bunch of hermits fasting in the desert." She shot a searching look at her brother. "What really went wrong at Quebec?"

"No discipline. Not your sins or mine, Aggie, just a bunch of raw recruits thinking they could beat trained troops by grabbing a musket and hollering 'God save the king!' And an amateur general who thought all he had to do to bring the French lilies tumbling down was to run the Cross of St. George up the mainmast. I told you before, Tom, courage can't conquer well-aimed cannon. But the trouble with you Massachusetts people is you think it can. And you think a man can win battles because he's shown he can make money. And as for God's part in it . . . well, the French were banking on a holy picture, and we had the Mathers asking him for direct hits. Frankly, Aggie," he said with a wry grin, "if I'd've been God, I'd've seen to it it all ended in a tie."

"Jonathan! That's blasphemy! And you, Tom Cowlett, stop giggling like a farmgirl watching her first bull."

There was a knock on the front door, followed by the sound of muffled weeping. The three exchanged glances, and Jonathan, glancing momentarily at his musket over the fireplace, rose quickly and went to open it.

"Martha! My God—it's Martha!"

Martha St. John came into the room holding Jonathan's hand. Her eyes were red and swollen and her shoulders were trembling. Her chestnut hair hung wildly around her face, wet with melting snowflakes. Her green dress—the one she had worn to both sailings—was splattered with mud, and there were rents and tears at the hem. Jonathan led her quickly to his chair, while Agatha hurried into the kitchen to bring her a cup of hot tea laced with rum.

"Here, child, drink this," Agatha said, and Martha took a sip, grimacing before she burst into tears again. "There, there, child, don't cry," Agatha said, gently patting her shoulder.

Jonathan came to kneel beside her. "What happened?" She shook her head, gasping when she saw the scar on his forehead. "It's nothing," Jonathan said. "Just a souvenir of Quebec." He fell silent, suddenly aware of Agatha and Tom Cowlett seated at the table, listening intently. Agatha arose and began clearing the table. "You'd better split some wood, Tom," she called over her shoulder. "It's snowing hard out." Tom got to his feet and went silently out the door.

"Please, Martha," Jonathan resumed, pressing her. "You've got to tell me."

"I can't. It's . . . it's too awful."

"Sir William? He tried to . . . ?" His voice turned hoarse and he glanced toward his musket.

She shook her head. "No. Not that. . . . It's been terrible. I . . . I've been a prisoner for the past three weeks. He wouldn't let me out of the house. He said I was still his ward, that it would be six more months before I came of age." She drew a catchy breath and glanced up at him accusingly. "Why didn't you come to me? I waited for you, but you never came. Every . . ." Her lips trembled. "Every night when you didn't come, I cried myself to sleep."

"Martha, I tried! But they wouldn't let me see you. Even today Samuel ordered me off the premises. Why didn't you run away?"

"I couldn't. All the doors were locked. Oh, Jonathan, you don't know how horrible it's been. Sir William came home a changed man. He would fly into rages and knock the servants down. Whenever he heard your name, he almost foamed at the mouth. If anything displeased him at dinner, he'd throw things into the fireplace. He'd stay longer at the table, too, along with his port. Tonight . . ." She lifted her head, calm, now, her green eyes fixed steadily on Jonathan. "Tonight, after dinner, I went to my room. A few hours later, Samuel came to tell me Sir William wanted to see me. There were two empty port bottles on the sideboard, and I realized he must be drunk." She shuddered. "He asked me if I had made up my mind yet. I said, no. Besides, I said, since I wasn't of age yet, I couldn't very well marry him."

"Touché!" Jonathan murmured, and Martha nodded and went on: "That made him wild. He threatened to turn me out of the house without bag or baggage. He accused me of meeting you behind his back and swore he'd have you put in the stocks. Then he . . . then he . . ." Martha tried to smile. "It would have been funny if I hadn't been so scared. All of a sudden he was like an angel. He told me of the wonderful life I would have if I married him. He reminded me of all the things he had done for me. He came around the table toward me with tears in his eyes. And then he grabbed me around the waist and kissed me."

"He *what?*" Jonathan shouted, bounding to his feet.

"He kissed me. It was horrible. His breath stank of wine and tobacco, and I could feel the wrinkles in his face."

Jonathan Clarke whirled and seized his musket, tearing open a cartridge with his teeth as though to load it. The door opened and Tom Cowlett staggered in, bent beneath a load of firewood. He immediately dropped the wood crashing on the hearth and took the piece from Jonathan's hands. "Nah, nah, Jon. Easy, now." Jonathan flushed and returned to Martha. "Go on."

"I pushed him away," Martha said, momentarily closing her eyes. "He fell down and began to roar. I ran out into the hall. Samuel had just unbolted the front door and gone outside to lock the gate. I ran right past him into the street." Martha gulped. "And then I came here."

Jonathan stared at her, puzzled. "But what about Sir William? Didn't he come after you in his carriage? You'd think he'd call the constable."

"He can't!" Martha cried triumphantly. "I'm of age! I'm free! The constable can't touch me." She reached into the bodice of her dress and drew forth a square of parchment. "All that time I was a prisoner, I had plenty of time to look for my baptismal certificate. I found it inside the Bible in his study. And I'm twenty-one and a half years old. Besides," she said, a gleam of satisfaction growing in her green eyes, "I think Sir William fell down the front stairs."

For the next few weeks, Martha St. John lived with the Cowletts. She slept upstairs with Agatha, while Tom slept on the settee downstairs and Jonathan on a mattress laid on the floor. A month after she ran away from Sir William's home, Martha St. John was married to Jonathan Clarke. The Reverend Increase Mather performed the ceremony. Undismayed by the size of the congregation beneath his pulpit—only the wedding couple and Tom and Agatha Cowlett, with little Jeddy, now one year old, seated openmouthed between them—choosing for his text "They shall cling together and be as one flesh," Parson Mather preached a sermon long enough and bombastic enough to satisfy a full church.

Smiling the thin mirthless smile that was his one concession to congeniality (he often admitted that levity was perhaps his overweening sin), Parson Mather descended the pulpit bearing a large Bible. He pecked Martha on the cheek—quickly, lest the flesh of a woman tempt him—and shook hands with Jonathan. "The good book is the gift of your Aunt Agatha," he said to Martha. "I have inscribed it."

It was a handsome bible, bound in calfskin with a silver clasp. It was heavy, too, and Jonathan had to help Martha hold it as they read:

March 2, 1691—Married this day, Jonathan David Clarke, lately of Albany, Colony of New York, now of Boston, and Martha Mary St. John, also of Boston, Colony of Massachusetts, North America, by Reverend Increase Mather.

"Oh, Aunt Aggie," Martha cried, turning eagerly to Agatha, "it's just what we wanted. There's lines for the names of all the . . ." She blushed. "All the family . . . and all the important dates." She let Jonathan take the book and turned to kiss Agatha. But the brims of their bonnets got in the way. They laughed, thanked Parson Mather for a wonderful sermon and ceremony, and went outside.

Walking back to the Cowletts', Agatha grumbled to her husband, "If I'd heard that kind of talk at our wedding, I don't think I'd've gone through with it." Everyone chuckled. Even Jeddy tried to caper, and fell down. Agatha pulled him to his feet and brushed him off. "I love your bonnet, Martha," she said.

Martha blushed happily. Jonathan had bought it for her for a wedding present. It was white silk with green lace around the wide brim, and it matched her green dress. So did the little pocket which Martha held proudly in front of her. Agatha had said Jonathan had a right to buy her a new white wedding dress, but Martha declared it wasn't right to spend all that money on something she would never wear again. Besides, he'd already spent too much on the bonnet and pocket. He'd said they had cost only a few bob, but she knew they cost twice as much.

Agatha had prepared a sumptuous wedding dinner. There was roast goose and roast chicken, both served in giblet gravy, the last of the potatoes that Agatha had preserved in sand the preceding fall, and brown betty served with a delicious hard sauce. As usual, Tom Cowlett had found a bottle of sack, and—surprise of the evening—a bottle of French champagne.

"To the bride," Tom exclaimed, getting to his feet with Jonathan and saluting Martha with his glass. "May all your troubles be little ones."

Martha turned red, and Agatha said, "Now, Tom," scoldingly. Martha sipped her champagne. It had a funny taste and she wasn't sure if she liked it. The bubbles got in her nose and made her want to sneeze. But Tom and Jonathan thought it was delicious, so Martha said she liked it, too. After dinner Martha arose to help her adopted aunt clear the table, but Agatha shooed her off. "Go on, child, it's your wedding night." Martha blushed again. It seemed to her that that was all she had done since morning. Somehow, everything Tom or Jonathan said had a double meaning. Seeing that Jonathan already had his hand on the stair rail, she followed him upstairs. Inside the room, they embraced. She felt his body hard against her own, and began to breathe heavily.

"You're not afraid, are you?" he whispered, and she shook her head. "I'll undress in the dark and get in bed first," he said. Martha nodded, listening to the rustling sound of his clothing falling to the floor, and then the creak of the bed.

"All right, Martha," he called softly, and she began to undress. She put on her nightgown. "Light the candle," Jonathan whispered. She did. She heard him draw his breath sharply. Silhouetted as she was against the candlelight, he could see the contours of her body. "Take off your nightie." She hesitated, and he said, "Go on."

Martha let her nightgown fall around her. Again, she heard Jonathan gasp. She stood there in the candleglow, her long chestnut hair falling about her white shoulders, her large eyes indistinct dark pools, her parted lips as pink as the nipples of her full breasts coming erect and firm in the chill air, while the candlelight, glinting softly in the triangle of hair between her thighs, made pinks and whites of her ridged belly. "Turn around," Jonathan called, and she did. He saw the sensual curve of her hips, her white buttocks swelling seductively toward him, and he said, "Come." She moved to blow out the candle. "No," he said. "I want to see you. I want to drink you in with all my senses." And she came: soft, clinging, fragrant—and submissive.

The following day, Martha and Jonathan sailed downcoast to Wood's Hole, making for the island of Nantucket the next day. Martha had never been at sea in an open boat before. At first she was afraid, until she gradually became aware of her husband's skill with sail and rudder. Impressed by his calm confidence, she relaxed, watching with delight the approaching shore and its line of little weather-beaten cottages.

They walked hand in hand up the cobblestone street of the town, pointing out the quaint shops and taverns to each other, gawking at the great houses of the merchants. Then they strolled out to the harbor.

"How would you like to live here?" Jonathan asked.

"I'd love it. I've heard the mists and fogs are wonderful for flowers. The roses grow wild on the beach. And they say it's much warmer in winter than the mainland."

Jonathan nodded. "With what money I've got left, I could buy a little ship. A coastal trader." He pointed to a small lateen-rigged vessel moored at the wharf. "Like that."

"No," Martha said, shaking her head vehemently. "I don't want you to go to sea. You could be shipwrecked." She gestured savagely toward the square promenades facing seaward atop some of the harbor cottages. "I don't want to spend half my life watching from a widow's walk."

"But it's something I can do."

"You can teach, too. You could open a school."

"You know, that's what Tom Cowlett has been saying. And I've been thinking seriously about it." Behind them the sun was setting in a brazen red ball. The sky above it was streaked with mauve and pink. "We'd best be getting back to the inn," Jonathan said.

They passed a two-story brick building. Carved into the arch above the door were the words "NANTUCKET LATIN SCHOOL." In the window a small sign in a copperplate hand said: Instructor Wanted."

"By God, I'm going in," Jonathan said, and opened the door. Inside, a tall thin man with a long New England face introduced himself as Harold Phelps, the headmaster. He asked Jonathan for his credentials.

"Two years at King's College."

"New York man?"

"I was. Taught school in Albany a little. I'm living in Boston, now."

Phelps's face hardened. "You said your name was Clarke? Jonathan Clarke?" Jonathan nodded. "Did you know this school was founded by Sir William Phips?" Jonathan gulped and shook his head. "Sir William was out here for a few days. Left only this morning. Came here March 2. That mean anything to you, Mr. Clarke?"

My wedding day, Jonathan thought, getting to his feet. "Thank you for your trouble, Mr. Phelps," he mumbled. "No, no . . . I'll let myself out." Hot tears of rage in his eyes, he rejoined Martha on the street. She saw the whiteness of his face, the scar on the forehead livid, and she knew that something had gone wrong. They walked back to the inn in silence. The beauty of the western sky, now layered in broad bands of blue and pink and mauve, was lost upon them.

A few days later they sailed back to the mainland. As Jonathan helped Martha ashore, she saw that his saturnine face seemed thinner, longer. There was misery in his gray eyes. That night in their bedroom she asked him if he wanted her, but he said no. In the morning she saw him sitting at the table with paper and quill, and she guessed that he was calculating how much money he had left. At dinner Tom Cowlett cheered them both by telling Jonathan he had found a place for him at the shipyard. But Jonathan was no carpenter and didn't last three days. "God a'mighty," Tom told Agatha, "I couldn't believe a man as smart as your brother could have so many thumbs."

Soon the burden of feeding five mouths instead of three began to tell on Tom Cowlett. He did not complain, but he seldom sat chatting and smoking with his brother-in-law after dinner anymore. Martha noticed—as Jonathan did not—that Agatha's meals were becoming plainer and skimpier. Flesh meat became rare, bowls of samp more frequent. She also noticed that Jonathan was stirring more rum than usual into his tea. His face was haggard. He sometimes went for days without shaving. At times when they were alone, he would rail bitterly against himself.

"Look at you," he said to Martha. "You married me in silk, and now you wear calico."

And then—on the day that Jonathan decided that he would have to return to Albany, sending for Martha when he had earned enough to resume married life—he bumped into Parson Mather on the common.

"Mr. Clarke! This is indeed fortunate. Are you still available to teach?"

Jonathan nodded eagerly.

"Harvard College needs a Latin instructor. Do you still have your Latin?"

Jonathan Clarke groped wildly in his memory for some Latin phrase that might impress the parson. He had studied the language, of course, and done well in it. But his grasp of it had atrophied with disuse. Yet, he was certain that, given time to refresh his fluency, he could teach it. Suddenly a familiar phrase flashed into his mind, and he burst out: *"Omnia Gallia in tres partes divisa est."*

"Come, come, Mr. Clarke. Be serious. Every schoolboy knows that all Gaul is divided into three parts. Here, let me say something in Latin and you translate." He frowned in thought. "Ah, yes. *'Nil desperandum Christo duce.'* "

Clarke smiled to himself. With typical vanity, the parson had quoted his own watchword for the Quebec expedition. Trying to seem impressed, he translated: " 'Do not despair when Christ leads.' "

"Excellent! You're just the man Harvard is looking for. If you go there in the morning, and tell them I sent you, I'm sure the post will be yours."

Jonathan Clarke literally ran back to the Cowlett house. "Martha!" he shouted, bursting inside. "Martha! I've got a post! I've got a post!" Martha did not reply. She was seated at the table, her chin in her hands. Jonathan did not notice the despair in her swollen eyes. He rushed to her side and knelt beside her. "Didn't you hear me? I've got a post! Aren't you glad?"

Martha lifted her tear-stained face. "I would be," she said dully. "But the king has made Sir William governor of Massachusetts."

Martha Clarke came out the front door of the Cowletts' house and walked toward the oxen and wagons standing in the street. Both vehicles were piled high with furniture and other possessions: hogsheads crammed with clothing, cooking utensils, and Tom Cowlett's new set of carpenter's tools. Tom had already finished packing his wagon and had climbed up on the box beside Agatha. Jonathan was busy harnessing his oxen. Martha turned to look at the little house in which she had found sanctuary, joy—and then despair. She could not believe that she was leaving it, going to live in the settlement of Deerfield on the far northern frontier. Yet, it was true. Tom Cowlett had proposed the move on the very night after she had told Jonathan of Sir William's appointment.

"A bunch of fellers from a place called Deerfield came to the yard a few days ago," he told Jonathan. "Lookin' for a carpenter. Told me if I'd go and live with 'em they'd grant me a hundred acres of farmland and give me the chance to build my own mill." Jonathan and Martha exchanged glances of dismay. Were the Cowletts abandoning them, too? "Don't you folks worry," Tom rushed on understandingly. "There's a chance for Jonathan, too. They say their settlement's growing and they need a school. They asked me if I could find 'em a schoolmaster. What d'ye say, Jon?"

Jonathan shook his head. "No frontier for me, Tom. I can't forget Schenectady. The danger is real. You've got to think of Agatha and Jeddy, Tom."

"Aggie's all for it. We talked it over. Work at the shipyard's slowin' down—and this is the chance of a lifetime. Shucks, Jon, King William's war is fizzlin'. The kings have all fergit about America. They're too busy tearing each other apart in Ireland and Europe. Besides, Frontenac's a sick old man and the frontier has been quiet for more'n a year."

Jonathan frowned and glanced questioningly at Martha. "We could try it," she said, putting her hand on his. "We've got to do something."

Jonathan Clark's eyes moved hesitatingly from Martha to Agatha to Tom. Sensing that he was weakening, Tom pressed him further. "They need a magistrate, too, Jon. They admitted that none of 'em was educated enough to handle the job. Said that if they got along with the schoolmaster they'd probably 'lect him magistrate."

"All right," Jonathan said. "We'll go."

And so they *were* going, Martha thought. The Cowletts had sold the house for enough money to buy the oxen and wagons (the Clarkes would pay them back as soon as they could), a new set of tools for Tom, and enough left over to build the mill. "Connecticut River runs by the settlement," Tom had said. "Fast. Just right for a mill."

Martha turned for a long look at the house. Then she walked to the wagon. Jonathan helped her up on the box beside him. He looked at her tenderly. His gray eyes were full of love. "I'm proud of you, Martha," he whispered. "And, by God," he said savagely, flicking the reins over the oxen's back, "I'm going to make you proud of me again."

Martha put her hand on his knee reassuringly. She blinked back the tears. The wagon lurched as it hit a rut between the street and the Common. Martha quickly put a hand to her stomach. But she had felt no pain. Martha had heard that riding in a cart or a wagon was bad for expectant mothers. It could bring on a miscarriage. But she was confident now. Tonight, she thought, she would tell Jonathan that she was pregnant.

Queen Anne's War

6

"Uncle Jon! Uncle Jon! The war's over! The war's over!"

Jonathan Clarke looked up from his desk in the schoolroom at Deerfield. "You sure, Jeddy? Where'd you hear it?"

"Yup," the boy replied, bobbing his blond head vigorously. "A man from Boston was over at Uncle Tom's mill. He said all the kings sat down at some place in Holland and promised not to fight no more."

"Anymore," Clarke corrected absently, and then, still the schoolmaster testing the boy's memory: "Where in Holland?"

"Ryswick," Jed Gill answered proudly.

Clarke nodded his approval, studying Jed thoughtfully. Jedediah Gill was a sturdy lad who showed promise of growing into a strong, healthy man. He was bright, too. Clarke had noticed that, and he was already thinking of sending the boy to Harvard College when he reached sixteen or seventeen. But he was only eight now, although he'd soon be nine. Clarke's eyes fell on the small white scar on the boy's forehead, and he felt the scar on his own. Strange how both their bodies bore memories of Sainte-Helene.

Clarke sighed. "All right, Jeddy," he said gently. "You can go. Thanks for coming to tell me the great news."

The boy grinned, his cheeks dimpling, and he ran outside.

74

"The war's over, the war's over!" he chanted, running among the cabins. "No more Injuns, no more scalpin'! King William's still our king."

So it's all come to nothing, Jonathan Clarke thought grimly: a standoff. Kings! Why did good people have to suffer and die just to satisfy their vanity? Because Louis wanted to put William's crown on James's head, Jeddy's parents are murdered and scalped three thousand miles away in the northern wilderness and I had to kill Sainte-Helene. And in the end, what? The mixture as before! He sighed, remembering the alarms of the numerous scalping scares during the past five years, and the one substantial attack of French and Indians that they had beaten back. Otherwise, Tom Cowlett had been right. The frontier was quiet and they both had prospered. Tom's farm was now among the most productive in the neighborhood, and his mill was even more lucrative. Jonathan Clarke's school had become so popular that it attracted students from the villages of Hadley and Hatfield a few miles away. And as Tom had predicted, Jonathan had been elected magistrate, and then captain of militia.

That rank had come to him after the big attack. Unlike the householders of Schenectady, the residents of Deerfield had listened to Jonathan when he pleaded with them to fortify their settlement. Under his direction they built a palisade eight feet high around the meeting house—which also served as the schoolhouse—atop Meeting House Hill. There were blockhouses at the corners of the four-sided palisade, and the fifteen largest private houses inside it were also fortified, with layers of bricks between the inner and outer walls to make them bulletproof and overhanging upper stories for firing down on attackers seeking the cover of the house. The remainder of Deerfield's forty-one houses—smaller in size— were strung out in the meadows bordering the Connecticut River or along the road to Hadley and Hatfield. When the enemy did strike, the people living in them were able to take refuge inside the palisades "fort" and help to repel the attack. In fact, the French and Indians had been so discouraged that they had retreated without burning the defenseless outer cabins. It was then that the grateful villagers, together with those of Hadley and Hatfield, had elected Jonathan their militia captain.

Reflecting on the event with pride, Jonathan Clarke suddenly clapped shut the book before him and got to his feet. Tomorrow, he had remembered, was muster day.

That night after Martha had put little Rachel to bed in the tiny room adjoining the kitchen, Jonathan took down his musket from its pegs over the fireplace.

"Where's my gun oil?" he asked Martha.

"Gun oil? You mean that nasty-smelling stuff you had on the mantel. I put it out in the shed, it smelled so bad."

Jonathan went out to the shed and came back with a saucer in his hand. "Doesn't smell that bad," he said, sniffing it.

"You just don't have any sense of smell," Martha said, going to the stove to seize the heavy iron kettle and lug it out to the well.

"Here," Jonathan said, putting aside his musket and the oil. "Let me carry that."

"Jon Clarke, will you please stop acting like I'm the spoiled little girl back on the Green Lane. I know it's heavy, but I can carry it—and you know I can."

"All right," Jonathan said grudgingly, sitting down before the hearth again. He watched her go out the door. Martha had matured much in the six years they had spent in Deerfield. Her soft girlish beauty was gone. In its place was a deeper, matronly beauty. She carried herself with great but unconscious dignity. Pulling his scourer from his musket, Jonathan recalled how she had struggled not to cry when she saw their new home. It was only a rude cabin, with one big room and a fireplace. With Tom Cowlett's help, though, they had partitioned it into a kitchen and parlor, and then, after Rachel was born, added a tiny bedroom for her and a spacious loft serving as their bedroom. Jonathan dipped a wool rag into the oil and wound it around the scourer. Then he inserted the rod in the musket's muzzle and worked it up and down, both cleaning and oiling the bore.

Martha came in the door, almost staggering under the weight of the kettle filled with water. "Oh, my Jesus," Jonathan said, jumping to his feet. "Are you daft?" He took the kettle from her and swung it up onto the stove.

"Daft?" Martha repeated petulantly. "You wouldn't have called me that before we were married, Jon Clarke."

"You wouldn't have tried to kill yourself like that before we were married, either," Jonathan said with a grin. He tossed the oily rag into the fireplace and slid the scourer back in place beneath the musket barrel.

"Why do you have to clean your own musket?" Martha asked. "You're the captain, aren't you? Besides, why do you carry one? None of the other officers do."

"The armies of free men don't have batmen," Jonathan said with contempt in his voice. "King's armies do. Kings with their mercenaries and their whips."

"Jon Clarke, what's getting into you lately? It's those books you've been reading, I know it is. You'd better not let anyone else hear you talking about kings that way."

"They won't. Oh, I'm a loyal enough subject, Martha. I just never heard of King Adam or the Emperor Noah, that's all. Do you remember what they used to chant in Wat Tyler's Rebellion?"

"Of course, not. How could I?"

" 'When Adam dug, and Eve span,' " he quoted softly, " 'who was then a gentleman?' "

Martha shook her head ruefully. "You're going to get us all into trouble someday," she warned. "And especially little Jeddy Gill. He worships the ground you walk on. Aggie says he quotes you all the time, just like you were the Lord himself."

Jonathan grinned, putting his musket back on its pegs. "Sure, I don't have to carry a musket. But I found out what a pistol's worth at Quebec. And that isn't much. Where's my uniform coat? I think I'd better try it on."

"Upstairs. Did Tom Cowlett say when he's going to finish the dresser for us?"

"A week or two," Jonathan said, going up the stairs. He came down wearing his red-and-blue militia coat. Martha looked at him proudly. He was handsome in his captain's uniform. She gasped. "You've lost a button!"

"No, I didn't," he said, pulling a large brass button from his pocket. "I saved it, see?"

Flouncing her chestnut hair, Martha took the button and began sewing it back in place on the coat's red facing. Jonathan watched her bite the thread with her strong white teeth. "Where's your uniform shirt?" she asked, her words slurred by the thread she was moistening. Jonathan ran upstairs again and returned with a ruffled white shirt. "It's filthy!" Martha wailed, shaking it out by the shoulders. Rumpling it

in a ball, she stuffed it inside the iron kettle, added soap, and
stooped to light the wood in the stove.

Soon the water began to boil and the room smelled
steamily of soft soap. Martha's face was flushed with the
heat. Her long eyelashes were wet and dark above her green
eyes. Jonathan came to her and put his arms around her and
held her hard against him. For a moment Martha rested her
head on his shoulder—until he put both hands on her buttocks and she could feel his penis hardening. Then she
pushed him away. "Don't you think of anything else? I've
got to dry your shirt and iron it. No!"

"Oh, come on. Rachel's asleep. You can do the shirt in the
morning."

"No, I can't. Oh, all right. But first let me wring it out and
hang it up to dry."

In the darkness of the loft, Martha still smelled faintly of
soap.

Martha was busy ironing the ruffled shirt when Jonathan
came downstairs in his singlet and breeches. He walked
toward the fire, rubbing his hands against his biceps, shivering. "Sure is cold upstairs," he mumbled. "Looks like winter's
here for good."

"I swear t' God, Jon Clarke," Martha grumbled, "I do believe you must be a princess. I can't believe you were ever at
Quebec. Why, I thought it was stifling up there."

"You're built a little different," Jonathan said, grinning. He
sniffed the aroma coming from the kitchen. "Smells good.
What's for breakfast?"

"Blood sausage and cornbread. And some eggs, too." Martha carefully set her iron on edge and hurried into the
kitchen. She returned with a heaping plate and set it before
him. She watched him eat greedily, satisfaction in her eyes.

"Where's Rachel?" Jonathan asked, looking around him.

"Gone. The moment she saw Jeddy Gill walking down the
Hadley Road, she was out of here like a shot. Didn't even
finish her breakfast," she added, pointing to the half-finished
bowl of corn mush on the table. "I tell you, Jon, I don't
know what this generation is coming to. Spoiled rotten. Imagine not finishing your breakfast."

"She's sure fond of that boy," Jonathan said, spreading
apple butter on his cornbread.

"She just worships the ground Jeddy Gill walks on. Wants to be just like him. Climb trees and go swimming in the river. Here all along I'd thought I'd had a girl."

"She'll get over it," Jonathan said, getting to his feet. "Wait and see, she'll grow up to be every bit as much a lady as her ma."

Martha glared at her husband. She's still beautiful, Jonathan thought, but when did she begin to turn shrewish? You'd think it was my sister talking. Women are the devil, he thought. Still glaring, Martha moistened her fingertip with her tongue and touched it to the bottom of her iron. It was cool. She went to the kettle and added more hot water to the iron, returning to the ironing board to finish Jonathan's shirt. "There," she said, holding it up before her.

Jonathan put it on. He patted his belly. "Your sausage is better'n Aggie's. I do believe you've got me spoiled rotten, too."

"Oh, you!" Martha snorted, helping him into his coat. She looked at him proudly. He put on his tricorn and took down his musket, making for the door. She followed him. "Aren't you even going to kiss me good-bye?"

He turned with a grin. "I was thinking of the letter I have to write the county for more lead for bullets." he pecked her on the cheek.

"Thanks," Martha said sarcastically, straightening his coat. "I'll remember that kiss next time you want to go upstairs."

Jonathan laughed and went outside. There were white patches of frost on the ground. He looked up at the sky. It was blue, but the horizon beyond the black line of trees across the river was gray. Snow, Jonathan thought: this'll probably be the last muster until spring. He walked toward the Hadley Road, where Tom Cowlett was waiting for him.

" 'Mornin', Cap'n," Tom said, coming to attention and saluting.

" 'Mornin', Sergeant. Where'd you get the new cockade?"

Tom Cowlett fingered the green cockade sewn to the upturned brim of his hat. "Aggie made if for me. Color of the company flag. New shirt, too," he said proudly.

Jonathan gazed with approval at Cowlett's deerskin hunting shirt with the fringes on the shoulders and down the sleeves. "You are a doodle-dandy," he said teasingly. "Now, which one of the Small girls do you have in mind?"

Tom Cowlett grinned, falling into step beside Jonathan. He was no longer the meek and obliging husband whom Agatha was accustomed to order around. His very step was different. He rocked forward on his toes instead of shuffling as he did when fetching for Agatha. Clapping Jonathan on the back, he chuckled and said: "Rebecca, that's the one I like. Pretty as the nigh side of a peach. Got bumpers, too. She may be Small, but they ain't small. By Jesus, Jon, a feller could hang on to Becky Small." He winked. "What say we give the Small girls a toss after muster? They're willin'. By Jesus, I hear tell half those Hadley girls is willin'." He moistened a finger and held it up to the wind. "Bundlin' season's a-comin'," he said, winking lecherously again.

Jonathan laughed. "Not me, Tom. I'm satisfied with what I've got."

"Who wouldn't be? Martha's the prettiest lass in Deerf— No, by Jesus, in the whole danged county."

Jonathan nodded absently. He was thinking of the fury of Martha's lovemaking the night before, how she had surprised him, clutching him fiercely, biting his ear. It was as though she were the aggressor. Jonathan knew that Martha was anxious to have another baby, to give him a son, and he wondered if her rising ardor were not due—

A girlish giggle broke out of the bushes beside the road, and both men stopped. They could hear Jeddy Gill's voice scolding: "Darn it, Rachel—you promised! You said if I let you come you wouldn't make any noise or anything. And now all you have to do is hear Pa and Uncle Jon coming and you start giggling. Just like a girl!"

"I am not! Don't you call me a girl, Jeddy Gill!"

Both men laughed, and the bushes fell silent. "All right, come out, we know you're there," Jonathan Clarke called. There was a rustling noise and the abashed children stepped out onto the road. Their coats were covered with nettles and their faces were scratched from branches. Rachel's chestnut hair was awry, and Jonathan wondered how much she resembled her mother. Jed had his eyes lowered in embarrassment, but Rachel confronted her father angrily.

"He called me a girl!"

"I thought you were one," Jonathan said, concealing his amusement.

"Well, maybe . . . but I can do anything a boy can."

"Such as what? What were you two doing in there?"

"We was waiting," Jed began, and Clarke said, "were."

"We were waiting to follow you to muster."

"Now, Jeddy," Cowlett broke in gently, "you know your ma and I told you you couldn't go to muster."

"But I want to, Pa." Jed turned appealingly to Clarke. "Just once, Uncle Jon," he pleaded. "I just want to see them shoot off their muskets. It's the last muster till spring. Please?"

Clarke shook his head. "You're too young, Jeddy."

"I'm going to be nine next month!" Jed shot back hotly. "You said yourself you'd let me shoot a musket on my birthday."

"No, Jed—that has nothing to do with it."

"But how'm I gonna kill Frenchmen and Indians like you say I have to, if you won't let me go to muster?"

Jonathan studied the boy admiringly. "By God, Jed, I believe you've got the makings of a Boston lawyer. But you still can't go. I just don't want you to hear the language down there."

"I've heard it already! Why, you should have heard Pa the other day when the saw broke in the mill. Ma said a man'd go on like that in front of children was a lost soul."

Tom Cowlett made a choking noise, and Jonathan turned away momentarily to hide the twinkle in his eye. "I'm sorry, Jed," he said, swinging back to the boy; and then, soothingly: "Tell you what. You and Rachel run back to Aunt Martha's. Your ma's coming over, and they're going to start making the Christmas cookies. Maybe they'll let you help."

"Oh, gee, Jeddy, let's go!" Rachel cried, jumping up and down exuberantly.

"Cookies!" Jed snorted scornfully. "That's woman's work. I'm gonna be a soldier when I grow up—not a cook. I'm gonna kill Frenchies."

"Oh, c'mon, Jed," Rachel pleaded. "Please? Maybe they'll let us lick the bowl and eat the spoilt ones. Please?"

"Oh, all right." Jed had seen the scar on his adopted uncle's forehead begin to turn white, always a sign of his displeasure, and he decided he had gone far enough. Seizing Rachel's hand, he ran and skipped with her back to the Clarke cabin.

Striding down the hill, Jonathan and Tom could see the men of the train band gathered along the fence opposite Small's barn. There were about twenty of them. Most of them were leaning against the fence with straws in their mouths, chatting. Jonathan started when he saw a short, powerfully built man marching purposefully down the hill below them. "Parson Lowry," he said to Tom, and Tom said, "What's the parson a-doin' here?" "He wants to be chaplain," Jonathan said sourly. "He told Martha at Sunday meeting if the militia wanted God on their side, they needed an intercessor." Tom chuckled. "God on *our* side, eh—I'd ruther be on *his*." Just then Mark Small led a bull into the field toward the heifers, and the militiamen began to make obscene remarks, exploding in boisterous shouts of laughter.

"How dare you!" Parson Solomon Lowry roared in a voice that made even the bull turn its head. "You call yourselves God-fearing men to be mouthing filth like that in front of womenfolk!" Parson Lowry pointed toward the other end of the fence, where about a dozen Hadley girls dressed in their Sunday best were standing. They lowered their heads demurely. The men lowered theirs sheepishly, shuffling their feet. Parson Lowry turned to greet Jonathan. "Captain Clarke," he barked, stroking his prognathous jaw, his humorless pale eyes still indignant, "I do believe your men can stand a little churching. Why, the filth I just heard . . . I wouldn't have under my feet what they had in their mouths."

"My apologies, Parson. I guess they didn't realize there was a man of God around."

"Christian men must *always* act as though they were in the presence of God himself," the parson snapped, laying a thick hand on the white stock beneath his chin. In the other he held a Bible.

"My wife tells me that you would like to become our company's chaplain," Clarke said. "That is true, Captain," the parson replied, and the militiamen, with suppressed groans, picked up their muskets and began climbing the fence into the field. "Oh, my Jesus," Seth Ankers, a tall thin man with a leering face, whispered to big Lem Waters. "There goes muster fun." Watching them form ranks, Clarke said: "That's very kind of you, Parson. But do you think you really should put yourself to so much trouble?"

"There is no labor sweeter than the salvation of souls. I

think of it as no less than a duty." He sniffed. "One could almost smell the Unclean One around here, Captain. Evidently, some of your men have forgotten the Second Commandment."

"The, ah, Second . . . ?"

" 'Thou shalt not take the name of the Lord thy God in vain.' That, Captain, and a few others."

"Again, my apologies. Would you care to address the company?"

"Not today," he said grimly, thrusting his Bible under his arm. "One of the Grimsby girls in Hatfield is with child. I intend to find out who the father is." His jaw lifted. "You may tell the men that I shall address them at the next muster. I have in mind a brief homily on the moral rectitude which Our Lord and Savior expects to find in the Christian soldier."

"Indeed, Parson. We will be honored . . ."

Clarke watched Solomon Lowry stride down the road, his eyes straight ahead, his massive head held high, God tucked under his arm in a thick black book, with even his bulging calves inside their black stockings bursting with righteousness. Relieved to see him leave, Jonathan climbed the fence, followed by Tom Cowlett. Both took their places before the company. The drummer boy began to beat "Connecticut Halftime" and Corporal Adam Brown marched out in front of the men with the company's green flag fluttering from his spontoon. Clarke studied the men. No two of them were dressed alike. Some wore homespun or black cloth; most had hunting shirts like Tom's. They stared gravely at their captain, and Clarke said: "Men, Parson Lowry has kindly consented to become our chaplain. At great sacrifice to himself, I might add. How about three cheers for the chaplain?" A weak burst of halfhearted hurrahs rose from the company, and Sergeant Cowlett shouted, "Tennn—shun!" They snapped to awkwardly, their muskets held loosely by the barrel, some on the right, some on the left.

"Sound off!"

Cowlett called the roll.

"Seth Ankers."

"Here."

"Adam Brown."

"Here."

So it went, on down the alphabet. Sometimes though, someone answered for an absent friend.

"Jamie cain't come. His cow's freshenin' . . ."

"Amos cut his toe yestiddy choppin' wood . . ."

"He's gone down East. His pa died . . ."

At last Tom Cowlett finished calling the roll. He swung around to face Jonathan and saluted. "All present or accounted for, Sir."

Jonathan nodded his satisfaction. "Drill them in the manual of arms, Sergeant." Cowlett did another half-turn and roared: "Right shoulder, arms!"

There was a spattering of hands hitting rifle stocks as the men shouldered their muskets: half to the right, half to the left. One of them cried out and clapped his hand to his forehead where his comrade, who had gone to the wrong shoulder, had nicked him with his musket muzzle. Captain Clarke closed his eyes and groaned inwardly. Soldiers! He opened them reluctantly, watching in pained silence while Sergeant Cowlett put them raggedly through the rest of the motions. Turning with a staisfied look on his face, Cowlett reported: "Manual of arms completed as ordered, Sir."

"Good, Sergeant. I will now make my inspection."

Jonathan handed Tom his musket, and Tom handed it to the drummer boy, who took it in surprise and handed it on to Corporal Brown, who let the green flag fall while reaching for it. Hastily retrieving his pike and flag, the corporal dropped the musket clattering on the ground. Bending to seize that, he expelled gas with a sharp ripping sound. Choking cries of laughter came from the girls at the fence, and Jonathan, noticing them for the first time, began his inspection with a red face.

"Seth Ankers, where's your ramrod?"

"Dunno. Las' I saw of it, the boys was playin' war. One of 'em had m' musket, t'other had m' ramrod."

"You've lost it, you lunkhead—and you know it! Here," he said, reaching for Lem Waters's musket, "give me your ramrod." He pulled it free, took Ankers's musket, and shoved the ramrod down its barrel. It only went halfway. With a sour look, Clarke pulled it free, swung the musket upside down in the air and sharply slapped the stock. A stream of marbles cascaded onto the ground and peals of laughter broke from the rail fence.

"Tarnation!" the red-faced militiaman swore. "I'm gonna whup their backsides when I get home. Told me they'd lost 'em. What a place to hide 'em. Just like that snake they put in there last summer."

Clarke handed the man back his gun. "Private Ankers, fined two shillings. One for losing your ramrod, one for a dirty gun."

"Tarnation, Cap'n! You know I can't afford that."

"Pay it," Clarke said grimly, stepping sideways to confront Corporal Brown. "Give me your flints and powders." Brown tugged at his pockets to produce the flints, pulling his powder pouch from his belt.

"Three flints," Clarke exclaimed. "The law says you've got to have four. One pound of powder and an Indian ax or a bayonet. Where's the other?" Brown shrugged. "Likely back home in the shed," he mumbled. "Feared I'd be late, and I guess I must've just grabbed the three."

"You'd better have it next muster," Clark warned, hefting the pouch in his hand. "Powder seems all right, though."

He moved on to the next in line, a big, muscular blond youth wearing an embroidered deerskin hunting shirt. "Lem Waters, turn around and bend over."

"Aw, Cap'n . . ."

"Lem Waters, you had a hole in your breeches last muster. I want to see if it's mended like I told you to."

Flushing, eyeing the giggling girls at the fence, Waters bent over.

"The hole's still there!"

"I got underpants under it," Waters said, and the men around him snickered.

"Silence!" Clarke thundered; and then, to Waters: "The law says every man must be equipped for a month's march."

"I don't march on my behind, Sir."

Loud guffaws broke out among the men, and Clarke bellowed: "Knock it off, or I'll march you right through lunch!" The ranks fell silent, and Clarke called: "Fall out." They broke ranks, some of them snickering again, gathering around Waters and chaffing him.

Jonathan walked toward Tom Cowlett. "Do you think we should drill them in the field or have lunch first?"

Tom was hungry himself, so he said, "Let 'em eat," and Jonathan told him that he'd better go in and tell Mrs. Small to bring out the meal. With her three pretty daughters helping her, Mrs. Small brought out hot mush with corn bread and seven cool jugs of beer. The men lay or sat in the stubble and ate and drank, and then Sergeant Cowlett ordered them into ranks again and marched them around the field. Jonathan was pleased to see that they kept in step, even the two odd men bringing up the rear of the column of threes. Corporal Brown was excellent as the fugleman, Johathan thought, keeping perfect time and using his green flag for a guidon. Feeling better, Jonathan watched Tom march them back to the rail. Then he gave them the order, "Muster completed, fall out!"

To Jonathan's surprise, the men did not immediately begin returning to their homes by twos and threes as they usually did. He knew that some of them had late chores to do before night fell, and it was getting colder. The sky had clouded over and there was more than just a hint of snow in the air. But the men lingered on, mingling with the Hadley girls, telling jokes and playing the dandy. They got Mrs. Small to bring out more beer, and then they got the drummer boy to play "The Highland Laddie." Somebody produced a fife. Soon they were drinking the beer and dancing with the girls, and when the snow began to fall they all ran into the Small barn.

Tom Cowlett had tried to get a dance with Becky Small. But she preferred Lem Waters. Lem whirled her around as easily as though she were no bigger than Rachel Clarke, and he laughed boisterously while he danced, his thick blond hair flopping like a rug at the base of his neck. Tom was disappointed, and he didn't offer a word of protest when Jonathan suggested that they had better be going before the road was deep in snow.

Walking home with the thick wet snow pelting their faces, Jonathan noticed that the closer they got to Deerfield the more Tom's footsteps slowed into a shuffle.

Although winter had arrived late, it quickly turned fierce: a howling white beast. Jedediah Gill always swore that he would never forget the winter of Ninety-eight. The snow that began on muster day kept falling right until the end of the year. It wan't too heavy, though; not more than a foot deep by Christmas. But on Jed's ninth birthday a blizzard struck and it did not stop snowing for a week. At first the snow made Jed Gill glad because it meant that he and Rachel Clarke wouldn't have to go to school and could play all day in it. They found some flat boards outside of the Cowlett mill and fitted them together for a toboggan, riding down the slope onto the frozen river, shouting with glee. They built snowmen and then snow forts and had a snowball fight. But when the snow did not stop they began to hate the thick white flakes falling steadily night and day. By the end of the blizzard, the snow was over five feet deep, piled high against the cabins. Jed and Rachel had to help their parents free the windows of snow to let in the sunlight. They helped, too, when their parents dug a snow tunnel from one house to the other. The snow was too high to clear a path, so they dug the tunnel instead, crawling on their stomachs from one house to another. At first Jed and Rachel thought that this was fun, but then, when the snow overhead froze, it became too cold to crawl through the pitch-black tunnel. That was when the Clarkes and Cowletts decided that it would be better if they lived in one house—the Cowletts'.

That way, the warmth of all their bodies would contribute to heating the one cabin, and Jonathan and Tom could work together cutting and hauling wood. They didn't cut and split small logs to lay sideways in the fireplace; instead they cut big whole round logs which they slid in the front door right into the fire. Every hour or so they would shove the log forward into the coals. When it burned down, they had another log lying on the floor ready to take its place. Then they would go outside and cut two more. Jonathan and Tom kept the fire going all the time, taking turns watching it during the late night hours.

Even so, the cabin was cold,—and the kitchen was almost freezing. Martha and Agatha were glad when it came time to prepare the meals, because that meant they could light the wood fire in the stove and warm their numbed fingers. Fortunately, the dry warm autumn had enabled both families to lay in supplies of food. Barrels of salted cucumbers and sauerkraut stood in the kitchen and in the loft there were sacks of potatoes preserved in sand, along with radishes, beets, turnips, peas, and beans. Cabbages hung from the beams of the kitchen ceiling in pairs, and there were sacks of corn meal. Oats, too, for Tom Cowlett had worked from sunup to sundown during the fall, picking his ripened grain and threshing it. Tom also had wisely stacked his hay on the lee side of the barn, where he could get at it through the snow. If he had stored it in the woods, it would have been lost. The hay meant life for his shaggy animals huddled together for warmth in the barn. The cows gave milk, but Tom dreaded milking them. Their cold teats numbed his bare hands, and the milk froze almost the moment it hit the bucket. Tom also stacked cow manure against the stable's weather wall. It always froze, but it did act as a kind of insulation; and Tom knew that if the firewood over ran out, they could burn the frozen manure.

Nobody bathed, except to wipe the sleep from their eyes with a cloth dipped in basins of ice-cold melted snow. Nobody talked much, either. At times Jonathan and Tom would lie in front of the fire drinking rum and molasses and talking in low voices. Or Martha would read to them all from the Bible that Agatha and Tom had given her. Jed loved to hear his Aunt Martha read from the Bible. Her voice was low but clear and carrying, and her face became animated as she read. It was as though the children of Israel were right there with them in the Cowletts' cabin. Jed's favorite passage was from Deuteronomy: "If at any time thou come to fight against a city, thou shalt first offer it peace . . . But if they will not make peace, and shall begin war against thee, thou shalt besiege it. And when the Lord thy God shall deliver it into thy hands, thou shalt slay all that are therein of the male sex with the edge of the sword." *The edge of the sword.* That was what Jed Gill would do when he reached manhood and marched against the French.

Even after the snow stopped, the wind never seemed to cease. Lying fully clothed in bed at night with Rachel, their two small bodies pressed together for warmth, Jed could hear the wind wailing and whistling, whining and howling. It blew the snow rattling against the windowpanes like handfuls of tiny stones. Sometimes they would awake in the morning and see the floor covered with a fine powder of snow that had been blown through the log chinks. It was in bed with Rachel that Jeddy innocently discovered how different a girl was from a boy. For warmth, he somtimes put his hands between his thighs over his genitals. When Rachel cuddled against him, his hands slipped between her thighs and found nothing. Jed was surprised, momentarily wondering what girls had between their legs. But he quickly forgot about it and fell asleep.

When he awoke, a thaw had begun. The cabin was warm. Jed could hear the sound of melting snow dripping from the roof. Two days later, Jonathan and Tom took their shovels carved out of oak planks and dug a path from the Cowlett cabin to the Clarke's, and the following day Jonathan went out hunting deer. He came back with a shriveled little doe draped across his shoulders. The poor animal had hardly any flesh on its bones, and what was there tasted like leather, but it was the first fresh meat they had eaten since New Year's.

Next morning, just before dark, Jed Gill awoke to hear the sound of the ice breaking up on the Connecticut River. It came in one long traveling report, just like Jed imagined an earthquake would sound. The rising yellow sun shone over the black line of trees, and the air was warm and moist. Now all Jed could hear was the sound of water; it was everywhere, rushing, running, falling, flowing, gurgling, seeping, swishing. . . . It flowed black and swift between the patchy white riverbanks, and overflowed in the low places into the thawing meadows. Jed Gill jumped out of bed and ran to the front door and threw it open in delight.

It was spring.

To Jed Gill, spring meant sugaring-off. Each day, while the thaw continued, Jed anxiously tested the ground with the toe of his boot, or gauged the ebb of the river by the widening darker line of bank above the surface. Even though he was only nine, Jed knew that you could not hold a sugar camp until the ground was dry; and if you couldn't do it in early spring, when the sap in the maple trees were running, you had to wait until late winter—if the winter was mild. One night, though, he almost jumped from the table in delight when Tom Cowlett said: "Good news, Jeddy—Uncle Jon's opening a sugar camp day after tomorrow." Jed had difficulty sleeping that night, and the following night he was up and dressed well before dawn.

At first light, he made his own breakfast of mush and milk and dashed outside to start piling the big five-pail iron kettles on the oxcart. Then he put the ten-quart butternut-log sap troughs and the oaken sap buckets on afterward, and as soon as his foster father came outside wiping his lips with the back of his hand, he helped him harness the oxen to the wagon. Hearing the creaking approach of his uncle's wagon, he ran out onto the road eagerly, expecting to see Rachel up on the box with her father. But she wasn't there.

"Where's Rachel, Uncle Jon?"

"Home with her ma. She cried a little, but sugarin' isn't woman's work." Jed's face fell, and to ease his disappointment, Clarke said quickly: "We'll be staying out there over-night, anyway."

"Over*night*? Oh, *boy!*"

Clarke grinned, glancing at the sky. It was an enchanting spring day, like a fairy godmother's gift in reward for having endured the ordeal of the long, cruel winter. Above the river, the early-morning mists were shredding and dissolving in the warmth of a mild spring sun. The tree line, bitter black for so many months, was now soft with the reddish pink of budding leaves. Creation was everywhere renascent and vibrant. Across the river Jed Gill saw squirrels and wild hare dashing about the woods. He could hear the trilling of wood thrushes and the cardinal's slow sweet whistle. Fat-breasted robins ran stiff-legged in the swamp grass beside the road, searching for worms, keeping clear of the blue jays hopping among them. The Ankerses' calico cat crept stealthily toward them, and the robins took flight, their warning chatter counterpointing the saucy screeching of the jays.

It seemed to Jeddy that his mind was clearer, his breath flowed cleaner through his nostrils. Without understanding why, he felt an exaltation of his soul and his senses as he rode up on the box with his foster father, turning, again and again, to see the tail of the snaking column of oxcarts growing longer and longer. Now there were men walking beside the wagons. Most of them carried muskets, and their eyes swiveled regularly to the woods beside the cart road and across the river. A half-hour from Deerfield, they all had tied kerchiefs over their mouths to keep out the dust stirred up by the wheels and the great powerful horned oxen plodding along at a three-mile-an-hour pace.

An hour and a half after leaving town, they came to the sugar camp in the grove of maples the people of Deerfield had been using for a decade. With one single screech of joy, the boys of the settlement jumped down from the carts and sprinted into the clearing. The older men walked after them, grinning, carrying their muskets, which they stacked in the clearing. Jed Gill deliberately stood apart from the other boys. He was proud that his uncle, the magistrate, was in charge of the camp, and he wanted the other boys to realize that he was not just another youngster. He followed Clarke from tree to tree, watching gravely while his uncle selected the best maples by cutting a notch with his hatchet at a point five feet above the ground, and then driving in the basswood spouts with the special tapping gauge that was the emblem of his rank as master of the camp. Then the yelling boys came running up to place the troughs beneath the spouts, and within a half-hour the sap began dripping into them.

From the grove behind him, Jed heard a great shout of laughter. Turning, he saw Lem Waters come staggering off the road, bent under an enormous load. He stopped and heaved it from his wide shoulders and it hit the ground with a shattering crash. Jeddy ran up to take stock of what Lem had carried. To his astonishment, he counted one big kettle, two sap buckets, an ax, a knapsack, a sack of provisions for three days—which for Lem Waters would be substantial—a blanket, and a musket and ammunition.

"Hey, Lem," Seth Ankers called, "y' fergit Becky Small?"

Another shout of laughter arose in the camp. Lem grinned, pulling his thick blond hair out from beneath his shirt collar, where it had gotten stuck. "Wagon broke down just as I was passin' Cowlett's," he explained. "Broken axle. It was either shank's mare, or miss the sugarin'."

"You *walked* all that way with all that gear?"

Lem nodded proudly.

"On yer behind?"

This time the outburst of laughter was so great and the chuckles so long in lingering that Jed Gill guessed he must have missed the joke. But he was still chuckling himself when he ran back to the slowly filling sap troughs.

Now the grove was ringing with ax blows. Fallen trees which would provide dry wood were chopped up. Jed Gill left Clarke to run to his foster father's side, watching him cut down saplings and fashion Y's out of them. These were sunk in the ground and long poles laid through the forks. Then the cooking kettles were hung on the poles and the boys rushed up to drop armloads of firewood under the kettles. Tom Cowlett walked back to his wagon to fetch his tinderbox. Jed watched him gravely as he removed the round cover, took out the flint and steel and a couple of "spunks"—strips of wood dipped in sulphur—and struck the flint and steel together to send sparks flashing into the spunks. He had to do it four or five times before the spunks caught and he could blow them into flame, stuffing them beneath the dry leaves under the kindling. Soon the fires beneath the kettles were blazing, and Jed ran to join the other boys pouring the sap from the troughs into the buckets and then lugging them to the boiling area, where they were poured into the kettle.

The boys began to race each other, trying to see who could carry the most buckets. Jed Gill was the smallest boy there, but he still tried to keep up with the others. Running back from the kettle, he bumped into Jared Ankers coming the other way with a full bucket. Jared fell down and spilled his sap.

"Damn you, Jed Gill," the Ankers boy swore, getting to his feet. He was three years older than Jed, but he was thin and slouch-shouldered. "I ought to punch your head," he shouted. His younger brother, Sam, came up. "Go ahead, hit him!" Sam yelled in his shrill voice. "He did it a'purpose."

"I did not!" Jed cried.

"Hit him anyway," Sam shrieked, dancing around the two of them. "He thinks he's better'n us 'cause his uncle's the magistrate."

Jed Gill stared at Sam Ankers in distaste. He never did like Sam, he thought, remembering how Sam would lick the frozen snot under his nose in winter.

"Mr. Clarke ain't rightly yer uncle, anyway, is he?" Jared growled, advancing on Jed with clenched fists.

"None of your business!"

"I've a mind to give you another nick," Jared muttered, staring at the mark on Jed's forehead. "All that mush about bein' tomahawked afore you was born."

"My Uncle Jon saw it!" Jed said fiercely, refusing to back away from the bigger boy. "You calling him a liar?"

"He's a York man, ain't he?" Jared sneered, screwing up his thin face. He drew back his balled right fist. "Holler 'quits'!" he shouted.

Jed shook his head. Jared Ankers let his hand drop. "Cain't hit a body that much smaller'n me," he muttered, and then, suddenly moving around Jed and pinioning him from behind, he shouted: "You hit 'im, Sam, while I hold 'im."

Grinning sadistically, Sam ran up and swung. Jed ducked, but the blow still hit him on his forehead scar. He shook his head, kicked backward viciously, and freed himself when Jared yelled and grabbed his ankle. Then Jed Gill lowered his head and charged Sam Ankers, his arms flailing like a windmill. Frightened by the fury of the smaller boy's attack, Sam turned to flee—just as one of Jed's fists struck his nose.

"Ow, ow, ow, ow!" Sam Ankers moaned, holding his nose and beginning to cry. Blood trickled through his fingers, and he began to cry louder.

Jonathan Clarke heard his screams and came running over. "Here, here, what's this about?" he called, seizing Jed by the shoulder.

"Jed Gill give me a bloody nose," Sam Ankers wailed. "I didn't do nothin', hones' I didn't. Jed Gill hit me when I wan't lookin'."

Jonathan glanced sternly down at Jed. "Is that true?" he asked, his hand tightening on his shoulder, his other hand straying to his belt buckle.

Jed's face whitened. His lips began to tremble. He couldn't trust himself to speak. He just shook his head fiercely.

"Answer me, boy."

"Whoa, Cap'n," a deep voice said. "Not so fast." Jed saw that it was Lem Waters. "I seen it all, Cap'n," Waters said. "Them Ankers boys tried to gang up on little Jeddy. The big one held 'im while the other one walloped 'im." He grinned. "That Gill boy's a tiger for sure. He licked 'em both."

The hand on Jed's shoulder relaxed. "You can go, Jed," Clarke said softly, a hint of pride in his voice. Jed nodded and walked toward the river with lowered head. His shoulders began to shake. He began to sob quietly. Bubbles of mucous burst from his nostrils. He tried to stop sobbing, but he couldn't. He hadn't quit, he told himself fiercely, and he'd won! Why was he crying? He looked up at the sky with defiant, tear-stained eyes. Why did you make me cry, God? he asked bitterly; but then, horrified by his own blasphemy, he said, "I didn't mean it, Lord—honest I didn't."

At the riverbank he stopped, studying the swift-flowing stream. He thought he saw a big bass jump, and stared hard at the place, looking for another. Suddenly he realized that he had stopped sobbing. He was just sniffling, and soon that stopped, too. His eyes still burned, but Jed concluded that no one would know he had been crying and walked back to the troughs.

To his surprise, the other boys crowded around him eagerly, shaking his hand and clapping him on the back.

"Good for you, Jeddy—them Ankerses had it comin' . . ."

"For a little feller, you sure hit 'im a lick . . ."

"You hurt your fist? Lemme see it . . ."

Jed proudly extended his fist, looking around for a glimpse of the Ankers boys. But he didn't see them again until that night after the sugaring was done and everyone had gathered around a great bonfire in the center of the clearing to eat the food they had brought with them. There were crocks of sweet cider for the boys, and, of course, jugs of rum and beer for the men. Jed listened enraptured while the men reminisced about other sugar camps they had held, especially the winter ones. They began to sing softly:

> God makes sech nights, so white and still
> Fer's you can look and listen.
> Moonlight an' snow, on field and hill,
> All silence and all glisten.

Then they fell silent, pulling at their fragrant pipes or taking another swig from jugs cradled over their shoulders by its neck, only to start another ditty, often a drinking song:

> To the tavern let's away!
> There have I a mistress got,
> Cloistered in a pottle pot;
> Plump and bounding, soft and fair,
> Buxom, sweet, and debonair,
> And they call her *Sack*, my dear!

Jed Gill was enchanted. He watched the firelight reflected off their sunburned faces, now red, now yellow, as the tongues of flame rose and fell. It was only their faces that he saw; the rest of their bodies were in darkness. They seemed like disembodied heads in a ring. Above him Jed heard the hooting of owls and the soft rustling of other birds stirring in their nests. Through the gaps in the trees he could see the stars swinging overhead as though at the end of a long dark tunnel. Then the spell was broken when his foster father seized his shoulder and led him off to sleep on the ground between him and Jonathan Clarke. Jed was going to protest that he wasn't sleepy, but he fell instantly into slumber, the uncompleted hoot of an owl in his ears.

Jed Gill awoke in the dark with a deep sense of alarm. There was no sound in the clearing except the snoring of some of the men. Occasionally a maple knot exploded in the dying fire, scattering sparks. Otherwise, it was still and black and Jeddy Gill was afraid. He sensed danger, an intruder. . . . Over there . . . by the sugaring kettles. . . . Did he see a shape move in the darkness? Was that a twig snapping? Jed caught his breath. There had been a clink against a kettle. Someone *was* there. An *Indian*? . . . A *Frenchman*? . . . Jed put a trembling hand out slowly toward his foster father, but then withdrew it, remembering how deeply he slept. He turned stealthily on his stomach and put his other hand over Jonathan Clarke's mouth. He could feel the stubble of hair on Clarke's lip. Then he withdrew it quickly. He had felt saliva on his palm and guessed that Clarke was awake.

"What is it?" Clarke hissed.

"S-someone's there," Jed whispered. "By the sugar pots."

Clarke sat erect and stared through the darkness. Yes, he *did* see a shape by the kettles. A large one. Was it Lem Waters? he thought. No, by God, it's a bear! At once Clarke felt for the musket beside him. In the dark, he opened the pouch at his belt and fumbled for a cartridge. He bit off the paper end and poured the powder down the muzzle, saving a few grains to sprinkle on the firing pan. Then he knelt erect, pushed the balled paper cartridge into the muzzle, inserted the bullet and shoved both down the barrel with his ramrod. Holding the musket in his right hand, he crept toward the smoldering fire on his knee.

Jed Gill knelt erect, too, peering into the darkness, his hand over his mouth, his whole body shaking. He saw Clarke stop by the fire, which now silhouetted him. Clarke shoved something into the coals, and suddenly there was light. It was a betty lamp ignited by the coals. Clarke jumped up and held the lamp before his face. A few yards away he saw the bear, a huge, black creature weighing at least four hundred pounds. The bear was seated on its haunch with a cold kettle on its lap. It cradled it with one arm while the other it scraped pawfuls of sugar from the inside of the pot and stuffed them into its mouth, licking the paw clean each time. It blinked in the light until it sensed Clarke's presence. Snarling, its drawn lips baring its white teeth, it clambered to its feet. Clarke fired. The bear toppled forward with a roar. Its upraised rear legs flailed the air wildly, and then, with a trailing whimper, it shivered and fell still.

The camp erupted in an uproar. Shouting men with muskets came from every direction toward the kettles. Clarke was surprised to see Jed Gill run up and kneel beside the dead bear, weeping.

"What're you crying for, Jed?" Clarke asked, puzzled, squatting beside the boy and taking him in his arms. "I thought you did right well, waking me up like that."

"I . . . I didn't want it to be a bear," Jed wailed, still blubbering while the astonished men of Deerfield gathered around him.

"What's wrong with a bear, Jed? Plenty of good fresh bear meat for our families. The hide for a bear rug. Bear grease for soap and candles. Four big paws for bear-paw shoes. Even the head for a trophy for you. That's why I shot it through the heart, Jeddy—so's you could have the head."

"But I didn't want it to be a bear," Jed wailed again, this time even more fiercely. "I wanted it to be a *Frenchman!*"

7

"Tom, I think Jeddy's ready for Harvard College," Jonathan Clarke said to his brother-in-law. They were seated at table in the Cowlett house, where the two families had just celebrated Rachel Clarke's thirteenth birthday with a meal of salted venison. Agatha Cowlett and Martha Clarke were in the kitchen cleaning up, and Jed and Rachel had gone skating on the frozen river under a clear moonlit sky.

"Ready for Harvard!" Tom Cowlett repeated in astonishment. "But Jeddy just turned fifteen last month."

"He's ready, though. He knows everything I know, and it'd be a shame to let him stagnate out here a few more years not learning anything. Besides, look at him. He's really grown the last few years. He may have reached his full height already."

Tom nodded, reaching for his pipe and lighting it. "Oh, he's big enough. Bigger'n me and almost as tall as you. But college . . ." He shook his head wonderingly. "Are we really that old, Jon?" The two men studied one another. Tom Cowlett's rough-hewn face was seamier and there was a bald spot in the middle of his sandy hair. Jonathan Clarke's saturnine face seemed longer, thinner. His thick head of black hair was turning pepper-and-saltish. Tom grinned. "Trouble with us, Jon, is we've been working too hard."

"Maybe you have, Tom," Jonathan said, laughing. He looked around him admiringly. "And you deserve all you've got. Beamed ceilings. Plaster walls. Real glass in the windows. Smokehouse in the attic. Cellar full of rum and cider." He belched slightly. "I don't know where you got that pipe of Madeira from, but it sure is good. By God, Tom, you must be one of the richest men along the Connecticut River."

Tom Cowlett blushed modestly. "Aggie'n me's been lucky. Leastways, Jeddy won't have to work as hard as us. That's one good thing. Guess leavin' Boston wasn't such a bad idea, after all."

"Not really," Jonathan said slowly. "But it's still the frontier here. And now we've got another war on our hands."

"Them French won't try us again so fast," Tom said fiercely, reaching for his pipe. "Not after what we done to them last time."

"Men have short memories. But we are stronger, now. Those twenty volunteers from the General Court will help, too."

"Fer God's sake, Jon," Tom Cowlett said in exasperation, lighting his pipe. "What's it all about this time?"

"Same thing." Clarke grunted. "Power. The kings are at their favorite sport again. Only this time it's a queen on our side. Queen Anne didn't like it when Louis the Fourteenth put his grandson on the Spanish throne. She thought that was too much power for Louis. So she talked Holland and Austria into going to war with her against France and Spain."

"What in tarnation do we care about the quarrels of Europe? We'd both be better off—us and the French—if we'd act like we never heard about it. We get nothin' but misery out of it. After King William's war was over—with all the killin' and burnin'—both sides give back all the prisoners and forts they took just like nothin'd ever happened. We even give back Port Royal!"

"I know. But you see, the French almost have to fight us. They don't have nearly as many people and they're always afraid their Indians will declare for us. If that happened—if their Indians went over to the English—with them and the Iroquois against them, the French would be wiped out. That's one reason they don't attack the Iroquois. They're afraid of stirring them up. So they hound their Indians against us, and that keeps them on the French side."

Tom Crowlett scratched his head in bewilderment. "Why should the French Indians want to come over to us?"

"Simple. We pay more for their furs. The hatchets and blankets and kettles and stuff we trade for the pelts are of better quality than the French, and we give more."

"Tarnation! You'd think Governor Dudley'd make the French Indians know how they're bein' tricked."

Jonathan Clarke smiled. "He'd like nothing better. D'you want to be his messenger to the Abnaki, Tom?"

Tom Cowlett grinned ruefully and scratched his head again. "Maybe leavin' Boston was a little previous," he mumbled.

Jonathan got to his feet. "I don't know about that. We're in pretty good shape. I've got the Court's volunteers patrolling inside the palisade at night, and our own people on sentry go. The blockhouses are manned. They'd need cannon to take Deerfield, now, Tom—and they're not easy to drag." He put on his blanket coat. "Not for three hundred miles through the woods and the snow." Tom Cowlett nodded, watching in admiration as his brother-in-law opened the door and stepped outside to begin his nightly inspection.

The night was bitter cold and there was a stiff wind blowing. Through the open gates Jonathan could see that the wind had blown the river clear of snow. Good skating for Rachel and Jeddy, he thought, watching high white plumes of snow being whirled across the meadows like waterspouts. Above him a frosty white moon crowned the apex of a vast black vault glittering with stars. Clarke saw with approval that the palisades patrol was moving briskly by twos around the compound. He returned their salutes. To either side of the gates stood Lem Waters and Seth Ankers with loaded muskets. They were the sentries.

"Better get those gates shut, Lem," Clarke said.

"We will, Cap'n. Just as soon as your girl and the Gill boy come back in."

Jonathan nodded. He looked at Seth Ankers. His pinched face was blue with cold and his teeth were chattering.

"Colder'n a witch's tit out here," Seth complained, clapping his mittened hands together. "When's our relief comin'?"

"Eight o'clock. About half an hour. You'll be back on watch at midnight."

"First thing I'm gonna do when I get indoors is make me a hot buttered rum."

"Uh, uh," Clarke said warningly. "No drinking on duty."

"Just a tot?" Ankers whined pleadingly.

"Not a drop. And remember, Lem—if my daughter and Jed aren't back inside within fifteen minutes, send someone out to fetch them. That gate has to be shut tight at eight."

"As you say, Cap'n."

Jonathan Clarke walked back toward the Cowlett house, frowning. He didn't like seeing Seth Ankers on watch at night. He just wasn't trustworthy. Jonathan made a mental note to remind Sergeant Tom Cowlett not to post Ankers on night duty anymore.

Jed and Rachel were delighted to find that the wind had swept the river bare. They sat on the riverbank strapping on their skates, gazing up at the moon through the sheets of blowing snow.

"Funny, looking at the moon and stars through snow like that," Jed said.

Rachel glanced up and down the river. "Nobody else is out. We've got the river all to ourselves." She jumped to her feet, tip-toed down to the ice and took a few quick steps. Then she swept lightly downriver, halting with a graceful turn, spraying ice. "Least you'n me aren't slugabeds on a night like this."

Jed came onto the ice. He studied Rachel with rising interest. When she had whirled around before, he suddenly realized that she was becoming a woman. At dinner he had vaguely noticed the slight curve of budding breasts beneath her dress; but now, watching her glide easily over the frozen river, the *clunk* of her blades striking the ice echoing crisply in the icy stillness, she excited him.

Rachel came to a scraping halt beside him. Her breath made vapor puffs. Her cheeks were reddening and her green eyes danced. "Race you to the mill and back," she called tauntingly.

"All right. I'll give you a head start." He motioned downriver. "Soon as you go around the bend, I'm comin' after you."

"You'll never catch me! What do I get if I win?"

"A big hug," Jed said, watching her carefully.

"A hug!" Rachel cried scornfully, tossing her chestnut hair. "What's *that*?"

"And what'll I get if I win?"

"What do you want?"

"A kiss."

Rachel's mouth flew open in astonishment. Then her eyes blazed. "Jeddy Gill, I ought to tell your ma."

"What's wrong with a kiss? I was at a party in Hadley last week and there was a lot o' kissin'. It was fun."

Rachel turned abruptly and sped downriver. A kiss! she thought with feigned anger. Why, I never . . . Still, the suggestion did not entirely displease her, and a mischievous glint returned to her eyes. The hide-hole! she thought, bending low as she turned the curve in the river, one arm behind her back, the other pumping for balance. She would hide there!

Instantly Rachel swerved to the shore and clambered up the bank tip-toe. She came to a huge elm tree and disappeared at the base of it. As always, she was surprised how roomy it was inside, even if it was pitch black. But the darkness did not frighten her. She was used to it. She and Jeddy had made the hide-hole one summer's day two or three years ago. They had found the elm rotted at the base and had scooped it out. They had made it their sanctuary. They would hide there when there were chores to be done, holding hands and listening in delicious delinquency while their parents searched the woods for them with angry calls. Now, Rachel squatted, trying not to giggle. See if he catches me now, she thought.

When Jed Gill swept around the river bend and saw the frozen stream was empty, he immediately guessed where Rachel had gone. He glided ashore, removed his skates and crept silently toward the elm tree. Then he dropped inside with a cry of "Gotcha!"—seizing Rachel and kissing her full on the mouth. To his surprise, she did not resist, but kissed him back. They clung to each other in the darkness, lips roving hungrily over lips. Jed freed himself and placed a hand on Rachel's breast. "Don't," she pleaded softly. "Don't, Jeddy . . ." He persisted, and she said nothing. He could hear her panting, and he slid a hand between her legs where she was squatting. "No, Jeddy, no . . ." she moaned. "We'll get into trouble . . ." Again he persisted, and again she said nothing. On fire with desire, Jed Gill struggled out of his blanket coat and slid it under the reclining Rachel. Then he began pulling down her knickers.

The wind that had swept the river bare had also piled a snowbank up to the top of the outside of the Deerfield palisade. Jed Gill had noticed it when he walked back to town with Rachel. Anybody could climb it and drop inside the palisade easy, he thought, resolving to tell his foster father about it. But then, both Rachel and Jed had been so flustered by Seth Anker's supicious stare as they walked through the gate that Jed forgot about it. He fell asleep with the comforting sound of the voices of the changing watch in his ears. Four hours later he awoke to the same sound—and thought of the snowbank. Why wake Pa, now? he thought drowsily, wriggling in the warmth of his bed. For another instant he thought of Rachel: how warm and lovable and desirable she had been. Now he knew why people got married; and he was going to marry Rachel some day; yes, he was. . . .

Outside, Lem Waters and Seth Ankers were soon stamping their feet and beating their hands together. Seth snickered. "What d'y think them two was up to, Lem?"

"What two?"

"Young Gill and the Clarke girl."

"You've got a dirty mind, Seth."

"No, I ain't. By God, that Clarke girl's becomin' a woman a'reddy. I been noticin' it."

"You would."

Seth coughed suggestively. "How about a swig o' rum to warm y' up, Lem?"

"No."

"Aw, why not?"

"Cap'n says so."

"*Him*! By Jesus, it ain't him what's standin' out here freezin' his dollywhacker off. *He's* as warm in his bed as a London whore, snuggerin' up to that red-haired wife o' his. Maybe givin' her a toss right now."

"Shut up, Seth. Why is it all you ugly little fellers got such dirty minds? You take that tongue o' yourn off Cap'n Clarke, y'hear? He's a good man. He knows what he's a-doin', too."

Seth Ankers stuck his mittened hands into his pockets and shivered. "God A'mighty, it's cold," he mumbled. He walked toward the locked gate and glanced swiftly up and down the enclosure. "Hey, Lem," he called. "We're all alone."

"What's that?" the big man cried, hurrying up beside Seth.

"The patrols. They're gone. All them fine fellows from the General Court has skedaddled."

"Probably just stepped out of the cold," Lem muttered, and Seth said: "Cain't really blame 'em, can you, Lem—so why don't we just step out of it, too?" He paused, watching his calico cat come walking toward him daintily pulling its paws from the snow. Seth's eyes widened in incredulity. "By Jesus, Lem—look at that, will you? Lookit my cat! His ears is froze and the points broke off."

"Well, you can shave my ass with a cross-cut saw," Lem Waters breathed. "Damn if he ain't got round ears, now—just like a big mouse."

"Y'see, Lem—that's what I call cold. So what's wrong with us stepping into my cabin for a sip o' rum? We won't stay but a minute."

"All right," Lem said, putting his hand on his mop of blond hair. "Damn if my hair ain't froze up, too."

Two miles downriver, fifty Frenchmen and two hundred Abnaki and Caughnawagas lay shivering in a pine forest. They had arrived there late in the afternoon of the preceding day, having come three hundred miles through the snow-covered wilderness on snowshoes. Making camp, they ate the last of their pemmican and lay down in the cold darkness, not daring to make fires. Two hours before dawn they arose, removed their packs and showshoes and set out for Deerfield.

There was a frozen crust on the snow thick enough to support a man. But it still made crunching noises as they walked. From time to time they stopped, hoping to create the illusion of a rising and falling wind. Within an hour, they stood in the meadows below the town. They were disheartened to see the high palisade with the blockhouses at the corners, until they noticed the snow banked against the wooden fence like an inclined path. Delighted, they loosened the hatchets in their belts and made sure there was powder in the priming pan of their muskets. Then, by twos and threes, they trotted through the meadow and up the snowbank, dropping silently inside the sleeping settlement.

With a single hideous scream, they attacked.

Seth Ankers was standing in front of his kitchen stove, stirring maple sugar into a mug of hot buttered rum, when the door began to buckle beneath the blows of a screeching band of Indians. It fell inward with a crash and Lem Waters aimed his musket at the first of the intruders rushing inside and dropped him. Then Lem clubbed his musket, whirling it viciously around his head, forcing the startled Indians to cower against the cabin walls. Lem rushed outside, yelling—but a Frenchman in an officer's uniform knelt in the snow and shot Lem through the head with a pistol. A young Indian rushing out of the Ankers house as though in pursuit grabbed the dying man by his blond hair and scalped him. Inside, an Indian with blue bars on his face killed and scalped Seth Ankers. He did the same to young Sam Ankers, but took Jared and six-year-old Anne prisoner.

Jonathan Clarke awoke in horrified disbelief. He pulled Martha from the bed and pushed her toward the window. "Quick—jump!" he ordered, tearing the oiled-paper pane apart with his fingers. Without waiting to see her go, he whirled and ran downstairs to get his musket. At the foot of the stairs, two Indians seized him and a third ran a spear through his middle. Screaming, Jonathan Clarke sank to his knees, his hands grasping the wooden shaft. Another Indian sank a tomahawk into the base of his bent head. Two others rushed into the kitchen and into Rachel's room. They saw the paper pane torn apart and came back out yelling angrily.

Outside, Martha Clarke lay writhing on the ground in her nightgown, surrounded by Caughnawagas and the Frenchman who had killed Lem Walters. The blue-barred Indian who had killed Seth Ankers knelt to tie her wrists with a cord. "No, Howling Wolf," the Frenchman said. "Her ankle's broken. She'll never make the trip." Howling Wolf glanced up, scowling. "A prisoner is worth more than a scalp." The Frenchman shook his head and Howling Wolf looked longingly at Martha, who stared at him in dread revulsion. "She's pretty. She'll make a good squaw." The Frenchman shrugged. "Suit yourself. But you'll only have to kill her along the way. Might as well get it over with, now." Sighing, the kneeling Indian put his cord back in his belt, drew his hatchet, and killed Martha Clarke. He arose, grinning, proudly shaking out her beautiful chestnut hair. "Pretty scalp," he said, giggling.

Rachel Clarke had climbed out of the window in terror. She ran around the cabin toward the open gate, barely conscious of the pain in her bare feet as they struck the frozen snow. Rachel was through the gate before anyone saw her. An Indian in ocher warpaint let out a war whoop and gave chase. A shot burst from the nearest blockhouse and the Indian fell, somersaulting through the snow. A big Frenchman took up the pursuit. A fusillade of shots burst from the blockhouse. Big as the target was, they all missed. Rachel ran on in horror, spurred by the shouts of her pursuer. He gained on her at first. But once they had left the hard-packed snow around the settlement, he began to flounder and fell behind. He could walk over the snow crust, but when he attempted to run, he was too heavy and his feet broke through it. Rachel skimmed over the frozen snow like a bird, and soon she was in the woods. Within a minute she had found the big elm and disappeared in the hide-hole. But the Frenchman did not give up. Until dawn and for at least an hour afterward, he prowled around the woods, whooping hideously. Rachel did not stir. She remembered what Jeddy used to say to her when they crouched in the hide-hole. "If an Indian ever chases you here, don't move. Especially when he yells. He wants to scare you so's you'll give yourself away." Rachel sat still in dark and silent terror. Jeddy? Was he . . .?

Because Tom Cowlett had made his front door so stout, the assailants had difficulty battering it down. Tom had time to seize his musket, pistol and cartridge bag and send Agatha scurrying downstairs into the cellar. Tom ran into Jed Gill's room but found the window smashed and Jed gone. Tom ran back to the cellar stairs, pulled the door down and bolted it. He joined Agatha, seated on a pipe of madeira, holding a fluttering candle in her shaking hands. "Oh, my God," Agatha moaned. "Oh, my God . . ." Tom listened to the rising tempo of blows against the door. After about five minutes, they began to subside. Then they stopped altogether. "Thank God," Tom whispered, letting out his breath. "They've given up." Agatha began to cry. Her shuddering sobs and shaking hands almost put out the candle. Tom took it from her and set it on a barrel of cider. He put a reassuring arm around her. For perhaps half an hour they sat there, clinging to each other, listening to the yelling and screaming as the massacre continued. Gradually, Tom became aware of a warmth creeping into the cellar. He heard a crackling noise overhead. "Just a second, Aggie," he said softly, getting to his feet. "I think I hear Jonathan's voice." Then he stepped behind his wife and shot her through the head. Drawing his pistol, he put the muzzle in his mouth and pulled the trigger.

It was in the light of the burning Cowlett house that Jedediah Gill was captured. Jed had crept on his belly from cabin to cabin, hoping to reach the gate and make a break for the hide-hole in the woods. But he was silhouetted in the leaping flames of the blazing house and two Indians seized him and wrestled him down. Jed's face was pressed into the snow, smothering his screams. He felt one Indian kneel on his back while the other yanked his arms backward with a painful wrench and tied his wrists together. Jed relaxed. He had been praying and bracing for the death blow, but now, he realized, they were taking him captive. They pulled him erect and the younger of the two pointed toward the meeting house where other prisoners were being taken. "You go there," he said, shoving him.

His soul writing in anguish, his mind full of dreadful fears for his foster parents and the Clarkes—he tried not to think of Rachel—Jed walked slowly toward the building. It was one of the few left standing in Deerfield. Almost all of the others were either burning or reduced to heaps of smoking rubble. A pall of black smoke hung over the settlement in the growing gray light of a chill and sunless dawn. Behind Jed, the two Indians began to argue. "He's my prisoner, Half Moon," said the bigger one, who had blue bars on his face. "No, Howling Wolf, he's mine. I saw him first and I tied him. He's mine!" Howling Wolf grasped Jed roughly by the shoulder and spun him around. "I'll kill him, then," he shouted fiercely, drawing his tomahawk. "Half Moon and Howling Wolf are friends. Why should we argue? Kill him and split the scalp money." Half Moon shook his head stubbornly. "My brother is dead. The Englishman with the long yellow hair killed him." He looked at Jed. "He's strong and young. I'm going to have him adopted into our tribe. I will make him my brother." Howling Wolf slowly lowered his hatchet. A cunning look came into his small, squinty eyes. "Will you buy my share?" Half Moon smiled. He drew Lem Waters's scalp from his belt. "I'll give you a scalp worthy of the Great Spirit Owaneeyo." Howling Wolf ran his tongue over his lips greedily. He put the grisly trophy on his belt beside the scalp of Martha Clarke, patting both in childish delight.

Jedediah Gill stared at the two scalps—one thick, blond, and masculine, the other the lustrous long chestnut locks of a woman—and he knew.

8

Jedediah Gill quickly realized how fortunate he had been in becoming the property of Half Moon rather than of Howling Wolf. Before the French and Indians began their long march northward, Howling Wolf had killed a five-year-old girl with a single blow of his tomahawk.

"She's too little to make the march," Half Moon had mumbled to Jed in explanation. "She'd slow us down."

Then why not leave her behind? Jed thought, but prudently said nothing. He had seen the glint of sadistic pleasure in Howling Wolf's eyes when he swung his hatchet so hard that it split the child's skull in two, scattering blood and brains on himself and those around him. Then Howling Wolf had turned to Jared Ankers and forced him to strip naked in the freezing cold and give him his clothes. Grinning, Howling Wolf shucked his filthy, vermin-infested hunting shirt and threw it at the Ankers youth. Jared put it on, his thin face twisted in revulsion. Moments later, he began to vomit. Howling Wolf kicked him viciously, making it known by angry gestures that he must pull his little sister, Anne, on a sledge. When Jed passed Jared on snowshoes, he saw that he was weeping. He felt sorry for him, almost wishing that he had not fought him and Sam at the sugaring that day.

108

Jed's snowshoes had been given to him by Half Moon. They had belonged to the brother killed by Lem Waters. Jed had been so tired when the column reached the pine forest where the raiders had hidden their packs and snowshoes that Half Moon saw at once that he could not make the march on moccasins. With surprisingly gentle patience, he showed Jed how to use them.

"No, no, Yellow Head," Half Moon said. "Don't lift your foot so high. You'll get racquet ache that way. Lift it just a little. Slide it forward over the edge of the other shoe. Good! That's it!"

Jed caught on quickly. By the time the column reached Greenfield Meadows, about five miles upriver from Deerfield, he was shuffling over the snow with confidence. Here the raiders encamped. They dug away the crust of frozen snow and spread spruce bows in the softer snow for beds. Most of them bound their prisoners to prevent their escape. Howling Wolf tied Jared Ankers and his sister to the sledge. After he finished gnawing noisily on a leg of salt venison he had found in theAnkers home, he threw them the bone.

"Howling Wolf is stupid!" Half Moon muttered angrily, slipping out of his pack and placing it beside the spruce boughs he had cut. "If he values his prisoners, why treat them like dogs?" He glared defensively at Jed. "Don't think all Indians are like that. Only sapheads like him. Besides, he's not a true Caughnawaga. His mother was a Catawba," he said contemptuously, as though that implied taint in ancestry explained everything. "Catawbas are bad people. They paint their arrowheads with rattlesnake poison. Their squaws sleep around." Stooping, Half Moon opened his pack and drew out three sausages and half a loaf of corn bread, which also had come from the Ankers home. "Here," he said, carefully cutting the loaf in two, along with one of the sausages, and ostentatiously handing Jed his exact half, "this is how true Indians share their food. With everyone—guests or prisoners."

Jed looked up from the food he had begun to gobble greedily. "But," he began hesitantly, "I thought you tortured and ate your prisoners."

Half Moon smiled, observing the young man's apprehension. "Sometimes. If they are our old enemies. But not always. These prisoners," he said, gesturing to the camp around him, "some of them will be adopted into tribes. Especially the women. Others will be sold to the priests. Or the French will ransom them. But I tell you, Yellow Head," he exclaimed fiercely, reverting to the earlier conversation, "our fathers have taught us' to be generous. If a stranger comes to my camp, I must give him the best that I have. The roast venison I am about to eat, and even sugar and bear's oil to make it sweeter."

Jed Gill finished his meal, wiping his fingers on his coat. What Half Moon had told him made him think of the Bible his Aunt Martha used to read to him: "And whosoever will force thee one mile, go with him other two." Remembering his Aunt Martha and the cold winter of Ninety-eight, he thought of the scalps on Howling Wolf's belt and turned away in tears.

"You are crying," Half Moon said in an accusing voice. "Great men do not cry."

"I . . . I can't help it," Jed stammered plaintively. "That scalp you gave Howling Wolf was my father's friend. The other—the red-haired one—was my aunt . . ." The tears came hotly again, and Half Moon turned away in embarrassment. "I guess my Uncle Jon is dead, too," Jed said, now half-ashamed at what he realized the Indian considered weakness. He wiped away the tears. "He was the finest man I ever knew."

"Better than your father, even?" Half Moon asked in surprise, his voice stern. "There is no man better than a man's father."

"I never saw mine," Jed replied, explaining how he was born.

"Schenectady? My father was there. That was many winters ago."

"Fifteen."

"You are fifteen, then? I am eighteen," Half Moon said proudly, "and I am already a brave. I will make you one, too." Jed said nothing, struggling again with tears as he thought of his foster parents. "I guess they're dead, too," he mumbled half-aloud.

"Who?"

"My foster parents. The people who lived in the house that was burning when you caught me."

"Yes, Yellow Head, they are dead," Half Moon said simply. "But you must be br—"

A wail burst from Jed Gill's lips, and Half Moon struck him hard across the mouth. "You are not fit to be my brother!" he hissed, drawing his tomahawk and lifting it. "If you cry again, I will kill you!" Jed Gill cowered away from the menacing hatchet. His frightened glance moved slowly from its glittering blade to Half Moon's blazing black eyes. "You have much grief, Yellow Head," Half Moon said slowly, softening his voice. "But all men have grief. You must learn to keep your grief to yourself. It is to women alone that the Great Spirit has given tears and lamentation." Jed nodded, relaxing and sitting up again after Half Moon put away his tomahawk. "Are you going to tie me up, Half Moon," he asked. The Indian shook his head. "I am not as stupid as Howling Wolf. If a wolf comes into camp, I want you to defend yourself. I will tie your arm to mine instead," he said, binding both their forearms by a thong. "Let us sleep, Yellow Head," he said, pulling him back on the spruce boughs. "It will be a hard march tomorrow."

Jed Gill lay back in the darkening night. He could hear the wind moaning softly as it blew harmlessly over the top of their hole. He was surprised how warm it was in the soft snow and fragrant spruce boughs. He thought of Rachel and screwed his eyes shut tight. He was afraid to weep, afraid that Half Moon would hear him. Still, the hot tears leaked out at the corners. Rachel! Oh, Rachel . . . did God spare you? He thought of the night before in the hide-hole—now an eternity away, as though an ocean of time and blood lay between him and those moments of ecstasy—and like a newly opened well a tide of grief rose up inside him that seemed unstoppable. It seemed to Jedediah Gill that his anguish would come spouting out his mouth in a wail of bereavement that he could not still. Suddenly, the night was filled with howling, wild yelling and singing. Opening his eyes, he saw flickering light fingering the blackness. For a moment, Jed Gill thought he was in hell—until half Moon shot erect beside him, dragging him up with him.

"What's that?" Jed cried.

"Firewater," Half Moon grunted in a tone of contempt. "They found rum in the village. Now they'll celebrate the victory. They'll get dlunk. They'll fight. And they'll kill each other."

"Can't you stop them?"

"Not me," Half Moon said sourly. "Me? Try to stop a dlunken Indian? Even our sachem wouldn't try, if he isn't dlinking with them himself. You know, you English aren't as clever as you think you are. If you really wanted to control the Indians, you'd do nothing but feed them firewater. They can't stand it. They don't dlink to enjoy themselves, like it says in the Bible, 'Wine to gladden the heart of man.' " Jed started in astonishment to hear an Indian quoting the good book. Half Moon chuckled and went on. "No, they dlink to get dlunk. If there isn't enough for everyone to get dlunk, they choose straws and the rum goes to the winners. They give their weapons to the losers in hopes that they'll keep them from killing each other." He paused, listening to the rising tempo of the howling. "But it sounds tonight like there's enough for everyone."

Jed was struck by the note of sincere sadness in the young brave's voice; but then, as though to fulfill Half Moon's fears, a horrible scream pierced the night. A few minutes later, they heard another scream. "Come, Yellow Head," Half Moon said in a scornful voice, pulling Jed down beside him. "We'll find out in the morning."

At dawn, Half Moon untied their wrists and walked toward the center of camp. He came back to Jed shaking his head. "It is as I feared," he said. "Howling Wolf killed an Abnaki in a dlunken argument over a black slave they'd captured. Then Howling Wolf went berserk and killed the black man." Half Moon bent and opened his pack. He took out two sausages, handing one to Jed. "This is all that's left. If we do not kill bear or deer along the way, we will go hungry tonight." They ate, put on their snowshoes, and waited for the rest of the column to move out before bringing up the rear.

Jed saw the dead Abnaki and black man lying not far from the black patch in the snow that had been the campfire. They had been stripped of their clothing. But Jed saw that the Indian's snowshoes and moccasins, lying in a snowdrift about ten feet from his body, had been overlooked. At once, Jed asked Half Moon if he might give them to Jared Ankers. "First time we stop," his captor said gruffly. Jed was delighted. If he could speak to Jared, he might get word of Rachel. He began to think well of Half Moon.

In the next instant he saw a murdered babe-in-arms and a ten- or eleven-year-old girl lying naked under an oak tree, and his old loathing and hatred for the Indians and the French returned. But there was no stopping that day. Because the crunching sound made by their passage over the frozen snow frightened away the animals, there was also no food; and because they were now in the depths of the great forest, the night was colder.

Next day, Jed felt so weak from hunger and numb with cold that he wondered if he could go on. At midday he heard shots ahead and then cries of delight. Some hunters had killed five moose, whose carcasses were quickly skinned and the raw meat shared out for roasting while the remainder was smoked and dried. Jed received Half Moon's permission to take the snowshoes and moccasins to Jared.

He found him sitting on a sledge with his head between his knees. His bloody feet were bound in strips of bark and there was blood in the snow around him.

"Where's your moccasins, Jared?" Jed asked.

"Wore out," he said in a hopeless voice.

Jed pointed to a bundle lying motionless on the sledge. "What's that?"

"M'sister. What's left of her."

"She alive?"

"Breathin'. But I cain't pull her no more. That devil of a Howling Wolf says ef'n I don't, he'll kill her. He says he ain't about to carry her on his back like the other Indians is doin'." Jared Ankers glanced up at Jed with dull, lifeless eyes. Suddenly they glinted in recognition. "Is that you, Jed Gill?"

Jed nodded, putting a finger to his lips, looking around for Howling Wolf. "Here, I've brought you some moccasins and snowshoes."

Jared sat erect. "Oh, my Jesus, Jed Gill, I think you've saved my life." He pulled the bloody bark off his feet, wincing when the flesh came with it. He put on the moccasins, standing erect in the snow, wincing again. Then he strapped on the snowshoes, and in a few minutes Jed taught him how to use them. "Much obliged t' you, Jed Gill," he wheezed, sitting on the sledge again. "Guess me and m' sis'll live a little while yet." He put out his hand. "I'm sure sorry about what me'n Sam done to you that day."

"Jared," Jed said, taking his hand and quickly dropping it when he saw a louse crawl out on his wrist. "Did you hear anything about Rachel Clarke?"

Jared shook his head, and Jed's heart sank. "Now, wait a minute," Jared said, scratching furiously at his hunting shirt. "Maybe I did hear she got away. Her parents was killed, I know that. But, Rachel . . . I sure didn't see nothin' of her in the meetin' house, and nobody tole me she was kilt."

Jed Gill's eyes gleamed with hope. "Thanks, Jared," he said, taking his hand again. "And forget about that fight at the sugaring."

That night, Jed Gill's spirits were so high when he prepared to go to sleep that even Half Moon teased him about it. "Moose meat agrees with you, brother?" he chuckled, and Jed smiled. It was the first time the Indian had seen his captive happy, and he was pleased at the sight of Jed's strong white teeth. Yellow Head will be a great warrior, he told himself. But the following morning Jed almost stubbed the curving toe of his snowshoe against the naked body of a pregnant woman. Tearing off his mittens, he knelt beside the corpse to put his hand on the belly. The flesh was ice cold. The child within was dead, too, he realized, and he stumbled erect, floundering on through the snow with his eyes blinded by tears. Half Moon's face darkened, and he hastened to overtake him; but then, remembering the circumstances of Yellow Head's birth, the fire left his eyes and he slowed down. Next day, the trail was strewn with the naked corpses of four more murdered Englishwomen. The sight made Jed Gill begin to hate Half Moon. He had been beginning to become fond of the young brave. They had been on the march more than a week and begun to share the kind of ordeal that binds men together. They had things in common to talk about before going to sleep at night. But now what seemed to him the senseless, brutal murder of defenseless captives made him despise Half Moon.

All day long as he trudged through the snow, he thought of ways of killing his captor and escaping. But he knew in his heart of hearts that he was shamming. There was no way that he could get at Half Moon. He was too wary. Wherever they went, Jed had to walk in front. When they lay down together bound, Half Moon slept with his tomahawk secured to his right wrist. Besides, even if he succeeded in getting away, how would he survive in the cold, barren, snow-covered forest? Still, Jed Gill could not admit to himself that he was powerless to avenge his murdered brethren. He promised himself that when the good weather came, he would slip away from Half Moon's village and make his way home by following the banks of the frozen rivers they were traversing north. He vowed that one day he would kill ten Frenchmen and Indians for every one of his countrymen who had been murdered; and he, too, would take scalps. He prayed to God for the strength to carry out his oath. He did not pray to Jesus Christ, the author of the new dispensation of love, who, in his Sermon on the Mount had blessed the peacemakers and had said: "Love your enemies: do good to them that hate you: and pray for them that persecute and calumniate you." Instead he prayed to that God of Battles, the author of the Mosaic law of "Eye for eye, tooth for tooth," and he remembered the fierce exaltation of his boyhood, when, in the winter of Ninety-eight, his Aunt Martha would read his favorite passage: ". . . thou shalt slay all that are therein of the male sex with the edge of the sword." Yes, he would avenge her, too, Aunt Martha . . . and Uncle Jon . . . and his foster parents . . . yes! and above all, his *own* parents!

Yet, the slaughter of helpless prisoners too weak to go on continued. On the night of the day on which Jed had seen the scalped body of little Anne Ankers, he refused the food that Half Moon offered him.

"Why do you not eat, my brother?" Half Moon asked with troubled eyes. "If you do not eat, you will die." Jed Gill looked away. He was afraid that the tears which his captor so detested might spring to his eyes again, and he also feared that he might say something foolish such as not taking life from the hands of murderers. "Is it that your heart is sore?" Half Moon persisted. "You grieve for those who have been killed? But you do not understand. They cannot go on. The little girl . . . her brother could no longer pull her. He could not carry her. Howling Wolf would not carry her, so he killed her. Is that not merciful?"

"Mercy!" Jed cried in horror. "You call that *mercy*?"

"Is it not better to kill them instantly than to leave them to linger and die in cold and hunger? Or to be eaten alive by wolves?"

"But why do you take them prisoner if you know that you're going to kill them?"

"We don't know. We take prisoners because prisoners bring more money than a scalp. It is only when they break down along the way that we kill them."

"Why don't you just leave them behind? I mean, the women and children?"

"We leave no one behind. Only those we cannot over-power. Those who held out in the blockhouses, they were left behind. We could not waste more time and men trying to overcome them. But those who were in our power we took with us. That is war."

Jed shuddered. "A while back," he began slowly. "I heard you quote from the Bible. Are you a Christian?"

"A Catholic, yes," Half Moon said carelessly.

"But doesn't the Catholic Church teach you that it's a sin to kill women and children?"

"Not in war. In peace, yes. Even our fathers believed it was wrong to kill your neighbor in peacetime. Even men. But in war . . ." He seemed to ponder, before his face brightened. "When we left our village, the priests told us to baptize the children before we killed them. This would save their souls and send them to heaven as true Catholics." He shrugged. "But there was so little time . . ."

Jed was shocked. "Hypocrites!" he burst out. "Murderers and worse than murderers! How can you believe such men?"

"They are good men, Yellow Head. They teach us to try to love one another. They teach us to plant, and they mill the grain for us. They try to keep the traders from cheating us, from getting us drunk on brandy and swindling our furs. The Onontio and the traders hate them because they will not let them treat us like dogs. And they are brave men."

"Brave? A man who would kill a baby to save its soul is brave?"

"French priests are very brave," Half Moon said gravely. "My father saw the Mohawks torture a Jesuit to death. They did what they could to make him cry out." Half Moon drew a finger across his mouth. "Cut off his lips." He held up his hand. "Cut off his fingers with clam shells, knuckle by knuckle, joint by joint. Made him walk over hot coals. Everything. But he never said a word until just before he died he forgave them. And now, my brother," he said gently, handing Jed the half-gnawed leg of wild turkey, "will you please eat?"

Wordlessly, mechanically, his tortured mind focusing on some future encounter between himself and one of Half Moon's priests—one of those black-robed disciples of the devil—Jed Gill began to eat.

About a hundred miles north of Deerfield, the column split up into small bands.

"We have no more food," Half Moon explained. "We must hunt for ourselves."

Jed was glad of the division of forces, if only because Howling Wolf went with the troop bound for Montreal, taking Jared Ankers with him. And because Jed was the only prisoner in the tiny party of ten Caughnawagas, now led by Half Moon, it meant that he would see no more corpses along the way. It also meant that they could move faster, even though it was early March and a thaw had left the rivers coated with slush and icy, ankle-deep water.

The thaw had also uncovered the forest forage, bringing out the deer and wild geese. Each day, two hours before sunset, they came to a halt while four or five of the best shots combed the woods for game. The others gathered firewood and cut spruce if there was still snow on the ground. If the earth was bare, they made lean-tos with saplings and bark stripped from linden trees, the one tree which yields its bark in winter. It was a rare day without a kill, and because they carried the remnants of the previous night's meal with them, they seldom went hungry.

Half Moon proved an excellent shot. He was especially adept at bringing down water fowl, with musket or bow. Jed pleaded with him to let him join a hunting party. "I'm a good shot," he boasted. "My Uncle Jon gave me a musket for my eighth birthday, and I've been shooting ever since." Half Moon smiled. "You will get a new musket when you become my brother." Eventually, they were forced to leave the rotten ice of the cracked and melting rivers and plod slowly along the banks through mud that sucked off their moccasins. Jed realized that the Caughnawagas' war paint had worn off long ago. Their tattered clothing hung loosely on their shrunken bodies. They stank hideously, and Jed wondered if he smelled that bad himself. He was surprised to see that their facial skin remained smooth and beardless. Although he was at least three years younger than the youngest, he could feel a soft downy fuzz on his upper lip and chin.

A month and a half after the column had divided, Half Moon's band reached the outskirts of Caughnawaga, nine miles below Montreal. Jed Gill was startled when the braves around him gave the scalp haloo, a long piercing yell given for every scalp they carried. This was followed by shrill shrieks of joy and the slow firing of muskets. From the village came answering shots, shouts, and laughter. Within a ragged circle of houses, perhaps two hundred Indians of all ages and sexes began to gather. Drums began to beat. They began to dance, pointing with glee toward Jed, toward his yellow hair, grown long on the march. Suddenly, they ran into the encircled area and formed two lines about four feet apart. They brandished sticks and clubs.

"You must run the gantlet, Yellow Head," Half Moon said. "You must run for your life."

"Are they going to kill me?" Jed asked, the scar on his forehead turning white.

"Not if you are quick. See, they carry no tomahawks. But you must run the gantlet. It is the way of my people. If you show them that you are quick and brave, they will welcome you into our tribe." He pointed his musket into the air. "Run!" he shouted, firing it.

Jedediah Gill trotted slowly toward the head of the gantlet, feigning fear. Shrieks of derision greeted his approach, especially from the old women. They beat their sticks on the ground in joyful anticipation. "He's afraid! He's afraid!" they jeered. "He will not run." Slowing, Jed pretended to turn—and then sprang swiftly between the rows of astonished Indians, dashing past a quarter of his would-be tormentors before they could raise their weapons. Howls of frustration followed Jed down the line, but he did not hear them, he was running so fast. At first, the blows he received were light and glancing. The Indians had not had time to gauge his speed. But they quickly learned to be ready for him and hit him hard. Jed felt a painful tattoo about his shoulders. A blow above his right eye staggered and slowed him. Another across his shinbone brought him to his knees. Little boys jumped upon his back and bore him to the ground, biting his ears and scratching at his face. A sturdy squaw with a papoose on her back bent to seize his hair and pull out a handful with a triumphant yell. Blood filling his right eye, his ears now full of a horrible din, Jed shook off the boys and pushed himself erect. He started running once more, again with such a swift start that he shot past a good half of those remaining in line. Perhaps only thirty yards remained to the end of the gantlet. Jed dug his toes into the dirt. His breath came in painful gasps. Blows fell upon him from each side, but he staggered on, lurching toward the end of the line and safety—just as someone threw sand into his eyes. Blinded, he felt hands seize him and spin him around. Jeering voices taunted him. "See, he runs both ways!" He sank to his knees, digging his knuckles into his tortured eyes. He arose again, wavering, and then, with a cry of rage and hatred, like a blinded Samson, he struck out wildly around him with his fists until a big brave with a club struck him senseless to the ground.

By the time Howling Wolf's party came to a little Indian village about thirty miles south of Montreal, Jared Ankers believed that his time had come. For weeks, he had had nothing to eat but the marrow he could suck from the gnawed bones of wild turkeys contemptuously thrown at him by Howling Wolf. Now, lying in the snow in the village square, too weak even to lift his lolling head, his skin wrinkled and shriveled on his sticks of arms and legs, he begged his captor to kill him.

"I might as well," Howling Wolf muttered, glaring down at Jared in disgust. "The condition he's in now, I wouldn't get a sou for him."

"Why don't we eat him?" a Caughnawaga brave asked.

"*Him*? You wouldn't get enough meat off that stinking skinny carcass to feed a papoose. No," he said, drawing his tomahawk and stooping to seize Jared by the hair, "I can still get five dollars for his scalp."

"Don't kill him, Howling Wolf," another Caughnawaga brave said. "I'll buy him from you."

"For what?"

"My aunt and uncle live in this village. Their son died a year ago. He'd be the same age as him," he said, pointing to Jared, now conscious in the snow. "I'd like to give him to them for a new son."

A familiar glint of greed crept into Howling Wolf's little eyes. "How much?" he asked, licking his lips.

"Two scalps."

"Two scalps! For a *live* prisoner?"

"You were just about to settle for his scalp alone," the brave replied, grinning. He glanced at Jared, whose body was beginning to be convulsed with shudders. "Better hurry up before he's not worth even that."

Howling Wolf kicked Jared viciously in the ribs. "All right," he growled, and the brave pulled two scalps from his belt.

Next day, Jared Ankers awoke to find himself lying on a pile of skins in an Indian lodge reeking of bear grease and sweat. But it was warm, and Jared himself was warm for the first time since he had been captured. Opening his eyes, he saw an old Indian woman crouching above him. She pulled him erect and began hugging and kissing him, weeping so hard that her tears ran down onto Jared's face.

"My son, my son!" she wailed, giving Jared corn and water. "Eat, Nunganey—drink!"

Next day, she took Jared to the graveyard where her son was buried. They were accompanied by her other two sons, older than Jared, and friends. The dead son's grave was enclosed by pickets, with smooth places to either side. The old woman's family and Jared sat on one side while the friends sat on the other. Both parties began to dance, dragging Jared around the grave, while the friends gave him presents of sugar, corn and tobacco. For the first time in months, Jared Ankers began to laugh. Life felt good again—until the old woman's husband returned to the lodge from a hunting trip.

The old man took an instant dislike to Jared. He kicked him out of the lodge, beating him about the head with the flat of his tomahawk, forcing him to drag his slain deer from the river to the lodge. When Jared sank to his knees in exhaustion, he struck him with a paddle. When his wife sought to intervene, he knocked her down. That night, Jared was made to sleep by himself in a corner, apart from the rest of the family and far from the fire. In the morning, he was sent to the spring to bring water. The presents he had been given were taken from him.

Eventually, Jared Ankers became a human pack animal. He was compelled to haul water and cut wood or carry loads of dried meat on his back from the scene of the hunt to the village. He was given just enough food to give him the strength to carry on, although sometimes his Indian mother would hide corn and give it to him when the old man was absent. Even his foster brothers tormented him, taking turns at beating him. At night, he was made to lie between the fire and the door of the lodge. Anyone who went out or came in kicked him as they passed. If they went out to drink, they threw cold water on him.

In despair, Jared thought of taking his own life. But all of the family's weapons were kept carefully beyond his reach. He did not even have a knife to cut what food was given to him. He thought of drowning himself, but the St. Lawrence was still frozen and the spring was not big enough.

One morning he was late bringing the water from the spring, and his enraged foster father seized him by the hair and dragged him outside, rubbing his face in a mass of dog excrement, as one would punish a cat. Then he threw Jared into a snowbank and went back inside the lodge.

That was where Father Sébastian Rale found Jared while returning to Caughnawaga from a visit to Quebec. Filled with compassion, remembering the parable of the Good Samaritan, Father Rale gently lifted the unconscious youth from the snow and placed him tenderly on his sleigh. Covering him with bearskins, he took him to Montreal, where he entrusted him into the care of his fellow Jesuits.

The Jesuits were kind to Jared Ankers. They nursed him back to health and put him to work in the refectory, meanwhile instructing him in French. They also insisted that Jared become a Catholic.

"We cannot have a heretic in this house," the rector explained in a soft voice. "You must embrace the one true faith, Jared. We would certainly not wish to send you back to your foster parents."

Frightened by the implied threat, Jared allowed himself to be baptized in the faith he had been trained to abhor. Soon he was serving at mass, outwardly devout—inwardly seething with hate and resentment.

"*Dominus vobiscum*," the priest would chant. "The Lord be with you." And Jared would respond, "*Et cum spiritu tuo*, And with thy spirit"—hating the Latin words, hating the priest, hating the Catholic Church and hating himself most of all. But as it had been in the Indian village, there was no way of escape. Life in the Jesuit house was too regimented.

One day Jared was summoned to the drawing room to meet "a very important person," as the schoolboy who brought the message had said. The visitor, a big man with a thick scar on his cheek, sat behind a desk. "I am Captain Yves Ravenel," he said in a deep voice. "I have just been talking to your parents."

"My parents?" Jared repeated in a puzzled voice. "But my parents are dead."

"Your foster parents," Captain Ravenel said, his dark eyes boring into Jared's. "From the Indian village." Jared's lips parted in fear and the captain continued: "They say they want you back."

"No!" Jared cried aloud. "Never! I will never go back. They can't make me."

"Perhaps not." Captain Ravenel said easily. "But I can."

Jared licked his lips. "But . . . but why?"

"Unless you do as I say."

"And that is . . . ?"

"Governor Vaudreuil is anxious to have, shall we say, a friend, on the New England border. He has heard about you and desires you to return to Deerfield. From there, you will make regular reports to him on the English defenses. You will also go to Boston from time to time to study the harbor . . . how many ships are transports, how many are men of war."

"You want me to spy!" Jared burst out scornfully. "You want me to be a sneaking spy. I won't do it. You cain't make me!"

"No, I suppose not," Ravenel said, getting to his feet. "Perhaps you will find life easier with your foster parents."

"No!" Jared screamed. "Not that devil of an old man." Suddenly, he looked up defiantly, and made as though to leave. "I'm gonter see the rector," he mumbled. "He won't let you make me spy."

"Perhaps not," Ravenel murmured. "The Jesuits are quite adept at making difficulties. It is possible—even likely—that the bishop will take their part and you may not have to do as the governor wishes. But even the sons of St. Ignatius cannot change the law. If you go to the rector, you will certainly also go back to the village."

Jared began to blubber. He glanced around him wildly, as though he were trapped. "I'd sooner go to hell," he muttered, running a hand under his sniveling nose. "All right," he whined. "I'll do what you want."

"Very well," Ravenel said, seating himself again. "You will be well paid. In fact, we will give you enough money to set yourself up as a farmer. You will then have a respectable cover for your operations."

"But I just cain't just go walking back to Deerfield and tell everybody I'm back. I've got to have an explanation."

"You will. You will tell them you escaped. You will tell them that when you got to Montreal you were so sick no one would buy or ransom you. That your captors decided to burn you alive. That they tied you naked to a stake and shot powder charges into your flesh. That they set the faggots around you on fire and that just as the flames neared you a cloudburst put the fire out. That night, you will tell them, your captors got drunk and you were able to escape."

"Cloudburst puttin' out the fire," Jared sneered. "Ain't a body I know'd ever believe that."

"They will, when they see the scars on your body from the powder burns."

Jared Ankers sucked in his breath and his lower lip trembled. He put a hand fearfully to his shoulder and rubbed it. He swallowed and his adam's apple bobbed in his scrawny throat.

"Do not be afraid," Captain Ravenel said, softening his voice. "You will not be hurt. Before your . . . ah . . . credentials are burned into your flesh, you will be given enough brandy to drink so that you will feel nothing."

Jedediah Gill awoke with his being bathed in pain. His body was a sore and aching mass of cuts and bruises, especially around his neck and shoulders where most of the blows had fallen. His right eye was swollen shut. Jed smelled strong drink, and he realized that someone was bathing his wounds in brandy.

"Please," he murmured, "may I have some of that? I . . . I mean inside of me."

"Certainly," the man said in a soft voice. He came to the battered youth's side, and Jed saw that he wore a black robe. He gasped.

"Something is wrong?"

Jed shook his head, compressing his lips and turning his mouth away from the glass of brandy offered him.

"Is it perhaps that you are surprised to see I do not have a tail?" The priest smiled. He was a tall man with a hawkish nose and ascetic face softened by gentle brown eyes. "I am Father Sébastien Rale. Come, take the brandy. It will do you good. It is not poison." He smiled again. "As the good Parson Lowry must have told you, we Jesuits poison only souls—not bodies."

Jed Gill gasped again. A Jesuit! But he took the brandy and drank, choking slightly as the burning liquid slid down his throat, then relaxing while the warmth suffused his body. "How . . . how did you know about Parson Lowry?" he stammered.

"We have heard of him. Some of his descriptions of us are indeed ingenious." He sighed. "I had hoped the raiding party would bring him back a prisoner. It would have been interesting to debate with him. He seems to possess an extraordinarily large number of misconceptions about us and our faith. Tell me, my son, what has he taught you about us?" Jed hesitated, and the priest said: "Oh, come, come, now—you smell no sulphur on my breath." He lifted his sandaled foot. "See? Toes—no cloven hoof." Jed tried to smile, grimacing at the pain the movement cost him. "Parson Lowry says that if a Catholic priest is the son of Belial, the Jesuit is his father."

"*Touché!*" Father Rale cried, clapping his hands. "An excellent turn of phrase and a rare compliment indeed. As I say, I miss not having him here. It would have been diverting. Well, young man, I must say that you are lucky to be alive. You are extremely quick and very, very brave."

Jed felt himself blushing. But then his face sobered and he asked: "If you are their priest, why do you let them do things like that? Don't you think making a man run the gantlet is sinful?"

"It depends," Father Rale replied, a glint of interest rising in his eye. "If you take it from the standpoint of intent—there are three conditions required to make a sin mortal, you know: a grievous matter, sufficient reflection and full consent of the will—and here I would say that their intent diminishes the condition of sufficient reflection." Jed Gill listened entranced. He saw that Father Rale was completely absorbed in the point he was making and absolutely detached in examining it. He saw immediately why his own Protestant clergymen were so vehement—even venomous—in their denunciation of the sly, wily, casuistic Jesuit. Father Rale continued: "Their intent is not evil per se. They intend only to test your manhood. If you do run the gauntlet in a manly way, they will adopt you into their tribe. If you don't, and show cowardice or weakness, they'll paint you black with water and soot and burn you alive."

"But, Father Rale—surely it is a sin to burn a man alive. A terrible sin—a horrible one!"

"It is indeed," Father Rale murmured, looking away in embarrassment. "But it's difficult to convince them that it is. 'This is the way of our fathers,' they will tell you, which is their staple defense of every piece of savagery in their quiver."

"Then they really aren't converted!" Jed Gill cried, almost sitting erect in triumph. "Their Christianity is really only skin-deep. It's like a shirt they can wear or take off as they please. You make them accept the crucifix by putting a crosspiece on their spear, but they really haven't given up the spear point."

Father Rale's brown eyes glinted again with interest. "You are indeed an astute young man. But what you say is not entirely so. They are savages, my young friend; noble in many ways, but savages still. One cannot expect them to become saints overnight. It is enough to get them to accept baptism and to accept the Christian God—we never speak to them of the Trinity—in place of Owaneeyo. After that, we can teach them how to make the sign of the cross, to make the right responses at Mass, to confess at least once a year—at least among the women—and on their deathbed." He sighed. "It is difficult to do even this, when one considers that one's own country always stands ready to exploit their love of bloodshed. But at least in villages like this we do keep them from killing each other. It may not seem to be much, my young friend, but when one compares our success to that of your Protestant clergy—it is actually quite a bit."

Jed Gill said nothing. He was aware, of course, that clergymen like Parson Lowry had almost no interest in converting the Indians. But he would not admit it to this clever

Jesuit, who, he suspected, had a trick of letting him score points, only to be led deeper into theological thickets where he would lose his way, and perhaps, even, his . . . Father Rale smiled, reading his thoughts. He put a hand on Jed's shoulder. "With your youth, you will be well again in two weeks. I will come to see you often. We will speak again, eh, of the truths of religion?"

Jed nodded, closing his eyes, hearing the priest shut the door of the bark hut which seemed to serve as the village hospital. Jed fell asleep. He slept most of the time for the next few days, or pretended to be asleep when Half Moon came to see him. Jed wanted time to sort out his plans. He realized that he could not avoid adoption by the Caughna-wagas, but he was still determined to escape and return to Deerfield, where he hoped to find Rachel. Escape and Rachel—these were the twin preoccupations of his mind. To make it safely through three-hundred miles of wilderness, he needed one thing: a musket. Remembering that Half Moon had promised to give him one after he became his brother, Jed decided to present a cheerful face next time the young brave visited him.

"Ah, my brother, you are sitting up," Half Moon said. "That is good. You will be walking soon. I will tell my father to prepare for the adoption ceremony. You are looking forward to becoming an Indian?" Jed nodded, smiling shyly, and Half Moon chuckled. "You will be a great warrior, Yellow Head. All the village says so. They were angry at first, because you tricked them—that's why they hit you so hard—but now they are saying you ran so fast your Indian name should be Deerfoot. What do you say, brother?"

Jed scratched his blond hair, growing ever thicker. "I don't know. Yellow Head seems to fit me, but Deerfoot—that's . . . that's something that I earned."

"Well spoken. I will call you both. Yellow Head is the name I gave you and it shall be special between us. But everyone else shall call you Deerfoot." Jed nodded again, delighted, and Half Moon said: "I go now to see my father."

An hour later, the door opened again and an Indian maiden came in. "I am Redbud, Half Moon's sister," she said shyly, kneeling to place a bunch of wood violets in a bark vase beside Jed's bed of linden bark and bearskins. Jed saw that Redbud was very pretty. He felt a pang. She must be the same age as Rachel, he thought. "Hello, Redbud," Jed said, "I am Yel—"

"Everyone knows who you are, Yellow Head. Soon you will be my brother."

"Half Moon says my adopted name will be Deerfoot."

Redbud giggled. "I like that better. You were very fast, Deerfoot. And very brave." Jed blushed, and Redbud said gravely, "I never hit you. Not once. When I saw you make as though to run away, my heart turned over. I thought they would kill you." She giggled again, and her black eyes danced. "But you outfoxed them." Her face sobered as she noticed the welt on his temple. "Beartooth did that," she said. "I think he tried to kill you. You probably don't know it, but you knocked out one of his teeth. He was very angry. Beartooth has big arms but a very small forehead." She arose. "I must go, Deerfoot. I must help my mother prepare the altar for Mass tomorrow. But I will come back, and I will bring my pipe."

"I don't smoke," Jed said.

"I will teach you. We will smoke my pipe together."

Redbud arose with a smile and walked to the door, walking with the unconscious grace of a girl verging on womanhood.

Next morning the door to the bark hut opened again and Howling Wolf walked in. "Get up!" he snarled at Jed, glaring at him fiercely. Jed glared back. He knew that he was now under the protection of Half Moon and his powerful father, Tamarack, chief of the Caughnawagas. Howling Wolf bent to pull Jed erect, but Jed pulled his wrists free and stood up.

"You must go to Mass," Howling Wolf said. "Father Rale says you must go."

"I will not."

"Today is Sunday! You must worship God."

"I will do it in some other place of my own choosing."

"You must go! Here," Howling Wolf said, lifting his right hand and blessing himself. "Make the sign of the cross with me."

"I'd sooner cut off my head."

Howling Wolf seized Jed by the wrist, trying forcefully to guide his hand through the abhorred sign. To his surprise, Jed was too strong for him. "You ingrate!" Howling Wolf shouted, drawing his tomahawk. "Go down on your knees and thank God for saving your life!" Jed stared calmly at the upraised blade. "I already have in my own way," he said. Howling Wolf slowly lowered his tomahawk and put it away. "You go to Mass," he mumbled sullenly. "Or I'll bite off your fingernail." Jed extended his right index finger. "Help yourself." Howling Wolf grabbed Jed's hand and stuck the finger in his mouth, grinding his teeth into it just below the nail. The pain was excruciating. Jed felt the room reeling around him, just as Howling Wolf let go and grasped him around the waist, trying to pull him out of the hut. Jed grappled with him. Weakened though he still was, he realized that he was stronger than Howling Wolf; and at that moment, he swore to himself that one day he would avenge his murdered aunt. They were still struggling, and Howling Wolf was shouting curses when the door opened and Father Sébastien Rale strode in.

"*Nom de Dieu*," the priest cried, separating the two, his green silk vestments flying. "What is this?" Jed extended his finger. Blood was oozing from the white tooth marks. "Is this how heretics are converted, Father?" The priest gasped and whirled on Howling Wolf. "You filthy savage!" he hissed. "What do you think you're doing?" Howling Wolf lowered his eyes sulkily. "You said you wanted him to go to Mass," he muttered, and Father Rale said: "I did not! I told you to tell Yellow Head that I was inviting him to hear me say Mass, that I thought he should thank God for his deliverance. *Mon Dieu*," he breathed in exasperation, "do we bring converts to *le bon Sauveur* in blood and chains?" Howling Wolf raised his eyes defiantly, and Father Rale sighed helplessly. "Please leave," he said, and Howling Wolf went out scowling. "I . . . I'm sorry, Yellow Head," Father Rale began; and then: "What is your Christian name?"

"Jedediah. Jedediah Gill."

"Jedediah," Father Rale repeated softly. "The biblical name for King Solomon. How you sturdy old Puritans do love those Old Testament names. All you Seths and Sauls, Jacobs and Jethros, planting the New Jerusalem on the shores of the New World. Well, Jedediah, I must apologize. I am very sorry for what Howling Wolf did to you. And you must believe that he took it upon him—"

"—It's all right, Father," Jed said, interrupting. "It was just an excuse to bully me. He hates me. He tried to take me away from Half Moon. Then, when Half Moon wouldn't let me go, he wanted to kill me."

"I understand. We do not boast about Howling Wolf."

Jed pointed to the priest's green chasuble with the large gold cross embroidered on the back and said, "Perhaps. But I think I'm beginning to understand why your priests are better at converting Indians than our parsons."

"As I have said before, you are an astute young man, Jedediah. But it is true. The Indians do seem to be fascinated by the vestments and the ritual of the Mass. They say it is better 'medicine.' Well, much as I would like to pursue this conversation, I must return to the altar." He looked at Jed, a glint of supplication in his soft brown eyes. "You will not come?" Jed shook his head. "No, thank you." The priest smiled. "Someone has taught you good manners. I will remember you at the elevation, Jedediah," he said, and left.

The following day Half Moon came to see Jed. "Come, my brother," he said, smiling broadly and taking him by the hand. He led him to the center of town where other braves awaited them. They surrounded Half Moon and Jed. Still smiling, Half Moon seized a strand of Jed's long blond hair and yanked it from his head. Jed winced, and Half Moon chuckled. "I am going to pluck you like a chicken, brother," he said. One by one, while the other braves watched laughingly, Half Moon pulled the hairs from Jed's head until there was nothing left but an area about three inches square on his crown. This Half Moon trimmed with a pair of scissors, plaiting it into three locks which he dressed with silver brooches. Next he seized a sharpened turkey quill. "Stand still, brother," he said, and thrust it through Jed's nose. Jed was surprised that it was not more painful, and he hardly felt it when Half Moon pierced the lobes of both his ears. Hanging earrings and a nose pendant in the holes, Half Moon said: "Take off your white man's clothes, brother."

Jed stripped himself naked and put on the breechclout handed him. Now, the other braves came close to Jed, smearing his plucked head, face and body with blue, green and ocher war paint. Half Moon then placed a heavy belt of wampum around his neck like a stole and slid silver bands onto his wrists and right arm. "Now you are ready," he said, smiling once more, and led him by the hand into the center of the clearing, where his father, Chief Tamarack, stood clad in full war regalia.

"Coo-wigh! Coo-wigh!" Tamarack called through cupped hands, and the people of the village came running from all directions to form a circle around them. "We are gathered, my children," Tamarack said, taking Jed by the hand, "to adopt into our great nation my new son, Deerfoot." Cries of "Ho, ho, ho" and shouts of approval followed his announcement. Three young maidens approached, and Tamarack handed Jed over to them. They led him to the river and waded into it waist-deep. They began to push Jed down deeper into it, up to his neck. Jed panicked. He thought that Half Moon had deceived him and the three girls were trying to drown him. He fought them off. Roars of laughter arose from the villagers lining the riverbank. Two of the girls jumped on Jed's shoulder and pushed his head under. He surfaced spitting water and choking. He felt a small hand squeezing his genitals and heard a soft voice in his ear, murmuring, "We won't hurt you, Deerfoot. Please, Deerfoot, stand still." It was Redbud. Jed relaxed. Giggling, the girls began to scrub Jed vigorously all over his body. Again, a small hand patted his privates playfully, and the girls led Jed from the river to the council house where the entire village was assembled. The men wore war paint and their finest regalia, the women were braided and beaded. Everyone was smoking.

New clothes were given to Jed: a ruffled shirt, leggings beribboned and beaded, a pair of moccasins and garters dressed with porcupine quills and the red feathers of a scarlet tanager. He was painted once again to replace the colors washed off in the river. Then Half Moon took his hand and sat him on a bearskin rug, handing him a tomahawk, a pipe and a skunk-skin pouch containing a mixture of tobacco and dry sumac leaves. Finally, he was given flint, steel and spunk, and after a prolonged and profound silence, Tamarack arose.

"My son," he said, solemnly addressing Jed, "you are now flesh of our flesh and bone of our bone. By the ritual washing just performed, every last drop of white blood has been cleansed from your veins. You are an Indian, a member of the great Caughnawaga nation and a warrior. You are adopted into a great family, and now received with great rejoicing in the place of my dead son. You are now my son, and your name is Deerfoot. You are one of us by a strong custom and an old law. Deerfoot, my son, you have nothing to fear. We will love and defend you as we love and defend one another. You are a warrior of the Caughnawagas, Deerfoot, and you will be a great man."

Cries of approval followed Tamarack's speech, and the villagers trooped outside to the cooking pots filled with venison and green corn. Half Moon came to Jed and embraced him and handed him a wooden bowl and spoon. Jed walked to the pots and was given his share. He was surprised that the Indians seemed not to notice him. At one moment, he had been the object of the ceremony, the focal point, but now, having been adopted, he was truly one of them—just another Indian. Jed sat down with Redbud and Half Moon and began to eat.

A war dance in his honor began. An old Indian began to sing, beating time on a drum. A line of warriors holding tomahawks formed. They moved rhythmically backward and forward, facing the southeast, the land of the Tulhasaga, as they called the English, "the people of the Morning Light." Together, they stretched their weapons toward Massachusetts and gave a single hideous scream, dancing backward chanting the war song while those seated around them beat time with their hands, crying, "He-uh! He-uh!" And then, instantly, it was all over. The villagers returned to their wigwams, leaving Jed alone with Half Moon and Redbud.

Half Moon embraced Jed again, his eyes shining with joy. "Now we are truly brothers," he said, and Jed returned the embrace, forcing a joyous smile of his own. "We will hunt together for many moons," Half Moon continued, "and we will take many scalps. And here, brother, is the gift I promised you," he said, handing Jed a shiny new musket.

This time, Jedediah Gill's smile of joy was genuine.

The musket was like a passport to freedom. With it, Jed would be able to feed himself on the three-hundred-mile trek from Caughnawaga to Deerfield. But first, he must recover his shooting eye, grown imperfect during the many months of disuse. The day after his adoption, Jed went alone into the woods where he found an elm tree at the end of a little meadow. Taking his knife, he carved the silhouette of a man's upper body on the wide trunk. On this he carved a heart in its proper place and two eyes and a nose on the head. Then he paced off a hundred feet into the meadow, where he drove a stake; and then another hundred, where he drove another stake.

Each morning at dawn he arose and trudged out to the meadow with his musket and bullet pouch, firing away from the hundred-foot mark. When he finished, he pried out the bullets to melt them down and remold them. At first, he was dismayed by his bad shooting. Gradually, however, his aim improved, and on the fourth day he began to put two out of three shots into the heart or between the eyes. On the fifth day, when he left the village, he found Redbud trailing along behind him.

"Where are you going, Redbud?"

"To the meadow."

"Shooting is not woman's work."

"Watching is," she said with a giggle.

Jed stopped and gazed down into her twinkling eyes. "Redbud, when I was being washed, someone . . . someone squeezed . . ." Redbud began to blush furiously, and Jed asked: "Why did you do that?"

"I didn't!"

"Yes, you did. I can tell. And I think I'm going to tell Father Rale on you."

"You wouldn't!"

"Oh, yes, I would."

"No, you wouldn't."

"Why not?"

Redbud giggled again, her black eyes dancing. "Because I think you liked it."

Jed shook his head with mock reproach. "That's not what I expected to hear from a good Catholic girl."

"I'm not a girl anymore," Redbud said proudly.

"You're what? Oh . . ." Momentarily flustered, Jed looked away in embarrassment. "All right, you can come with me. But stay behind me while I'm shooting."

Inevitably, the sound of Jed's practice attracted spectators. Soon the village buzzed with gossip about Jed's growing prowess. One morning Jed was loading his musket when he saw Howling Wolf join the knot of onlookers on the edge of the meadow. Grinning, Jed turned quickly to put a bullet in the silhouette's heart, and then, reloading rapidly in less than thirty seconds, he put another between his eyes. Cries of approval rose from the crowd. Redbud clapped her hands. "What do you think of that?" she called tauntingly to Howling Wolf. "Not bad for a boy," Howling Wolf replied with a sneering laugh. "At that distance I could do better with my eyes closed." Stung, Jed fired two more quick shots. Each missed its mark. The crowd snickered. Howling Wolf laughed aloud. "If he gets rattled that easy, what would he have done if I'd been shooting at him?" The crowd laughed again. Howling Wolf swaggered up to Jed with a gloating grin. "You may have the foot of the deer," he said, "but the eye of the hawk belongs to Howling Wolf."

Jed turned scarlet. "I'll . . . I'll shoot against you any day," he stammered.

"For your musket?"

Jed glanced at the weapon in his hand in dismay, nodding silently.

"When?" Howling Wolf asked, his cunning little eyes resting greedily on Jed's new musket.

"Whenever you say."

Howling Wolf pondered for a moment. "I must go to Montreal today. I will be back in three days. A week from today?"

"Agreed," Jed said, and Howling Wolf let his derisive eyes rove over the crowd gathering around him, before turning back to Jed to say in a tone of contempt: "But the distance must be three hundred feet." A gasp arose from the onlookers. Jed gulped. "Agreed," he mumbled again, pushing through the crowd to go to the elm tree to recover his bullets. When he returned, he saw that Howling Wolf had left, followed by an admiring throng.

"You fool!" Redbud hissed at Jed. "You can never outshoot Howling Wolf. He is the best shot of the Caughnawagas. Even better than Half Moon."

Jed grinned. "No, he isn't, Redbud. I am."

"But you missed your last two shots! And at a hundred feet! How can you expect to outshoot Howling Wolf at three hundred?"

"Easy. I'm just as good at three hundred as at a hundred. I missed those shots on purpose, Redbud, just to suck him in. I hate him! I'd like to kill him."

"He is a Caughnawaga like yourself. You cannot kill him."

"I know. But maybe I can do something better. Maybe I

can humiliate him. I tell you, Redbud, I can shoot. I know I can. Half Moon didn't believe me when I told him I'd been shooting a musket since my uncle gave me one on my eighth birthday. But I have, and at three hundred feet I can put two balls within an inch of each other. And now that Howling Wolf has been stupid enough to give me a week to practice at that distance, maybe I can do better."

Redbud stared at Jed in admiration. "I like you when you talk like that, Deerfoot. You sound just like Half Moon."

Jed did not hear. He was studying his musket. He lifted it in one hand and held it out at arm's length. "See this, Redbud. People talk a lot about shooting, but they know nothing about it. They think it's just pointing a musket at someone and pulling the trigger. They know nothing about aim. Why, in the English Army they don't even have a rear sight on their Brown Besses. They don't even have the word 'aim' in their firing drill. And it isn't all aim, either—unless you've got your musket barrel propped over a log or something. No, sir!" he exclaimed, proudly bobbing the outthrust musket up and down. "The strength of your arms has as much to do with it as eyesight. You've got to be able to hold a musket as steady as a rock so's you can really sight in. See this? When I was a boy, my uncle had me holding a musket like this for hours at a time. Two hands, of course. But now I can do it one-handed. Here, try it yourself." Redbud took the proffered weapon and imitated Jed. After a few seconds she winced in pain and lowered it. Jed chuckled with masculine pride. "See what I mean? Here," he said, pulling off his hunting shirt and flexing the muscle of his right arm. "Feel that." Redbud put a shy hand on Jed's bicep, entranced by the whiteness of his bared skin in contrast to his bronzed face and shaven head. "It's so nice and white," she murmured, stroking it with the flat of her hand. Jed snorted in exasperation, and Redbud hastily added, "I mean, it's strong, too. You are very strong, Deerfoot." Jed grunted in satisfaction. He shouldered his musket. Unconsciously, he took hold of Redbud's hand. They began walking back to the village.

"Your hand is so small," Jed said. "That's how I knew who it was in the river . . ."

Redbud blushed. "Oh, you!" she burst out. "The way you talk, you'd think I did that to everyone! I never did *anything* like that before. You were floundering around so, I remembered what Half Moon does to his dog when he gets out of hand. So I just sq—"

"I'm a *dog*?"

"I didn't say that! You were just so scared. I only wanted to calm you down."

"Calm me down! I wonder how you'd try to stir me up!"

Redbud giggled. She squeezed Jed's hand, and then, as they neared the village, she withdrew it. "The old women will see and gossip," she muttered, and Jed nodded absently. His mind was back in the shooting meadow.

For the following week, Jed Gill was out at the meadow two and three times a day, firing from the three-hundred-foot mark. As soon as he shot up his supply of bullets, he recovered the lead from the tree to melt it down and remold more. When he was not shooting, he stood for hours at a time holding his musket before him in either hand. And by the time the day for the match arrived, the big elm tree was so riddled with bullet holes it was no longer usable as a target.

"Let us use that tree," Howling Wolf said to Chief Tamarack, pointing to a big white oak about fifty feet to the right of the elm. "I will carve the silhouettes on it myself."

"No," said the chief, shaking his head. "Neither you nor Deerfoot will do anything but shoot. I am chief. I will choose the tree and see to the carving."

"But Deerfoot is your son."

Tamarack flushed. "I am his father, yes. But I am Tamarack. Do you question my honesty?"

Howling Wolf hung his head sullenly. Upon his return to Caughnawaga he had found the village buzzing with tales of Deerfoot's accuracy at three hundred feet. Besides, the sun was shining directly in the eyes of the shooters, and Howling Wolf had deliberately chosen the white oak because it stood out more clearly than the darker trees. He watched anxiously while Tamarack, accompanied by Half Moon, Beartooth and other leading braves of the village, walked through the meadow grass to the fringing woods, but he relaxed when he saw Tamarack select the very oak he had chosen himself. He turned to watch the villagers filing into the meadow behind him. All of Caughnawaga was there. There had been no event as exciting as the shooting match in many years. Even though the sky was overcast with a strong suggestion of rain, they came and filled the meadow. Howling Wolf cast a covert glance at Deerfoot, standing about twenty feet away, talking casually to Redbud. He scowled. What did Redbud see in Deerfoot? He wasn't even a brave yet!

"We are ready," Tamarack said upon his return, and the crowd stirred in excitement. "Each man will have twenty shots. You will shoot by turn. Each hit will count for one point, each miss for nothing. You will shoot first at the heart, then between the eyes. Half Moon will verify the shots for Deerfoot, Beartooth for Howing Wolf. Who will go first?"

With a pretense of gallantry, Howling Wolf nodded in Deerfoot's direction, ignoring Redbud's scornful glance. Even Redbud knew that the pressure was always on the first shooter. Jed said nothing, smiling confidently as he stepped up to the aiming stake. Quickly throwing his musket to his shoulder, steadying for a second, he fired. At once, Half Moon and Beartooth left the protection of a big maple and ran to the oak.

"Hit!" they called, and the crowd cheered. Redbud clapped her hands in delight.

Howling Wolf came to the stake. He brought his musket up quickly and fired. Half Moon and Beartooth again ran to the tree. There was no call. They seemed to be arguing. Chief Tamarack walked down to the wood. He returned. "Shoot again," he said grimly to Howling Wolf. He did, and the cry came back: "Miss!" A mutter of surprise rose from the onlookers, and Jed stepped forward and fired once more.

"Hit!"

Howling Wolf was perspiring as he took his place again. But he placed a ball between the eyes of the target. Then Jed pierced the heart, and Howling Wolf missed it. He glared at Jed, belching loudly just as he squeezed the trigger. Jed missed. So did Howling Wolf. He began to hum a war song while Jed took aim. "Silence!" Tamarack thundered, and Howling Wolf fell silent. But then he broke wind loudly, and the crowd laughed. Jed turned and stared coolly at him. "Did you say something?" he inquired sweetly. "I thought I saw your lips move." The throng roared in delight. Glowering at Jed, Howling Wolf growled: "Shut up and shoot." Jed did, and scored a point. Now the spectators began to turn against Howling Wolf. He had been boasting for days of how easily he would outshoot the upstart Deerfoot. Now, as he floundered and fell behind, they began to root openly for Jed. But as the score mounted in Jed's favor, so, too, did the dark clouds gather. From behind the wood, the sky grumbled. Howling Wolf—almost hopelessly trailing 13 to 9, with six shots to go—took hope and began to stall. He asked and received permission to clean his musket. He took his time stepping to the aiming stake. He dawdled at choosing his cartridges, once deliberately spilling the powder so that he had to shake it out and open another cartridge. And then a jagged sheet of lightning flashed over the meadow, followed by a deafening clap of thunder, and a torrent of water fell from the skies. Tamarack didn't even bother to declare the match postponed, merely joining the drenched villagers in their race to their houses.

Next day, when the match was resumed, Howling Wolf insisted that he be allowed to select the target tree. "You chose it yesterday," he reminded Tamarack, "and you are Deerfoot's father."

"But I acted as chief," Tamarack argued.

"I know you did. And now, as chief, I appeal to you to be fair and let me pick the tree."

"You have spoken well, Howling Wolf. It shall be as you ask."

Grinning triumphantly, Howling Wolf walked to the wood and choose another white oak. Jed thought it a strange choice, so far to the right and partially obscured by a big, leafy beech tree. But he said nothing, although he did object strongly when Howling Wolf next proposed that the match should start all over.

"It was thirteen to nine, my favor—and that's how it should stand," Jed protested. "He's asking for a new match."

"That is not true, Tamarack. Even though I was behind, I still could have won. If a match cannot be completed, it must start all over. That is the way of the Caughnawagas."

Chief Tamarack closed his eyes, pondering. Opening them, he said: "Howling Wolf is right. The match will begin again."

Howling Wolf grinned once more. Jed was surprised by his change in attitude. The poor loser of the day before was now a man of complete confidence. He even allowed Half Moon to verify the shots alone when it was discovered that Beartooth was not present.

"This morning he told me his ear hurt," Howling Wolf said. "Maybe he went to Montreal. But you are still my friend, Half Moon, and I trust you to keep score."

Half Moon nodded and trotted across the meadow to his position about thirty feet to the left of the target tree. The crowd surged forward eagerly, and Tamarack cried: "Let the shooting begin."

Shaken by Tamarack's decisions and disturbed by Howling Wolf's cool confidence, Jed Gill missed his first shot. Howling Wolf smirked, walked to the aiming stake, lifted his musket to his shoulder, and after an unusually long pause of five full seconds, he fired.

"Hit!" Half Moon shouted, and the crowd stirred in surprise.

Recovering his composure, Jed put a ball between the eyes of the silhouette, but so did Howling Wolf. Again and again, Jed scored direct hits, but each time he was matched by Howling Wolf. Jed's solitary miss loomed larger and larger in the scoring, and the onlookers, sensing the closeness of the contest, grew so absorbed in the shooting that they watched it in silence.

Redbud was completely absorbed, but for a different reason. She suspected Howling Wolf of cheating. He *never* shot that well in his life, she told herself. Something is wrong. Watching Howling Wolf closely, she noticed that he did not reload his musket until Jed was at the aiming stake and everyone's eyes were on him. Then he did it quickly, shielding his musket muzzle from the crowd with his body. Then he *always* held his aim for five full seconds. Redbud was sure of this, for she counted time under her breath. Finally, at least once, possibly twice, she had heard a faint echo of Howling Wolf's shot. But it's not an echo! she thought suddenly. It's another *shot*! Timed to coincide with Howling Wolf's!

Quietly slipping away from the crowd, Redbud worked her way to the edge of the meadow—suddenly ducking down into the tall grass and beginning to wriggle toward the wood. The grass was hot and full of insects that buzzed around her ears and stung her, but Redbud kept on going. Once she felt eyes upon her, and looking up she saw a seven-foot black snake watching her warily with his head raised a foot above the ground. "Go away, grandfather," she whispered, "go away." As though reassured by her voice, the snake lowered its head and slithered off. At the halfway point, Redbud confirmed her suspicions. There *were* two shots! With rising excitement, she realized that as she drew closer to the target tree, the shot behind her grew fainter and the one in front louder. Raising herself on her hands and knees, she realized that she was about fifty feet from a leafy beech tree. She began to tremble. Someone was in it! About twenty feet high in a crotch of the tree there was a man with a musket!

Redbud dropped to the ground and wriggled rapidly back to the shooting area. She walked quickly to her father and tapped him on the shoulder. Tamarack pushed her away in irritation.

"Please, Father," Redbud whispered, pulling on the sleeve of Tamarack's hunting shirt. "It's important."

"Go away," Tamarack snapped gruffly. "Can't you see I'm b—" He paused, his eyes widening in disbelief when Redbud cupped her hands to his ear and whispered: "Howling Wolf is cheating. I can prove it." Glancing quickly at Howling Wolf, who was watching them intently, Tamarack drew his daughter aside and listened to her. When she had finished, he turned to the crowd and announced in a loud voice, "There will be a delay. Half Moon has requested an inspection of the target tree." Tamarack marched toward the wood. Halfway there, he heard a shot behind him. A warning signal! he thought, and began to run. Half Moon ran to join him as he reached the beech tree. "Climb up to that crotch and see if it's warm," Tamarack said. Half Moon scrambled up the tree. "It is warm," he called down. "Someone's been here. The leaves are singed with powder burns."

Tamarack nodded, bending his head to study the ground around the tree, while Half Moon climbed down again. "There!" he exclaimed, pointing to the imprint of a moccasin. "Now whose do you think that is?" Half Moon chuckled. "Beartooth, of course. No one else in the village has a foot that big. What are you going to do?"

"Nothing."

"But you've caught him red-handed!"

"No, I haven't. I can't prove anything. The only one who saw anyone in that tree was Redbud, and she didn't know who it was. Certainly, I can see how it was done. Howling Wolf probably loaded his musket with nothing but powder. Beartooth could see him lift his musket to take aim. That gave him five seconds to turn and take aim himself—from thirty feet away. Even he couldn't miss. That's how they did it, Half Moon, but there's no way we can prove it."

Half Moon's face flushed angrily. "But that's not fair to Yellow Head! He's been cheated. It's not fair!"

"My son," Tamarack said in a tired voice, "people who make loud talk about what Father Rale calls abstract justice either have a secret motive or they do not know men. I am the chief of the Caughanawagas, and I must rule my people wisely. Howling Wolf is a famous warrior. He has many friends in the village. If I were to make such a grievous charge against him, I would divide my people. Divide them uselessly, for I have no proof. No, Half Moon, I will not cut the Caughnawagas in two just so my adopted son may humiliate a foolish boaster." He smiled gently. "Besides, I have a feeling that Howling Wolf will not shoot so well anymore."

"But he is ahead by one point and has two shots left to Yellow Head's one."

"Your brother does not miss," Tamarack said quietly, and returned to the shooting area, where an obviously agitated Howling Wolf rushed up to him to explain to him how he had shot off his musket by accident. Tamarack listened impassively, before turning to the crowd to announce: "The match will begin again."

Howling Wolf advanced to the aiming stake, lifting his weapon. Redbud saw with satisfaction that he fired almost the moment he took aim.

"Miss!" Half Moon shouted, and the crowd sighed as though in relief.

Jed fired.

"Hit!"

The crowd murmured in excitement.

Howling Wolf came to the stake. He brushed the sweat off his lips with his hand and wiped it on his leggings. He raised his musket and fired.

"Miss!"

The crowd roared. "A tie! A tie!"

Chief Tamarack lifted his hand for silence. "There will be no tie. They will shoot at a tie breaker." From around his neck he took a leather disc about two inches in diameter fastened to a leather throng. "Take this to Half Moon," he said to Redbud, "and have him hang it on a limb and start it swinging." He turned to Howling Wolf. "You will shoot first, and I will give the word to fire."

Redbud ran through the meadow to Half Moon, who hung the disc on a limb. Waiting until he saw Howling Wolf walk to the stake, Half Moon swung the target like a pendulum and took cover behind a nearby elm.

"Fire!" Tamarack shouted, and Howling Wolf pulled the trigger jerkily. The disc disappeared! Even Howling Wolf gaped in astonishment, while the crowd around him cheered and cheered. The familiar grin returned to his face, and he brandished his musket over his head, capering in front of Jed and yelling, "I've won! I've won! Your musket belongs to me."

Again, Tamarack lifted his hand for silence. "No one has won until Deerfoot has shot. We will make another tie breaker. "Jed Gill shook his head. "No, my father," he said quietly, "there is still something left for me to shoot at. And if I hit it, it is Deerfoot who has won."

"You mean the *string*?" Tamarack asked in disbelief.

Jed nodded. He pointed at his smirking opponent. "Once before, that man who talks loud told my people that I might be a deerfoot but that I was no hawkeye. Now, I will show him I am both." Lifting his musket to his shoulder, he slowly squeezed the trigger. Those in the crowd who could see the slowly swaying thong gasped in amazement.

"Hit!" Half Moon yelled jubilantly. "Hit! Hit! Hit!"

An expectant silence settled upon the crowd. Even Redbud was quiet, her happily brimming eyes swiveling slowly, with all others, toward Howling Wolf, who had thrown his musket on the ground in a peevish rage. Aware of his fellow villagers' contempt of his petulance, he retrieved it and brought it to Jed, throwing it sullenly at his feet. Jed put out his toe, nosing it until he had his foot under it, when he flipped it into the hands of the startled Howling Wolf.

"Keep your musket, Howling Wolf," Jed said. "I want it to remind you of me."

9

Although Jed Gill had proved himself before the entire village, his victory had the reverse effect of inhibiting his planned escape. He had become so famous that there was no opportunity to slip off by himself unnoticed, thus gaining a full day's or perhaps even two days' start on his bolt for Deerfield. Moreover, with the approach of the cooler weather, he became much in demand as a hunter.

Day after day, he joined the hunting parties; and under the patient tutelage of Half Moon his skill as a tracker began to rival his prowess as a marksman. Half Moon taught him how to identify an animal by its footprints or its dung, where to look for deer beds or even deer parks in the swales of the forest, to search the surfaces of the ponds for giveaway signs of freshly pulled lilies. Best of all to Jed's mind—for it would serve him well in any attempt to escape—Half Moon taught him how to run great distances.

"You are very fast, Yellow Head," he said, "but you do not have the stamina of a true Indian. An Indian should be able to run down a bear or a buffalo with ease. I myself have run down deer. There is no four-footed animal I cannot tire in a single day." Half Moon paused, frowning. "Well, maybe not a wolf. . . . How far can you run, my brother?"

"Eight or ten miles at a time."

"That is nothing. I will teach you to run great distances. But it takes work. To run fast is a gift, but to run far is an art."

So Jed learned to run naked in the forest with only a tomahawk in the belt of his breech-clout. He taught himself to endure hunger and thirst as he ran, gnawing at the trot on tiny loaves of pressed dried meat and blueberries, sucking on the mouthfuls until the berry juice softened the meat and made it chewable. Above all, he learned to conserve energy, going up the hills at a light trot, going down them at a lope, lengthening his stride only in the straightaways of the meadows or the trails.

As the weather grew colder, the hunts became longer, for the earth no longer yielded its bounty of corn and nuts and berries, and the people of Caughnawaga now subsisted almost entirely on game. On his first winter hunt, Jed accompanied a party of about twenty braves, among them Half Moon, Tamarack and Howling Wolf. They set out on the St. Lawrence in a large birch-bark canoe. Ascending the tributaries of the great river, they paddled the canoe ashore, carried it up the bank and turned it over to form a shelter for themselves and their baggage. Then they began their hunt, taking deer and bear, and many raccoon and beaver. Jed realized at once that they were more interested in skins than flesh, guessing that they would carry back meat on their return voyage to Caughnawaga. Nevertheless, he was appalled by the amount of meat wasted in the mounds of half-eaten carcasses left to rot in the forest.

"Why don't you preserve your meat?" he asked Half Moon one night after they had feasted off an unusually fat bear.

"Like the white man?" Half Moon countered. "No. That is not our way. Besides, Indians do not like salt. I know the white man keeps stocks of cattle and fills his barns with grain, and I think that is because the white man does not really trust the Lord Jesus. You see," he said, waving an encircling hand at the forest around him, "the Great Spirit keeps us wonderfully supplied."

"Geat Spirit? I thought you were a Roman Catholic, Half Moon."

"Oh, yes," Half Moon replied with an easy grin. "When we are in front of Father Rale and the other priests, we speak of the Lord Jesus and God Almighty and his saints in heaven. But among ourselves, we speak as our fathers did—of Owaneeyo, the Great Spirit. It is all the same, Yellow Head," he went on gravely, pointing to the sky overhead. "There is only one Sachem. That is why we do not worry about providing for ourselves like your brothers of old. We know he will provide for us. Oh, yes, we go hungry sometimes, especially in the winter. But Owaneeyo does not let us die. He only lets us suffer a little so that we will realize that we are dependent on him." Half Moon yawned. "Come, my brother, let us sleep."

When they awoke in the morning, they saw that the ground was covered with two inches of snow and that the others were already at work burying the canoe and building bark lean-tos. "We will come back for the canoe in the spring," Half Moon explained. "But look, my brother—the snow is a good thing. Now the bears will be crawling into holes for their winter's sleep. Today we will hunt bear holes."

Throughout the day they prowled the woods, searching for trees with their bark scratched by the claws of climbing bears, and with holes above ground large enough to admit the beasts. When they found one, they cut a sapling or a smaller tree, leaning it against the large one just beneath it. While Half Moon stood ready with his musket, Jed climbed up to the hole with a stick to prod the hibernating bear out of his slumber. But they found only empty holes, until, just before sunset, they came upon a large elm with scratch marks and an opening too high up to be reached by a sapling. Fortunately, a tall red oak stood only ten feet away. Half Moon fetched a long pole and tied rotten wood to it with strips of bark. Then he lighted the wood and began climbing the red oak. When he rose opposite the hole, he stuck the firebrand into it. A growl of rage issued from the hole, and Half Moon shoved the pole in farther. Snarls and snuffles of pain came out of the hole. Half Moon could smell singed hair, grinning in delight when the bear backed out of the hole and began climing down toward Jed, who quickly shot him dead. The bear fell at his feet with a heavy thump. At once Half Moon came down the tree. He slit the bear's throat while Jed opened its belly. Together they plunged their bare arms into the opening to pull out its hot, stinking entrails. "Build a fire," Half Moon said, groping for the liver. He cut it free, wrapped it in caul fat, and spitted it on a stick, which he stuck over the fire to roast. Then the two happy hunters put a kettle on the fire before skinning the beast and building a small lean-to of linden bark. An hour later, they went to sleep, sated with both roasted and boiled bear meat.

In the morning, when they awoke, Jedediah Gill decided that the time had come to escape. He noticed that the hunt had been moving steadily eastward toward Massachusetts. He calculated that he was only about two hundred miles from Deerfield. When Half Moon asked him to start cutting up the bear meat while he returned to camp to fetch carriers, Jed made up his mind. Ten minutes after the departure of his adopted brother, he filled his knapsack with boiled bear meat, seized his musket and struck out east through the forest. Snow began to fall, but he pressed on. It grew thicker, swirling about him. The air darkened. It was like night in the forest. Jed could not see around him. He was lost. Now, so far from striving to escape, he began to fear for his life. He moved slowly from tree to tree, feeling with his hands until he found a hollow one. It was dry inside, and sheltered from the wind. He could stand in it, even sleep there if he curled up. Stripping off his blanket, he took his tomahawk and went outside to cut limbs from a fallen tree. These he leaned against the hole like a stockade, leaving a narrow opening for himself. Squeezing inside, he dragged a log in after him, which he used to block the hole, filling the voids between the limbs with small sticks. Next, he hacked down the rotten wood on the inside of the tree and beat it fine for a bed like the nest of a goose. Taking off his moccasins, he jogged in place for a half-hour to warm himself, after which he coiled up on the rotten wood with his head resting on his moccasins and his blanket over him. He went to sleep with the whine of the wind in his ears. Awaking, he could still hear it howling. He could not tell if it was day, because snow had filled the chinks in his stockade of limbs. It was utterly black inside the tree. Jed went back to sleep. Awaking again, he decided that it must be day and felt in front of him for the log. When he found it at last, he could not move it. It was heavy and weighted with snow. Jed was terrified. If he could not move the log, he would die of starvation inside the tree. He fought for control of himself, not to panic, to tear at the log with his hands . . . The thought of starvation reminded him of the bear meat in his pack, and he opened it and ate some in the dark. Curling under his blanket again, he began to pray. "Spare me, O Lord," he prayed. "Give me the strength to move that log. Thou gavest me the strength of soul to resist the wiles and snares of the Jesuit priests, now do thou give me the physical strength to move that log and I will remain steadfast in the pure faith of our fathers." Satisfied, he lay still for a while, meditating. He thought of Rachel and the hide-hole and the bear Half Moon and he had driven from its hole the day before and the hole that had saved him from the storm, and he wondered why holes in rotting trees had come to play so great a part in his life. Suddenly he thought: the hide-hole! That's *it*! That's where Rachel must have hidden to escape the Indians. Rachel is alive! He arose quickly, full of confidence, and attacked the log again. It moved! He wrenched it savagely. It moved again and came free. A shower of snow fell upon Jed, and he saw with great joy that it was daylight outside and the snow had stopped. He pushed at the tree limbs, but they budged only at the top. One by one he shoved them back against the the snow that trapped him, until he had freed an area large enough for him to scramble over them. Belting his blanket around him, seizing his pack, musket and tomahawk, Jed climbed out of his sanctuary into the bright light of a dazzling sun. It shone upon a blanket of pure whiteness that stretched away to infinity around him. Even the trunks of the trees were splotched with snow, and accumulations of three or four inches rested on their limbs. Jed had never seen so much snow fall in a single night. It must have been three feet deep. But he could walk on it. Stretching his arms wide, he lifted his face to the sunlit heavens in exultation. " 'I have cried to thee, for thou, O God, hast heard me,' " he prayed aloud in gratitude, quoting from the Psalms, " 'thou who savest them that trust in thee'." A shower of snow stored on a branch above him fell upon his upturned face, and his joyous heart turned cold. In this snow, he realized, he could never make it to Deerfield. Winter was here, the forest was a barren wilderness; the nuts and other forage covered with snow, the game cuddling for warmth in their nests and lairs or hibernating in their holes. In despair, he glanced back toward the camp of the Caughnawagas. He would have to go back, or die, he thought. He would tell them that he had gotten lost in the storm while tracking a deer. Would they believe him? he wondered wearily. Jed Gill hardly cared, listlessly shouldering his musket and floundering woodenly through the snow, guiding his way westward by the moss growing on the northwestern side of the straighter trees. Just before sunset, he came to the creek the camp was on. It ran black between the mounds of white on its banks. Jed drank some of its icy water to wash down the bear meat he had eaten, emptying the rest of the meat into the stream and carefully washing away all traces of it from the inside of his pack. Nearing the camp, he gave the scalp haloo and fired his musket. Half Moon was the first to greet him when he entered the clearing filled with lean-tos.

"Yellow Head!" he exclaimed happily. "We gave you up for lost. Where have you been?"

"I was tracking a big buck deer," Jed said, embracing Half Moon, "and I got lost in the storm. I spent the night inside a hollow tree and here I am."

"You lie!"

Jed Gill turned and saw Howling Wolf glaring at him accusingly. He came a step closer, followed by the other silent encircling braves. "You were trying to escape!" Howling Wolf snarled. "I know, because I was the first one to the bear, and I followed your tracks."

"I tell you I was tracking a big buck. Maybe twelve or fourteen points. Maybe you like bear meat better than venison, but I don't."

"I didn't see any deer tracks."

"Sometimes, Howling Wolf, your eyes aren't too good."

An ugly flush came over Howling Wolf's face, and he turned to speak to Chief Tamarack, who stood quietly beside him. "He's a liar, I tell you. He was trying to get back to Deerfield. He wants to be a white man again to kill more Indians and steal more land." Growls of approval rose from most of the other braves, but Tamarack said nothing. Jed looked into his eyes appealingly. "My father, I am telling the truth. Would anyone try to escape in a storm like that?"

"The storm came up suddenly," Howling Wolf interjected. "It made me go back to camp. But I know he was trying to escape," he insisted, glancing at the men around him, "because his tracks went straight, like a man in a hurry. If he was tracking, they'd've gone clooked." The point went home among the others, and they muttered angry approval. Encour-

aged, Howling Wolf turned to Jed. "Let me see your pack."
Jed took it off and handed it to him. Howling Wolf's eyes
flickered in disappointment when he saw that the pack was
empty. But then he felt it. "It's wet!" he cried, shaking it triumphantly. "Why did you wash out your pack, Deerfoot?" he
asked, smirking. "Was it because you wanted to clean out the
meat you took for provisions on your escape?"

"Of course it's wet," Jed answered carelessly. "So are my
leggings and my shirt. Did you ever walk through three feet
of snow without getting wet?"

Now Tamarack lifted his hand. "I believe you, Deerfoot,"
he said quietly, staring straight into Jed's eyes. "But you did a
foolish thing by getting caught in the storm. It was not
worthy of a brave of the Caughnawagas. We were worried
for you, my son. Your brother did not sleep all night, and I
had to keep him from going after you. He would have died
uselessly while you slept in safety inside your tree." Jed lowered his eyes in shame, and the chief continued: "You must
be punished for your rashness, Deerfoot." He held out his
hand. "Give me your musket." Jed raised his eyes in desperate pleading. But Tamarack was unmoved. "Your musket,"
he repeated, and without a word, but with despair in his
heart, Jedediah Gill handed over his cherished key to
freedom.

For almost three despairing years, Jed Gill continued to
live among the Caughnawagas, actually more of a prisoner
than an adopted tribesman. He was not held captive, nor prohibited from entering into the life of the village, its feasts, its
dances, its councils, or its hunts; and yet, much as he distinguished himself with the bow and arrow that replaced his
musket, he remained the object of those suspicions nurtured
by Howling Wolf. He was carefully watched, and when he
spoke in council, his words were always weighed and sifted
for ulterior motives. Jed knew that the constant serveillance
of him, together with his loss of his musket, made it impossible for him to escape. Even if he should find the opportunity to slip away, a bow was not the equal of a firearm, if
only because a quiver could not hold as many missiles as a
bullet pouch. Again and again, Jed appealed to Tamarack for
the return of his musket; each time, he was turned down—always at the instance of Howling Wolf.

"When we ate the Algonquin last month, why did not Deerfoot join the feast . . .?"

"He is not a true Indian. When we frolic with our prisoners, he always closes his eyes . . ."

"Why does Deerfoot not become a Catholic like the rest of us . . .?"

Jed was surprised and dismayed by Howling Wolf's growing influence over Tamarack. He asked Redbud about it one night when they met at the waterfall.

"It's not that my father is afraid of Howling Wolf," she said soberly. "It's because he is worried that he will accuse him of softness and spread more dissatisfaction among the braves. You see, Howling Wolf is really an evil man. He loves to make trouble, to make people unhappy."

"He loves to kill, too," Jed murmured, taking Redbud's hand in the dark. "At the ring hunt last fall he must have killed twenty deer. He left all but two or three of them there to rot. He didn't want the meat or skins. He just wanted to kill."

Redbud shivered, tightening her hand in Jed's. "That is true. He is like Atotarho."

"Atotarho?"

"You have not heard of him? His name is in many songs about Hiawatha."

"I've heard of Hiawatha."

"But not Atotarho? That's funny. You see, Hiawatha is to us Iroquois almost like Jesus Christ is to the white man. We are Iroquois, you know—a Caughnawaga is a converted Mohawk, and the Mohawk are the bravest of the Iroquois. The other tribes are the Cayuga, Onondaga, Seneca and Oneida. Long, long ago, Deerfoot, these five tribes did nothing but kill and eat each other. Then along came Hiawatha. He was an outcast, like Jesus," she said, mechanically bobbing her head in reverence at the name of the Savior. "He called himself the Master of Life," she said, raising her voice above the sound of the waterfall. "He was a great orator and a magician. He preached peace and he made magic to make the people listen to him, just like the miracles of Jesus," she said, bobbing her head again. "Hiawatha wanted the five tribes to combine in the League of the Five Nations and live peacefully side by side. But there was an Onondaga chief named

Atotarho. Some of the songs say he was Hiawatha's half-brother."

Redbud paused, watching the tip of a yellow crescent moon poking above the mountain beyond the waterfall. "Atotarho was a devil." She shivered. "Maybe he was *the* Devil. All the songs say he had a twisted body. There were seven crooks in it. His hands were like the paws of a turtle, with red streaks in them. His feet were the feet of a wizard. They were shaped like a tortoise's, with the claws of a bar. His hair was a mass of wriggling snakes. All the tribes were terrified of Atotarho. He had spies and assassins everywhere." Redbud shivered again, nestling closer to Jed, her eyes on the bright crescent now half above the mountain. "Whenever Hiawatha got one or two of the tribes to attend a peace council, Atotarho would send his killers to break it up. He killed all of Hiawatha's daughters, one by one."

"How many daughters?" Jed asked, stealing an arm around Redbud's waist.

"Some songs say three, others seven. Anyway, Hiawatha was ready to give up preaching peace. Then another preacher named Deganawidah came to him. He was a Huron. His name means 'He-the-Thinker.' He told Hiawatha he had a vision that all men everywhere would live in peace. But first, they had to convert Atotarho. Hiawatha said it couldn't be done, but Deganawidah said it could. So they strung the thirteen belts of wampum and wrote the famous Six Songs, and Hiawatha went to see Atotarho. When he saw him, he was terrified. He couldn't speak. But then Hiawatha unwrapped the wampum and began to sing the Six Songs. That cast a spell over Atotarho. While he was under it, Hiawatha combed the snakes out of his hair, straightened his body and gave him human hands and feet. After that, Atotarho agreed to join the League of the Five Nations."

"The Iroquois?"

"Yes. It means 'rattlesnake people.'"

"Do you think anyone could convert Howling Wolf?"

"No," Redbud said, snuggling closer to Jed. They stood up, gazing at the yellow crescent above them, now in full view. Jed's arm was still around her waist. He drew her closer, watching the moon glinting off the brazen hollows of her face below the high cheekbones. The floor of the forest was like a carpet of silver. Thick, braided ropes of white and silver water flowed musically over the falls. Jed bent his head and kissed Redbud. She pushed him away angrily. "Don't do that! You are spitting in my mouth." Jed chuckled and held her close again. "Don't Indians kiss?" he whispered into her tiny ear, biting it. Redbud giggled and shook her head. He nibbled playfully on her ear again and held her face tenderly in both his hands. "Now they do," he murmured, and kissed her again. Redbud pressed her own lips against Jed's and pushed her soft little body into his. Jed drew her down beside him, and Redbud clung fiercely to him and sobbed: "Oh, Deer-foot, I love you so."

For months afterward, whenever there was a moon, Jed and Redbud met at the waterfall. Jed had made some soap from bear fat, and they walked naked in the moonlight under the waterfall, where there was a large, smooth rock to stand on, and there they soaped each other down before they jumped, hand in hand, through the cascading water into the cold pool below. When they came out, Jed lay down on the bearskin he had brought with him, and Redbud knelt over him to pick the lice that had not come off in the washing and the swim. Indifference to dirt and vermin had been the one characteristic of Indian life that Jed detested most, and he delighted in lying down naked while Redbud went over his body with her cool, nimble fingers, plucking off the bugs and flicking them away. Once, when she knelt over him, Jed opened his eyes and saw her small firm breasts swinging over his head. He lifted his lips to kiss one and said: "Redbud, your name should have been Pinkbud." She frowned and said, "Why?" "For these," Jed answered, nibbling on the nipple of her breast. "But they won't always be pink," Redbud said, laughing at the puzzled look in Jed's blue eyes. "After a woman has a baby, they turn brown." Now it was Jed who frowned. "I don't want them to turn brown," he said, pulling her down beside him. She kissed him gently, and said: "I think they will, Deerfoot."

"Whaaat?" Jed Gill exclaimed, sitting upright.

"Yes, Deerfoot—I am going to have a baby." She put a hand on her stomach proudly. "It is yours. He will be like you."

"But, Redbud, what are we going to do? Do you want me to marry you?"

"Yes," Redbud said slowly. "But you can't." Jed gaped in bewilderment, and Redbud giggled. "You look so funny when you are upset. No, you can't marry me. Father Rale says so. Not unless you become a Catholic."

"Never!"

"I know, I know. You are all Christians, you white men, followers of the God of Love—and yet, you hate each other. Anyway, I knew you'd say that. But there is a more important reason why you can't." Redbud stood up and began putting on her clothes. She looked down at him fondly. "You will have to run away."

"Redbud," Jed said slowly, "I don't understand you."

"Yesterday, I was berry-picking when I heard Howling Wolf and Beartooth talking in a tree above me. They thought they were alone. They talked about killing you. You see, the Onontio is sending out another war party against Deerfield." Jed gasped, and Redbud nodded. "Yes, Deerfield—the home of your people. It is because the English tried to capture Quebec again this summer. They failed, but the Onontio is angry."

She tensed, listening, while Jed pondered what she had told him. Jed had forgotten the war that had claimed the lives of his loved ones. He had not heard of it since his adoption. But now, he thought miserably, the borders were to burn again. Hearing Redbud give a relieved sigh and say, "It's only a raccoon," he gave her his attention again. "You are to go on the war party, Deerfoot," she continued, watching him carefully. "Yes, Howling Wolf has convinced Tamarack that this should be the test of your loyalty. If you do not kill white men and take scalps, they will burn you on the spot." Jed Gill lifted his head proudly like an Indian brave, and Redbud said gently: "Do not pretend, Deerfoot. You cannot kill your people, and you know it. You are a white man. I knew it would never work. You were too old. If you had been a little boy of five or six, maybe it would have worked. But you still remember too many things that you've lost. I would have too, and I do not blame you. But listen to me, Deerfoot, Howling Wolf does not intend that you should live to reach Deerfield. He and Beartooth are going to kill you. They are going to say they caught you trying to escape to warn Deerfield, and they are going to accuse my father of helping you, so that Howling Wolf will be made sachem."

Jed nodded, standing up to put on his clothes, and Redbud continued: "When you are nearly there, Howling Wolf is going to propose a scouting party to capture English who are out in the woods so that they can get information from them. You and Beartooth are to be left behind to shoot game and guard the camp. Beartooth is going to pretend to have mislaid his tomahawk and ask you to lend him yours to behead the fish he has caught."

"My only weapon," Jed murmured thoughtfully.

"Yes. They are not going to give you back your musket. And you know how useless a bow and arrow are at close quarters. So it is then, Deerfoot, that Beartooth is going to kill you and tell everybody you tried to kill him and take his musket." She looked at him inquiringly. "You will know what to do?"

Jed Gill smiled grimly. "Yes, Redbud, I will know what to do." Suddenly he seized her by the waist and held her close. "Why do I have to run away alone?" he cried in anguish. "Why don't we both run away? We don't need a priest to marry us. Let's go west toward the lakes. We could live along a creek or a river. We'd be happy there."

Redbud shook her head sadly. "It will not work. I believe you when you say you love me, Deerfoot . . . but you love your people more."

"No!"

"You will give up Rachel?"

Jed Gill stared at Redbud in incredulity. The moon was sinking behind the waterfall, yet, in the diminishing light he could see the tears in her eyes. "You . . . you know about Rachel? How?"

"At night, when the people of our fireside are asleep in the long house, I have heard you call for her in your sleep."

"I don't even know if she's alive."

"But you love her, and you think she is." Redbud shook her head in sorrow again. "No, Deerfoot—you must go back to your people. Some day, you will be a legend in our village. And everyone will know that I was Deerfoot's woman. They will not despise me for it. They will admire me. Our son will be a great chief and I will call him Yellow Deer." She took his hand, and they walked together toward the village.

Behind them, like an eternal hymn of nature, they heard the singing of the waterfall.

The countryside was becoming familiar, now. A week ago, they had reached the mouth of the White River, where the Indian bands and their prisoners had split up nearly five years ago. With a suppressed shudder Jed Gill had seen the whitened skeletons of the Englishwomen murdered along the way, grinding his teeth when he passed the tiny bones of Anne Ankers.

There were about three hundred raiders—two hundred Caughnawagas and about one hundred Frenchmen—and they were moving rapidly along the Connecticut River. Half Moon was ahead of Jed, no longer behind him as on the trek into captivity, and Jed took this as a sign of his adopted brother's confidence in him. Jed could remember how radiant Half Moon had been that morning after he and Redbud had parted, announcing that he was to accompany the war party eastward. "When you have proved yourself, my brother, our father will return your musket and you will become a Caughnawaga brave."

Jed had feigned joy and enthusiasm. Now, trotting along behind Half Moon, he hated himself for his hypocrisy. Yet, he could remember the shrugging fatalism with which Half Moon had dismissed the murder of Anne Ankers and the others: "That is war." So be it, Jed thought grimly, and then, remembering Howling Wolf's accusations against him: Yes, I will become a white man again, and I will indeed kill many Indians—including you, Howling Wolf. Thinking of Redbud, Jed felt a pang of remorse. Redbud was an Indian. And their son—he, too, would have Indian blood in his veins.

The column halted. They had come to a fork in the trail. With rising excitement, Jed recognized the fork. To the left lay Northfield, about ten miles away; straight ahead was Deerfield, about forty miles away. It would be an easy run! He could do forty miles easily in six hours, and he mentally thanked Half Moon for his tutelage in distance running.

Just before dusk, when Jed returned to camp from the woods with an armful of brush, he heard Howling Wolf outlining his plan to the French commander. "*Oui*," the commander said, "*c'est un bon plan.* That is a good plan." He paused, murmuring in a low voice: "We do have a friend in Deerfield. But, still . . ." Jed Gill was thunderstruck. A *friend* in Deerfield. But who . . .? Jed's heart beat faster.

Now, more than ever, he must warn the village. After dinner he sat cross-legged, sharpening his tomahawk. He spent so long at it that Half Moon asked him if he planned to shave with it. "You have let your beard grow long, my brother," Half Moon said with a grin. Jed nodded grimly. "Yes—and I won't shave until I have taken my first scalp." Half Moon grunted in approval, and the two rolled over to sleep.

In the morning, the raiding party fanned out through the woods, leaving Beartooth and Jed in camp. Jed took his bow and arrow to go hunting. An hour later, he shot a deer drinking by a lily pond. Hoisting it across his shoulder, he returned to camp, where he found Beartooth sitting on a fallen log cleaning a mess of perch. "Have you seen my tomahawk, Deerfoot?" Beartooth asked. His voice was casual, but Jed could see that the pupils of his eyes had dilated. They were almost slits, like a fox's. Jed felt a calm descend upon him. "No," he said easily, "did you lose it?" Beartooth scratched his head. "I must have mislaid it. Could you lend me yours, Deerfoot? I need one to chop off the fishes' heads." Jed's hand went to the hatchet at his belt. "Of course," he said, pulling it free—and he struck it straight between the eyes of Beartooth. With the barest whimper of pain, the big Indian toppled backward off the log, his weight pulling the tomahawk out of Jed's hands. Jed jumped over the log and wrenched it free. He had to use both hands, it had penetrated so deeply into the dying man's skull. At once, Jed Gill shucked his hunting shirt and his leggings. Naked but for his breech-clout, he leaped the log again and took off running down the trail to Deerfield.

An hour later, running smoothly, Jed realized that he still held his tomahawk. He shoved it inside the back of his belt where the handle wouldn't strike his thighs, and increased the pace a little. From the woods to his right, Jed heard a crackling of musket fire. Bullets whispered overhead. Jed began to sprint, the stink of drifting black powder in his nostrils hastening him on his way. Angry yells pursued him. There were more shots. More yells. Jed went up a hill, running hard. At the top, he flung a look over his shoulder and saw five or six Caughnawagas kneeling on the trail with leveled muskets. Jed grinned. At that range, they couldn't hit the broad side of a barn. Suddenly he realized that he was out of breath. He went down the other side of the hill gasping. He had lost too

much wind taking the ascent so fast. He eased off, until he
flung another look over his shoulder and saw an Indian running behind him.

The pursuer wore red and yellow paint. Jed did not recognize him, except that he was tall and slender like most
Caughnawagas and he knew how to run. He grasped a tomahawk, holding it confidently in the throwing position. He
came closer, sprinting—gaining on Jed. Jed knew that if he
got within thirty or forty feet of him he could throw that
hatchet with deadly accuracy. Jed knew immediately what
the game was. It was an old Caughnawaga trick, to make the
fugitive run at full speed. The others behind the leader would
go at a slower pace. As soon as the first man tired, another
would move up—and so on. In this way, they could run
down any man in four or five hours.

Any man, yes, Jed Gill thought—but not Deerfoot. He began sprinting himself. He felt his throat going raw and a
stitch opening in his side. But he maintained the pace, hoping
to tire the leader. He had already picked out the points ahead
where he would ease off. Jed knew that trail like he had
known his little room with the Cowletts. It ran right past the
sugaring camp and into the meadow below the village. Jed
looked quickly behind him again and saw that his pursuer
was keeping even. Jed began to worry. Maybe he had un-
derestimated the man. Jed was breathing hard, gasping
again—his breath in his throat like a ragged blade, the stitch
in his side deepening. But Jed Gill wasn't just running for his
life, he was running for the lives of the people of Deerfield.
For Rachel, if she was still there. He knew that if the Indians
caught him, they would also catch Deerfield sleeping again.
He was certain that Howling Wolf's patrols would net a few
captives who would talk under torture, tell the French commander where and when to attack. But if Jed could warn the
village, he was also certain that the French would turn
around and go home. So Jed deliberately ran faster.

He had reached the point of maximum torment, where he
must put more pressure on his tortured lungs or collapse.
"That is when you run hardest, my brother," Half Moon had
said. "When your heart is bursting like that, you must swallow it. Eat your pain and gulp your wind down." Half Moon
was right. Jed could feel his second wind coming. The pain in
his side was easing, his breath was coming slower. Now he

ran in exaltation. His head was clear and his confidence returned. To his left, Jed saw a stand of pines beside a marsh. Sutter's Sinkhole! he thought—the place where he had shot his first deer when he was ten years old. That meant that Talking Creek was only a few hundred yards ahead. Fifteen miles to go!

Running around a bend, Jed saw the creek ford ahead. Oh, it was *wide*! Jed could never remember Talking Creek being that wide, sixteen feet or more. But he could not slow down to run through it. Besides, running in wet moccasins rubbed your feet raw. Lifting his head, Jed sprinted harder, soaring into the air with a mighty leap at the creek's edge, sailing over the water, and clearing the bank by a good foot. Now Jed ran with renewed exhilaration. He had never jumped nearly so far in his life. If he lived, he would tell his children about it. Rachel's? Redbud's? Cursing himself for a fool to think such disturbing thoughts, he looked behind him again.

His pursuer was just coming to Talking Creek. He was slowing down! He was *trotting* through it! That meant that he was tiring, that he would soon give way to another runner. Jed began to ease up. He wondered how he looked running through the forest like a man of two colors. His hands and forearms were bronzed like an Indian's. So was his plucked head with the tanager feathers flopping from his blond scalplock, and the V below his neck from the open hunting shirt. But the rest of him was white: fish-belly white, he thought, chuckling inside of him so as not to waste breath, and what would the good people of Deerfield think when he burst in among them looking like that?

Gradually the light began to fade. Looking up, Jed saw a canopy of tangled leaves overhead, knit together by creepers and vines. The trail became uneven, rock-strewn and ribbed with tree roots. In the gloom, Jed saw that a new man was pursuing him. He wore ocher instead of red and yellow paint. He had a long, thickset body, with short legs and powerful calves. Jed realized at once that he was faster than the first man. Obviously, he was the one chosen to run him down. But with a thick, heavy body like that, Jed reasoned, he couldn't have too much stamina. Jed decided to put the pressure on *him*. He would take the race away from him, force him to match Jed's longer stride step for step, and also take him flying over the uneven, unknown ground where he might easily stumble and hurt himself.

They ran for three or four miles that way, the Indian's powerful arms pumping steadily, his short strong legs twinkling over the ground. Jed couldn't widen the gap between them. But he was positive that the man had to be tiring. Running over unfamiliar ground cost too much energy, Jed thought; and even he, knowing his way, had to keep his eyes glued to the trail. He dared not risk tripping on a single root or slipping on just one loose stone. How could the Indian stay on his feet? His answer was a loud crash and a howl of pain behind him. Slowing to look over his shoulder, Jed saw his pursuer crawling to the side of the trail, dragging a limp leg. Jed eased off. A few minutes later, he flung another look backward. A third man was chasing him.

It was Howling Wolf!

Jedediah Gill could not mistake those blue bars on the man's face. No other brave in Caughnawaga would dare to wear that color and style of war paint that was Howling Wolf's cherished own. Jed Gill felt for the head of the tomahawk hanging at his back. His time had come! Imperceptibly, Jed stepped up the pace. Howling Wolf responded, but Jed saw that he was not doing it easily. He was not the runner Half Moon was. The trail swerved sharply right, going downhill. More daylight filtered down through the thinning overhead. Jed heard the whistle of a cardinal and then the shrill saucy cry of a blue jay. He caught a glimpse of gleaming black water flowing to his left, and he knew that it was the Connecticut. They were near the sugar camp!

At once, the cry of the birds reminded him of the Ankerses' calico cat frightening the robins in the swamp grass at the sugaring that day. That had been spring, but now it was fall, and the swamp grass would be eight or ten feet high! Jed reached behind him again and drew his tomahawk. His stride lengthened, and soon he was running as fast as he could. He was going to run away from Howling Wolf, run out of his sight, and hide in wait for him among the swamp grass.

Jed flew past the sugar camp. Reaching the first stand of swamp grass, he came to a sudden halt and slipped inside it. He crouched there, parting the tall reeds for a field of view down the trail. He winced when the long sharp blades of grass sliced his fingers. His grip on his tomahawk tightened. There was Howling Wolf . . .

Momentarily, the faces of his murdered loved ones swam at the back of his brain. He could almost hear Howling Wolf's hideous snicker when he patted the scalps at his belt. Howling Wolf was slowing, looking around wildly . . . Suspicion glinted in his cunning little eyes, and he slewed frantically away from the swamp grass just as Jedediah Gill stepped in front of him and swung his tomahawk at his right forearm. Howling Wolf screamed in pain and terror. His hatchet fell to the trail and he held his rent and broken forearm with his left hand. Jed struck him savagely on the kneecap, and he went down, writhing. Jed seized his neck with his left arm and drew it taut toward him while he held the head of his tomahawk in his right hand like a knife. "You won't take any more scalps, Howling Wolf," he whispered, and he drew the blade across the hollow under his ear. A stream of bright, hot blood spouted over Jed's naked chest. Pushing the body of the dying man savagely aside, he jumped erect and began running again.

A minute or so later Jed heard a long, rising scream of anger behind him. Looking back, he saw an Indian kneeling beside Howling Wolf's body. The man stood up, shook his tomahawk menacingly at Jed, and began pursuing him.

It was Half Moon.

Now, Jed Gill ran with tears in his eyes. The fact that Half Moon had his tomahawk out meant that he intended to kill his adopted brother if he caught him. Jed knew that it was foolish for him to weep, but he could not help himself. He had loved Half Moon. They *had* been brothers. . . . Jed's foolish sentimentality almost cost him his life. Half Moon sensed why he was gaining on Jed, and he began to run harder. He was only forty feet behind and was drawing his hatchet back for the throw when Jed saw his peril and called upon his remaining strength to pull away to a hundred feet again.

Half Moon never came closer. They entered the meadow within sight of the Deerfiled stockade with both men blowing hard. Jed Gill saw tiny figures standing outside the gate. He thought he heard faint cheers. About twenty feet behind him he did hear a heavy object strike the ground. Looking back, he saw Half Moon slowing down to a walk. He was empty-

handed, and Jed realized that he must have thrown his tomahawk in desperation.

Jedediah Gill waved in farewell salute to Half Moon of the
Caughnawagas, and then he trotted slowly up the grade
toward the village.

10

"But it's been almost five years, Parson," Jared Ankers said. "If Jed Gill ain't dead, then he's an Indian by now, and what's worse, probably a Roman Catholic, too."

Parson Solomon Lowry shuddered. He glanced nervously behind him, as though the Unclean One himself had infiltrated his parsonage. "Don't say that, Jared," he snapped testily, glaring across his desk at Ankers. "I can't believe that young Gill would sell his soul like that. Least of all for the life of a savage. After all, he was an educated young man when he was captured. His father told me he was planning to send him to Harvard College. He might have become a clergyman himself." Lowry shook his massive head. "No, I prefer to believe that he, too, is a martyr. Jed Gill is in heaven with our Lord and his loved ones. You've got to be mistaken, Jared. You've got to be."

Jared Ankers struggled to keep the irritation out of his tired voice. "Parson Lowry, if I tole you oncet, I tole you a thousand times: the Injuns done adopted Jed Gill. The Injuns in Montreal tole me that." An eager look crossed his thin pinched face. "It don't make no never-mind anyway, Parson. One way or another, he's dead—and you're free and legal to sell me the Cowlett property like you promised."

The parson nodded. "True. Mrs. Cowlett did tell me she and her husband intended to leave the church a . . . ah . . . bequest. Not the entire property, of course. But now, with no heirs to claim the inheritance, it would seem right and proper for everything to go to the church. That is, if Jed Gill is truly dead."

"He *is*!" Jared hissed fiercely. "Even if he ain't, even if he ain't a Injun, he ain't been back in five years, and as magistrate, Adam Brown can declare him legally dead."

A calculating look crept into the parson's eyes. "How much did you say you'd pay, Jared?"

"Two hundred pounds."

"Two hundred pounds! That's a sight of money. Why, my stipend here in Deerfield is only sixty pounds a year—and most of that is in kind. With that kind of money, we could double the size of the church and add a school. Where'd you get a fortune like that, Jared?"

"I tole you a dozen times, Parson," Jared replied, swallowing to make his Adam's apple bob. "Pa left it to me."

"But your father wasn't wealthy."

"He come into money," Jared mumbled, shifting his watery eyes from the parson to the rush light on his desk. "He hid it in a hollow tree in the woods. He tole me about it just afore the massacre. He said if anythin' happened to him, I was to git it and share it out with Sam and Anne." Jared blinked, his eyes coming back to the parson's. "An' you know . . ." he said falteringly, "you know what happened to them."

"Yes, yes, Jared," Parson Lowry murmured, almost clucking in his sympathy. "It was a terrible thing. Now, does this include everything—the mill, the farm and the land in town?"

"Everthin'."

"My, I don't know what to say. I am not, of course, a man of the world—and so I hesitate to put a cash price on anything. But still, for the farm, the mill and the land, Jared, wouldn't you say two hundred pounds was a trifle low."

"Too low!" Jared repeated indignantly. "Tarnation, Parson, it's too all-fired high!"

"Please, Jared," Parson Lowry interjected stiffly. "Your language. Even proper swearing . . . I will not tolerate it. Now, as I say, I do not wish to haggle. And I do believe that you, as a righteous, churchgoing, God-fearing man, have no intention of cheating the church. But . . . ah . . . it does seem a lot for two hundred pounds."

"Where else you gonna git it?" Jared burst out petulantly. "Ain't nobody in these parts got a hundred pounds, let alone two."

"Perhaps. Of course, I haven't inquired. And I should consult the deacons. Perhaps they might want to keep it and work it for the church's benefit. *Ad maiorem gloria Dei,*" he intoned pompously. "For the greater glory of God."

"*Them?*" Jared spat out the question contemptuously. "They ain't got the time or the kith or kin to work their own places."

"We might place it up for sale. Not just in Deerfield, but the whole country. Maybe even Boston."

"You go ahead, Parson. You won't find many a body biddin' on run-down property in a place what's been massacred. Leastways from Boston. But, you go ahead. That way maybe you'll get to like m' offer. Pa always said a thing ain't worth but what you kin git fer it." Jared arose as though to leave, and the parson lifted a thick white hand. "No, no, Jared. I'm sure we can work this out satisfactorily. Just as soon as the court rules in the church's favor, we can come to an agreement."

Jared shook his head doggedly. "I'd like a letter right now, if you don't mind, Parson. Just a promise to sell to me at my price." He grinned irreverently. " 'There's many a slip twixt the cup and the lip,' " he said, obviously delighted to trade quotations with the parson.

"My goodness," Parson Lowry murmured sarcastically, "I had no idea the Ankers family was so familiar with the classics." He drew a sheet of foolscap toward him, picked up the quill pen beside his three-legged standish of blotting sand, and began to write. It became silent in the room, except for the scratching of the pen and the ticking of the large brass clock on the wall behind the parson.

Suddenly shouts, cheers and the sound of shots came from outside the door. Jared Ankers's face blanched when he heard the firing. He glanced at the clock in frantic disbelief.

Never a man to lose his self-control, Parson Lowry put his pen down carefully, left his desk and marched to the door, opening it and going outside. Beyond the open gates of the palisade, on the ground above the meadow, a crowd of people had gathered. There were militiamen among them. They were cheering and shouting. Some of the women waved their wide-brimmed hats, and a few of the militiamen pointed muskets toward the woods and fired them. Solomon Lowry's prognathous jaw lifted in astonishment when he saw a naked Indian standing in the center of the crowd. It lifted higher in outrage when, coming closer, he saw that the Indian was embracing young Rachel Clarke, the schoolmistress at his parish church.

"Stop!" Solomon Lowry bellowed, and almost at once the cheers and cries faded away. "Do you call yourself Christians and Puritans to stand there in tolerance of such abomination? A naked savage . . . a naked heathen . . ." Solomon Lowry began to sputter.

"It's all right, Parson," Jed Gill said easily, releasing Rachel, who nevertheless still pressed her head to his chest. "It's me—Jed Gill."

"Jedediah Gill?" Parson Lowry breathed incredulously, hardly hearing Jared Ankers gasp in dismay behind him. His eyes traveled over Jed's bronzed head and hands, the blond scalp lock and incongruous blond beard. "Is it really you, Jedediah—returned from Babylon?"

"It sure is, Parson," said Captain Adam Brown, putting the tricorn he had been waving back on his head. "And you can thank the Lord, it is, too. C'mon, everybody, let's get inside. Sergeant Barter, I want you to post pickets in the meadow and a patrol outside the palisades." Turning to Parson Lowry, walking beside him at the head of the murmuring crowd, he explained: "Yes, sir—Jed Gill run away from the Indians to warn us. We was just comin' back from muster when we seen him runnin' through the medder. Jed said the Indians was goin' to attack tonight. He saved our lives."

"You don't say," Parson Lowry murmured, turning again to stare at Jed, at the stark whiteness of his naked body. "Yes, yes . . . of course we are all in his debt. But will someone please put a blanket over him? After all, there are womenfolk present." He shook his great head sorrowfully. "You'd think a young man of his upbringing would have a little more Christian decency."

Rachel Clark heard the parson's words, and she giggled, blinking away the tears of joy. She reached up to tug playfully on Jed's beard, giggling again. Then she nestled her head against his chest again and began to weep. "Oh, Jeddy, it's you, it's you!" she sobbed. "You're alive. I knew you were, I knew it!" Someone came up with a blanket, and Jed gently detached her and put it over his shoulder. "Now you really do look like an Indian!" Rachel exclaimed. "Oh, Jeddy—were they mean to you? Did they hurt you?" Jed nodded. "A little at first. But, wait a minute, Rachel. I have to talk to Adam Brown and the parson." Jed hurried ahead to join the others walking toward the rebuilt meeting house. He was pleased to see that most of the village had been restored, but saddened at the sight of the still-blackened ruins that once had been his home.

"Didn't anyone take over the Cowlett house?" he asked Parson Lowry. The parson shook his head, shooting a glance at Jared Ankers. "They couldn't. The estate isn't settled, yet." "But it's been almost five years," Jed said, opening the meeting-house door to allow the others to enter. "Things move slowly out here on the frontier," Parson Lowry replied, sitting at the table and motioning the others to do the same. "Now, Jedediah Gill, you tell us what we should do about these Indians."

"French and Indians," Jed said. "One hundred French and about two hundred Indians. Well, Parson, I think Adam Brown's really done enough with pickets in the meadow and patrols around the palisade. They won't come, though. I'm sure of that. Not after I've warned you. The French might, but the Indians won't. They don't like to attack strong points. They like surprises—like the last time." Jed paused. "D'y know, I never did find out how they got in so easily."

Adam Brown grunted disdainfully. "All the sentries and patrols was inside out of the cold. And the wind blew the snow agin the palisade and gave 'em a regular bridge over it."

The snowbank! Jed Gill thought with guilty horror. And he had neglected to warn his foster father! Jed stared at the others in consternation, but their minds were on the present; the past was long behind them.

"I don't believe it," Jared Ankers was saying. "I don't believe they's Injuns out there at all. Jed Gill's makin' it all up so's he could come home a hero."

"Oh, yes, they is," Adam Brown interjected before the surprised and angry Jed could defend himself. "I seen one of them chasin' Jeddy. He threw his tomahawk at him."

"Could have been play-actin'," Jared snorted contemptuously. "I'll bet it didn't come within a mile of Jed."

"It's obvious that it didn't hit me," Jed said easily, having recovered his composure. "But I'll tell you what, Jared—you go out there by the sugar camp right by the last stand of swamp grass. You might find a dead Indian there named Howling Wolf. Remember him?"

"You know dang well I remember him," Jared snapped, scowling. "You killed 'im?"

"Yes. But wait a minute. Maybe they took his body with them. They'll do that if they have the time. But go out there anyway, Jared—you'll find a lot of blood. Enough to convince even you."

"Could be deer's blood."

"Oh, no. Not that much. The biggest buck you could shoot wouldn't bleed like that."

Adam Brown spoke up. "How come so much blood, Jeddy?"

"I cut his throat," Jed said quietly, and Parson Lowry gave a quick gasp of horror. "If you still don't believe me," Jed continued, "maybe you can go with me tomorrow to the Northfield fork. I'll show you their camp."

Parson Lowry coughed gently. "Please, gentlemen, let us not talk at cross-purposes. Do you think we should close the gates tonight, Jedediah?"

"By all means. And keep your patrols *outside* the palisade. Frankly, I think the gates should be closed every night, rain or shine, winter or summer. I couldn't believe it when I saw them wide open. They would have swept you away."

Adam Brown nodded sagely. "That's what I've been sayin'. But everybody listened to him," he said, pointing a scornful finger at Jared Ankers. "Just because he'd been a prisoner up there in Montreal, they believed him when he said they wouldn't come."

An ugly flush crept over Jared's narrow face. "They *don't* come this time a' year," he protested. "They're too dang lazy. This kind'v weather they like to feast and lay around."

"Not when there's a war on," Jed said.

"You call this little piddlin' Queen Anne's War a war?"

"Governor Vaudreuil does. He didn't like it when you tried to take Quebec again, and—"

"—Not Quebec, really," Parson Lowry interrupted. "A ground force was advancing on Montreal from New York. Up Lake Champlain and the rivers. Then a fleet was to sail from Boston for Quebec. But the queen never sent the ships, and the whole campaign fizzled."

"Well, it still made Vaudreuil mad, and that's why he sent out this war party."

"Against Deerfield? Little Deerfield? What good would a few more scalps do Louis of France? You'd think they'd be after something big like Boston or New York. A real star for the bloody Sun King's crown."

"They'd love to, Parson—but they just don't have the men." Jed spoke like a man preoccupied, his thoughtful eyes on Jared. He was remembering what the French commander had said to Howling Wolf: *We have a friend in Deerfield.* Was it Jared Ankers? "Jared," he said aloud, "how did you get back to Deerfield?"

Jared Ankers's Adam's apple bobbed and he looked quickly away from Jed. "I escaped," he said, his voice rising. "It was about four years ago. Howling Wolf sold me to another Indian for a slave, an' after I lived with 'im about a year, I got sick and he decided to burn me alive. They tied me to a stake and shot powder into me, and just when they got the fire goin', a cloudburst broke an' put it out." Jared began unbuttoning his shirt. "You want to see the powder burns?" Jed shook his head, and Jared continued: "That night they got drunk on brandy and I untied myself and got away." Jed nodded again. "I believe you, Jared," he said. "I saw the same thing happen myself in Caughnawaga. They were going to burn an Algonquin, but the rain put out the fire." Jed Gill did not add that it would have been better for the Algonquin if he had died in the flames. That night Howling Wolf and three others slept on top of the captive so that he could not escape, and the following day they "frolicked" with him until dusk. Jed did not, of course, believe that Jared Ankers would not have met an identical fate, but he said nothing, pleased to see the flicker of relief in Jared's watery eyes.

Jed turned to Adam Brown, who had arisen and was speaking to him. "I agree with you, Jeddy—I don't think they'll come back. But we can make it hot for them if they do," he added proudly. "Got a four-pounder, now, mounted in the north blockhouse coverin' the medder. Just got it up from Springfield a week ago, an' I don't mind telling you it was one helluva—'scuse me, Parson—one powerful haul. Took a team o' oxen three days to get it here. Just a little bitty bar o' iron—no bigger'n half a fireplace log—but it weighs eight hundred pounds. Wisht it'd bin winter so's we could've put the gun and the balls on sledges. But what d'y think of a four-pounder, Jeddy?"

"Great! They're scared to death of artillery. Just the sound of it'll make them think twice. But you mark my words— they won't come back." Jed also got to his feet, drawing his blanket around him. "Guess I got to get civilized again," he said with a grin. "I don't know how I'll like it, sleeping under a roof." He glanced sideways at Parson Lowry. " 'Course, I can't stay with Rachel Clarke . . ."

"Stay with me," Adam Brown said eagerly, and Jed said, "Thanks, I think I will. Can I borrow your razor?" Adam nodded, and Jed said: "I'd like to take a patrol out to that Northfield camp tomorrow. Want to come along, Adam?" Brown nodded again. "You too, Jared?"

Jared Ankers shook his head. "Not me," he mumbled. "I've got to scoot right now ef'n I'm goin' to get to Hatfield afore dark."

Jed shrugged, turning to conceal the shrewd look glinting in his blue eyes. So, he thought, Jared Ankers was not planning to be in Deerfield tonight.

There was no need for Jed to take out a patrol to the Northfield camp to confirm his story of a war party in the neighborhood. A man out hunting and a woman who had gone berry-picking did not return to Deerfield that night, and it was immediately assumed that they had been carried off by the raiders. When Jed told Captain Adam Brown next day that that was how the war party intended to gain information about the village's defenses, Adam at once ordered all the villagers to leave their farms and groves and come within the safety of the stockade. Then he sent couriers to warn Hatfield and Hadley. Before he left his home, Adam lent Jed a suit of homespun and a pair of wooden shoes, and after Jed shaved off his beard, he went to pay a call on Rachel Clarke.

Jed was delighted to see that the Clarke home had been one of the few spared in the massacre. It was the same little house, just a bit more weather-beaten, and there were violets and daisies and black-eyed Susans and other wild flowers growing in a tiny front yard. Jed knocked, and the door immediately flew open. Rachel stood there, smiling, her green eyes dancing—but blushing furiously. Evidently she had been expecting him, for there were drinking cups on the table and a trencher full of a steaming stew. Jed stepped quickly inside and closed the door.

"Oh, you shaved off your handsome beard," Rachel said. "And you're not an Indian anymore. I'm going to miss him," she said, pretending to pout; and then, brightening: "What was your Indian name, Jeddy?"

"Deerfoot."

"Oh, that's nice. I like that."

"At first, they called me Yellow Head."

"That's nice, too—but I like Deerfoot better."

"I sure earned it," Jed said with a rueful grin, and he told Rachel how he had run the gantlet. Tears came to her eyes, moistening and darkening her long auburn lashes. Jed had been on fire with desire when he came in the door, but now the serenity of Rachel's beauty sobered and calmed him.

"You sure do look like your ma," he said. "Except your face is a little longer, like your pa's. Your eyes are a little slanty like his, too."

Rachel giggled and tugged at the corners of her eyes. "Chinese?"

Her laughter rekindled his desire, and he embraced her and kissed her ardently on the mouth. She came to him, and his hand sought her breast. She pushed it gently away. "No," she said. "That night in the hide-hole, you said you were going to marry me, and I let you do it." She began blushing again. "I shouldn't have. I should have made you wait for me."

"But I do want to marry you. Just as soon as I can get Parson Lowry to announce the bans."

"I like that!" Rachel snorted. "Here you go blathering away about a wedding without even asking me if I wanted to marry you."

"But you do, don't you?" Jed asked anxiously.

"You big booby. Of course, I do. Here, let's have something to eat."

They sat down together, side by side, and began spooning stew from the trencher. "Ummmm, this is good," Jed said. "What is it?" Rachel swallowed before she answered. "Just a plain old hotch-potch. Spoon meat and chopped vegetables. I'm not the cook your ma was."

"You will be," Jed said. "I learned a lot about hunting and fishing up there. We won't ever go without fish or game, believe me." Jed spooned more of the stew into his mouth and chewed it with slow relish. "Salt!" he exclaimed suddenly. "That's what it is—the salt. It makes everything taste different."

"Of course, it does. Who cooks without it?"

"Indians do. They hate salt. D'y know, Rachel, this is the first salt I've tasted in five years. And I don't know if I like it anymore. Like sleeping under a roof. Last night, after everyone was asleep in Adam Brown's house, I had to go outside and lie down. It was that stuffy inside. I guess I never realized how much of an Indian I was."

"There's a lot you'll need to get used to again," Rachel said banteringly. "Like wearing white men's clothes. Wherever did you get what you have on?"

Jed thrust out his arms and kicked his legs, and his homespun cuffs shot up to his forearm and his calves. "I didn't realize Adam was that much smaller than me."

"It isn't that Adam's so small, it's that you've gotten so tall," Rachel said, standing up. "Here, stand next to me. Land sakes," she cried, glancing up at him proudly, "you've grown bigger than Pa was. Here, come with me." She walked to the stairs and went quickly up to the loft, Jed behind her. "We were lucky they didn't burn our house down. Everything was saved." She opened a dresser of carved oak. "Your pa finished making this the day before the massacre," she said sadly. "All my ma's and pa's clothing is in here, just like it was the day . . ." Grief made Rachel's voice break, and she began to sob softly. "I . . . I can't say it. I . . . I've never said it." Jed nodded understandingly and drew her to him. She caught her breath and freed herself, opening the dresser and taking out her father's clothes and laying them on the bed.

"Why, that's Uncle Jon's best suit," Jed said eagerly, picking up a black frock coat and breeches, "the one he wore to Sunday meetings and when he was hearing cases on the

bench." He slipped off Adam Brown's shirt and put on the
coat. "Yes, and here's his shirts," Rachel said. "Six of them.
All ruffled, and five of them are almost new. And his lace
cravats. Pa sure loved lace cravats." She studied Jed in her
father's coat. My, he's handsome, she thought, saying aloud:
"Perfect! Just a little tight across the chest, but I can fix that.
See, Pa even had silk and thread for mending his clothes."
Jed looked at Rachel shyly. "You . . . you mean you want
me to wear your pa's clothes?" Rachel nodded, and he said:
"But won't it . . . won't it make you feel bad seeing me in
them?" Rachel shook her head firmly. "Not at all. Somebody's got to use them. Anyway, we're frontier folk, and we
can't afford to throw away perfectly good clothes just because
they belonged to a . . . to a . . ." Rachel bit her lip and
walked back to the dresser. "I'm going to wear Ma's things.
They fit me perfect. I've even got that beautiful green silk
dress she was married in."

"That one? Let me see it. I remember when we were little
and we sneaked up here one rainy day and played house.
You were going to put it on. Remember? Good thing you
didn't. Aunt Martha heard us and came up here mad as a wet
hen and made us go downstairs and scrub the kitchen floor.
Remember?"

"I remember. But I'm not going to let you see it. I'm going
to be married in it, too, and the bridegroom isn't supposed to
see what the bride's wearing until he meets her at the altar."

Jed laughed good-humoredly and put his arms around
Rachel's waist, looking down fondly into her eyes. "I love
you, Green Eyes," he said softly. "I think I've always loved
you, ever since I can remember." Rachel gazed up at Jed
adoringly. She put her head on his shoulder and said: "I
guess it's always been that way with me, too. I guess I always
expected to marry you. Funny, even though I always thought
of you as my brother, I always expected to grow up and become your wife."

"Kismet," Jed said softly. "It is written. Remember how
fond your Pa was of saying that. He was a powerful realist,
Uncle Jon, but he was a fatalist, too. He believed that men
were at the mercy of events. They were shaped more by the
tides of human history than they were able to control events
themselves. 'It is written,' he would say.' " Jed paused, pondering. "Who was that poet he loved so much? A name like a

weapon. Shakespeare! William Shakespeare. Your pa used to tell me that the world was just getting to know Shakespeare, but one day it would kneel at his feet. And whenever Uncle Jon said, 'Kismet,' he would quote a line from Shakespeare: 'There is a tide in the affairs of men, which, taken at the flood, leads on to fortune. . . .' Then he would tell me that there were new winds blowing in the world, new tides, new movements. . . . People were beginning to question the authority of kings. They were talking about freedom and the rights of individuals. 'They're just whispering, now, Jeddy,' he would say to me, 'because they're still afraid of the king's torturers and executioners. But one day they'll be shouting it from the rooftops.' He was right. Why, those Caughnawagas I lived with were freer men than we are. They may have had their chiefs and sachems, but the chiefs were responsible to the councils. No one was afraid just because a chief got mad at him. But with us, the wrath of the king is death."

Rachel stirred in her enchantment. "I believe what you've been saying," she said. "But I don't think it's that bad."

"It can be," Jed insisted. "And it has been. Mary Tudor burned Protestants, and her sister Elizabeth had Catholics drawn and quartered. And then Elizabeth's Archbishop Laud turned on us, just because our people rejected the Anglican Church."

"After which we hung innocent people in Salem just because someone said they were witches."

Jed Gill nodded soberly. "True. But that wasn't the same thing. What I'm trying to say is that it wasn't a man's belief that really mattered as much as the king's pleasure. And that's what we have to stop. And that's what I mean when I say, 'There is a tide in the affairs of men . . .' It's beginning to run now, and when it starts to rise to the flood, I'm going to take it." Jed's face darkened. "But, first, we have to drive the French from Canada. As long as they're there, harrying our borders, burning our frontiers, the people of New England can never be safe—they can never really organize and turn to . . ." His voice trailed off, and Rachel asked softly, "Turn to what?" Jed shrugged. "You know what."

"I do, Jed—and I'm glad you didn't say it aloud." Rachel put her arm in his. "Let's talk about something pleasant—like getting married." Jed grinned and kissed her on the forehead. "Rachel Gill it's going to be," he said. "Almost as good as

Rachel Clarke. And what a family the Gill family is going to be," he exclaimed, his eyes shining. "The Gills will be to America just like the sons of Noah were in the Bible."

"Please, Jeddy, don't get carried away. First you were talking you-know-what, and now you're close to blasphemy."

"No, I'm not! The sons of Noah were off to a fresh start after the flood in the Old World, and the sons of Jedediah and Rachel Gill will be off to a fresh start in the New World. Look at us, Rachel! My parents were murdered by the French and Indians in the first war between the French and English in America. Your father was at Port Royal and Quebec, and then both your parents were murdered by the French and Indians in the second war. Some marriages, they say, are made in heaven—but ours was born in blood. The Gills are a bloodborn brood. I know, it's a dreadful thing to say, but it's true! And we *will* drive the French from the continent, and we *will*—"

"Hush," Rachel said, gently putting a finger over Jed's mouth. "Please. No more tides taken at the flood. Not for today, anyway. Let's go downstairs and have a glass of cider." Jed nodded absently, still absorbed in his thoughts. He handed Rachel her father's coat. "I'll be proud to wear your father's clothes. There never was a finer man. But not until our wedding day." Rachel put the clothes back in the dresser and led the way downstairs, Jed clumping after her in his wooden shoes.

At the table again, Rachel poured glasses of cool cider and sat down beside him. She sipped it silently, before asking abruptly: "How are we going to get along?"

Jed grinned and said: "No girl as pretty as you are should be so practical."

"I can't help it. Ma brought me up that way. All day long I'd hear her: 'A stitch in time saves nine. A penny saved is a penny earned. Many a muckle makes a mickle.' And we will have to make ends meet. Of course, Parson Lowry will still be paying me thirty pounds a year to run the church school. It isn't much, but it'll help. Oh, you should have heard the fuss the deacons made when he mentioned it. A *woman*? A woman teach their children? Some of them said they'd sooner have their children illiterate than have a woman teach them. But you know the parson. He just told them that, inasmuch as no one else in the village was educated enough to teach anyone, it would just have to be me. But, still, thirty pounds . . ."

"But, Rachel—I'm not exactly a pauper. My pa was the richest man along the Connecticut River when he was killed. He taught me carpentering, too, and farming—and he had me working in the mill with him since my eighth birthday."

"But, you see, Jeddy," Rachel began slowly, "you don't really own that property yet. There are problems."

Jed raised his eyebrows. "Parson Lowry said something to me about the estate not being settled, yet. What did he mean?"

"It's Jared Ankers. He's after the Cowlett property. Ever since he came back here, he's been telling everyone that you joined an Indian tribe and became a Catholic."

"I never did!"

"Of course, you wouldn't. But Jared says the Indian who captured him told him that. When he told the Reverend Mr. Lowry that you went over to Rome, I thought the poor parson would have apoplexy. Jared wants Adam Brown to declare you an outcast. He says that you should be judged by the Penal Laws for Catholics in England and Ireland. That way, you'd be disenfranchised."

"Why, the dirty, sniveling son of a bitch!"

"Jedediah!"

"Oh, I'm sorry, Rachel—but I practically saved that ungrateful skunk's life," Jed said bitterly. "And this is how he repays me." Explaining how he had provided Jared with moccasins and snowshoes on the trek from Deerfield, Jed continued: "But what good would all that do him? He wouldn't get the property."

"No, but he thinks he could buy it cheap from the church. Parson Lowry has let it be known your ma promised him a bequest."

"I don't doubt that. But no more than a few pounds or so for a new Bible or a communion cup."

"Well, the parson has the idea—probably planted by Jared, he's sure a clever sneak, that one—that if there are no heirs, then the church should get everything."

"Everything! Parson Lowry says *that*? Why, that sneaking, sanctimonious—"

"No, Jeddy—he isn't dishonest. He's just a little too eager to serve the Lord."

"In his own way, which isn't necessarily the Lord's. Anyway, Ma would spin in her grave if the church got what she and Pa intended for me. She just wasn't that churchified. She was a believing Christian and tried to live up to it, but she sure hated all that praying and fasting." He grinned. "I remember the parson asking her one winter how come she had missed Sunday meeting both morning and afternoon. She told him that her foot stove was broken and she was afraid her feet would freeze off."

"Was it?"

"Not really. There was just a crack in it. I think she dropped it on purpose to put it there."

Rachel laughed, and then, sobering, she said: "So that's what you're up against."

"It really doesn't seem like much. It's Jared's word against mine. And he has no proof. Only what Howling Wolf told him, and that's just hearsay, and your pa told me a long time ago, Rachel, that hearsay just isn't acceptable in an English court of law. I'm sure even Adam Brown knows that. So, I don't think Jared—" Jed paused abruptly. "I've been thinking about Jared Ankers, Rachel," he said softly. "Does everyone believe that story about his just missing being burned alive?"

Rachel nodded, and Jed shook his head. "I don't."

"But he does have scars from the powder burns. Land's sakes, for the first few weeks after he got back, every time he met someone he'd roll up his sleeve or unbutton his shirt to show them to him. Adam Brown said he was sure glad they didn't shoot him in the behind."

"If the French wanted a spy in New England," Jed said, ignoring her giggle, "they could easily provide him with a story like that and the scars to verify it. They're not squeamish."

"If the French . . .?"

"Yes," Jed said, telling her of what he had overheard the French commander say. "So, you see, it's no coincidence that Jared convinced everyone that the Indians weren't coming, and then planned to be in Hatfield last night."

Rachel gasped, and her hand flew to her mouth. "He *is* that dirty thing that you called him! Why, now, I'm beginning to remember things myself."

"Such as what?"

"How he got all that money. People used to wonder about

it. He said he got it from his pa. He said he hid it in the woods just before the massacre."

"His pa!" Jed snorted scornfully. "Seth Ankers never had two ha'pennies in his pocket at the same time. He was always trying to cadge a shilling or two off Pa on muster day. And he never paid his fines."

"I know. Then, Jared never really did much after he came back. He hired a man to rebuild his family's cabin and work the farm. And he was always going away somewhere for two or three weeks at a time. He spent every summer in Boston."

"Boston, eh? More likely Quebec. Or Quebec *after* Boston and a little sniffing and snuffling for the Onontio."

"Onontio?"

"That's what the Indians call the governor of Canada."

There was a knock at the door, and Rachel arose to open it and admit Parson Lowry. "Good morning, Rachel," the parson said stiffly, frowning when he saw Jed. He coughed suggestively and said: "It would not seem . . . ah . . . seemly to find two unmarried persons of your age in the same home together alone."

Rachel blushed and Jed laughed and said: "That's all right, Parson—Rachel and I are going to get married. And we want you to announce the bans as soon as you can."

"I am most pleased to hear that, Jedediah," Parson Lowry said, relaxing slightly. "But I must tell you that my object in coming here might have considerable effect on your decision to marry."

"I think I know what you mean, Parson. Rachel has been telling me about what Jared Ankers has been saying about me. It's all a pack of lies, of course."

Solomon Lowry put his hands behind his back, leaning forward with extended jaw. "You did not join the Popish church?"

"Of course not! Do you, Parson Lowry, think so little of your own teaching?"

The parson beamed. "Ah, yes . . . of course. Of course."

"But I did become a Caughnawaga. On the surface, at least. I had to. Otherwise, they would either have tortured me to death and eaten me, or else burned me alive. But all the time I was with them, I thought of nothing but escaping and coming back to Deerfield. And, as you have seen, I finally did."

"Yes, of course. And we are all deeply in your debt, Jedediah. But the fact is that Jared Ankers has now withdrawn these charges. He still insists that they are true, but he is waiving them in the interest of a graver and more verifiable claim: that you are not the Cowletts' legal heir."

"Whaaat?"

"I am sorry, Jedediah, but Jared seems to have proof that your foster parents never adopted you legally. There is no record of such a procedure either in Boston or here."

"But maybe they were destroyed in the fire."

"The Cowletts' records would be, but not the county's."

Jed turned to look at Rachel in dismay. Incredibly, Rachel smiled and winked. She began to laugh. Jed Gill doubted his senses, but there was Rachel with her head thrown back and her green eyes twinkling while merry peals of laughter broke from her lips.

"Rachel, are you daft?"

"Not daft, just dumb. I guess it was that long face of yours that made me realize how stupid we've all been. Maybe it was just seeing you alive again that made me forget. Or else it was Jared Ankers with all his lies and insinuations. Can't you see, silly—if you're not your ma and pa's heir, I am!"

"Oh, my God," Jed Gill groaned in relief, holding his head in his hand; and even Parson Lowry was so overcome by the obvious nature of Rachel's revelation that he neglected to rebuke Jed for having violated the Second Commandment.

"Of course!" Rachel continued, "Pa was Aunt Agatha's brother, and I was her niece. Am I right, Parson?"

Solomon Lowry did not answer momentarily. His broad mouth was gaping, revealing a set of strong separated teeth. "Ah, yes . . . of course," he murmured at last, passing a hand over his bald forehead. "It was entered in my own records the day I baptized you. The Cowletts were your godparents." His face hardened. "I shall have a few words to say to Mr. Jared Ankers," he muttered.

"Please do, Parson Lowry," Jed Gill said with a smile. "And don't forget the wedding bans next Sunday meeting."

11

Like Rachel's parents, Jedediah and Rachel Gill decided to spend their honeymoon on the island of Nantucket.

After the ceremony, Adam Brown, who had served as Jed's best man, drove the wedding couple to Hadley in his oxcart. At Hadley, Jed and Rachel rented horses. Jed wanted Rachel to ride behind him on a pillion, but Rachel scoffed, "Pshaw! A pillion is for old ladies. I'm riding my own horse." So they got a smaller gray for Rachel, which she rode sidesaddle, and Jed mounted a big glossy bay. They rode together down the Hadley Path through Belchertown and Ware to Brookfield, where they followed the Bay Path to Springfield.

The narrow paths led through dense forests reverberating to the massed screeching of tens of thousands of migrating birds perched on the tree limbs in neat serried rows, or along the banks of streams still so full of leaping, flashing fish that Jed remarked it would be easier to go after them with your bare hands than with a seine. Sometimes, they would have to wait for ferries; and if they were alone, they would dismount and hug and kiss. At other times they crossed the water on the new "cart bridges," in actuality nothing more than rickety makeshifts, precarious floating bridges which bumped and bounced on the surface of the stream, always threatening to dump those who rode them into the water.

At Springfield, Jed and Rachel stayed at the Bartlett Tavern. It was run by the Widow Bartlett, an enormously fat woman with a fallen stomach and bright red dewlapped cheeks. She was merry enough for all her wheezing and grunting when she moved, and she smiled knowingly when Jed came into the hall with Rachel shyly trying to hide behind him and asked for a night's lodging.

"One-shilling-sixpence for you and the missus," she wheezed, "and sixpence for the horses."

"*Two* shillings?" Jed asked, aghast, and the Widow Bartlett nodded, running her eye approvingly over Rachel, who had at last ventured into view like a bashful child. "Then we'll be wanting a room to ourselves," Jed said, lifting his shoulders belligerently. Rachel turned scarlet, and the Widow Bartlett's eyes twinkled. "You can have the back room upstairs," she said. "But if the inn gets crowded, I might have to stick someone in with you."

"Stick some—" Jed Gill's blue eyes blazed in indignation. Rachel took his hand and squeezed it gently, and he calmed down. "What are you charging for the privacy of a private room?" he asked sarcastically, taking his purse from his pocket again.

"Fivepence," she said cheerfully, and Jed handed her the coin, which she put in her pocket with a cherubic smile, jangling the fip in with the others there. Deborah Bartlett could spot a pair of newlyweds halfway up the Bay Path, and she had been subjecting them to her own outrageous style of extortion—"I may have to stick someone in with you"—since she took over the inn on the death of her husband ten years ago. Once, the dread of a third party on the wedding couch had compelled an elderly magistrate with a wife thirty years his junior to cough up two staggering shillings. Remembering that triumph, the Widow Bartlett inquired, "Supper?" and when Jed nodded, she pointed to the tap room and said, "In the tap."

It was a warm, congenial room with sturdy ceiling beams turned black by smoke. There was a fireplace with a brass fence around it and a small bar. They were alone in the tap and they sat at a table near the fireplace. Widow Bartlett waddled in and took their order, which was the only dish on the menu: boiled pork and roast pheasant with pig greens and sauerkraut.

"We'll have a bottle of sack, too," Jed said, and Widow Bartlett grunted in pleasure at this unexpected sale and waddled back to the kitchen.

"A *whole* bottle?" Rachel asked, her green eyes widening in dismay. "Can we really afford it?"

"It's our wedding night," Jed said, arising to walk over to examine a notice on the wall. It was from the local magistrate and it sternly warned the landlord not to "knowingly harbor in house, barn, or stable, any rogues, vagabonds, thieves, sturdy beggars, masterless men or women." It also frowned upon what it called "the Sports of the Innyard," listing them as "carding, dicing, tally, bowls, billiards, slide-groat, shuffleboard, quoits, loggets, nine-pins or any other idle and foolish pastimes." Jed shook his head and returned to his seat. "I'll tell you," he said angrily, "this Puritan petty persecution is something else that's going to sink in the tide taken at the flood."

"Shhh!" Rachel warned as two men in farm boots came into the room, just as Widow Bartlett brought them their meal. "Someone might hear you."

"Can you believe it?" Jed persisted, ignoring her alarm, "that notice on the wall prohibits every innocent game imaginable. What do these Puritans have against pleasure? What do they think the good Lord gave us our senses for?"

"To mortify them, of course," Rachel said, helping herself to pheasant. "Ummm, this is good—and with pan gravy, too."

"Right. If Parson Lowry had his way, we'd all walk around blindfolded, button-lipped, earplugged, and nose-pinned."

"That's only four. What about the fifth sense?"

"Touch?" He grinned suggestively, and Rachel laid down her spoon and murmured in a low voice: "Don't you say another thing." Jed laughed and poured himself more sack.

More men were coming into the room. They were locals, apparently regulars at Bartlett's Tavern. They began to talk in loud voices about the second expedition to Port Royal which had failed two years before. A thin pockmarked man with a deep voice blamed the entire fiasco on the commander, Colonel John March. "Wooden sword, that's what he is," he said, finishing his denunication of Colonel March with a loud belch.

"You're right there, Cap'n Soames," a short bald man with an enormous mustache chimed in. "Look what Phips did at Port Royal with a roll of drums. Now, there was a man, Sir William."

"But he was no match for old Frontenac at Quebec. You ask me, Phips was another wooden sword. So was Nicholson at Lake Champlain this summer. Just a little bit of ordinary English courage and Montreal would have been ours."

"You cain't rightly blame Nicholson," said the stout man. "You cain't fight a plague with gunpowder, y'know. It was them filthy Iroquois what done it. They was afraid the French'd get licked proper leavin' us in charge on the continent. So they poisoned the creek with animal skins and shit, and when Nicholson's men drunk the water they got the plague."

The thin man nodded gloomily. "That's what I heard, too. Why us English keep trustin' them two-faced varmints, I'll never know. Anyways, it was Vetch more than Nicholson. The whole campaign—Montreal by land and Quebec by sea—was Samuel Vetch's idea. Comin' back from London like that all puffed up like a bullfrog on a lily pad. Tellin' everybody how he done dined with the queen and she was gonna send us the ships and men to git rid of the French for good." He paused as Widow Bartlett lumbered by, moving to clear the dishes from Jed and Rachel's table. "Hey, there, Debby—a couple more pitchers of beer, eh?" Turning back to his fellows, he rubbed his chin and pursued his monologue: "Like I said, all that money wasted, an' me an' t' other officers drillin' them pore fellers ever' day waitin' for the queen's ships. Six months of it! And then she sends the ships to Portugal, instead. And what about them pore fellers gettin' sick o' the plague an' dyin' at Wood Creek?"

There was a silence in the taproom while the men filled their tankards from the pitchers Widow Bartlett brought them. Jed Gill glanced at Rachel and put a finger to his lips. She nodded. She, too, had been listening intently. It had made her feel important and mature to sit there in the taproom listening to the older men around her discussing the affairs of the world.

The stout man blew foam from his tankard, careful not to

soak his mustache. "Y' gonna 'list again next year, Cap'n Soames?"

"Cain't say. Depends on what kind of guarantee they kin git from the queen. I'll say this, though—New York's sure hot fer war. Feller from Albany stopped here las' night and said New York's sending Nicholson to London in December. And Peter Schuyler—the big Dutch patroon—is takin' no less than five Mohawk chiefs across the ocean, too."

"*Five*! How come so many?"

"Impress the queen, I guess. No, I think I've got it backwards, Will. Impress, the *Mohawks,* I mean. Show those Injuns an English queen in all her jewels and London after dark, an' mebbe they'll stick to us a little closer."

The men pounded their tankards on the tables in approval, and the man named Will called for three more pitchers of beer this time. Widow Bartlett brought them with a cheery smile on her cupid's-bow mouth, carrying three of the huge containers in one hand as lightly as though they had been glasses.

"She is *strong,*" Jed muttered to Rachel. "With hands and wrists like that, she sure could steer a straight furrow."

Rachel giggled and whispered, "If you could find a horse strong enough to pull her and the plow, too."

The men had begun to sing, and both of them fell silent. Listening intently, a slow smile came over Jed Gill's face. "Listen," he whispered eagerly to Rachel, "it's the song the men used to sing at the sugaring."

> . . . Buxom, sweet and debonair,
> And they call her *Sack,* my dear.

There was a roar of laughter at the conclusion of the song, and another rattle of tankards on tabletops. Widow Bartlett came hurrying with more beer, just as the taproom door opened and a tall, long-faced man in a black doublet, hose and cloak burst into the room, crying: "Hah, now, what's this, you varlets? Roistering and breaking the public peace!" He strode angrily to the bar to count the empty pitchers Widow Bartlett had placed there. "Not another drop for them, y'hear," he shouted at the Widow Bartlett, and the poor woman broke into tears, her dewlapped cheeks quivering as she wailed: "I've just filled up three more pitchers! What am I to do with them?"

"Throw them away!" the tall man snapped. "Foul, filthy stuff that it is, anyway. The devil's own drink, to make a man waste his time and his substance on it. Throw it out, I tell you!"

Still wailing, she marched toward the door with the pitchers in her hand. Before Rachel could stop him, Jed lifted a hand and said: "Here, we'll have a pitcher of that." Turning her tear-stained face gratefully toward him, Widow Bartlett moved to comply, but the tall man in the cloak and doublet stepped quickly between her and Jed. "Who be you, you pink-cheeked knave, to interfere with a tithing-man about his duties?"

"Tithing-man?" Jed repeated in a puzzled tone, his eyes roving in contempt over the man standing over him. He reached for his purse. "Are you some kind of church beggar?"

A gasp arose from the men sitting silently at their tables, and the tithing-man reached down to grasp Jed by his coat lapels. "You insolent puppy," he snarled through gritted teeth. "What be your name and where be you from?"

Jed was about to tell the tithing-man that it was none of his business, until he felt Rachel's imploring eyes on him and saw Widow Bartlett shake her head warningly. "Jedediah Gill and his wife, Rachel," he answered in a steady voice, "married this day in the village of Deerfield."

"Prisoner Gill, it will be, if you don't curb that tongue of yours." He pointed to Jed's table and shouted at Widow Bartlett: "Clear the table! He's had enough to drink, too."

His eyes blazing again, Jed put his hand on Widow Bartlett's thick wrist. "Who is he to say when and how much a man may drink?"

"I'll show you who I am!" the tithing-man snarled, moving toward the door. "I'll have the constable on you, and you'll spend your wedding night in jail."

Jed Gill opened his mouth to shout his defiance, but it was instantly covered by the pink, perspiring and pudgy palm of the Widow Bartlett. "Please, young sir," she pleaded. "Please . . . He is an officer of the law. He's the tithing-man. The magistrates have placed the order and regulation of all the town's taverns and ordinaries in his care." She withdrew her hand cautiously. Jed's mouth was still open, but this time in incredulity. Widow Bartlett laid a substantial pink finger over it, and Rachel, again fixing him with her imploring green eyes, whispered: "Please, Jeddy—don't. It's . . . it's our wedding night . . ." Jed's sullen eyes swiveled from both women toward the tithing-man; but luckily for him, he had turned from Jed to the man at the tables. "Off with you!" he shouted. "Back to your beds, before I chide you away!" One by one, they arose and went meekly out the door, the belligerent Captain Soames quietly leading the way. Jed watched them go with unbelieving eyes, until he felt Rachel tugging frantically on his elbow. "Hurry," she panted, pulling him out of his chair. "Hurry, before he chides you away, too." Seizing Jed's hand, she led him almost at a run out of the room and up the stairs to their bedroom. "Oh, Jeddy, Jeddy—you have such a terrible temper," she murmured, closing the door behind her and kissing him full on the mouth, more to close his lips than to express her love.

"The son of a bitch!" Jed swore, lighting the betty lamp with trembling hands. "Telling free men how much they can drink and how long they can stay up. What right does the church have to inter—?"

Rachel kissed him again, standing on tiptoe. When she withdrew her lips she put her hand over his mouth. "Shhh! He's probably at the foot of the stairs listening."

He was, but Widow Bartlett had followed him into the hall, a glint of shrewish satisfaction in her eyes. "How, there, Mr. Yawkey," she yelled at him as he knelt on the stairs with his hand cupped to his ears. "Who's to pay me now for the three pitchers of beer thrown away?" He motioned her to silence angrily, but she deliberately raised her voice and shouted: " 'Tis the day's profits I threw out with them, Mr. Yawkey. A poor starving widow woman like myself, and the magistrates sending you in here to drive away my custom. What's to become of me?"

Upstairs, Rachel put her hand over her own mouth to stifle her giggles. She realized the fat innlady was deliberately spoiling the tithing-man's attempt at eavesdropping, warning them with her loud voice. Jed knew it, too, and his good nature began to return.

"Will you shut up?" the tithing-man snarled.

"I will not. You may be able to close my tap, but you can't close my mouth."

"I'll have you in the stocks as a common scold." He grinned maliciously. "That is, if you can fit."

"Get out of here, you lanky hank of a snoop," Widow Bartlett yelled, her cheeks shaking with anger. "I ought to sit on you, that's what I ought to do." She turned as though to flop down on top of him. and the tithing-man scrambled nimbly to his feet. Aware that he had gone too far, he grinned sourly and made for the door. "I'm almost positive I heard the varlet up there curse," he grumbled. "If it hadn't been for you, it would have cost him five shillings. That and maybe another ten for interfering with an officer of the law." Ducking his head inside the taproom for a quick official glance, he went outside.

Upstairs, Rachel and Jed clung together, shaking with silent laughter. Rachel was so pleased that Jed had recovered his good humor that she immediately began undressing beneath the betty lamp, hoping to forestall any renewal of a diatribe against the petty persecutions of the Puritans. Jed watched her with swiftly rising desire, quickly slipping out of his own clothes. In a few moments they stood in the center of the room naked, clinging fiercely to each other, warm flesh pressed against warm flesh, and in another few moments Jedediah Gill's grudges against his sovereign and his church were forgotten—to the delectable profit of that fifth great sense of touch.

Three days later Jed and Rachel Gill walked along the oceanfront at Nantucket hand in hand. It was Indian summer and the wild roses still bloomed pink and fragrant among the sand dunes. Rachel was enchanted. She had never seen the ocean before, and she looked from side to side with stretched neck or in front of her on tiptoe, as though seeking to find a limit to the vast expanse of water. They were enthralled by the sights and sounds of the harbor, too, the ships coming and going, and by the quaintness of the village. "How would you like to live here all your life?" Jed asked Rachel, unaware of how he had echoed her father's question to her mother twenty years earlier.

Rachel shook her head. "I love it," she said, "but it's too far from the mainland. Besides, I want to see what Boston is like. The Widow Bartlett said it's grown into an enormous city. There must be ten thousand people living there," she said.

A week later, the newlyweds cantered into Boston Common and Rachel was immediately dismayed by the clamor and commotion of the metropolis. Gradually, however, she became used to it and eventually found it exciting. They had no trouble getting lodging, for Rachel, who had a knack for finding out things, soon discovered that Boston boasted of no less than thirty-four ordinaries or taverns. Jed and Rachel put up at the Traveler's Rest and immediately rushed out to explore the city.

They went to the Green Lane first. Rachel was anxious to see the great house her mother grew up in. "There it is," she said, pointing to it eagerly. "It's even bigger than ma said it was. All brick, too, just like she said. My, but Sir William must have been rich. He's dead now, though. Didn't last more than a year after he lost the governorship. I wonder who's living there, now." They looked for a name, but couldn't find one. Strolling on, they came to another mansion almost as grand as Sir William's. The name "VETCH" was etched in frosted glass in the arch above the door. "Vetch," Rachel murmured thoughtfully. "That must be the Samuel Vetch the man in Springfield was talking about. He sounded awfully important." Jed nodded absently. "Let's go find the street where ma and pa lived," he said, and they walked back to the Common.

By luck their first sally down an alley took them to the Cowletts' old house. "That's it!" Rachel cried. "I'd know it in a minute! Aunt Aggie told me she had a brass busybody shaped like an hour glass outside her parlor window, and there it is." She pointed to the mirror which, fixed to reflect inward, helped to sate the curiosity of the Boston housewife without distracting her from her daily household chores. "All the other houses have busybodies, too," Jed pointed out. "Yes, but this is the only hour-glass one," said Rachel. She studied the name "WESTON" burned into the board nailed to the fence. Murmuring, "It isn't like New Englishmen to waste things," she stood on tiptoe and peered over the fence at the other side of the board. "There!" she cried triumphantly. "COWLETT. Just like I told you." Jed laughed with pleasure. Looking up and down the alley, seeing no one, he seized Rachel and hugged and kissed her.

"You be careful," Rachel warned, drawing away and glancing anxiously around her. "Don't forget what nearly happened in Springfield."

"I won't if I live to be a hundred," he said grimly; but then, brightening: "That's what I like about Boston. I haven't seen a constable yet. Or a tithing-man. And only one parson. I like Boston."

"So do I," Rachel said. "Why don't we live here?"

"How can we? Everything we own is in Deerfield."

"We could always sell it."

"We wouldn't get much. An acre in Boston is worth about five hundred or even a thousand in Deerfield. Besides, I wouldn't know what to do here. There aren't many farms or mills in the city, and the ones that are here we could never afford to buy."

Rachel fell silent, walking pensively beside him. She yearned to have her own little house in Boston, just like the Cowlett's, near the Common within reach of all the amenities of a city. "It's so hard living on the frontier," she said slowly. "I don't mind it so much in the spring and summer. But the winters are so long and cold and dark. There's nothing to do. Everyone we loved or knew there is gone, now. We'd be almost strangers." She shuddered slightly. "The war is far from over, and we've got another winter coming on."

Jed nodded soberly. "That's all true, Rachel. But, say we can even sell the property in Deerfield. Get four or five hundred pounds for it. What would we do in Boston?"

Rachel pursed her lips thoughtfully. They had turned into the Common and were approaching the Traveler's Rest, when Rachel stopped and pointed at the tavern. "We'd buy a tavern!" she cried.

Jed Gill stopped short. He scratched his head. A dubious expression on his face was gradually replaced by one of calculation. "Not a bad idea," he said slowly.

"It should be easy to locate one," Rachel said, her eyes bright with enthusiasm. "I told you there were thirty-four of them in town. A lot of them are owned by women, so I could help you run it. And we'd specialize in game! You could hunt in the woods outside of town." She looked up at him pleadingly. "Please, Jeddy—let's. . . ."

Jed fingered the scar on his forehead, and said: "I'd have to have a horse to carry back the game. Maybe a cart, too.

We could buy one of those waterfront places. Something a little run down that I could fix up myself. I could make the signboard myself, too." Rachel took his hand and squeezed it happily. " 'Gill's Tavern and Landing,' " Jed said dreamily. " 'Venison and Pheasant Our Specialty.' " Rachel laughed in delight, her eyes moisting. She squeezed Jed's hand again and stood on tiptoe to whisper in his ear, "Do you want to go upstairs before supper?"

"You scarlet woman," Jed snorted teasingly, holding the tavern door open for her. "But I guess Boston really is the best place to get the Gill family started."

Part II

Part II

12

"One breast of pheasant for the gentleman at the harbor window," Rachel Gill called to her husband as she approached the roasting spit. Jed nodded and quickly brushed the flies off a plucked pheasant lying on an oak block beside the roasting spit, lifting it high in the air with one hand while thrusting the spit through it with the other. Then he put the spitted bird on a wheel and began to turn it.

Rachel and Jed Gill were very proud of their roasting spit. It stood in the center of the highly polished mahogany bar above a bed of coals contained in a copper-lined iron pot. It was the chief attraction of Gill's Tavern and Landing, filling the taproom with aromas of roasting game so delectable that it made the mouths of their guests water. On pleasant days, Jed left the taproom door open so that the delightful odors of his cuisine might be wafted outside onto the wharf to lure its strollers inside.

Turning the pheasant slowly, Jed Gill studied the guest at the harbor window. He was obviously a man of consequence, judging from his nonchalant air of confidence. He was of above average height and sturdily built. Jed admired his dress, wishing that he, too, could afford such a powdered white wig, and rich but modest coat of brown velvet with

191

matching breeches, white lace trimmed with yellow at his throat and wrists, yellow silk stockings and brown leather shoes with gold buckles.

"Pheasant's ready," Jed called to Rachel in the kitchen. He lifted the spit from the wheel, neatly sliding the pheasant off it onto the block. Selecting a heavy, sharp knife from the rack above the block, he dexterously separated the breast from the body and placed it on a bed of rice on a warm serving platter held by Rachel. Next, he wrenched off a leg, mincing some of the meat and placing it on a frying pan, mashing it against the hot iron. Adding flour and butter, he stirred in onions, herbs, three tablespoons of Madeira and the pheasant's liver chopped fine. Soon an aroma so savory arose from the pan that the man at the harbor window, who had been absorbed in the unloading of a West Indian merchantman on the wharf, turned his head toward the spit. Jed smiled. He began spooning the Madeira sauce onto the breast of pheasant and rice. He poured the remainder into a bowl and said to Rachel, "Take him this, too. He might like to dunk his biscuits in it."

Rachel nodded and brought the meal to the guest with a quick, gay smile. He said something, and Rachel turned to fetch a mug of beer from the bar. The man began to eat, and Jed Gill was pleased to see him chew his first mouthful with obvious relish. Then three ship's captains came stomping into the taproom, calling loudly for ale and venison, and Jed became preoccupied again in spitting a haunch of meat from the doe he had shot that morning. It was only an hour later, when the taproom had cleared, that he noticed the well-dressed man was still seated at the harbor window, sipping a glass of Madeira.

"I think that man at the window is Samuel Vetch," Rachel whispered to him.

"Samuel Vetch? You mean the man who owns the house we saw on the Green Lane?"

Rachel nodded, lowering her eyes. "He's looking at you, Jeddy. Look, I think he wants to talk to you."

Jed saw that Vetch was indeed beckoning to him, and he hastened to slip a black waistcoat over his white shirt, coming around the bar to join him at the window table.

"Let me congratulate you, Sir," Vetch said in a low, agreeable voice. "That was probably the finest breast of pheasant I've ever eaten."

"Thank you, Mr. Vetch," Jed said, flushing with pleasure.

"Oh? You know my name?"

"My wife recognized you. We are indeeed honored to have you dine at our tavern."

"The pleasure is all mine. As I said, you are an uncommon fine cook. I never tasted game so soft and sweet. Here, will you have a glass with me?"

"Indeed, I will, Sir—but let it be my pleasure." He turned toward the bar. "Rachel . . . a bottle of the best Madeira, please, and fresh glasses." Jed sat down opposite Vetch, who regarded him with open admiration. Rachel brought the bottle and glasses and Jed began to pour. "This is my first time in your place," Vetch continued. "But it will not be the last, I assure you. Have you been here long?"

"Six months."

"Less than a year, by God, and already the town is talking about you. My friend, General Nicholson, sent me here."

"General Nicholson?" Jed repeated in obvious delight. "Has he dined here?"

"Oh, yes—several times. But, tell me, where do you get such excellent game?"

"I go hunting twice a week out in the woods across Boston Neck."

"You must be an uncommon fine shot to keep a tavern as busy as yours supplied with game."

"I don't miss, Mr. Vetch," Jed said with simple pride. "And if it starts to rain . . . well, I'm almost as accurate with a bow and arrow."

"Where did a young fellow like you learn to shoot like that? And with a bow and arrow?"

"I was captured by Indians five years ago. I lived with them for four years."

Jed finished pouring the Madeira, while Vetch studied him thoughtfully. "Jedediah Gill, eh? I think I've heard of you. Weren't you at Deerfield?" Jed nodded, and raised his glass. "To the destruction of the French," he said, and Vetch smiled, murmuring: "I'll drink to that." He sipped appreciatively. "Your cellar isn't bad, either, young man. So you hate the Frenchies, eh?"

"I have reason to. They and their filthy Indians murdered

my parents before I was born, and then they murdered my foster parents."

"Before you were born? How was that?"

"A tomahawk opened my mother's womb. I was born in her death blood."

"Zounds! You've an uncommon past for a young fellow. Where was that?"

"Schenectady."

"I remember Schenectady. I was in Albany at the time, with my father-in-law." He glanced up at Jed. "Ever hear of Robert Livingston?"

"Of course," Jed said, visibly impressed. "The Livingstons are one of the wealthiest families in New York. My uncle told me about them."

"Well, when we got the alarm, we rode out with a local magistrate." Vetch frowned in recollection. "Name of Clarke."

"He was my adopted uncle," Jed said grimly. "The man I just mentioned. The French murdered him, too—with my aunt. At Deerfield." Jed's powerful hand closed around his glass, and Vetch, fearing he might break it, gently laid his finger over it. Jed relaxed, and Vetch asked: "When you were with the Indians, did you learn to speak their language?" Jed nodded. "Any French?" Jed nodded again. "A little. I used to talk to a Jesuit up there."

"This is uncommon good luck, meeting a young fellow of your talents just when I needed them most. Knows the Indians. Speaks their language. Knows a little French. Can shoot the eyes out a pheasant. We can use a man like you at Port Royal."

"Port Royal?"

"Yes. And d'y know where I've just come from, young fellow?" Vetch paused, glancing around him mysteriously. "The General Court. It's all laid on for Port Royal, young man— Jed, isn't it? It's all laid on for Port Royal, Jed."

"Port Royal? All the gossip in here said Quebec."

"Well, it *was* Quebec. But then the Ministry changed its mind. Damn the Ministry! A mind like the wind! Every ship brings a change of plan. Or a change of heart," he grumbled. "Like last year. Poor Nicholson sweating out the fever in that pest hole at Wood's Creek, waiting for me to move against Quebec—and then the Ministry sends our forces to Portugal instead. And who do they blame? Who do they curse in their tankards? Who do they want to see swinging on a rope? Samuel Vetch, that's who—Samuel Vetch and Francis Nicholson. Goddam the Ministry, I say! A pack of la-de-da foxhunters trying to play soldier." Samuel Vetch threw back his head to finish his Madeira. He put his glass down suggestively close to the bottle, and while Jed refilled it, he wiped his lips and glanced cautiously around the taproom. "Forget what I said, lad—I mean, Jed," he muttered. "But it is Port Royal. Nicholson has the chief command, with myself and Sir Charles Hobby his seconds. Like to come along, Jed?"

"My Uncle Jon was at Port Royal." Jed said musingly. "He was Sir William Phips's right-hand man."

"You don't say! Ever talk to you much about the port? I've studied Canada, lad, and I know it. I don't mind saying I know the St. Lawrence as well as any Frenchman. But Acadia, now, I don't have a bloody clue."

"I've never been there. But my uncle told me a lot about it. He was a seaman, too. He said you've got to be careful going into the harbor. The entrance is narrow and the tide runs like a mill race."

"By God, this is uncommon good luck!" Vetch cried, striking the table with his fist. "You've got to come along with me, Jed Gill. Young as you are, I daresay you'll be the handiest man we can ship aboard. I can't make you second like your uncle, but if you come with me, I'll make you second to my second."

Jed Gill's eyes blazed eagerly. But then, seeing Rachel standing behind the bar and watching them intently, the light died, to be replaced with doubt. "We've only just begun here, my wife and I," he began. "I don't know as it's fair to her, leaving her alone to run the place by herself . . ."

"Nonsense! Young as she is, she's a very capable woman, I can see. If it's help she'll need, I can send over a couple of black boys until you return. And I can do more, Jed Gill," Vetch said, his mysterious air returning as he pulled a piece of parchment from his coat pocket. "By order of the Queen, the Honorable Samuel Vetch is to be governor of Port Royal after it's captured," he read. "And the General Court hereby votes that a pipe of wine, twenty sheep, five pigs and one hundred fowls are to be presented to General Nicholson for the service of his table. Hear that, Jed—and do you know who's going to provide for the general's table? Gill's Tavern and Landing, that's who—and there's no telling, lad, what else will be coming your way after I'm governor. Now, what d'y say?"

Jed Gill pondered. He glanced at Rachel, still watching them with a frown. *There is a tide, which, taken at the flood, leads on to fortune. . . .* Jed smiled and held out his hand. "I'm your man, Sir," he said.

Beaming, Samuel Vetch grasped it. "Now, all we need is the ships," he growled. "It's those damned la-de-da lollygaggers in the Ministry again. The ships were due in mid-March. Here it is June, and they're still not here. And we can't do a thing until they get here, either. The General Court isn't about to waste a lot of time and money waiting for ships that never come like the last time." He arose, smiling affably again. "But the moment they get here, I'll expect to hear from you."

"You will, Sir," Jed said, getting to his own feet, and glancing apprehensively at Rachel. "But I'm going to have the devil's own time of it explaining things to my wife."

Redbud's time had come.

With her mother and other female relatives of her clan she had gone to the house of the women to deliver Deerfoot's child. Her father, Tamarack, as chief of the Caughnawagas, also accompanied her, but he did not enter the women's house. Instead, he erected a sweat house outside it to purify himself before addressing Owaneeyo.

Tamarack made a circle of hoops of bent saplings stuck in the ground. To these he attached blankets and skins to form sides. Next, he rolled hot stones from a nearby fire into the center of the circle. Then he entered the circle carrying a kettle of water mixed with cured herbs. When he was crouching inside, the squaws put a blanket over the circle and Tamarack began to pour his aromatic water on the hot stones. As the steam arose and engulfed him, he began to chant to the Great Spirit. Soon, as the sweat poured from his body, he began to entreat the Great Spirit.

"Oh, ho, ho! Great Being," he began, "I thank you for the many blessings thou hast bestowed upon the Caughnawagas and for having filled the belly of my daugther, Redbud, with new life and for bringing her healthy to its birth.

"Oh, ho, ho! Please grant that the child will be a boy and that he will become a great warrior and a chief.

"Oh, ho, ho! Grant that he will be able to run like a deer, to shoot with the eye of the hawk and to fight with the strength of the bear.

"Oh, ho, ho! Grant that he will be fierce to his enemies and gentle and true to his fellow Caughnawagas and that they will return his love for them.

"Oh, ho, ho! Grant that no harm will overtake the mother or the baby during childbirth and that they will both be well soon.

"Oh, ho, ho! Grant that we will kill many bears for a birthday feast and that we shall kill plenty of turkeys and deer to stew with our fat bear meat."

There was a pause, and then, in a lower voice, and as though in perfunctory deference to his new religion, Tamarack continued: "In the name of the Father, and the Son, and the Holy Ghost, amen. Almighty God, who made the world and the earth on which we tread, who made Adam out of dust and Eve from the rib of Adam, who brought Noah safely through the flood and set his ark to rest atop Mount Ararat, who brought the children of Israel out of the bondage of Egypt, who sent his only Son into the world to save our souls, grant that my daughter, Redbud, may give birth to a healthy baby boy, in the name of our Lord and Savior, Jesus Christ, amen."

Redbud did not hear the entreaties of her father. She lay racked with pain on a bed of animal skins in the women's house. "My back," she moaned, "the pain in my back. . . . I thought it would be in front. But, my back. . . . Aaaaaah!" She screamed aloud and her mother said to her sternly, "Lift your knees, my daughter. You must help him come. You must push. Push. Puuusssh!" Redbud obeyed, straining her stomach muscles. She felt her spincter muscles open and was powerless to close them against the rush of excrement. "Redbud!" her mother scolded in disgust. "I told you to cleanse yourself." Redbud did not answer. Her eyes were closed and she was gasping in pain, straining, straining, straining. . . . She fainted momentarily, regaining consciousness at the movement of the child within her. She felt his head pressing against the walls of her vagina, tearing it. . . . Redbud screamed again and again,—and once again fainted. She

awoke to a vague awareness of the women around her crooning in delight and singing happily. There was no more
pain. . . . Redbud felt drowsy and fell asleep again.

Reawakening, Redbud felt her mother kneel beside her and
whisper in her ear: "It's a boy. A big boy. A healthy boy.
God be thanked."

"Where is he?"

"They are rinsing him off with warm water. We had to
throw the skins outside."

Redbud giggled. "I'm sorry, Mother. I . . . I didn't know."

"No one does the first time," her mother said sharply.
"Here he is." Redbud sat up, tenderly receiving the baby into
her arms. He began to bawl, and she looked at him in dismay. Then he opened his unseeing eyes and Redbud cried
aloud in delight. "They're blue! His eyes are blue! Just like
D—" She paused and bit her lip, aware of her mother's stern
gaze. "But his hair is *red*!" she wailed. "I wanted it to be *yellow*!" Putting out a tentative finger, she touched one of the
red-gold ringlets on the child's head. "But it's so pretty," she
murmured. "Like the sunset. I will call him Red Deer." The
name made Redbud think of Deerfoot, and she began to cry.
Hugging the baby to her breast, she lifted her tear-stained
face to her mother and asked shyly: "Will the nipples on my
breasts turn brown now?"

The ships arrived in July, 1710, and Jed Gill immediately
hurried to Samuel Vetch's home to report for duty. He was
ushered into a tall, sunlit, book-lined chamber, where he
found Vetch seated at his desk talking to a slender man in a
militia captain's uniform.

"Jed, I'd like you to meet Captain Soames. Nathan, this is
Jed Gill, my right-hand man." Soames, whose face was heavily pockmarked, looked at Jed with open surprise, and Vetch
chuckled. "Just a baby, eh, Captain? Not yet twenty-one, but
he knows the Indians and the French like nobody else in the
colony."

Jed Gill blushed momentarily, starting as the captain said,
"Pleased to meet you, Mr. Gill," in a voice so deep that Jed
immediately recognized him as the outspoken man in Bartlett's Tavern in Springfield.

"I think we've met before, Captain," Jed said, smiling. "Or
at least bumped into the same tithing-man."

Soames peered at Jed in astonishment, grinning when he recognized him. "If it ain't the young hell-raiser was gonna spend his wedding night in jail. You sure gave old Yawkey a turn, young feller. I never saw the tithing-man in sech a tither."

Jed chuckled, and Samuel Vetch glanced back and forth between them. "You know each other?" he asked. Captain Soames said, "Not really," explaining the scene in the Widow Bartlett's taproom. "Damn meddlers," Vetch sniffed after he had finished. "Got the same problem here with the Mathers. Every time the governor wants to do something different, someone quotes to him from the *Essays to Do Good*. They're not so strong in Salem as they used to be, though—not since they hung the witches. Well, gentlemen, things are moving along. The House voted thanks to the queen yesterday, and today they're closing the harbor to outward-bound ships. A bit high-handed perhaps, but it's the only way to get the fourteen transports we need. And not a ship gets out till we get 'em. The House voted to raise nine hundred men in Massachusetts, too. There'll be another six hundred coming from New Hampshire, Connecticut and Rhode Island, too—with about four hundred British regulars. Marines. Best damn troops in the world. Half of 'em wild-eyed Irish. They took the queen's shilling in their cups and they've been taking it out on the Frog-eaters ever since. Two thousand men, all told—more than enough for Port Royal, if you ask me. The militia will be mustering today at Dorchester and Cambridge. Soames, I want you to take Cambridge and do your stuff." Vetch winked at Jed. "You've heard the captain talk?" "Oh, yes, Sir," Jed said, grinning. "It was hard to avoid it." Vetch grinned himself. "Out Springfield way they say he can shout down a bull. Well, gentlemen—hop to it," he concluded, rising to shake their hands.

Outside, Jed and Captain Soames mounted waiting horses and rode toward the Charles River.

"Two thousand men!" Jed exclaimed as they clattered over the bridge to Cambridge. "Where will they put them all?"

"Quarter them on the townfolk."

"But supposing they won't take them."

"They cain't refuse. They gotta take 'em—'any law or usage to the contrary notwithstanding.' That's the House speakin'."

"Do they pay the householders for their keep?"

"Sometimes. Sometimes not. Depends on how much money's left in the box."

"But that's outrageous! These are free men, subjects of the qu—"

Captain Soames reined in his horse and brought Jed's mount to a halt, too. "Young feller," he said, tapping Jed's knee, "you'd better put a halter on that sense o' justice 'o' yourn. I won't say you're the first young feller I've heard rantin' about freedom and a man's rights and all that other mush what's comin' out of France these days. Fact is, I seem to've heard a peck of 'em the last couple years. I will say, though, none of 'em gets fired up as quick as you kin. But, you listen to me, Jed Gill: that's the way we raise an army in New England, and they ain't no other way."

"But it isn't fair!"

"War ain't the time fer bein' fair. An' lemme tell you somethin' else: war ain't the time for freedom, either."

Jed said nothing, and they rode across the bridge in silence. Coming to the green in Cambridge, Jed was astonished to see company after company drawn up there. He followed Captain Soames as he strode purposefully through their serried ranks, mounting a small bandstand on which a drummer and a fifer stood to either side of a militiaman holding the Union Jack aloft. The drum began to beat and the fife squealed out the camp duty, bringing the men to attention.

Captain Soames stepped foward. "Stand easy, men," he bellowed, and a murmur of astonishment rippled through the sea of blue coats.

"Be he a man or a bull?" exclaimed one of the foremost militiamen, and his company burst into laughter.

"This is no laughing matter, men," Soames called, his deep voice seeming to rise out of his socks. "We're at war, and the colony needs men. I'm calling on all of last year's soldiers to reenlist. If you do, the court promises that you'll all come home as soon as we take Port Royal." He paused, hoping to hear eager shouts of approval. None came, and the captain held up a Brown Bess musket. "The court says if you reenlist you kin keep yer musket."

"Fer what?" a man in the rear ranks yelled. "Don't even

have a front sight to it. Cain't hit the broad side of a barn with a Brown Bess."

The assembled militiamen roared with laughter, and Captain Soames flushed. "How about some volunteers?" he shouted. "The colony will pay every volunteer a month's pay in advance and provide him with a brand-new coat."

"What's the coat worth?" came the query.

"Thirty shillings."

"Whose?"

"The queen's."

"Ow," a distinctly cockney voice rose from the crowd, "screw the bleddy queen."

There was a moment of shocked silence, until another voice rose in a mock falsetto. "Screw the queen? Why, you cain't even get close to her majesty."

Now the crowd of blue-coated militia collapsed with laughter, and the officers among them ran through the ranks trying to restore order. Even Captain Soames turned away, his eyes twinkling. " 'Taint easy getting these fellers to 'list again," he muttered. "Cain't blame 'em, either—after the messes of the last two years." He gazed wistfully over the heads of the milling militiamen toward Boston harbor. "Wisht t'Gawd I was 'listin' sailors. All you got to do there is get a press gang together and stop at all the brothels and taverns. Well," he said ruefully, "here goes." He ordered the fife and drummer to play the men to attention again and yelled: "I am empowered by the House of Representatives to inform all colonels of militia, that, if volunteers do not come forward, or last year's soldiers do not reenlist, the said colonels must draft as many men as are needed to fill their quota of ten men to a company. The said colonels are also instructed to appoint officers to conduct the men to their quarters." Swallowing, Soames assumed a solemn air and concluded: " '. . . any law or usage to the contrary notwithstanding.' "

A concerted cry of dismay arose from the assembled militiamen, but then, drums began to beat and fifes began to play, officers began to shout orders, and within fifteen minutes a crowd of about 450 protesting men was rounded up and marched to the end of the green, where they were quickly set to work erecting tents.

"Y' see, Jed Gill," Captain Sloames said, regarding Jed

with mournful eyes, "they ain't any way y' kin raise an army by bein' fair."

Because of the usual delays, the expedition for Port Royal did not sail until September 18, 1710. One by one the ships of the fleet—five small warships and about thirty transports, supply ships, and hospital ships—unfurled their flags and their sails and made for the harbor mouth. With Colonel Vetch and Captain Soames, Jed Gill was aboard the fourth-rater, *Chester*. Apart from his honeymoon sail to Nantucket, it was Jed's first venture upon the ocean and his very first time on the open sea. Severe winds baptized him with sprays of seawater as he sat on a capstan—"A green Gill if I ever seen one," Captain Soames punned heartlessly—struggling to control an eruptive stomach, and arising at times in an unsuccessful effort to walk on the swaying, heaving decks of the ship. "Don't eat none, Jed, that's the secret," Captain Soames advised, and Jed wailed: "I *can't* eat. Don't even *mention* food." Winking slyly at the sailors around them, Soames cried, "Oink! Oink!" and Jed groaned and leaned over the rail with open mouth and arched throat, a plume of vomit arching from his mouth. The sailors roared with laughter. Jed hung weakly to the rail, his only solace a resolution to murder Nathan Soames the moment he recovered. That occurred a few days later, and on the twenty-fourth, Jed stood confidently on the port quarter of the *Chester* as the fleet approached Port Royal's narrow entrance. Entering it, Jed noticed how the incoming tide seemed to buoy the ship and carry it along. Turning to Captain Soames, he asked: "Did Colonel Vetch speak to the admiral about what my Uncle Jon said about the tide here?"

"He did," Soames replied gruffly, "and the admiral told him he didn't need the advice of a beardless landlubber who'd never been to sea."

Jed shook his head ruefully, turning to watch a small transport following in the *Chester*'s wake. Lighter than the warship, it was immediately lifted upon the fast-running tide and swept toward the rocky shore of the harbor mouth. Jed gripped Soames's arm anxiously. Both men could hear cries of alarm from the transport, trying desperately to veer away from the danger. Suddenly, all its sails came tumbling down in an effort to slow its movement. Jed saw a splash beside the prow of the ship, guessing that the anchor had been dropped. But the tide carried the vessel inexorably toward the rocks. Now, Jed and Soames could see soldiers leaping over the sides of the transport. Some of them came up and began swimming ashore. Others did not surface.

"My God, can't we do something?" Jed cried. "Those poor fellows are drowning!"

"Not much we kin do," Soames said laconically, glancing toward the bow of their own ship. "See, there, Jed—all them ships is in trouble." He pointed toward the line of vessels beating against the wind toward the shelter of Goat Island, in sight of the French fort. "They've got all they kin do to keep clear of the rocks themselves. Seems like the admiral might've listened to Colonel Vetch. But that's one of the bad things about bein' a admiral. It makes y' deaf."

Jed did not hear him, gazing with horrid fascination at the stricken ship being driven squarely among the rocks. He could hear the faint sound of smashing timbers. Then he saw with relief that small boats had been launched and were moving among the swimmers, picking up survivors. Still, when the *Chester* dropped anchor off Goat Island an hour later, Jed learned that twenty-six sailors and soldiers had been lost.

On the following morning, his mood of sorrow changed to one of high excitement with the landing operations. While bands played martial tunes, he had entered one of the landing boats with Colonel Vetch and Captain Soames. Vetch was in command of two battalions assigned to come ashore on the north side of the port, General Nicholson with the other two battalions to land on the south. As the boats neared shore, Jed Gill kept an anxious eye on the French fort. Once again, its guns remained silent. Jed was a little disappointed, and his frustration grew the next day when the French concentrated all their fire on Nicholson's force pushing across Allen's River to entrench itself about four hundred yards from the fort. Vetch's troops were not fired upon.

"Some campaign," Jed sniffed in disgust as he sat down that night to share his mess with Captain Soames.

"Some folks likes glory, but I'll take it this way," Soames said. "Besides, I don't think them Frenchies is really got their hearts in it. From what Colonel Vetch an' me could see on reconnaissance today, I don't think there's many of them inside that fort. An' when we bring our own artillery up tomorrow, I think they'll quit.

A few days later Jed accompanied Colonel Vetch, Captain Soames and Vetch's battalion commanders to General Nicholson's headquarters for a council of war. Jed stood outside the general's tent watching the English artillery—siege guns and mortars from Nicholson's artillery train, squat coehorns from the ships—being dragged into position. Suddenly he heard the tap of a drum and saw a blindfolded French ensign in a white coat being led into camp by a militia captain. The two went straight to Nicholson's tent. A few minutes later, Samuel Vetch poked his head out and called to Jed: "Young fellow, we can use your French." Jed ducked inside the shelter, standing shyly at attention. Vetch handed him a sheet of foolscap with the gold lilies of France embossed upon it. "Can you translate?" he asked. Jed nodded, cleared his throat and addressed General Nicholson, seated at a field desk. "It's from Governor Subercase, Sir," he said, and the English general waved a hand impatiently and snapped, "What does he say?"

" 'I now write to tell you, Sir,' " Jed translated, his voice quavering slightly, "that to prevent the spilling of both English and French blood, I am ready to hold up both hands for a capitulation that will be honorable to both of us.' "

"Hear! Hear!" the assembled officers shouted jubilantly. "Three cheers for General Nicholson!" They gave the exuberant "Hurrahs!" while their general smiled broadly. Looking up at Jed, he said: "Tell the ensign to tell the governor that my terms will indeed be honorable. In the meantime, I shall continue to emplace my artillery."

Next day, to Jed's surprise, both sides began firing at each other; but they ceased almost as quickly as they had begun, and Jed realized that the artillery duel had been only a token exchange designed more to save each side's honor than to cause damage. A few hours later Subercase agreed to talk, and the next day he accepted Nicholson's terms granting the garrison honors of war and safe passage home in English ships.

"See?" Captain Soames crowed to Jed. "I tole you they was gonna quit!"

Jed nodded in disgust, but he was happy to march with Soames and about two hundred militiamen to the gates of the fort, where the English formed two ranks. General Nicholson marched between them, followed by Vetch and Sir Charles Hobby, and then his field officers. The gates swung slowly open and Governor Subercase marched out, handing the keys to the fort to Nicholson with a graceful bow. Nicholson returned the bow and turned the keys over to Vetch as a symbol of his office. Then the French band inside the fort broke into a gay, Gallic air and Subercase's soldiers came marching out with shouldered muskets and waving flags.

"See!" Captain Soames whispered into Jed's ear. "I tole you they wasn't many of 'em. I'll bet we outnumber 'em by six to one."

Jed Gill nodded silently, watching the ranks of white-coated French disappear in the direction of the waterfront. A week later, Jed was also marching toward the ships. Governor Vetch had asked him to stay in Port Royal—renamed Annapolis Royal—as his aide. But Jed was unimpressed with the barren little capital of Acadia, and yearned to be back with Rachel in the familiar warm bustle of Boston. So he went back aboard the *Chester* with Captain Soames.

"Well, young feller, you're a veteran, now," Soames chortled as they strode up the gangplank.

"Of what?" Jed countered sarcastically. "I think I was in more danger beside my roasting spit."

13

"Why, it's Mr. Vetch," Rachel Gill exclaimed as the tavern door opened and Samuel Vetch strode into the taproom. "Jeddy," she called into the kitchen, "Mr. Vetch is here." Jed Gill came out of the kitchen, where he had been filleting a big sea bass he had caught in the harbor that morning. He wiped his right hand on his apron and held it out with a smile. "This is a surprise, Sir—what brings you back from Annapolis Royal?"

"You don't know?" Vetch replied in surprise, seating himself at the bar. "I can't believe anything that big could be kept that secret. Not in Boston. You really mean you haven't heard about the Quebec expedition, either?"

"Quebec? Not a word of it. And we get our share of gossip in here."

Rachel nodded in assent, filling a mug from the beer cask on the wall behind her. "Here, Sir—have a mug of nice cool beer. It'll cool you off."

"It is hot down here," Vetch said, mopping his brow with a lace handkerchief. "A lot hotter than Annapolis. Thank you," he said, putting the mug to his lips and drinking deeply. "Aaah, that's good. Well, anyway, Jed Gill, we're going to capture Quebec for fair, this time. And all of Canada. The queen is hot for it. Those Mohawk chiefs we sent over a year or so ago made a big impression on her. She's all for driving the French out of the New World for good." He drank again, and added: "Of course, the new Tory government's for it, too. They'll do anything to embarrass the Whigs . . . rub some of the shine off the duke's victories."

"Marlborough, Sir? But I thought he was the hero of the age—the toast of all England."

"He was. And still is, to a great extent. But the Tories are working on that. They've got Dean Swift's pen on their side, now, and—"

"—*Jonathan* Swift, Sir," Jed broke in, his eyes shining with delight. "The Irish writer?" Vetch nodded, and Jed rushed on. "I think he's great! I think I've read everything he's written. *The Tale of a Tub* . . . *Battle of the Books* . . . all of them. He feels just like I do about religion and government. Corruption everywhere. Rotten. I tell you, Sir—"

Samuel Vetch held up his hand with a gentle smile. "Still on fire for justice, eh? Well, so's our friend Swift, especially now he's turned Tory. He can't forgive the Whigs for letting the Irish clergy starve. So now he's burning 'em with that poison pen of his. And what he's saying about Marlborough! No other man in England would dare one sentence of such criticism. And Swift's turning out whole pamphlets."

"But Marlborough is a great general, Mr. Vetch. The greatest since Alexander and Julius Caesar. What about Blenheim and Ramillies?"

"Swift says the duke's victories helped Holland and Austria more than they hurt France and Spain or helped England. So he's rubbed a lot of the shine off Marlborough's name, and now the Tory government figures it can finish him off by taking Quebec. First, by drawing troops away from the Continent they'll cripple the duke's movements and limit his chances for more victories. Then, if they can make America an English continent, they'll put all that he's done so far in complete eclipse."

Jed Gill's lips twisted in scorn. "So that's the way they run things!" he cried bitterly. "I saw more honor among the Indians. Our civilized masters are no better than pirates and highwaymen. All lace and perfume, but they still stink!"

"Jedediah!" Rachel exclaimed, aghast. "You mustn't talk like that. Please, Mr. Vetch, he doesn't mean it. He just gets carried away. It's those books he reads. . . . My father was the same way."

Samuel Vetch smiled at Rachel and patted her wrist reassuringly. "Of course, he means it," he said, his eyes twinkling at the glowering look on Jed's face. "And I wouldn't have him any other way. I was just like him at his age. But I'm older now, and maybe a little wiser. Certainly a little more scarred and bruised. But, he'll change. This is the way the world is run, and it's never been any different."

"It will be," Jed muttered, ignoring the reproof in Rachel's green eyes. "And I won't change, either. I'll change the world first."

"Bravo!" Vetch cried, clapping his hands in delight.

Jed grinned sheepishly. "Well, whatever the reason, it's a good thing we're going to get rid of the French. How big is the army going to be?"

"Twelve thousand men."

Jed's eyes bulged in astonishment. "God in heaven," he murmured. "My Uncle Jon told me Phips had only two thousand, and he could have won."

"Quite so. But I tell you, Jed Gill, the queen is on fire against French America. Seven of Marlborough's best regiments, six hundred Marines—and fifteen hundred of our own. That adds up to twelve thousand men."

"Who's in command?"

Vetch could not conceal his disgust. "Jack Hill," he replied. "General Jack Hill."

"Never heard of him."

"Well . . . Now, hold on to that temper of yours, Jed Gill. The fact is that Hill is the brother of Mrs. Masham."

"Never heard of her, either."

"She's Queen Anne's new favorite. The Duchess of Marlborough fell from grace, you know, and now this Mrs. Masham woman is in."

"But she has no title," Rachel interjected. "What does she do for the queen?"

"She's her tire-woman," Vetch said, again in a voice of disgust.

Rachel giggled, and Jed scowled and asked: "Tire-woman? What's that?"

"Hairdresser," Vetch said, actually chuckling when he saw Jed fling the dish rag the length of the bar and pound the mahogany with his fist. "Jesus Christ!" Jed swore. "A hairdresser's brother. And they've put the fate of our continent and the lives of twelve thousand men in his hands. If this is that worldly wisdom you were talking about, Mr. Vetch, I think I'm going back to the Indians." Pausing to draw breath, Jed realized that he might be abusing Vetch's patience and good nature, and he continued in a more controlled voice: "Excuse me, Sir, I don't mean to be offensive—but does General Hill know *anything* about war?"

"Not that I know of. He's a great favorite at court. I met him when I was in London. Beautiful manners. I daresay there isn't a man in the world could really dislike Jack Hill." Vetch paused, frowning. "I hope to God that doesn't include the French in Quebec," he muttered. "Of course, Hill is just in command of the land troops. Admiral Hovenden Walker will command the fleet."

"Never heard of him, either," Jed said, shaking his head ruefully.

"Neither did I until General Nicholson told me about him. Francis doesn't think much of him. Says he's the soul of incompetence."

Jed Gill groaned aloud. "I can't get mad anymore, Mr. Vetch—I just can't. I'm just sick, that's all."

"Oh, it isn't really that bad, Jed Gill. There's some very competent officers in the army and navy. They'll make up for their superiors' deficiencies, I'm sure. Why, General Nicholson will be in command of the Montreal expedition. He's an excellent soldier. He'll be leading a force of about twenty-three hundred men—mostly New Yorkers and Iroquois—against Montreal. Up the lakes and down the rapids." Vetch coughed. "And I, my dear young friend," he said, with a self-deprecating smile, "will be in command of our New Englanders at Quebec."

"Oh, Mr. Vetch, how wonderful!" Rachel exclaimed. "I'm sure you'll make Jed and me very proud of you."

"That's great, Sir—just great!" Jed cried, reaching under the bar for a bottle of Madeira. "That calls for a drink," he said, placing three glasses on the bar and filling them. "To your victory," he said, lifting his glass, and then, in a grim voice: "And the destruction of the French." Vetch inclined his head gracefully, and drank. "Superb, as usual," he said, smacking his lips.

"Mr. Vetch," Rachel began shyly, "would you be our guest for dinner tonight? We'd be honored."

"Yes, please do," Jed put in eagerly. "I've been cleaning a striped sea bass. I was planning to serve it with a shrimp-and-wine sauce. And we've just got a cask of excellent sack. Please, Sir—a slice of the breast and a glass of the best."

Vetch smiled. "I accept. But on one condition." Both Jed and Rachel exchanged glances, nodding their heads in assent. Vetch smiled again, downing the last of his Madeira with a pleased chuckle. "The condition is that you, Jed Gill, shall come to Quebec with me."

"Jedediah Gill, you are not going off to war again."

Jed and Rachel were undressing in the bedroom of their living quarters above the tavern. Jed scowled when he heard Rachel's voice. It had the tone of finality he had learned to dislike. Gradually, as they had fallen out of the romantic love that had bound them, and into the more bearable fondness of a devoted union, Jed had been astonished to learn that the little girl who had adored him and the youthful sweetheart who had spoiled him had grown into a mature woman with a mind and will of her own. "Uncle Jon taught you too much" became a favorite saying of his whenever Rachel not only disagreed with him but also went on to demonstrate the logic of her position. Now, watching Rachel undress beneath the betty lamp, Jed bit his lips, wondering how to overcome her opposition to his going to Quebec with Samuel Vetch. Rachel was naked to the waist, now, her hands on her hips, facing him defiantly. The flickering light made bright points on the pink nipples of her breast. The nipples made Jed think of Redbud. Redbud! He felt a pang of remorse. Did she have her baby? *Their* baby? Was it a boy? Did she name him Yellow Deer as she had said she would? Jed glanced anxiously at Rachel, wondering: shall I tell her? No, he thought: she wouldn't understand. Instead, he came to her and bent to kiss her breast and nibble gently on her nipple.

"No," she said, stooping to push him gently away, "not unless you promise not to go to Quebec."

"That's a typical woman's trick," he complained. "You're taking advantage of your sex. Besides, I have to go. I promised Mr. Vetch."

"You can tell him you changed your mind."

"Rachel, I can't do that. It just wouldn't be honorable."

"If you don't, you won't have a wife when you come back."

"Whaaat?"

"I mean it. I had a terrible time by myself when you were in Port Royal."

"But you said yourself Vetch's black boys were a great help."

"But they weren't a husband. There was nothing to do and no one to talk to after the tavern closed. I hated it—and I'm not going through it again." Rachel reached for her nightgown on the hook, preparing to slip it over her and finish undressing beneath it. "But, Rachel—I *have* to help drive the French out of Canada. It was your own father who taught me that. He trained me to hate them and he made me promise every day of my life to avenge my parents."

"Pa's dead, now," Rachel said with impeccable illogic, slipping the gown over her head, stretching her breasts taut as she did so.

"Yes, he is!" Jed shot back scornfully. "Murdered by the French. I tell you, Rachel, I'm going!" Rachel's voice was muffled beneath the gown. "So am I, if you go." Exasperated, but still unable to stifle the desire growing within his loins, Jed moved to lift her nightgown above her head. Rachel smiled to herself beneath its folds. Struggling halfheartedly, she allowed him to remove it and stood before him half-naked again. Once more, Jed bent to kiss her on the nipple. He drew down her knickers, and she stepped out of them. He swung her into the air, kissing her again on the breast and depositing her gently on their bed, where he plunged his nose into the pungent and abundant auburn hair at her crotch. Spreading her legs, he knelt between them. But Rachel covered her crotch with her hands. "Promise me you won't go," she whispered, fixing him with her tantalizing green eyes. "Oh, all right," Jed Gill gasped, feeling his loins throb—and she withdrew her hands, and he entered her.

Men are stupid! Jedediah Gill thought bitterly, rowing his fishing boat out onto the waters of the harbor. Esau sold his birthright for a mess of pottage, and Jedediah Gill sold his soul for thirty seconds of ecstasy. It was not, of course, thirty seconds; for Jed's desire had returned during the night, and

he had awakened a willing Rachel; and he had begun the day
with the same insatiable sensuality. But thirty seconds sounded better to Jed, and he cursed himself again for a dishonor-
able lecher. What, now, would he say to Samuel Vetch?

A horn blew loudly somewhere above him, and looking up,
Jed saw a huge ship-of-war bearing down on him. He pulled
frantically on his oars to get out of its way, leaning on the
oars as it swept majestically by, a great, massive wooden fort
that missed him by only a foot. He sat there, bobbing in its
wake, gazing upward in fascination at the smartly uniformed
Marines who leaned over the rails shaking their muskets at
him in mock reproof. He could hear a band playing and officers shouting orders.

Another horn sounded, and Jed saw yet another warship
making toward him, but not nearly so close: another . . .
and another . . . and another. . . It was the British fleet! Jed
sat fascinated in his boat all morning, watching the warships
and the transports arrive. Soon the harbor was crowded with
them, and it reverberated to the booming guns of the colonial
ships saluting them. Jed saw that the ships were headed for
Nantasket Roads, apparently intending to anchor off Noddle's
Island to unload their troops. He rowed after them. But the
distance was far too great. He would never be able to row to
Noddle's and get back in time to tend to his crab and lobster
pots. Reluctantly turning his boat, Jed rowed back the way
he had come. Behind him, faint on the wind, he could hear
the bands playing. An hour later, when he turned for a last
look, he was astonished to see an entire camp—with neat,
serried rows of tents—springing up on Noddle's Island.

"Jared Ankers is in town," Rachel announced when Jed returned to the tavern.

"Jared Ankers! What's he doing here?"

"I don't rightly know," Rachel said. She was drying and
polishing glasses and stacking them neatly upside-down on
the bar. "He says he's an aide to Admiral Walker." Jed's
mouth opened in disbelief, but Rachel continued on. "He says
he's been in London for the past year. Got to meet the admiral there. He says the Ministry was frantic trying to find
someone who knew something about Canada."

"So our nasty friend just happened to be handy. I wonder

who introduced him? Some other loyal Englishman in the pay of the French?"

"Now, Jeddy, you don't really know Jared is a spy. He was very nice. Asked to be remembered to you and everything."

"I don't *know* he's a spy, but I'm pretty damn sure of it. I'm going to have to speak to Mr. Vetch about Jared."

"Mr. Vetch?" Rachel repeated sharply, a steely look coming into her eyes. "What do you have to see him for?"

"I . . . I'm not," Jed stammered. "When he comes in here again, I mean."

Rachel shot a chilly glance at her husband. "We had other visitors," she said. "The constable and an officer of the queen. In fact, it's been a busy day. What took you so long?"

"The harbor was so full of ships I had a time of it checking my pots. What's all this about the constable and the queen's officer?"

"The whole town's in a tizzy, and I guess the colony is, too. The fleet arrived without notice, and nothing's ready to feed and quarter the troops. The Assembly's issuing orders so fast there's a new one out before the ink dries on the last one. The constable and the officer told me we can't raise our prices."

Jed's blue eyes blazed, and the scar at his temple whitened. "Who are they to say what we can charge?" he cried indignantly. "By God, even England herself wouldn't be that high-handed. It's Oliver Cromwell all over again. A regular dictatorship! So we have to sell our supplies at low fixed rates, and when the fleet sails and the rates rise, we won't have anything left to sell. I won't do it, I tell you!"

"You'd better," Rachel said calmly, placing the last glass on the bar and flipping her cloth over her shoulder. "The constable said he's got the authority to search the town for food and liquor. If we don't sell at the prescribed price, he can seize them."

"You mean break in here by force?"

"Yes."

"By God—" Jed began, but Rachel held up a restraining hand and said: "There's more. They can quarter troops on us, if they want—eight pence a day per man—and they're even impressing pilots and rounding up mechanics and laborers and making them work on Sundays."

Despite his anger, Jed Gill grinned. "On Sundays, eh—I

wonder what the Parsons Mather will have to say about that."

Rachel did not reply, looking up when the door behind Jed opened and Samuel Vetch came in. "Well, well, Mr. and Mrs. Gill, you both look fine today."

"Not so fine my sense of justice isn't bruised again," Jed said.

"Oh, I take it you mean all the . . . ah . . . acts of the Assembly. Can't be helped, young man. The fleet had such an uncommonly fair voyage they just burst in on us without warning. So the Assembly has to cram months of preparation into a few weeks. It'll make for some ruffled feathers. I imagine, but it can't be helped."

"The people haven't taken to the troops," Rachel said slowly. "Especially the officers. They're awfully arrogant."

"Yes, I know. They don't like our . . . ah . . . democratic ways. Sometimes I get the impression they don't believe we are really legitimate Englishmen. Bastard brothers beyond the sea. That sort of thing. Jed, can you provide me with some juicy venison and a bag of pheasants?"

"Now, Sir? Venison and game aren't good to eat at this time of year. The meat's flabby. Chances are it'll be wormy, too. That's why we serve almost nothing but seafood in the warm weather."

Vetch's face fell. "Oh, dear," he murmured. "I've been bragging to Admiral Walker about your delicious food and was going to have a private dinner for him." He frowned, but then his face brightened. "At least I might present him a pipe of your excellent Madeira. How about it, Jed Gill—can you spare a cask for your old friend? You name the price."

Jed nodded, eager to do Vetch a favor before telling him he was not going to Quebec. "Of course, Mr. Vetch," he said. "Where do you want me to deliver it?"

"Oh, I'll take care of that. I'll have my man take it over to the admiral's headquarters on Noddle's Island."

"No, no, Sir—I'll bring it over. Besides, I'd like to see the camp."

"Very well," Samuel Vetch said. With a smile for Jed and a bow for Rachel, he left the tavern.

In the morning, Jed loaded the cask of Madeira onto his fishing boat. Because the weather was hot, he put it under a pile of nets and blankets and began rowing toward the island.

When he reached it, he found a mounted British subaltern awaiting him on the wharf. "Is this for the admiral from Colonel Vetch?" the officer asked, and Jed nodded and the officer ordered two soldiers to put the cask on a cart and tow it away.

Jed secured his boat and began to prowl about the island. He was amazed by the order and precision of the camp. Troops were drilling everywhere, raising clouds of dust. Above the squealing of the pipes and the rattle of drums he could hear the voices of the sergeants hoarsely bawling orders. Just in front of him he saw a long, low building and heard drums beginning to beat a muster. Columns of soldiers brilliant in red coats and immaculate white cross-belts marched into the open area in front of the building to form a hollow square. The drums ceased and then Jed heard the tap of a single drum coming from the long, low building. A door opened and a drummer marched out followed by a soldier stripped to the waist walking between two sergeants. Jed was struck by the singular physical beauty of the half-naked soldier's muscular torso. He wondered what the occasion was, until he realized that the man was a prisoner and that the long, low building was probably a guardhouse. The drum still tapping, the sergeants led the man to a thick post standing in the middle of the square. They put nooses over his wrists, passed the rope over a notch at the top of the post, and hauled him up until he was standing on tiptoe, his powerful shoulder blades standing out like fins from his broad back.

Jed Gill gasped. *A flogging!*

Now a colonel in full dress accompanied by his officers came to stand in front of the guardhouse, watching. The sergeants stepped back, and the regimental sergeant major stepped forward from the assembled regiment while the drums beat a roll. Reading from a paper, the sergeant major cried aloud in a parade-ground voice: "Private Rory Quinn, Captain Gosse's Company, tried before court-martial and found guilty of drunkenness. Sentenced to fifty lashes with the hide whip. July 26, 1711. Lashes to be administered before entire regiment on parade, by order of Colonel . . ."

Jed did not catch the commanding officer's name, for the drums had begun to roll again, and the colonel called out grimly: "Sergeant Major, do your duty."

Saluting smartly, the sergeant major stepped toward the

right of the stake where a six-foot hide whip lay coiled like a blacksnake. He shook it out and snapped it gently. The drums rolled once more, and the whip sang out toward the bound prisoner. It snapped against his flesh with a hideous cracking sound and left a red welt squarely across his back, except for the bunched space between his shoulder blades. The man did not quiver.

"One," the sergeant major intoned, and cocked his whip arm once again.

Crrrack!

"Two."

Crrrack!

"Three."

Jed watched in horrified fascination. The whipping was as precise and rhythmic as the beat of a drum. Each welt appeared an inch below the other, until there were ten parallel red stripes on the man's back. Still, he made no sound. Jed admired his stoicism. But now the sergeant was starting at the top again. The whip sang and cracked for the first overlay. Blood spurted from the double welt. It trickled down his back, seeming to race the spurts from the other welts until it won by an inch and disappeared inside his trousers. The third overlay began, and the man's back was now wet with blood. Still, he did not cry out. Jed watched him pressing his mouth against his shoulder, gnawing at his flesh—biting himself like a wolf. It was not until nearly the end of the third overlay that he screamed.

Jed glanced at the officers. Their faces were grim, expressionless. Jed hated them and the entire British Army. He hated the sergeant for his cruel calm, the pitiless skill of his flogging, as though he exulted in the art of turning the living flesh of a brave man into a bloody chunk of skinned meat covered with crawling black flies. Tears came to Jed's eyes when the soldier defiantly stiffened his back for four more silent stripes after his first yell, but then he collapsed against the post screaming hideously.

Jed did not hear his final screams. He had torn his tear-filled eyes away and began to walk rapidly back toward the wharf, fearful of what he might say when the flogging was over. He jumped into his boat and began rowing back to Boston, conscious of nothing but the black hatred raging in his heart. He was halfway home before he noticed something strange about the pile of nets and blankets in the stern. It seemed to rise and fall. Jed thought he detected the gleam of a scarlet coat through the voids of the nets. A British soldier!

"Who's that back there?" he called sharply.

"Faith, and it's me, Danny Quinn," a voice answered in a thick Irish brogue. The pile heaved and the man sat up, wrapping himself in the blankets to conceal his telltale coat. He was big and handsome, with jet-black hair and the darkest blue eyes Jed had ever seen. He grinned sheepishly at Jed and said: "I hope yez don't mind me stowin' away in your boat."

Jed did not answer. He was studying the man's face. He seemed to resemble the soldier who was flogged. "You said your name was Quinn?"

"Aye, Danny Quinn of the County Wexford."

"Do you have a brother in the army?"

"That'll be big Rory. Ah, poor divil, I guess they've flogged him by now."

"They have. I saw it."

"Ah, Jaysus—did they make Rory cry out?"

"Not for a long time. Twenty-five lashes, I think. If it'd been me, I'd've been yelling at five. Your brother is a brave man."

"He is that, and it's kind of you to be saying it. But he's a bit daft, you see. 'Twas him that got us into the tavern where the recruiter was buying drinks, and before we knew it they'd gotten us drunk and we'd taken the queen's shilling. And now poor Rory gets drunk on his own and they give him fifty lashes."

"Is that why you're deserting?"

"No. I hit the sergeant that was arresting us, and they had me down for a thousand."

"A *thousand* lashes? I can't believe it!"

"Ah, sure, 'tis nothing. When I was in France, they sentenced a sojer to more than ten thousand stripes. But they stopped at eighteen hundred, and him almost dead. Ain't they the tender lads, though, the British officers."

"My God! What kind of men are they?"

"Divils," Quinn muttered laconically. "Divils in satin and lace. 'Tis the divil's own invention, Sir, the British Army. They told us of all the grand places we'd see and the pretty lasses we'd meet. But 'twas nothing but sweat, sodomy and the lash." He looked nervously behind him again. "You'll not be turnin' me in, Sir? They'll be after hanging me, now, you see."

"Never! I'd sooner return a man to hell." Jed began to row harder, wondering where he could hide the man. "But I can't keep you anywhere in Boston. There's a pretty stiff fine for harboring deserters. There's sheriffs and constables scurrying all over hunting for them. I understand there's been quite a few." They were nearing the wharf. "You'd better get back under those blankets and nets," Jed continued, and Quinn lay down again, pulling the coverings over him. In a few minutes, the boat bumped against a piling and Jed made it fast to the wharf. "Stay here," he whispered. "I'll be back after dark to bring you some civilian clothes. And, remember—don't move."

Walking back to the tavern, Jed was still wondering what to do with Quinn. Even the outlying villages were too dangerous. Springfield! At the very western end of the state. He could send him to the Widow Bartlett's. She surely could use a big strapping fellow like Quinn around her place. Entering the tavern, he saw that the taproom was empty. Rachel was in the kitchen, and the barmaid was polishing glasses. Jed went quickly upstairs and found a worn old doublet and trousers, which he rolled into a ball. Opening the window, he pushed the clothes out onto the edge of the roof overhang. Then he went downstairs. "I've got to go back to the boat," he called to the barmaid. Going outside, he stood on tiptoe to retrieve the clothing and walked back to the wharf with it under his arm.

Climbing carefully into the boat, he whispered, "It's me, Danny," and the big man threw off his covering. "Here, put these on, and stuff your soldier's clothes into the fish box." Danny Quinn complied quickly. In a few moments, he was a civilian. He grinned in the dark. "A bit tight, Sir," he said softly, "but thank God yez're as big as yez are."

Jed pressed a pound note into Quinn's hand. "Take this. And make for Springfield in the western end of Massachusetts. Springfield, y'hear?" Quinn nodded, and Jed said: "Here's a little map I made to show you how to get there. Ask for Bartlett's Tavern. It's run by the Widow Bartlett. Tell her Jed Gill sent you. The young fellow who almost spent his wedding night in jail. You got that—Jed Gill?" Quinn nodded in the dark. " 'Tis a foine name, Sir." Jed chuckled. "I'm sure the Widow Bartlett will be glad to have a big fellow like you helping her at the tavern." Quinn coughed. "Widow, Sir? what would her age be?" Jed chuckled again. "Fifty-five years and three hundred pounds." "Ah, sure, you can't have all the luck," Quinn groaned. "But it's grateful I am to you, Jed Gill. You've saved me life, you have. I can't repay you now, Sir, but I will someday. And in the meantime, it's me own sainted mother'll be praying over you like you was the second person of the Holy Trinity." They shook hands and left the boat. Jed led Quinn to the Common and showed him the way west. "Move at night and sleep by day," Jed said, and they shook hands again and parted.

Back at the tavern, Jed saw that the taproom was filling up. There was a murmur of voices, the loudest of them a pair of British captains.

"Sour lot, these provincials, wouldn't you say, Gosse?" one of them said in a voice of disdain.

"Quite so, my dear Fox. A bad business, I'd say, giving them their own charters. You'd think there were no king in Israel, the way they go on. Every man guiding on himself. The admiral has written the queen about it, you know. He's told her the people here grow more stiff and disobedient every day."

"General Hill's simply beside himself."

"Charming man, the general."

"Beautiful manners, of course. Quite wasted on this ignorant rabble. What's needed is someone with a bit of steel in his spine. Someone like the duke."

"Careful, Gosse."

Captain Gosse smiled thinly, plucking fastidiously at his lace cuffs. "Oh, I daresay there's none of the Ministry's spies about. Unless you are going to report me, my dear Fox."

Shaking his head amiably, Captain Fox said, "I say, Gosse, I am thirsty." He lifted his hand in the air and snapped his fingers imperiously. "Ho, there—innkeeper!"

Jed Gill waited three full seconds before he turned his head in the officers' direction, giving no sign that he recognized them as having been witnesses at the flogging. He walked slowly to their table. "Yes?"

"What do you have to drink, my good fellow?"

"Beer . . . sack . . . rum . . . brandy . . . Madeira . . ."

"Madeira, eh?" Captain Fox exclaimed. "You don't say!

We'll have a bottle. And the food? We've heard yours is the best on the waterfront."

"Thanks," Jed grunted grudgingly, deliberately omitting the "Sir." "Tonight's special is shad baked in cream with spinach stuffing."

Captain Fox's eyes sparkled. "I say, Gosse, sometimes these provincials amaze me. The last time I had shad baked in cream was at White's. That will do me, my good fellow," he said to Jed, and Captain Gosse inclined his head in agreement.

Good fellow, eh? Jed thought grimly, walking back to the kitchen. They'll find out. He gave the order to Rachel and returned to the bar, still staring into space and listening intently.

"I say, Fox," Captain Gosse was saying, "I do hope her majesty listens to the admiral's proposal. After we throw the French out of Canada, come back here to tidy up the provinces. Take their charters away and put them all under one government. A *strong* government run from London. No nonsense."

"I agree. I say, this Madeira is uncommon good. I wonder where the fellow gets it. But, you're right, Gosse—and we've got the forces to do it. In fact, I'd say we've got to do it. Once these fellows get the French off their back, they'll be even more stiff-necked."

You're right there, Jed Gill thought. He turned to enter the kitchen, pausing when he heard Captain Gosse say: "Were you at the flogging today, Fox?"

"Wouldn't have missed it for anything. Cheeky beggar. I'd rather expected to hear the music a dozen lashes sooner. Sorry the colonel didn't give him a few more stripes for stiffening his back that way."

"Well, you can't say the sergeant major didn't do his duty. He's an artist with the whip, old Jack. I daresay there's no one in her majesty's army can make the leather sing like Sergeant Jackson." Captain Gosse frowned, plucking at his cuffs again. "Quinn has a brother, you know. Both in my company. Trouble-making Irish if I ever saw one. The brother was scheduled for the post tomorrow. One thousand lashes."

"My word!" Fox exclaimed, almost spilling his drink. "I've never seen more than five hundred. I'll be there, my dear Gosse—rely on it."

"No, you won't, my dear fellow," Gosse said gloomily. "Quinn's escaped. Hit the turnkey on the head with his manacled fists, took his keys and unlocked his irons. Walked out of the guardhouse in full uniform as pretty as you please."

"Shocking!"

"The colonel's outraged. He's offered to promote the man who brings him in. But so far they haven't seen hide nor hair of him. Oh, we'll get him, my dear Fox. He's probably hiding somewhere on the island. The provost marshal says he couldn't have got away by water." Captain Gosse ground his teeth together. "When we do get him, I'm going to have him flogged—and *then* hanged."

"Quite right," said Captain Fox, and Jed walked back to the kitchen with a little smile tugging at the corner of his mouth. "Shad ready, yet, Rachel?" he called, and Rachel nodded, turning from the stove to hand him two plates. "Where'd you put those rotten clams?" Jed asked, and Rachel pointed to a slop bucket. Jed walked to it and stopped to seize a clam. He held it to his nose. "Whew!" he snorted in disgust. Putting the clam on a block, he minced it. Then he carefully inserted a pinch of the mess inside the shad's spinach stuffing. "That should suit those fine gentlemen out there."

"Jedediah Gill!" Rachel exclaimed in consternation. "You can't do that! It'll ruin our reputation."

"They're leaving in three days. They can tell everyone in Canada how bad our food is."

"You might poison them!"

"It won't kill them—but they'll wish they were dead. Nothing like a bit of tainted fish to rowel up a man's stomach. I hope they put them in the same hospital with their flogged soldier, so's he can hear them moan."

Jed carried the plates out to the waiting captains. Smiling warmly, bowing graciously, Jed placed their meals before them. "Enjoy your dinner, gentlemen," he said, and walked back to the bar.

That night after Rachel and Jed went to bed, Jed said to his wife: "Rachel, I'm going to go to Quebec."

"But you promised!" Rachel wailed.

"I know I did. But you tricked me. You got me all riled up so that I didn't know what I was saying. It was like Jacob tricking Esau. But after what I saw at the flogging today and what I heard that arrogant pair of officers saying—I have to go."

"Then I won't be here when you get back," Rachel said in a dull voice that carried no conviction.

"Yes, you will. I'll get Mr. Vetch to send over his black boys again, and I'll ask him if Mrs. Vetch can't visit here some nights."

"Thanks a lot," Rachel murmured sarcastically.

"Rachel, I've got to go! The queen certainly wants to drive out the French, but I think she wants to take away our liberties, too. I told you what those officers said. And Mr. Vetch suspects that the reason the queen sent so many troops was to have them on the scene when she revokes our charters."

"But what's that got to do with you?"

"*Somebody* has to know something about war! Your father always said raw militia can't stand up to well-aimed cannon. When the time comes, we're going to need combat leaders. And I'm going to be one of them."

Rachel said nothing. Jed wondered if she were weeping. He thought of "Rachel weeping for her children, and refusing to be comforted for them, because they are not," and wondered if his wife was afraid that he would be killed. He put out his hand to feel her cheek, but it was dry. To his surprise, Rachel murmured, "We'll talk about it tomorrow," and then rolled over to embrace him. She came to him, all girlish tenderness and ardor, her lips as soft as rose petals. Before he fell asleep, Jed Gill concluded that a woman was a much more mysterious being than he had believed.

Three days later, when the mighty British fleet set sail for Quebec, Jedediah Gill accompanied Captain Soames and Colonel Vetch aboard the warship, *Edgar*, the flagship of Admiral Hovenden Walker.

14

On the stern of the *Edgar* as it cleared the harbor mouth and
turned to port to sail northward along the coast, Jedediah
Gill thrilled at the sight of the great armada forming in line.
There were nine ships of war (plus four others on patrol
duty), two bomb ketches and some sixty transports and other
ships. It was a splendid sight—the sails turning faintly pinkish
in the glow of the rising sun—and it turned out to be a bliss-
ful voyage until the fleet sailed into the Gulf of St. Lawrence.
There, a sudden storm compelled the ships to seek shelter in
Gaspé Bay. A few days later they steered north and then navi-
gated into the waters of the mighty St. Lawrence River.

"What island is that, Sir?" Jed asked, pointing to a huge
land mass rising off the starboard quarter.

"Anticosti. We'll soon be into the widest part of the river."
Vetch stared forward and muttered, "I don't like it. I'm not a
sailor, but I've been here several times before. There's an
uncommon stillness in the air, and it could be the lull before
one of the river's typical east winds."

A few hours later Jed was standing on the stern when
Vetch, who had been to speak to Admiral Walker about his
misgivings, rejoined him.

"What did the admiral say?" Jed asked.

Vetch made a wry face. "He told me he was not accustomed to taking the advice of landlubbers."

"Sounds just like Port Royal," Jed said, his voice and face somber. He looked astern, turning, craning his neck from side to side. "My God, I can't see land on *either* side. This is a *river*?"

"We're at the widest point. Seventy miles wide." Night was falling, and Vetch watched the light fading from the skies with anxious eyes. Wisps of fog curled around the tops of the masts. "We've been steering north too long," he muttered. "I think we're nearing the north shore. There's some pretty treacherous shoals up there. Around an island called Egg Isle."

Up forward on the bridge, Admiral Hovenden Walker called to the captain of the *Edgar*. "I say, Paddon, we're not far from the south shore. Signal the fleet to bring to, under mizzen and main topsails, heading south. I'll be in my cabin if you need me."

The *Edgar*'s signal guns began to fire, and the ships of the fleet changed course. Still standing on the stern, Samuel Vetch relaxed. "That's better," he said to Jed. Within a few minutes, a breeze began to blow from the east. The fog began to thicken. In his cabin, Hovenden Walker undressed and lay down in his berth, quickly falling asleep. He was awakened by Captain Paddon, who cried: "We've sighted land, Sir!"

"Must be the south shore," Walker mumbled. "Damme, Paddon, signal the fleet to wear and bring to with heads northward."

Once again the signal guns spoke above the murmur of the rising gale. The ships changed course again. "This is not good," Vetch said to Jed. His hand tightened on Jed's arm. To port the sky was clearing magically and the stars were shining with peculiar brilliance. But then great flying wreaths of clouds rushed beneath them and obscured them. Soon there was a screeching of wind howling above the surface of the river, whipping it into a frenzied froth. A driving rain struck Jed and Vetch full in the face. The ship rose and plunged as though it were out upon a wild sea, and the two men clutched each other to stay upright. A vent appeared in the fog and Vetch saw the white caps of breakers on all sides. "Land!" he shouted. "My God, it's the *north* shore."

Samuel Vetch rushed forward and down below to the admiral's cabin, throwing the door open and shouting: "Up, Sir, up—there's breakers all around us!"

"Damn your cheek," Admiral Walker roared, coming erect in his berth. "You damned provincial landlubber, get out of here!"

Appalled, Vetch turned and ran back on deck. The admiral, still muttering darkly, sank back on his mattress. But the sound of trampling and shouting overhead alarmed him, and he arose and was slowly putting on his dressing gown and slippers when Samuel Vetch appeared once more and cried: "Admiral, for the love of heaven, we need you topside!"

Growling, "Out of my way," Walker pushed past Vetch and slowly climbed the ladder. Emerging on deck in his slippers and robe, he was not a sight to inspire confidence in his frightened sailors, some of whom had already run for the davits and were swinging out lifeboats. Seizing a speaking trumpet, Walker bellowed: "Avast there! Get away from those boats!" Even with the trumpet, his voice was too weak to carry above the sailors' shouting and the shrieking of the storm. Captain Soames ran to Walker's side, crying, "Give me the trumpet, Sir—I've got a loud voice." Too shaken to reply, Walker silently relinquished the horn and Soames put it to his lips to repeat the admiral's orders. His voice burst upon the terrified seamen like a thunderclap. At once, they stood in their tracks and the sailors at the davits left off lowering the boats.

Suddenly, the wind tore a hole in the fog and the moon shone through, illuminating breaking surf to leeward. "What do you make of it, Paddon?" Walker asked the ship's captain. "It's the south shore, of course, isn't it?" Paddon shook his head. "The French pilot we captured swears it's the north shore. Shoals of rock everywhere. That's why I let down the anchor, Sir."

"*Anchor?*" Walker roared, aghast. "My God, cut the cable! Haul on all sail and beat to windward for an offing."

Slowly, the ship drew off, with all eyes but those of the scurrying seamen turned anxiously toward the sky. Ruptured cloud masses raced wildly across its face, howling dreadfully. The wind blew crackling gusts of water off the surface of the water and hurled them against the ship and its decks with the sound of pistol shots. A plume of water struck Jed Gill in the face with such force that he screamed aloud as though his eyes had been scalded, and for a moment he feared they had been blown out of their sockets. Gradually, the *Edgar* withdrew farther out on the river. The gale still tormented her, but she was safe. So were all the other warships and most of the other ships, although the miserable night was made even more dismal by the sound of ships' guns firing distress signals. But shortly before dawn there came the terrible sound of crashing timbers from the direction of the north shore. Faintly on the dying wind came the sound of injured men screaming, of calls for help. There was a rush to the starboard rail, but nothing could be seen. Gradually, the light of dawn seeped through the fog. Then the wind rose and shredded it, scattering wisps of mist like a flower girl tossing petals. Jed Gill stared through the thinning fog in horrified fascination at the sight of perhaps a dozen British ships driven among the rocks and reefs surrounding a humpbacked island and breaking up there.

"Egg Isle!" Samuel Vetch groaned.

The cries of hundreds of drowning, struggling soldiers and sailors were not audible above the rising wind, but Jed could see through his glasses the black dots of heads bobbing on the water, the larger oval shapes of floating casks. Broken masts and spars, gun carriages and splintered chests were driven over the rocks by the boiling white water and washed up on the beaches. Regularly, the black dot of a human head would strike a rock and vanish.

Admiral Hovenden Walker and Captain Paddon stood not far from Jed Gill and Samuel Vetch, watching through their own glasses. Jed saw that the admiral's face was ashen. His hands trembled. He put down his glasses and spoke in a low voice to Paddon, and soon the *Edgar* was signaling the fleet for the smaller ships to work their way inshore to bring off survivors from the rocks of Egg Isle.

It took three days for the ships to save about five hundred soldiers and sailors. But nearly one thousand were lost, and Admiral Hovenden Walker immediately called for a council of war.

"Councils of war!" Colonel Samuel Vetch snorted, taking his place beside Jed Gill in the stern of the boat that was to row them to the *Windsor*. "Do you know who shouts the loudest at councils of war? The faint-hearts, howling down the fighters. And they always outnumber them, damn their lily livers. Why do so many cowards want to command? And I'll tell you why timid commanders always call a council, Jed Gill. To excuse their own cowardice! 'Therefore, taking counsel from the experience and wisdom of my assembled officers . . .' Therefore and wherefore, the twin crutches of the solemn donkeys who back into history with their arses presented to the enemy."

"You sound just like my Uncle Jon, Sir," Jed said, chuckling heartily as he reached out to seize the Jacob's ladder dangling down the *Windsor*'s side. The two men climbed aboard. The officer of the deck saluted and said: "You're the first to arrive, Sir. The general's quarters are below." Vetch thanked him and strolled aft. "Let's wait a bit, Jed," he murmured. "It wouldn't do for a provincial to precede a regular. Might start a civil war." Jed grinned and accompanied him to the stern, where they studied the anchored ships of the fleet. Then they turned to watch the arrival of General Hill's colonels.

Jed started when he saw a soldier standing sentry by a lifeboat. Could it be . . . ? Was it the man he'd seen flogged? "Excuse me, Sir," Jed said to Vetch, and walked up to the soldier. "Is your name Rory Quinn?" The man's eyes swiveled in their sockets toward Jed. "It is that, Sir."

"I saw you flogged, Rory," Jed said softly. The man's eyes glinted like blue steel. "It was by accident. I just happened by." Jed lowered his voice. "I can't apologize for the British Army, Rory, but for the honor of England I can say that I'm sorry."

Quinn's eyes softened. "Honor is it, Sir? Sure, you're the first honorable thing I've seen in England since I took the Queen's dhirty shilling."

Jed smiled. "How's your back?"

"Better, Sir."

"How are Captain Gosse and Captain Fox?"

Quinn's eyes widened in astonishment. "How did you know, Sir? They brought them to the hospital half-dead, they was that sick. Groaning and moaning and calling for the chaplain."

"What, from a little food poisoning?"

"Was that it, Sir? Sure, the regimental surgeon near went

daft trying to doctor 'em. Bleedin' 'em an' leechin' em, an' all."

Jed smiled again. Stepping closer to Quinn, he whispered: "Your brother Danny got away."

Quinn's eyes shone but he kept his lips compressed. "S'truth, Sir?" Jed nodded, stepping back to address him with an authoritative air meant to disarm the officer of the deck, who was watching them. "He hid in my boat, and I rowed him back to Boston. I gave him a change of clothes and money. He should be in Springfield in the west by now."

Quinn brought his musket smartly to port arms as though in response to an order, and Jed turned to rejoin Vetch. Together they went below to General Hill's cabin.

Admiral Walker and General Hill sat together at a table surrounded by their chief commanders. Jed Gill was surprised to see Jared Ankers standing behind the admiral, and he smiled to himself when he saw Jared staring at him in astonishment. Jed studied General Jack Hill. He could see why he was never described as anything but debonair. He was elegantly clothed in the uniform of a brigadier and wore an immaculate white wig. He greeted his officers warmly, bestowing upon each a glance of special favor as though each were a prized and cherished acquaintance. When Admiral Walker opened the meeting, he listened to him with an air of deference.

"We have suffered a severe loss, gentlemen," the admiral said grimly. "Not a disaster, perhaps, but a blow which, to be truthful, was not quite unexpected in an armada of this size proceeding up a great and treacherous river with no pilots to guide us." Walker paused, and Samuel Vetch thought grimly to himself: you mean sailing up a seventy-mile-wide river fifty miles off course! "The loss of a thousand lives—one-twelfth our strength—before we have even joined the battle, would give any commander pause," the admiral continued. "And I might say that neither I nor General Hill envisioned such enormous casualties when the battle itself was joined. The question now arises, gentlemen, whether or not we should proceed. I, for one, as the officer responsible for the safety of the queen's ships and stores and the lives of eleven thousand of her brave soldiers and seamen, give it as my considered opinion that the task—if not impossible—is at least fraught with dangers of the most melancholy consequences. Because

of the delays caused by the colonies having been most grossly
—I might have said most reprehensibly—unprepared for the
victualing and supplying of the fleet, to say nothing of the in-
clemency of the weather, we are fast approaching a season of
the dire Canadian winter." The admiral shuddered. "It will be
a time when *the ice in this mighty river freezing to the bottom* could utterly destroy and bilge our ships as though they
were being squeezed between rocks." A chill seemed to creep
into the cabin following that doleful sentence; but Jed Gill,
who had been watching Jared Ankers carefully, was sure he
had detected a glint of mirthful satisfaction in Jared's eyes.
So *that's* who's been scaring the pompous old pussycat out of
his wits. Jared's really earning his French pay this time.

"It is, perhaps," the admiral continued, "a blessing in dis-
guise that we should have suffered our misfortune so far
down the river. For I view it as a distinct possibility—if not a
certainty—that, upon arriving before Quebec, we should have
found our provisions reduced to a very small proportion, not
exceeding eight or nine weeks at short allowance, so that
eleven thousand men must have been left to perish with the
extremity of the cold and hunger. Nay, I must confess that
the very contemplation of such a calamity fills me with fore-
boding and horror. How dismal would it be to behold the
earth and seas locked up by adamantine frosts, and swollen
with high mountains of snow, in a barren and uncultivated
country. How horrible and melancholy has it been to contem-
plate the prospect of vast numbers of brave men famishing of
hunger, of seeing them drawing lots to determine who should
die first to feed the rest."

A shocked murmur arose in the room. Jed Gill, still scruti-
nizing Jared, swore that he saw a suppressed smile tugging at
the corners of his little pinched mouth. "But, as I say, gentlemen," the admiral concluded, "we have called you here for
your advice and counsel. The opinion I have given comes
only from a brother officer, albeit one who has been entrusted
with the safety of this enterprise by her majesty the queen.
We shall be pleased to hear from you."

At once, Samuel Vetch arose, pretending not to notice the
irritable disdain with which he was regarded by Admiral
Walker. "I think we should proceed to Quebec, your Excellency," he said. Another murmur, one of scornful disapproval, arose—and Vetch saw that General Hill's polite smile

of inquiry had frozen on his lips. "After all, Sir," Vetch went on, "Sir William Phips got to Quebec without pilots. And he sailed two weeks later than we did. Besides, all our warships are safe, and we've still got eleven thousand men, Sir—five and a half times as many as Phips had."

"I am aware, Colonel Vetch," Walker replied frostily, "of Sir William's expedition, having taken the care to provide myself with a copy of his log. I am also aware of his failure, one which, I might add, was not complicated by the misfortune of a disastrous storm."

General Hill broke in, leaning his chin delicately forward on an impeccable white hand. "It seems to me, my dear Walker, that the entire question turns on the competence of the pilots. It would seem that our best course at this juncture would be to have them brought in and examined."

"Yes, yes, of course," Admiral Walker replied testily. "But first I would like to question Colonel Vetch. Would you, Sir, be willing to act in the capacity of pilot?"

"I am sorry, your Excellency. I was never bred to the sea. It's no part of my province. But I do know the river, and I think I can be of service by showing you where the most dangerous spots are."

Walker smiled with polite deprecation. "Yes, I see, Colonel Vetch. So good of you." He turned to Hill. "I think, General, that we had best begin examining the pilots."

One by one the pilots were brought in, and they all disclaimed any working knowledge of the river. "I told you that when you impressed me," one salty old sea dog with a white beard complained. "But you brought me here anyway."

"Hold your tongue, varlet!" Captain Paddon snapped. "Or I'll have it pulled out of your head."

While the pilots were being questioned, Jed Gill conferred in whispers with Colonel Vetch. "All that nonsense about the Canadian winter, Sir—it's absurd. I'm sure the admiral got it from the man standing behind him. He's a French spy. I can't prove it, but I'm positive." Vetch was astounded. "Perhaps you'd better relieve the admiral of his misapprehensions." After the pilots had filed from the room, Vetch stood up and spoke to Walker. "With your permission, Excellency, my young friend here has something to say about the climate here."

The admiral glared at Jed. "What are your credentials, young man?"

"I . . . I was a prisoner of the Indians along the river for nearly five years," Jed replied in a faltering voice, aware that his legs were trembling and that a battery of unfriendly eyes was trained upon him. "With all due respect, Sir, the . . . the St. Lawrence doesn't really freeze to the bottom in winter. In fact, many Canadians go ice-fishing in the basin of Quebec."

Swiveling in his chair, Walker spoke to Jared. "What say you to this, Mr. Ankers?"

"It ain't true," Jared replied calmly. "This man is trying to lead you into a trap, Sir."

"That's a lie!" Jed shot back angrily. "You're a liar, Jared Ankers! You always were! Admiral Walker, I grew up with this man. He was captured in the same raid I was. He's not telling you the truth, Sir. He's a French spy!"

A scraping of chairs in the cabin, as the officers turned around to peer at Jed, mingled with exclamations of amazement. Admiral Walker brought silence by striking his table with the flat of his hand. "Poppycock!" he sputtered. "A man introduced to me at court by a member of the Ministry is an agent of the French? Sit down, young man! I'm not going to listen to any more damned nonsense."

"Thank you, Sir," Jared Ankers simpered. "I never seen this feller before in my whole life. An' if they's any French spy in this room, it's him tryin' to do you all in."

"Quite right, quite right," Walker muttered, glaring again at Jed. "By rights, I should put you in irons."

"Oh, no, Sir!" Colonel Vetch cried in a voice of horror, shooting to his feet. "I can vouch for Jed Gill. He's a hero in his vil—"

"Please, gentlemen, please," General Hill interrupted in a tired voice. "Let us not allow this council to degenerate into a debate over the Canadian winter. We have heard from the pilots, and now, I should think, my dear Walker, the whole question turns upon what your naval captains think of going forward. In your opinion, gentlemen, should we proceed?"

"Positively not!" Captain Paddon growled.

"Not in these currents and without pilots," said the captain of the *Windsor*.

"It would be reckless to the extreme," a third captain said.

To a man, Admiral Walker's ship captains declared it was

impossible to go to Quebec. Walker turned to the *Edgar's* captain and said: "Paddon, you will please signal the ships to change course." Samuel Vetch was still standing. He fixed the admiral with a less-than-deferential eye and said in a loud voice: "As I stand here, the only man from the colonies with a command of any importance, I must, for the honor of those who placed me here, go on record as utterly opposed to any deviation from our purpose. The late disaster cannot, in my humble opinion, be in any way imputed to the ignorance of the pilots. Sir William Phips arrived before Quebec under the guidance of even less informed pilots. No, your Excellency, the catastrophe was not due to navigation but the course we steered, which most unavoidably carried us upon the north shore. Who directed that course, you best know, Sir. And our return without any further attempt will be a vast reflection on the conduct of this affair, and it will be of very fatal consequence to the interest of the crown and the British colonies."

Vetch sat down to an enormous and hostile silence, broken only when General Hill spoke to him as though in careless afterthought: "Quite so, my dear colonel, you are indeed in a peculiar position. I should suggest that you put your objections in writing and forward them to the Ministry. Gentlemen, this council is now declared ended."

Vetch and Jed Gill were the first to leave the cabin, going outside with fists clenched and tears of shame and frustration forming in their eyes. On deck, they saw that it was dark. The running lights of the ships bobbed on every side. There was some confusion at the quarterdeck among the departing captains and colonels calling for the boats that were to take them back to their ships. "I don't want to mix with that mob," Vetch murmured in distaste. "Anyway, I told our bos'n to keep clear. He's probably either fore or aft. I'll go forward to look for him, Jed, and you go astern." Jed nodded and walked slowly aft. Failure again! he thought bitterly. And that lying swine of a Jared Ankers! He reproached himself for having given Jared those lifesaving moccasins. I should have let Howling Wolf finish him off!

His eyes now accustomed to the dark, Jed peered over the stern rail. He could just make out the shapes of the ships. He could hear their anchor chains clanking slowly up the hawse pipes. There was a soft footfall behind him . . . Jed whirled, just as a shape lunged out of the darkness. He saw a faint gleam of steel and threw up a protective hand, deflecting the point aimed at his heart into his shoulder. "I'm gonna kill you, Jed Gill!" Jared Ankers's voice panted, and the knife came free and was plunging down again straight for his heart—when there were more footsteps and a soft Irish voice calling, "Doon, Sir . . . doon!" Then Jed heard the sharp spat of wood on bone, and the shape slumped to the deck. Soundlessly, Private Rory Quinn stooped and seized Jared Ankers and threw him over the side. The splash when he hit the water was smothered in the noise of the commotion at the quarterdeck, and Jed turned to Quinn with an extended hand: "Thank you, Rory—you saved my life."

"Ah, sure an' I owed you a life, Sir, you helpin' me brother Danny get away."

Both men leaned over the rail, studying the dark surface of the river. "Do you think he'll be able to make it ashore?" Jed asked.

"Not with the taste of the butt I give him, Sir. His crock is cracked for sure. But, you, Sir—yez'd better get over to sick bay and have a look at that hole in yer shoulder." Jed Gill put a hand to his wound and felt the thick blood oozing out. He could feel it trickling down his chest inside his shirt.

Even with this little souvenir, he thought wryly, it's still more dangerous at the roasting spit.

The War Against the Abnaki

15

The tall, carved oak door in the governor's chamber in the Château St. Louis in Quebec closed noiselessly, and Father Sébastien Rale, his feet moving soundlessly beneath his black soutane, glided forward to greet Philippe de Rigaud, the Count Vaudreuil, Governor of Canada.

"Sit down, my dear Father Rale," Vaudreuil said, seating himself behind his massive desk and leaning forward toward his visitor. "As an intelligent and observant man, Father, you must realize that the Treaty of Utrecht solved nothing. True, we have lost Port Royal and Nova Scotia. But the question of boundaries remains unsettled. The treaty, of course, provides for boundary commissioners, but let us pray to *le bon Dieu* that they never meet; for if they do, they will surely quarrel and start another war. So you see, Father, it is just as it has been since 1689—the mixture as before."

"I do not understand, Excellency. I have just come from the bishop, and he told me only that you wished to see me. You have a mission for me, Monsieur?"

"I do, with the full approval of Monsieur the bishop. But I must fill you in, first, Father. As you know, the war ended in 1713 and it is now 1720. In those seven years, the wretched *Bastonnais* have been returning to the lands from which they were driven in both wars. They have been crossing the Kennebec River into lands which are the sacred soil of France."

"But don't the lands belong to the Abnaki?"

"They do, under the protection of King Louis. But as you know, the wretched *Bastonnais* will swindle an Indian out of his land for a bottle of rum. Now they are reclaiming the lands with those absurd titles of theirs. This is encroachment. The Kennebec has always been regarded as the dividing line between France and England in the New World. Worse, the Abnaki have mistakenly concluded that the Treaty of Utrecht has ended French power there. They have sent messengers to the English asking for peace. They have even made a treaty with them, declaring themselves subjects of the English crown. As a result, there has been a steady stream of settlers into the region of the lower Kennebec. We cannot permit this, good Father. This is soil sacred to France. Its very name—Maine—comes from the beautiful province in our dear homeland. Moreover, the Kennebec leads to the Chaudière River, and the Chaudière leads to here—right where we sit, my dear Father Rale—to Quebec, the heart of New France."

"But, how can you stop this, Excellency? Surely, you do not plan to send troops? It would start another war."

"*Evidemment*. Obviously. The answer is not to confront the *Bastonnais* with French military power. It is to restore the Abnaki to their allegiance to France. Then they will take care of the English settlers. Eh, Father—*comprenez vous*? And it is you, my dear Father Rale, who will do this for King Louis."

"Me? But I am only a poor priest. A missionary."

"Yes, and there are times when a priest and missionary is worth three regiments of foot."

"I serve no earthly master!"

"Well said, Father. It is a phrase and a sentiment worthy of a Brébeuf or a Gabriel Lalemant. But there are no more martyrs in New France, Father. They have done their work and our Indians are converted. The Iroquois no longer chastise us. The age of the glorious apostleship to the savages is over. I have informed myself of your bravery, Father Rale, of your diligence and devotion. In another time I am sure you would have won your crown in heaven with your life's blood, like Isaac Jogues or Charles Garnier. But you are a missionary, not an apostle. You are a shepherd tending your flock. You must know, my dear Father, that religion is the chief bond by which these savages are attached to us. And you, as a Jesuit, are charged above all others to keep this bond firm. Finally, may I remind you that you are also a subject of the French crown."

Father Rale lifted his chin. "If I can serve my king by serving my God, I am content."

"Again, well said, Father." Vaudreuil arose and walked to a wall map of the region between Canada and Acadia. "This is Maine," he said, pointing with a finger. "And this is the lower Kennebeck. See how it curves here? There is a meadow there, and on the meadow above the river is the village of the Norridgewock Abnaki. Norridgewock is like an advance outpost of New France, Father. It blocks the easy river route to Quebec. It is a rallying point for all the other Abnaki. From it, you may begin your mission of returning our allies to their former allegiance."

"When do you want me to go there, Excellency?"

"As soon as you can."

Upon his arrival in Norridgewock, Father Sébastien Rale called for a council of the local chiefs and those of the surrounding Abnaki. He opened his gathering with the question: "Why do you allow the English heretics to settle on your lands?"

"They say it is their land," an old chief named Wawatam said, rising to his feet. "They say they bought it from us."

"For a bottle of rum?" Father Rale asked sarcastically. "A string of beads? They are thieves!"

The old chief shifted his feet in embarrassment. "They say it is legal. They show us deeds with our totem marks on them. They say if we do not let them settle, their new king will punish us."

"King George? That duck-bottomed Dutchman sitting on the English throne? The King of France has never granted any of these lands to that pig of a German. They belong to you, under the protection of King Louis. And you cannot sell these lands, because they belong to the whole community."

"But we are chiefs," Wawatam objected.

"Who drank the rum? Whose squaw wore the beads?" There was an embarrassed silence, and Father Rale pressed on. "Certainly not the tribesmen. And even if you had had the consent of the tribesmen to sell—which you didn't—you still could not do it. You chiefs of the Abnaki hold these lands in trust for your children, for your children's unborn children. To sell them is to violate that trust, and those pieces of paper which the treacherous *Bastonnais* wave under your nose are just that: worthless scraps of paper. You must recover your lands. You must drive the English off them."

"But the English are strong. They beat the French in Queen Anne's War."

"That is not true, Wawatam," Father Rale said slowly, astonished by the old chief's bluntness, but careful not to insult him. "The *Bastonnais* are great liars and twisters, and I'm sure they told you that because the king gave them Port Royal, they won the war. But King Louis never wanted Port Royal. It was a burden on the crown. We are building a better port and a stronger fort at Louisbourg. But the *Bastonnais* wanted Quebec, Wawatam. They sent a great armada—a hundred ships and fifteen thousand men—to get it. Did they tell you what happened at Quebec, Wawatam?" The chief shook his head, and Father Rale gave an exultant laugh and said: "The great God and the Holy Virgin who favor true religion sent a terrible storm which wrecked their fleet and sent them scurrying back to *Bas*ton. Some day, my children, we will go to Egg Isle in the St. Lawrence, and there you can count the whitened skulls of the English soldiers and seamen." He paused for effect. "Five thousand of them."

Cries of amazement arose from the assembled chiefs, but Father Rale was quick to notice that Wawatam and three or four other chiefs seated close to him said nothing. When the outcry ceased, Wawatam said: "But that was the great God. It was not the French."

"But he is on the side of the French. Do you want to be on the other side from God, Wawatam?"

"The white man's war is not the Indian's war," the old chief said slowly. "We don't want to fight for the English, but we don't want to fight them, either. We hate them, but we need them for trade."

"You cannot trade with the French?"

"The English have better goods."

"Yes, when you can make a fair trade," Father Rale replied sarcastically. "Why is it that when the English come to trade for your furs they always get you drunk, first? And where are the trading posts that Governor Shute promised you in the treaty, Wawatam?" When the old chief lowered his head in silence, the priest pursued his point. "There are none, are there? Instead, there are forts. Forts to guard your land that they stole from you. You must realize, you chiefs of the Abnaki, that the loss of your land means the loss of your freedom. It has been well said that the Spanish in America want gold, the French want furs and the English want land. Land, land, land! It is the English God. They lust for it insatiably. Look about you! Wherever you go, you see the English surveyors' marks on the trees. But they go deeper than bark. They cut straight and deep into the soul of the Abnaki."

Angry shouts of approval followed Father Rale's reference to the hated surveyors, and the priest pressed on, encouraged. "The English say they want to live peacefully with you side by side," he sneered scornfully. "They say they love you. But what do they really say among themselves. They say, 'The only good Indian is a dead Indian.' I tell you all, chiefs of the Abnaki, the English will take from you all the land they can get, until there is nothing left for you but a little hollow in the hills where you can live like moles." Father Rale raised his voice dramatically. "Chiefs of the Abnaki, you have to— you *must*—recover your lands!"

Once more furious cries of approval arose from the assembled chiefs.

"Kill their cattle!" they shouted.

"Burn their haystacks!"

"Poison their wells."

Father Sébastien Rale beamed in delight, carefully keeping his eye on the silent Wawatam and his friends.

"That is good," Father Rale said. "But remember, my children, no shedding of human blood—for now."

In the ensuing months, plumes of smoke spiraled skyward from burning barns and hayricks west of the Kennebec. Father Sébastien Rale was delighted, until the enraged officials demanded reparations from the wayward Norridgewocks. To Father Rale's angry surprise, Chief Wawatam persuaded his frightened tribesmen to give four hostages to the English and to promise to pay two hundred beaver skins in damages. At once, the priest sat down to write to Governor Vaudreuil:

> There is an "English party" in the village which is busily undoing the good work I have been able to do so far. It is my belief, Monsieur le Gouveneur, that an old chief here named Wawatam is secretly in the pay of the English. It is he who has persuaded the Norridgewocks to do their bidding, and it is my fear that they might go over to them.
>
> These savages are as unstable as water. As often as I harangue them, they denounce the heretics or boast to my face of the brave deeds they will do against the English. But once they are out of my sight, they are persuaded by this reprehensible Wawatam to confer with the English, whereupon they return to the village and accuse me of lying.
>
> They are now preparing a council to discuss the English invitation to an interview at Georgetown, a settlement on Arrowsick Island at the mouth of the Kennebec. It is my conviction, M. le Gouveneur, that we must control this council. Therefore, I am requesting that you send to me some trustworthy braves among the converted Indians of Canada, whose attachment to France and the Church is beyond all doubt, and who have been taught to abhor the English as children of the Devil. I suggest Abnaki from Becancour and St. Francis, Hurons from Lorette, and Iroquois from Caughnawaga. I particularly recommend that you send to me the brave young Caughnawaga chief named Half Moon. . . .

"Why do you wish to go to Norridgewock, Redbud?" Half Moon asked. "Is it because it is so much closer to Deerfield?"

Redbud flushed and bit her lip. "You think I'm running after Deerfoot. I'm not. I want to be with Red Deer."

"Red Deer is twelve now. The presence of his mother on a journey will embarrass him. Besides, women cannot join war parties."

"I do not wish to go on a war party. I have a friend in Norridgewock. She is the squaw of the chief named West Wind. I will stay with her."

"Redbud, you are still in love with Yellow Head."

"Maybe I am," Redbud said, lifting her face defiantly.

"Why do you not become the squaw of some strong brave in our village? You are still the most beautiful of the Caughnawaga women. You could still bear children."

"After a woman has known a man like Deerfoot, there can be no one less than he."

"So you think the white men are better than the men of your own race?"

"No. In strength and morals and courage, I think the red men are superior. We did not know how to lie and steal until the white men came. But the white man is clever. He makes things that do his work, like wheels and plows and sails. He lives off the beasts, with his horses and cattle and sheep that haul and carry for him or give him milk and cheese and meat and woolen clothing. Or his gunpowder and his cannon. These are the things that give him his advantage over us. But he is not better than us. Inside, he is greedy and scheming and covetous. Covetous, that is a word that Father Rale used to use. The white man wants the world."

"If you feel that way, how can you love Yellow Head?"

"He was not like that." Redbud's face softened. "Maybe it was because he was young. We were both young. And we loved each other with the passion and the joy of youth. Sometimes it . . . sometimes it hurt." Redbud's voice was sad and wistful. "We weren't together long enough to get to know each other . . . to find fault . . . to let the children come between us . . . to let our love grow cold. That is why I cannot forget, Half Moon—I have only love to remember."

Half Moon was exasperated. "How can you love him?" he exclaimed scornfully. "A man who betrayed your brother, who killed two of your fellow tribesmen, who warned the enemy and disgraced you and your family. All this he has done to you and yours—and you still love him? You are mad, Redbud!"

"Is that what they say about me in the village? Because I see things too clearly, I have to be mad? Anyway, Half Moon, I wish to go with you to Norridgewock. When the canoes gather at the riverbank tomorrow morning, I will be there." Half Moon said nothing, and Redbud put a tender hand on his shoulder. "Thank you, my brother," she murmured.

When Half Moon and the other Indians from Canada arrived at Norridgewock, old Chief Wawatam realized instantly that his cause was hopeless.

"War!" he shouted with the other chiefs, when the question was put to a vote in council. But he did not accompany the band of 250 warriors who paddled down the Kennebec under the leadership of Father Rale, another Jesuit and two French officers. Upon their arrival at Georgetown, the Frenchmen stayed in the boats while Half Moon led the war band toward the fort. There, they paraded back and forth, waving French flags, dancing, bobbing their hideous painted faces up and down, shaking their spears and muskets and howling threats at the English. A drum beat a parley, and an English militia captain came out accompanied by two lieutenants. "What do you want, you filthy savages?" he yelled, keeping carefully close to the gates.

"Our land!" Half Moon shouted in reply. "We have come to tell you English to leave the Abnaki lands forever. If you do not go, we will burn your houses to the ground!"

"You have broken your word," cried the captain, inching quietly back toward the gate. "What of your treaty?"

Symbolically, Half Moon pulled a piece of parchment from his shirt and set it afire. "There is your treaty," he said contemptuously, dashing it to the ground and stamping on it with his moccasin. "And this is what we will do to you English if you do not leave the Abnaki lands."

Half Moon kept his word. A few weeks later he reappeared with his Indians, burning twenty-six English homes and attacking the fort, retreating only after the English received reinforcements.

Father Sébastien Rale was overjoyed.

Te Deum laudamus [he wrote to Governor Vaudreuil]. We praise thee, Lord. We have begun to succeed, your Excellency. The burning of the homes of the heretics is now almost a daily occurrence west of the Kennebec, and the English fort has been put on notice that its days are numbered. Now, it seems to me, would be the time to introduce a few troops of regulars into the affair. Perhaps they might be dressed as Indians in paint and breechclouts.

My dear Père Rale [Vaudreuil wrote in reply], you are to be congratulated for the skillful and discreet manner with which you have conducted so delicate an operation. However, to send French soldiers against the English would be to abandon the discretion which you have so far admirably maintained. The crown is most anxious to avoid another war. The English, of course, must be driven over the Kennebec; but to this end we must let the Indians act for us. To this end also, our most gracious king has instructed me to allow you a pension of six thousand livres, which you may distribute among the Indians in the form of presents of arms and ammunition, or of food and clothing for the squaws and children while the warriors are away raiding the English. I salute you, my dear Père Rale, and pray to the most Holy Virgin that she may look over you.

Monsieur le Gouveneur [Rale wrote in his next communication], I am overcome with astonishment. It is as though *le bon Dieu* has favored you with the gift of prescience. For you could hardly have imagined, when you implored our Blessed Mother to look after me, that the Holy Virgin would be so quick to answer your prayers. Yes, M. le Gouveneur, I write to you as one preserved by the miraculous intervention of the Blessed Virgin Mary.

Only a few weeks ago the wretched *Bastonnais* placed upon my humble head a reward of a thousand pounds, hoping thereby to lure my Indians away from their allegiance to me. My children's reply was to return to the warpath, pillaging and burning, and this time, I regret to report, killing English settlers. Presently, *les Bastonnais* raised a band of three hundred militia, which they dispatched to Norridgewock with instructions to demand from the Indians "the person of the said Jesuit, Rale, and the other heads and fomenters of this rebellion." Upon refusal, the English war party was to seize my unfortunate person and carry me away to Boston for trial.

Warned of the English approach, I immediately rushed to the chapel, where I swallowed the consecrated wafers and hid the sacred vessels, hurrying to the woods to take shelter there in a cave behind a waterfall. I swear to you, Excellency, it was the Virgin herself who directed my steps to that cave. I had never seen it before, and yet I found myself inside of it, crouching there in my wet and muddy soutane, telling my beads while all around me I could hear the wretched *Bastonnais* thrashing through the underbrush and cursing and calling for me by name.

Unfortunately, sundry of our correspondence has fallen into English hands, and I write to tell you that you must be prepared to deny the allegations which undoubtedly soon will be placed before your gracious king in Paris.

It is also painful to report that an incursion of our Indians, incensed by the attempt to seize my person, though successful in the extreme through the burning of the village of Brunswick and the capture of nine families at Merry-meeting Bay, has thoroughly enraged the English to the extent that the governor of the colony of Massachusetts and its Council have now declared war against the Abnaki and their allies.

It was New Year's Day, 1723, and Lieutenant Governor William Dummer of the colony of Massachusetts was surprised and dismayed to be summoned to the office of Governor Samuel Shute. Dummer had spent the previous evening and much of the early morning saluting the new year with sack, Madeira and mulled port. His smile, as he entered the governor's chambers, was not gay and his step was not sprightly.

"My word, Dummer, but you look peaked," said Governor Shute.

"Yes, I am feeling rather dainty. It must have been the mulled port. I have never believed that one can improve a fortified wine by stirring it with a heated poker. But I shall manage."

"Quite so. But, now, I must tell you, my dear Dummer, that I have found these people in the House and the Assembly impossible. I do believe they are more interested in victories over the governor than victories over the Indians. As you know, they wouldn't grant me the money to build those trading posts I promised the Abnaki. They refused money for presents for the Norridgewocks, and as a consequence I had to take old Wawatam off the payroll. If I plan a campaign, they want to control supplies and conduct operations under a committee of their own. Imagine! A *committee* conducting a campaign. Instead of springing to arms, they'll spring to the ballot box. They think they can solve everything by a vote. They may even try to win the war by passing a resolution disqualifying the Abnaki. Look what they did to my man, Walton. The only thing they didn't like about him was that he was appointed colonel commanding by *me*. So they have brought charges against him, as you know."

"Yes, I know," William Dummer said, laying a delicate finger against his throbbing temple. "A pity one can't reason with them."

"It is just not possible, my dear Dummer, and this, I must say, is the last challenge. If I knuckle under to them here, there will be no more royal authority in the colony. And I would have served my king as the most cowardly sort of craven." Governor Shute paused dramatically. "So I am leaving for England today."

"Good Lord, Sir—you can't mean it!"

"I do, indeed," Shute said grimly. "Only the few servants I'm taking with me know about it, and now you. I want to lay my case before the king and Council before these dreadful libertarians can set their agents at court to work blackening my name. And so, my dear Dummer, as a present for New Year's Day 1723, I am leaving you the colony of Massachusetts—with all that irascible, stiff-necked, purse-pinching, crackbrained crowd of parliamentarians that goes with it."

"You are too kind," William Dummer murmured wryly.

Because William Dummer was that rare being among humans—a patient man—he was able to persuade the Assembly to grant him the necessary money to prosecute the war against the Abnaki and their allies. In the first year of his office, his new commander, Colonel Westbrook, successfully led an expedition against the Penobscot at the town of Panawamske. Finding the village empty, they nevertheless burned it, together with its chapel. In the following year, the jubilant Dummer prepared another stroke against Norridgewock itself.

"The chief fomenter of the rebellion is the priest Rale," the lieutenant governor said to Colonel Westbrook. "Seize him, and the Indians will come to us with their hands up."

"I agree, Sir."

"I understand the village is heavily fortified?"

"Not anymore, Sir. At one time it was surrounded by a nine-foot stockade. But that old Wawatam got them to knock it down. Now it stands open and shouldn't be too difficult to storm. Besides, I've brought an exceptionally able Indian-fighter from Boston."

"Boston? Do they fight Indians there? I thought it was only the king's officers."

Westbrook smiled. "He just lives there, Sir. He's really a frontiersman. He was captured in the Deerfield massacre and lived nearly five years among the Indians. His name is Jedediah Gill, and I can tell you, Excellency, I've already learned from him. He told me the Indians have two tactics against the English. First, the Indians never bunch together when they march and fight, while we English always do—and that's true. So we're easy to hit. Second, when they're in the woods and find a body of English, they always know that's all there is, because we never divide our forces. So they're never afraid of being struck by a second force. But they always divide and scatter so that we can never get at a main body."

"Very interesting, Colonel. And please remember—the priest Rale is to be taken alive. Also the young chief, Half Moon, if you can."

"It will be a pleasure," Colonel Westbrook said grimly. "And the only reward I want is a front seat at their trial."

On the eighth of August 1724, Colonel Westbrook put 208 men in four companies aboard whale boats at Fort Richmond and sent them upriver to Taconic Falls. There they disembarked, leaving forty men to guard the boats, and marched through the forest of Norridgewock.

On the advice of Captain Jedediah Gill, Westbook had divided his force into four companies under the overall command of Captain Harmon. Jed Gill marched side by side with Harmon. Toward evening, Harmon and Gill heard shots and screams up ahead.

Jed Gill stiffened in horror when he heard the screams. It had been fourteen years since he had heard that voice, but he

knew it. He ran swiftly up the trail until he came to a clearing filled with wild blackberry bushes. A terrified squaw
struggled in the arms of two English scouts, one of whom
held his hand over her mouth. Another Indian woman lay on
the ground.

Jed ran and knelt beside her. "Redbud, it's me, Deerfoot,"
he cried, seizing her hand and bringing it to his lips.

"Deerfoot," she gasped, struggling to come erect. He
pushed her back gently. "Let me look at you, Deerfoot," she
pleaded, and he helped her sit up. She gazed at him with lov-
ing eyes, until she became convulsed with pain again and
sank back on the ground. With horror Jed Gill saw the
spreading red stain at her breast. Her voice sank and he bent
closer to listen. "Kiss me, Deerfoot," she said, and he pressed
his lips softly against hers. "Remember? At . . . the . . .
waterfall! You taught me . . . how . . . to kiss?" Tears came
to Jed's eyes, and he kissed her again. "Our son . . . Red
Deer . . . is at Norridgewock. Take care of him, Deerfoot."
The light was fading fast from her eyes, and Jed had to come
still closer to hear. "I loved you, Deerfoot—there was no one
else. Please . . . don't hurt Half Moon . . . or Father Rale."

Jed nodded, clutching her hand. "We have orders to take
them alive," he said.

But Redbud of the Caughawagas did not answer.

She was dead.

The woman whom the scouts had captured was the squaw
of the chief, West Wind. She gave the English a complete
description of the village. She said that it was empty in the
afternoon, when most of the men were working in the cornfield above it. On the twelfth, Captain Harmon took about
eighty men upriver toward the cornfield. Captain Moulton,
accompanied by Jed Gill, took about the same number
through the woods to Norridgewock.

At about three o'clock, Moulton's men, spread out as skir-
mishers in Indian fashion, emerged from the underbrush in
front of the unguarded village. Not a sound issued from the
cabins. The chapel was also quiet. "Let them see us," Jed
whispered to Moulton. "They'll get excited and fire every
which way. Tell your men to hold their fire until the Indians
have emptied their muskets."

Moulton nodded, and the order was transmitted to his

men. Five minutes later, a yawning Indian strolled out of a cabin. Jed started. It was Half Moon!

Moulton's men shot erect, and the startled Half Moon let out a war whoop and dived back into his cabin. Immediately, screaming squaws and children burst from the cabins and ran for the river. Half Moon emerged again, saw Jed Gill, and with the cry of "Die, you traitor" raised his musket and aimed it at Jed.

Now perhaps sixty Indian braves ran into the square, firing madly. One of them bumped Half Moon's arm just as he pulled the trigger, and he missed. Now the ranked English fired a volley. It riddled the Indians. Perhaps twenty of them leaped into the air or were bowled over backward, to writhe screaming in the dust. The rest of them reloaded and fired again. A man beside Jed moaned and pitched forward. Jed aimed at a Norridgewock sprinting for the river, hitting him just as he jumped for the water. He disappeared beneath the surface. All of the squaws and children were in the river now, trying to wade across through the low water. Some of the braves swam over. Jed was disgusted and angry when he saw the musket balls making spouts among the terrified women and children. Many of them sank out of sight. Other Indians had jumped into their canoes, jumping out again when they realized the paddles had been left in the cabins.

Yelling madly, the English crowded down to the riverbank. They lay on their bellies to pick off Indians in the water or scrambling up the farther shore. The ragged reports of their guns counterpointed their shouts and the screaming of the stricken or the whimpering of children.

Behind him, Jed Gill heard an outburst of shots. He rose and ran toward the chapel. About a half-dozen English lay on their stomachs shooting at the little peak-roofed structure topped with a rough log cross.

"That son of a bitch of a priest is in there shooting at us," a man yelled. He saw a tall lean man with a sharp face. Jed recognized him as one of the scouts who had killed Redbud. A shot came from the chapel, and the man clutched his wrist and yelled in pain. "I'm gonna come in there and kill you, you black-robed devil!" he shouted, shaking his fist at the chapel.

"No, you won't," Captain Gill said. "We're taking Father Rale alive."

"Says who?"

"Governor Dummer, Colonel Westbrook . . . and me. Did you hear that?" The man glowered silently, staring at his wrist, on which a red welt had risen.

"Cut a tree for a battering ram," Captain Gill called to the other men, and they scrambled erect and made for the woods. For about ten minutes, the clearing rang to axe blows, and then the men reappeared dragging a fallen beech. Seizing it under their arms, they ran toward the door.

Wham!

The frail little building swayed, and the door buckled.

Wham!

The log cross came tumbling down and the door swung backward, hanging on a hinge. The English cheered and charged inside, led by Captain Gill. A musket fired, and one of the men groaned and sank to his knees. Jed Gill saw Father Rale standing at the altar. The little brass tabernacle door was open, and an empty gold chalice stood in front of it. Jed guessed that Father Rale had been swallowing the consecrated hosts. Jed turned and motioned his cheering men to silence. He walked slowly toward the priest, who was bent over reloading his musket. Jed was amazed at how Father Rale had aged. His jet-black hair was pure white, and his smooth saturnine face had begun to wrinkle.

"Put down your gun, Father," Jed called softly. "You're under arrest."

"Eh? Is it you, my young friend?" Father Rale stood erect, straightening his black soutane. "But neither of us is so young anymore, eh, Deerfoot? And by whose authority do you arrest a French subject on French soil?"

"King George of England."

"But King George and King Louis are not at war. You had better do better than that, my young friend."

"Massachusetts is at war with the Abnaki and their allies," Jed replied, growing exasperated.

"I see," the priest murmured sarcastically. "King George has given you the power to declare war. Most gracious of him."

A growling came from the man behind Jed, and the sharp-faced man snarled, "Let's stop his filthy mouth and string him up!"

"Right!" another man shouted. "Hang the popish swine."

"He's the bastard what's behind all the killin' an' burnin'."

They moved past Jed toward Father Rale, and the priest lifted his musket. "One more step, and one of you dies," he said softly.

"Get away from him!" Captain Gill ordered, and the men faltered. "Please, Father," Jed pleaded. "Give me your musket. You're outnumbered."

"The person of a priest is inviolable, and it is my sacred right to defend myself."

"But if you shoot one of my men, I won't be able to stop them from killing you."

"If I were afraid of death, would I have come to Canada?" He turned to the militiamen and cried in a stern voice, "Be gone, you ruffians! You stand on the altar of God, already desecrated with your presence. Leave this holy place at once!"

"Like hell!" the short man snarled, raising his musket and aiming it at Father Rale. "I'm gonna put a ball right inside your Goddam Injun-lovin' heart!"

"Allow me," Father Rale said, unbottoning the top of his soutane and baring his white-haired chest. He moved closer to the militiaman. "Now, even heretic carrion like you can't miss." With an oath, the man fired, and Sébastien Rale pitched forward dead.

"You fool!" Jed Gill hissed, kneeling beside the fallen priest. "Taking him back to Salem for trial was half the purpose of this mission!" Realizing that the priest was dead, Jed arose and drew his pistol, wheeling savagely on the man who had killed him. "You're under arrest!" he began, pausing when he heard a commotion outside the chapel. Men were hooting and jeering.

"Hang 'im!"

"That's right—string 'im up right now."

"No, no—let's scalp 'im alive first."

Hurrying outside, Jed saw a group of men hustling a young Indian toward an oak tree with strong low limbs. The youth's hands were bound, and there was a rope around his neck. Jed Gill gasped. Although the boy was unmistakably an Indian in his features, his hair was dark red and his eyes were blue. Jed ran forward to push the militiamen aside and confront the boy. "Is your name Red Deer?"

"Y-yes," the youth stammered, licking his lips and glancing around him with frightened eyes.

Jed motioned with his pistol toward Red Deer's bonds. "Untie him," he said.

Cries of rage and protest arose from the men. "*Untie* him? We're gonna *hang* 'im!"

"No, you're not," Jed said quietly. "Unless you want to hang yourselves for the murder of an English subject."

"Captain, you're plumb crazy?" the sharp-faced man yelled. "He's not English—he's an Injun!"

"He's both. He's my son. And the son of any English subject is an English subject himself."

There was a silence. One by one, the men peered at Red Deer's face, noticing for the first time the light copper hue of his skin and the color of his hair and eyes. One by one, they scratched their heads in perplexity and strolled away, mumbling to each other in low voices.

Jed untied Red Deer and put his hands on the boy's trembling shoulders. "I am your father, Red Deer," he said softly.

The youth's lips trembled. He bowed his head, digging his knuckles into his eyes, and Jed turned mercifully away, realizing that Red Deer was struggling against a flood of shameful tears. In a moment he felt him touch him and say, "I thank you, Father—you have saved the life you have given me."

Jed nodded, overcome. He took the boy's hand. "It is getting dark, Red Deer. Come, we must find a place to sleep."

That night, as Jedediah Gill lay under the stars with Red Deer asleep beside him, he pondered what to do with his son. He had never told Rachel about Redbud. He was afraid that for him to introduce his half-breed son into their home—where there were already three Gill sons, and another child expected—would wreck their marriage. Rachel would be scandalized. Fond as she was of him, she would be crushed by the self-righteous condemnation of her Puritan neighbors. They would make her an outcast. No, he could not bring Red Deer back to Boston.

But what could he do with him? With her dying breath, Redbud had asked him to take care of their son—and he had promised that he would. Setting him free to fend for himself in the wilderness, or sending him back to Caughnawaga, would be a base violation of that sacred pledge. But what to . . . ?

Jed sat erect in the dark. Daniel Quinn! Danny Quinn, the Irish deserter from the British Army whom he had helped to freedom. Jed had heard from him every year or two since the Quebec disaster. The Widow Bartlett had died of a fall down the tavern's cellar stairs, and she had left the place to her daughter, whom Danny had married. They had a family of their own. But Danny Quinn had never left off begging for a chance to repay the great favor done him by Jed Gill. Now was his chance! Jed would take Red Deer to Springfield and ask Danny to raise him to manhood. In the intervening years, Jed would have time to think of some way to introduce the young man into his household. But, for now—it was Springfield and Danny Quinn!

Jed fell asleep, and when he awoke in the morning, he was more confident in his plan. Sitting up, he saw the militiamen down at the riverbank pulling drowned Indians from the water and scalping them. Jed shuddered in disgust. He remembered how, as a prisoner of the Caughnawagas, he had secretly vowed to take Indian scalps. But he realized that he could never do it. He thought of Half Moon. Was his adopted brother's body among those now lining the riverbank? He shuddered again, and put out a hand to wake his son.

"Come, Red Deer, we must go to see if my brother Half Moon is among the dead."

"My uncle?" Red Deer said, rubbing his eyes. "He is not here. I was hiding in a tree, and I saw him escape downriver by swimming underwater."

Jed Gill smiled in relief and patted the boy on the shoulder. "That is good news, my son. Come, let us get something to eat. We have a long journey ahead of us."

King George's War

16

"Happy birthday, Pa!" Happy birthday, Martha!"

With one voice, the three Gill brothers and their mother rose from their chairs to serenade their father and their sister, who shared the same birthday.

At the head of the table in the splendid dining room in the house on the Green Lane once owned by Sir William Phips, Jedediah Gill smiled fondly at his family. At his right hand, his black-haired daughter laughed almost as heartily as a man, until the tears came to her light blue eyes. Martha's laughter momentarily softened the firm line of her jaw, but after she had wiped her eyes and her face resumed repose, the faintly belligerent thrust which even Martha's striking beauty could not camouflage—and which reminded Jedediah Gill so much of his foster mother—was there again.

The two decades which had passed since the destruction of Norridgewock had not laid an exceptionally harsh hand on Jedediah Gill. His blond hair had turned iron gray, of course, and he wore it shorter, in a way that made it stand up bristling. Although prosperity had planted a paunch at his middle, his step and his grip were still firm, and his blue eyes, only slightly darker than Martha's, were still confident and friendly—still capable of blazing instantly in anger or indignation.

After the singing stopped, Jedediah arose and walked to the other end of the table, leaning down to kiss Rachel tenderly on the lips. His children clapped their hands in delight, and the oldest, Malachi Gill, tapped his silver spoon against his wineglass to make the Irish crystal ring as musically as a bell. "Again!" Malachi cried "Once more!" Immediately, the other children set their glasses ringing. Rachel's eyes widened in horror. "Stop that! Land's sake, those glasses cost a pound apiece."

Micah Gill chuckled. He was the youngest son, and although all the other Gills resembled each other. Micah was the reincarnation of his grandfather, Jonathan Clarke. "Come on, Ma," he teased. "What's a pound or two to the man who practically owns the Boston waterfront?"

"That's not so," Rachel replied, smoothing the gleaming white linen tablecloth before her with her fine hands. "There was a time when your pa and I had to live off the scraps from the guests' plates."

Rachel Gill's children hooted at her in fond derision.

"Was that before or after Pa bought the Cartwrights' fishing fleet?" Mordecai asked, and even Jedediah joined in the ensuing laughter. Rachel pretended not to hear, studying her hands. They were still shapely, and she was still proud of them, but they were full of pain and had begun to swell at the knuckles. Malachi tapped his glass once more, and said, "The idea was for you to kiss Ma again, Pa."

Jedediah shook his head and returned to his place at the head of the table. "My kissing days are over, Malachi." He glanced meaningfully at his three sons. "And it's about time yours started. "I'm fifty-five today, and I still don't have any grandchildren."

"I don't have the time, Pa," Malachi said. "It's been less than three months since I hung out my shingle, and some days I barely have time to eat. I never saw so many people with colds and agues.

"What do you give them, Mal?" Mordecai asked.

"Hot buttered rum and mustard plasters, just before bedtime. I swear, Pa, I ought to get a percentage of your rum profits."

"J. Gill & Sons imports mustard, too," Jedediah said, winking at Mordecai. "But I still think a fellow your age should be married, Mal. A doctor needs a good woman to do for him."

Malachi shrugged, and Mordecai pointed to his sister and asked: "How about Martha? She turned twenty today."

Martha blushed and her father leaned over to pat her fondly on the arm. "Martha's staying here to do for her pa in his old age. Right, Marty?" Martha nodded, still blushing, glancing appealingly at her mother.

"I'm doing all my courtin' in the courthouse," Micah Gill put in, an impish smile on his saturine face. "I know there're lots of pretty lassies available, but I tell you, Pa, that abstract law is beautiful stuff. Parson Lowry keeps telling me I ought to get hitched, but I told him I'd sooner go to war."

Everyone laughed but Mordecai. "Maybe King George'll give you your chance," he said somberly.

Jedediah shook his head. "Not in this war, Mordy. King George's War is strictly a European squabble. It won't spread to America like the others."

"Why not?" Rachel asked casually, carefully watching the black slave from the West Indies clearing the table.

"Because they're *all* in it. It's not just mainly England and France, like the last three. George and Louis the Fifteenth have bigger fish to fry."

Martha spoke up with the self-righteousness of youth. "I don't like that Frederick of Prussia. He promised Maria Theresa he'd help her keep her Austrian possessions. Now, instead of protecting her, he's robbing her."

"With the help of France and Spain," Micah added, reaching for the bottle of brandy brought in by the black woman. "But I really don't believe that King George is fighting Frederick just to protect the beautiful young queen of Austria. George of Hanover is about as chivalrous as a cow. He's just worried about his possessions in Germany, that's all."

"I agree with you," Jedediah Gill said, a pensive note stealing into his voice. "But I could wish for one more try at Quebec. Damn that Hovenden Walker's lily-livered soul! If the queen had sent us half a man to lead an army half as big, Canada would be English now. But she sent us a pair of pygmies leading an elephant."

"Well, you can forget Quebec this time, Pa," Mordecai said, watching Micah pour brandy into his snifter. "Besides, I think keeping the war in Europe will be all to the good for the colonies. We won't lose any men or money, and we should be able to turn a pretty penny supplying British forces on the continent."

Martha Gill regarded her brother with a sour eye. "Spoken like a true Mordecai," she said contemptuously. "You're the only man I know who'd go into battle with a ledger and a bottle of ink."

A dark flush suffused Mordecai's oval face. Rachel Gill rapped the table sharply with her knuckles. "Martha Gill, you watch that sassy tongue of yours! You've got no call talking to your brother that way, even if it is your birthday."

Martha glared defiantly at her mother, but said nothing. Jedediah spoke quickly to Mordecai: "Speaking of supplies, is the fleet back from the banks?"

Mordecai gulped his brandy and shot an agonizing glance at his mother. "All but the two the French captured," he blurted out. "Shucks, Pa, I didn't want to give you the bad news on your birthday. But, now that you've asked—a squadron of French corsairs out of Louisbourg took the *Redbud* and the *Red Deer* in a running fight."

Jedediah Gill blanched when he heard the names. They were his two newest and best ships. When Rachel had questioned him about the unusual names, he had told her they were Indians who had been kind to him in Caughnawaga. Now, his dismay gave way quickly to rage. "Louisbourg!" he swore, striking the table so hard it rattled the glasses. "God damn that filthy pirates' hole! I know, I know, Mr. Lawman," he snapped at Micah, whose black eyes twinkled in patronizing amusement, "you're going to tell me there's a war on and its legal. But, war or peace, those thieves up in Louisbourg keep snapping up our ships. And I say that it's damn well high time we did something about it!"

"But, Pa," Mordecai pleaded, distressed, as always, by his mercurial father's abrupt changes in mood or attitude, "you just said the war wouldn't spread to America."

"That was before I learned I'd lost my two best ships," Jedediah grumbled. "And I repeat: we've got to take Louisbourg, even if we have to do it ourselves. By God, I'm going to put it up to Governor Shirley!"

"Too late, Pa," Micah grunted laconically. "I think the

governor's already proposed it and the Assembly turned him down."

"Where'd you hear that?" Jedediah growled in a tone of doubt. "It's new to me."

"You've been away, Pa. While you were in Philadelphia visiting Benjamin Franklin, the governor called a secret meeting of the legislature. It was right after the French burned Canso and tried to take Annapolis Royal. But nobody put two and two together. Nothing like it had ever happened before. At least, that's what the old-timers at the courthouse told me. And nothing leaked out." Micah began to shake with silent laughter. "Not until one night at Ward's Inn in Salem. I was there trying a case. There were a lot of delegates boarding at the inn. There was this old rustic from the frontier. Maine, I think. He had a room right over the taproom, and the night before they put Shirley's proposal to a vote, he went down on his knees to pray to God for guidance. Well, he prayed so damned loud everybody in the taproom heard him—and the secret was out. The whole town knew it, and Shirley got so mad he accused the delegates of giving him away, and they got so riled up they turned him down. They said the colony couldn't do it on its own. Frankly, I think they were right."

Jedediah Gill stared frostily at his son. He fingered the white scar on his forehead thoughtfully, and then, haughtily swiveling his eyes around the table, he said:

"*I* don't."

Jedediah Gill knew the character of the governor of Massachusetts better than his sons did. Jedediah had known William Shirley since he arrived in Boston from London in 1731 to seek his fortune as a lawyer. He had been a lodger at the family tavern until he had become prosperous enough to buy his own brick house on the Green Lane, and in 1741 the king had made him governor of the colony. Jedediah respected Shirley as an able, hardworking administrator and a true friend of the province. He was also aware of Shirley's secret insatiable thirst for distinction, particularly as a military strategist, and he was not surprised when the governor came to the waterfront offices of J. Gill & Sons one day and was ushered into the counting-room, where Jedediah and Mordecai were busily at work.

"Welcome, Governor, welcome," Jedediah said, motioning to Mordecai to give their distinguished visitor his chair. "A glass of Madeira? A pipe? It isn't often that J. Gill & Sons is so signally honored."

Shirley shook his head, waiting for the door to close behind Mordecai before he spoke. "Gill," he said, coming directly to the point, "do you feel like giving up the expedition to Louisbourg?"

"I do not. And I think you ought to get the legislature to reconsider its vote."

"You're the very man I want! That's exactly what I wanted to hear! Now, listen to me, Gill—you're a big man in Boston and you're respected in the colony, too. I always regretted seeing you leave the House."

"It was getting to be too much for me, Governor. The tavern had grown so big . . . and there were my timber interests . . . and then the fishing fleet. It was just too much."

"I understand. But what I'm getting at, Gill, is that if a man of your caliber were to join me in getting up a petition to reconsider the proposal, I think the delegates would go along with it."

"By, God, I'll do it!" Jedediah exclaimed. "And I'll get every merchant of substance in Boston to sign it, too. They hate those sons-a-bitching Frenchies in Louisbourg. What's more, I'll go to Salem and Marblehead and all the other coastal towns."

"Excellent, my dear Gill, excellent! I am sure our petition will carry the day. And now, if you will, a glass of Madeira *and* a pipe."

A month later Jedediah was again in his counting-room with Mordecai, when Micah Gill knocked on the door and entered. "Pa, did you hear?" he cried. "The governor's named William Pepperell to command the expedition."

"Pepperell? Pshaw. He wouldn't be my choice."

Mordecai glanced up, reluctantly tearing his eyes from his beloved ledger. "But, why not, Pa? William Pepperell's a very fine man. He must be the richest man in Maine."

"Wealth doesn't necessarily fit a man for war," Jedediah replied, remembering his Uncle Jon's furious strictures on that point. "I know, they think it does over here, but you wouldn't find any of the kings of Europe putting a rich civilian in command of his armies. They want professionals."

Micah nodded. "I agree, Pa, but we don't have any professionals over here. There isn't a single soldier with experience. Why, we don't even have an engineer."

"*I've* got experience," his father said proudly.

"But you retired from the militia last year. And you're fifty-five."

"Peppcrell's forty-nine. And he's never heard a shot fired in anger. Not that I think the governor should give the command to me," Jedediah went on with unconvincing modesty. "But at least he should have given it to a man of action. Someone like William Vaughn. Dammit, it was Vaughn who first proposed the expedition to Shirley. And it was really Vaughn who got the legislature to change its mind. Vaughn's a man out of the same mold as Samuel Vetch. He's got force and daring. Men would follow Vaughn. I tell you, Mordecai, William Pepperell couldn't lead me to the outhouse."

"But, Pa," Mordecai persisted stubbornly, "he practically owns the towns of Saco and Scarborough."

"Dammit, Mordecai, must you always think in sums? I'll wager if we opened up that head of yours we'd find you had a ledger for a brain."

Micah chuckled, chanting in a low voice: "Good ol' Mordecai, sitting on a fence, trying to make a shilling out of eleven pence." Mordecai flushed, and Micah took a newspaper from beneath his arm and unfolded it. "It says here there'll be about four thousand men in the expedition. Three-quarters of 'em from Massachusetts. The rest from Rhode Island, Connecticut and New Hampshire."

"No one else?" Jedediah asked. "Damn those southern colonies! I know its no use the governor writing them. They'd only say they were busy with the Spanish. Hasn't been a Spaniard down there in thirty years. But what about Maryland and Pennsylvania, New York and the Jersies? Does New England always have to do it all?"

Micah grinned. "Geography makes history, Pa. Those Louisbourg pirates just don't sail that far south. And you really don't expect those Quakers in Philadelphia to fight, do you? They won't even defend their own people from the Indians. War is immoral, they say. So what did they do? They tried to buy the Indians off."

"How much?" Mordecai asked, and Micah and his father exploded with laughter.

"You can't beat him, Pa," Micah gasped. "He's got a price tag on everything. "Mordy, what do you figure your soul is worth?"

"I haven't had an offer yet," Mordecai said, grinning weakly.

"Speaking of Philadelphia," Jedediah said, "I was talking to Ben Franklin's brother yesterday. He says Ben wrote him to say that fortified towns like Louisbourg are tough nuts to crack, and we don't have the teeth for it. I wrote Ben myself to say we seem to have the *only* teeth on the whole damn seaboard. And I told him he'd better come back home to Boston where people don't hide behind the Bible when there's fighting to be done."

"Good for you, Pa,'" Micah said, getting to his feet. "I've got to be going before old man Revere closes his shop. He's making me a pair of horse pistols."

"What for?" Mordecai asked.

"For the expedition, you dummy. I'm going in Vaughn's regiment."

"*Regiment?*" Jedediah exclaimed angrily. "Is that all they gave William Vaughn?" Micah nodded, and his father shook his head in disgust. "I thought Governor Shirley could rise above politics," he muttered. "Well, Micah—welcome aboard. I'm going with Vaughn, too. He asked me to go with him no matter what his command was, and I said I would."

Mordecai's normally sober eyes twinkled maliciously. "Does Ma know you're going, Pa?"

"I'll take care of your mother," Jedediah said stiffly; and then, to Micah: "Is Malachi going, too?"

"Nope. He says he's just got his practice started and he can't leave it. He told me to tell you not to get upset—that he'll go on the next one."

"Next one, eh?" Jedediah repeated moodily. "Maybe he's right. There always does seem to be a war going on. At least for the Gills. My parents were killed in one, and I was born in one. I was captured in one and my stepparents and your mother's parents were killed in one. Then I sailed to Port Royal and Quebec in another one, and was wounded in the war with the Abnaki." He paused, thinking of Red Bud and Father Rale, of Half Moon and Red Deer. To the surprise of his sons, a tear glistened in his eye and slid down his nose. "That's two generations of Gills," Jedediah murmured, "and now there is a third generation going to war in America."

For all of his inexperience as a soldier, William Pepperell was a man of good will, good sense and almost inexhaustible patience. He was aware that William Vaughn possessed the talents suited to the battlefield, while his own were rather more compatible with the council table, but he nevertheless accepted the command. Not without first having consulted Parson Solomon Lowry, for William Pepperell was above all else a religious man.

"I wouldn't take it," the parson grunted bluntly. "If you lose, they'll mock you in the streets and call you wooden sword. If you win, they'll envy you even more than they do now. Besides," Lowry muttered, stroking his heavy jaw, "if it weren't a chance to purge the continent of Roman Catholicism, I'd be against it. It's turning the people away from the Great Awakening. George Whitefield and myself and the other parsons had the people on their knees. We had the wheel of prayer whirling, we had them praying and fasting to beat the devil, Mr. Pepperell. And now from fighting the devil, they must turn to fighting the French."

"But, don't you think the expedition is in the cause of heaven?" Pepperell asked. "Like a crusade?"

Parson Lowry nodded. "That's the only thing it has to recommend it. Otherwise, it's a harebrained scheme. On second thought, Mr. Pepperell, I think you had better accept the command. If only to keep it out of the hands of a wild man—a smoker and a drinker—like William Vaughn. Or worse, a vainglorious pomposity like the governor of New Hampshire."

Pepperell smiled thinly. "Benning Wentworth does have a fondness for fame. Governor Shirley soothed his vanity by telling him it was only his gouty legs that kept him from the command."

Solomon Lowry heaved himself to his feet with a grumble. "Sometimes the governor of Massachusetts is a bit careless with the truth. Well, good day, Mr. Pepperell—and as I say, as your parson, I should advise you to accept." Straightening his shoulders, the parson marched through the door held open by a servant, lifting his outthrust jaw in disapproval when he passed William Vaughn in the corridor.

Inside Pepperell's chambers, Vaughn seated himself with a grin. "I hear you are lieutenant general three times, Sir."

"Yes, it is a little silly. One commission from Massachusetts and one each from Connecticut and New Hampshire. But, tell me, Vaughn, what do you think of the New England navy?"

"Not much. A dozen so-called ships, and not one of them really battleworthy. The *Massachusetts* is the best, with twenty-four guns. And she's really only a converted brig. Some of the others have as few as twelve guns. Two French men-of-war could smash the lot of them to splinters."

"Yes," said Pepperell, a frown on his long, heavy face. "That is my chief worry. The governor wrote Commander Warren at Antigua to bring his squadron to the rendezvous at Canso. But Warren wrote back that although he and his officers were eager to help, they dared not without direct orders from the Admiralty."

"Damn the Ministry," Vaughn growled. "Don't they understand the value of Louisbourg? It controls not only Cape Breton Island but Acadia as well. It'll give us a base almost a thousand miles closer to Quebec."

"That's exactly what Governor Shirley said in his letter to the Duke of Newcastle. Acadia and the fisheries are in great danger. But there's been no reply, and it looks like it's up to ourselves alone."

"With a ten-shilling navy and tuppence worth of artillery," Vaughn muttered. "The cannon are much too light. The heaviest are the twenty-two-pounders. Then there's the ten eighteen-pounders that New York sent us, along with their refusal to join the expedition. We don't have anything nearly heavy enough to bombard the fort, granted that we can get into the harbor without naval gunfire support."

"Oh, it isn't all that bad, my dear Vaughn. Governor Shirley seems to think we can turn their own artillery against the French. There's nearly thirty forty-two-pounders in their Grand Battery. Shirley says we could capture it and use the guns to knock down Louisbourg's walls."

"I see," Vaughn murmured sarcastically. "Rather like selling a bear's skin before you kill the bear. Our governor fancies himself a clever strategist, it would seem."

"You don't know the half of it, Vaughn," Pepperell groaned, lifting a thick sheaf of foolscap from his desk. See this? It's the governor's plan for the capture of Louisbourg. It's incredible. A night landing. The army divided into four divisions, all supposed to move like clockwork in the dark over unfamiliar terrain. each one with an independent mission. Imagine! Alexander himself couldn't do it. The governor leaves out the rocks, the waves, the wind, the weather. There are no marshes, hills or hollows to be crossed—no thickets stuffed with enemy soldiers. In fact, he leaves out the French, too."

"My God," General Vaughn exclaimed in dismay. "You can't follow a crazy plan like that."

"Of course I can't! And I won't. Fortunately, at the end of all this," Pepperell said, shaking the sheaf of foolscap in his hand, "the governor graciously gives me permission to use my own discretion."

"Thank God," Vaughn groaned, rising to his feet. "You know, at first I was a bit disappointed not to get chief command of the expedition. And I didn't like being given just one regiment. Of course, I'll do my very best for you, General. But I don't mind telling you that knowing what I know now, I don't envy you."

"Neither do I," said Lieutenant General William Pepperell.

17

Jedediah Gill thought there was something familiar about the sturdy figure of the parson striding up the gangplank ahead of him. He stared at the muscular calves bulging from their black stockings and realized at once that the man he was following aboard the transport was the Reverend Solomon Lowry.

Tapping him on the shoulder, Jedediah said: "What are you doing here, Parson Lowry?"

"Going to battle, of course," the parson said, turning. "Why, it's Jedediah Gill. Yes, Jedediah, I am going to battle. I shall stand at Armageddon and do battle for the Lord!"

"But, Parson, you're at least seventy-five years old."

"Wasn't that execrable idolater of a Frontenac over seventy when he went to war? Should the Lord's saints do less?"

Micah Gill, who had been marching behind his father, came up beside the two men and pointed to the heavy ax over the parson's shoulder. "What's the ax for, Parson?"

In reply, Parson Lowry seized the handle with both hands and lifted the blade high over his head. "I shall hew down the Temple of the Antichrist!" he bellowed. "I shall chop up the silken couches of the Whore of Babylon!"

Micah turned away to hide a smile, and Jedediah looked

up at the skies darkening overhead and said, "That's all very well, Parson, but I think you'd help the expedition more if you prayed for some good weather."

"I shall do that, too. But, never fear, Jedediah, we are in the Lord's hands—and we shall get to Canso without incident." Shouldering his ax, Solomon Lowry stepped on the quarterdeck and went marching below, undismayed by the ear-splitting roar of thunder and the flash of lightning that followed his words.

A furious northeaster struck the fleet on the voyage to Cape Breton Island, scattering some ninety transports and twelve warships, and sickening those members of the invasion force who were not veteran sailors. Parson Lowry could be heard in his bunk, his iron voice alternating between groans and supplications to the Lord. Micah Gill, who was surprised by the stability of his stomach on experiencing his first storm at sea, stood at the rail with his father and Colonel Vaughn, watching fearfully through glasses as their ship was blown closer and closer to the rockbound shore. Eventually, all the ships which had been blown toward the coast stood with furled sails, rolling in the immense seas, driven ever closer to the shoals garlanded with sprays and plumes of white water, awaiting either destruction or the providential abatement of the storm. It did subside—a "miraculous" turn of fortune which the men aboard Micah's ship attributed to the prodigious praying of Parson Lowry—and the far-flung ships of the fleet began to reassemble. On the morning of April 5, 1745—ten days after the armada had sailed from Nantasket Roads—sixty-eight transports put into the harbor of Canso, about fifty miles from Louisbourg. Over the next few days, all of the remaining vessels came limping safely into port.

Canso was the English settlement which the French had burned, provoking the New England retaliation, but General Pepperell's men found it deserted. Pepperell immediately set his soldiers to work building a new fort, while sending his bantam warships out to sea as cruisers. They returned within a few days with six French prizes, together with the doleful news that the fort of Louisbourg and its harbor were still locked in ice.

"It will be impossible to land," General Pepperell told Colonel Vaughn. "Worse than that, if French ships-of-war arrive before the ice melts, we won't even be able to approach the harbor. We'll have to go home—just like Admiral Walker."

Pepperell's spirits rose the following day upon receipt of a report that his little fleet had attacked the French frigate, *Renommée*, thirty-six guns, and so mauled her that she had put about and sailed back to France. Three days later, his lookouts reported a large ship flying British colors approaching the harbor. The commander of the New England army was delighted to learn that it was the frigate, *Eltham,* escort to the annual mast fleet from England. Commander Warren, who had received orders from the Duke of Newcastle to proceed at once to Pepperell's aid, had ordered the *Eltham* to Canso, and the next day, to the cheers and booming ship salutes of the New Englanders, Warren himself appeared in the massive sixty-gun *Superbe,* accompanied by the *Launceston* and the *Mermaid,* forty guns each.

General William Pepperell was jubilant. "I tell you, Vaughn, it's nothing short of a miracle. Of course, I won't say it was *all* due to Parson Lowry's sermon yesterday. But, that was mighty powerful preaching. 'Thy people shall be willing in the day of thy power.' I didn't miss a word."

"I did," Colonel Vaughn said dryly. "I clocked it, too. Three hours."

Pepperell smiled thinly. "I know you're not much on religion, Vaughn, but even a sceptic like yourself can't deny that the Lord is on our side. The French Navy just can't stop us, now."

Four days later, Pepperell received a report from Commander Warren's bloackading fleet that Garbarus Bay was free of ice, and in two more days, on the first fair wind, the invasion force sailed out of Canso, reaching Louisbourg the following morning.

Once again, Micah Gill stood with his father and Colonel Vaughn on the quarterdeck of their ship, glasses pressed to his eyes. Louisbourg lay on a tongue of land between its harbor and the sea. On the left of the harbor, reefs and shoals barred entrance. On the right was a small rocky island on which the French had built their Island Battery. Ahead was a bigger fortification, almost the size of a fort, called the Grand Battery.

"We could never force our way in there," Jedediah Gill

mumbled. "Not even with our navy. We'd be raked fore and flank."

"Quite so," said Vaughn, "but we're not planning to force an entrance." He pointed to his left. "Up there is a place called Flat Point Cove. We're going to make a feint there, draw the French in, and then row like mad for Fresh-Water Cove, two miles farther east."

"Good plan," said Micah, and Vaughn replied, "Yes, Captain Gill—and your company is to be the spearhead. Get your men boated at once."

His eyes sparkling, Micah moved to obey, only to feel his father's hand on his arm and hear him say, "Yes, and get me a musket."

"Pa, you can't go! You're too damn—"

"Don't tell me I'm too old!" Jedediah snapped. "My eyes may not be as sharp as they used to be, but I'm still the best damn shot in this whole damn army. Get me a musket, y'hear?"

Shrugging helplessly, Captain Gill went below, reappearing at the head of his troops with a musket in his hand. "Here, you old fire-eater," he growled, handing him the gun. "Wait'll I tell Ma about this." Chuckling, Jedediah joined a platoon of soldiers clambering into one of the boats. Micah swung aboard, standing erect in the stern and calling through cupped hands to two other boatloads of soldiers. "All right, lower away and make for Flat Point Cove. When you get there, pretend you're afraid of the surf and rocks and draw off. Engage the French from the water to keep them busy."

The boats were slowly lowered into the water. Jedediah watched as they were rowed toward Flat Point. He could see a column of about a hundred white-coated French soldiers marching swiftly toward the threatened area. Reaching it, they vanished from view.

"They've got entrenchments there!" he called warningly to Micah. "They're waiting for your men."

"Of course, they are! But, you see, our ship is drifting west opposite Fresh-Water Cove. As soon as our men get the French occupied at Flat Point, we're going to make for Fresh-Water. Once we seize a beachhead there, the other boats will follow to widen it. Then the rest of the landing force can come in."

Jedediah nodded in admiring approval. "Excellent plan,"

he said, his eyes resting proudly on his son. He put his glasses to his eyes again. The two boats were headed straight for a cluster of rocks pounded by the surf. Suddenly, the militiamen stopped pulling on their oars and began to backwater. Jedediah heard a volley of musketry. Answering shots came from the English. The French fired again, and the English backed still farther away. Jedediah could hear the French cheering. A large white flag bearing the golden lilies of France waved triumphantly on the beach.

"Lower away!" Captain Micah Gill bellowed to the men on the davits. Jedediah felt his stomach turn over, the boat fell so swiftly down. It struck the water with a sharp *spat!* raising geysers of water on both sides. For a moment, Jedediah feared it would capsize. But the militiamen did not panic, immediately seizing their oars.

"Row!" Micah shouted. "Row, Goddamn you, you mothers' mistakes!"

The men pulled, and the boat surged forward, but Captain Gill was not satisfied. "Faster!" he yelled. "Double the beat and I'll double the rum ration."

Jedediah could not have believed that the boat could go faster, but it did. Though it was a cool day, he saw beads of sweat popping from the foreheads of the men at the oars. Suddenly, a great outcry came from the beach. One by one, white coats burst into view and began trotting briskly toward Fresh-Water Cove.

"Keep it up, boys!" Micah called jubilantly. "We've got 'em beat. Keep it up!"

Now the two boats at Flat Point had changed direction and were following Captain Gill's boats. Their oars flashed in and out of the water. Jedediah watched the oars on his boat digging deep into the blue water, making little whirlpools and dappling the water with foam.

Shots came from the shore, so harmless and so badly aimed that Jedediah couldn't even hear them moan in passing. They were only a hundred yards from Fresh-Water. The beach was of stones, and a high tide was driving a roaring surf up to its edge. But as the breakers receded, Jedediah saw that there would still be space enough to land. Glancing to his right, he saw that the French were running, now. Their tricorns were falling off but they did not stop to retrieve them. They were perhaps ten yards away, when Captain Gill called, "Heave!" and the oarsmen gave one last mighty pull and the boat crested a roller and was thrust up on the beach. The keel made a grating noise on the stones, until, once free of the water, the boat keeled over on its starboard side.

"First platoon, form a firing line," Captain Gill ordered. "Second platoon, get the boat up into the woods."

Immediately, half the men began dragging the boat up the beach, while the other half ran to take cover among the stones to face the oncoming French. Jedediah joined them. He flopped down next to a freckle-faced youth of about eighteen, peering eagerly forward while the French formed in close battle order. A bugle blew, and they came forward at the double. "Watch this, sonny," Jedediah Gill, said, squinting down the barrel of his musket. He fired, and the youth gaped in disbelief when one of the white coats, fully fifty yards away, sank to the ground. Jedediah grinned again and reloaded.

"Who's that firing on his own?" Captain Gill shouted angrily.

"Me," Jedediah replied, firing again. A second Frenchman spun out of ranks.

"Goddammit, Pa, wait till I give the order!"

Jedediah said nothing, reloading again. Then, shouting, "Tell your Ma about this one," he fired a third time, and a third Frenchman fell.

Suddenly, the French halted, knelt and fired. Two New Englanders flopped on the sand, holding their wounds and groaning. Rising under the cloud of black-powder smoke drifting overhead, the French gave a loud shout, leveled their bayonets, and charged.

"Fire!" Captain Gill yelled.

A volley crashed out. Jedediah saw six more Frenchmen fall, before a curling cloud of powder smoke obscured his view. When it lifted, he saw that the enemy had broken and was fleeing. Some of them threw away their muskets as they ran.

The acrid powder smoke in his nostrils like a stimulant, Micah Gill jumped to his feet, crying, "After them! We want prisoners!"

Cheering, the New Englanders rose in pursuit. But the French had had a head start, and they were running for their lives. Only three of them were overtaken and brought back, and when three of the six who had fallen in the volley were found to be wounded, they, too, were imprisoned.

By the time Captain Gill and his men returned, the other two boats had landed and disgorged their passengers. Micah at once formed his men in a perimeter around the beachhead. He handed a Union Jack to the freckle-faced youth who had lain beside Jedediah, and said, "You climb a tree, Adam Jenkins, and wave this flag at the fleet."

Signal guns were fired from the English ships when the flag was seen, and a grand concourse of landing boats began to move toward Fresh-Water Cove. They came swarming ashore, the men cheering wildly as they leaped onto the beach. By nightfall, almost two thousand men had landed safely, and the remainder came in the following day.

"Congratulations, my dear Vaughn," Lieutenant General William Pepperell cried cheerfully when he was helped onto the beach by a pair of sturdy militiamen. "Thanks to you, we've got the French flanked."

A few days later, Captain Micah Gill was summoned to the makeshift tent—an old sail stretched over poles—of Colonel William Vaughn.

"The one thing we need most, Gill, is information," Vaughn said. "General Pepperell just has no idea what forces the enemy have. All he knows is that the French commander is the Chevalier Duchambon, who is not supposed to be much of a fighter. In fact, that may explain why the French haven't made a sally while we're out here in the open. But the general needs to know what the enemy's strength is. How many guns, how many men, whether they're regulars or militia, what their morale is, that sort of thing. We thought we might get something out of the fellows you captured, but they're just ignorant privates. So, I want you to take a patrol toward Louisbourg looking for prisoners. You might even try the settlements around the town. Take enough supplies for four days. If you're not back by then, I'll come out looking for you. Any questions?"

"None," Captain Gill replied, saluting smartly, and he returned to his own area, ordering his sergeant to notify the first platoon to be ready to go on patrol the following day. "Issue them enough food and ammunition for four days, Sergeant," he said. "And I want you to detail Private Adam Jenkins to me as a courier."

Walking back to his tent, Micah saw his father in front of him. He saw him stop, seized by a paroxysm of coughing. Jedediah was bent over, mopping his watery eyes with a piece of sailcloth. Turning to Micah, he straightened up quickly. "What a time to get a cold," he mumbled.

"What did you expect," Micah snapped irritably, "lying out in the mud and fog with fellows half your age? I told you not to come, Pa, and now if you die of the ague or go home all twisted up with the rheumy, Ma'll never forgive me."

"I'll get over it," Jedediah said, smothering a sneeze. "Cold or no cold, I'm having the time of my life. I tell you, Micah, these fellows are the toughest bunch of rapscallions I ever saw. I've been watching 'em unload the ships——helping them, sometimes. Those big flatboats they got don't get in close enough. So they have to carry the loads ashore on their heads. They go wading through that ice-cold surf up to the waist without a whimper. Then they sleep on the ground at night, soaking wet, the chill coming out of the ground and the fog all around them. Shoes worn out, clothes in rags— some of 'em barefoot—and they still go on. You've got to hand it to them, Micah. New England men are the stoutest fellows in the world. And that goes for Old England, too." Micah nodded, watching in dismay while another paroxysm of coughing seized his father.

"I'll get over it," Jedediah mumbled again. "Have you been up to the gun-hauling yet?" he asked eagerly, and when Micah shook his head, his eyes lighted up again and he continued: "Something to see. It's about two miles from here to the first battery, and it's almost all marsh. First cannon they tried—only an eighteen-pounder—sank right down in the mud." Jedediah made a sucking noise with his mouth, and said: "Just like that, wheels, gun; carriage, and all—gone. Lucky they had a shipbuilder up there. He got 'em to make sledges of timber sixteen feet long and five feet wide, and they put the guns on them. Then they harnessed two hundred men to the sledge, just like oxen, with rope traces and breast straps, and they dragged the guns through the marsh. But I tell you, I heard Colonel Vaughn saying he doesn't know what we'll do when we get those big French guns."

"*When* we get them," Micah said; and then, an anxious

note creeping into his voice: "Now, look, Pa, you've got to take care of yourself. If you don't, I'm going to put you aboard the first ship back to Boston."

"Damnation, Micah, I *am* taking care of myself. You forget your pa was an Indian once. I'm not sleeping in the mud like most of them. I've built me a sod hut with spruce boughs for a thatch. Rain or fog, I'm dry." Jedediah's eyes gleamed. "The whole company's buzzing about the patrol, Micah. Got a place for me?"

"I do not."

"You didn't want me in the boat, either, but you saw me shoot."

"Pa, a patrol isn't the place for a fire-eater. We want live prisoners, not corpses."

"I sure wish Malachi was here," Jedediah said sulkily. "He wouldn't stand for his little brother talking to his pa like that."

"*Mr.* Gill," Micah snapped in exasperation, "I'm in charge here, and you're not even a proper soldier."

"Sidewinders," Jedediah muttered in a tone of injured pride, turning to stride stiffly away. "I've gone and brought a generation of sidewinders into the world."

Captain Gill watched him go with a grin. Then he continued on to his tent, where he filled his pack and examined his pistol. In the morning, Micah led about a dozen men eastward into the woods toward Louisbourg.

Captain Gill was surprised how quiet it was. The nesting birds had not yet returned from their migration to the south, and only the occasional whistle of a cardinal or the squalling of a squirrel disturbed the dripping silence of the faintly green forest. Micah had scouts to the front and flankers out to either side to guard against ambush, but his patrol encountered not a single human being. Micah wondered why the French were so inactive. They were the ones who should be patrolling, not the English. At midafternoon, they came to a pond. Micah let the patrol move on ahead while he sat down amid the croaking of the bullfrogs to write his report. He handed it to Private Jenkins and told him to take it back at top speed to Colonel Vaughn. Then, aware that his men had gotten far ahead of him, Micah hurried to overtake them.

Trotting beneath an elm tree, he thought he heard a rustling noise overhead. He looked up. A dark shape blotted out the sky, and in the next instant he felt a body strike him and a strong arm encircle his neck and drive him to the ground. A powerful odor of bear grease came into his nostrils. An Indian! The arm around his neck drew tighter, choking him. He struggled until he felt the point of a knife pressed into the hollow of his ear. Micah lay still while his arms were pulled painfully behind him and bound with leather thongs. His feet were also tied, and a blindfold was wound roughly around his eyes. Then he felt himself hoisted into the air and borne away.

A half-hour later he was thrown onto the ground, the blindfold was yanked away and his arms and legs were freed. Sitting up blinking in the fading light of day, Micah saw that he was in a rude Indian camp. A half-dozen lean-tos had been erected in a clearing. In the center of the clearing were about a dozen Indians in war paint and a single white man wearing the white uniform of a French officer. A torch of pitch was brought forward and lighted. The officer said something in Indian dialect, and two Indians came to Micah, jerking him to his feet and bringing him to face the officer. Turning to another Indian, the officer spoke in French, and the Indian nodded and stepped toward Micah.

"What are your name and rank?" he asked in English.

Micah was surprised by the questioner's perfect diction. He was also startled to see that his eyes were blue and that his hair, reflecting the flickering light of the torch, seemed to be a dark red. Otherwise he had the oval face and high cheekbones of a true Indian.

"Gill," Micah answered. "Captain Micah Gill."

Now it was the Indian who seemed shaken, even astounded. He glanced sideways at the French officer and asked in a low voice: "If your father's name is Jedediah, shake your head."

Incredulous, Micah shook his head, and his questioner raised his voice again and said: "What is your regiment?"

Shaking his head again, Captain Gill replied: "I cannot tell you. That is against the rules of war."

The Indian turned to the officer, speaking to him in French. The officer glanced sternly at Micah and spoke at length to the interpreter, who came back to Micah and said: "Captain Gill, you are a prisoner of the French crown in America. You will be taken to Louisbourg for questioning.

You will be treated with courtesy and honor, but you must be prepared to answer all questions. Captain du Bois says the rules of war apply only to regular officers holding commissions in the king's regiments. They do not apply to militia. Captain du Bois says if you fail to answer questions, you will be treated as a civilian—a spy—and hung."

Micah Gill's eyes shifted to the officer, who inclined his head in a cold little bow. Micah returned his gaze to the Indian. Was he trying to say something to him with his eyes? Warning him? "Do you understand?" the Indian asked, and Micah replied: "Yes, but I still cannot answer." Again a warning seemed to shoot from the interpreter's eyes, and the Indian turned quickly to speak casually to the officer, who nodded in satisfaction. Then he spoke in dialect to the other Indians, and Micah felt himself seized, bound and blindfolded again. He was lifted into the air and carried about twenty feet, after which he was placed facedown on a pile of putrid animal skins. From the cold water, fragrant with the scent of spruce boughs, that dripped down on his neck and ran into his ears and nose, Micah guessed that he was inside a lean-to.

They *can't* hang me! Micah thought fiercely. They can't! It's against the rules of war. If they do, General Pepperell will raze Louisbourg to the ground! Yes, he thought with grim sardonicism, and a lot of good that will do you after you are dead. Micah stiffened. Someone else was in the lean-to beside him. He could hear him breathing. "Do not fear, I am your brother," a voice whispered. It was the interpreter! "I will save you, my brother," he continued. He began loosening Micah's bonds. "I am going to speak to your guards. I will tell them Captain du Bois told me to inspect your bonds. I will come inside and pretend to draw them tight. You will scream. But I will leave you free. When I go out, I will give the guards a drink of brandy. We will drink and talk together. Then I will leave the brandy with them and go. They will drink it all, never fear, and fall into a drunken sleep. That is when you will leave. Step softly. Be sure everyone is asleep. I will meet you at the pond. Do you understand?"

"Yes," Micah whispered. "But why are you leaving?"

"I will tell you in the morning, my brother."

Micah opened his mouth to ask why the Indian kept calling him brother, but the man quickly clapped his hand over it and whispered, "Shhh! I must go outside before the guards come in here." He crawled soundlessly away.

A few moments later Captain Gill heard him speaking to the guards in dialect. They all chuckled at something that he said, and then he came striding into the tent. "Ah, my English songbird," he said in a loud voice of feigned contempt, "you will sing well for the Chevalier Duchambon tomorrow, eh? But, first, let me make sure you do not fly away." He bent over Micah, grunting in pretended exertion, whispering, "Scream!" Micah screamed, flopping up and down on the ground as though in pain, while the Indian freed his hands and feet. "There," the Indian said, and went back outside.

Micah heard him speak again to the guards and heard the popping of a cork. The guards laughed in pleasure. Micah removed his blindfold and saw the guards silhouetted at the mouth of the lean-to. In turn, they leaned back and lifted the bottle to their lips, wiping their mouths with the back of their hand each time, belching gently or grunting "Ah!" in approval. Micah noticed that his liberator placed the bottle only momentarily to his own lips, and guessed that he was not swallowing any brandy. Eventually, he arose and left, leaving the guards with the bottle. They called after him jovially, their voices thick with drink. Micah watched tensely while his captors tilted the bottle again and again. One of them rolled over and lay motionless. The other arose and came back into the lean-to, swaying drunkenly.

Micah tensed. Drunk as he was, the guard could still give the alarm if he found him unbound. Micah quietly put out a foot. The guard tripped over it and fell heavily to the ground, a loud "Whoosh!" issuing from his mouth. Micah leaped on top of him, groping for his mouth. But it was not necessary. The Indian had passed out. Micah felt for the man's knife, found it, and cut his throat. He crawled outside and cut the throat of the other sleeping Indian. They could still awake and arouse the camp, he thought.

Sprawling on his belly, the dripping knife in his hand, Micah Gill began crawling toward an opening in the woods marking the trail his captors had followed. An owl hooted above him, and Micah lay still. It could be a signal. The owl hooted again. Micah heard soft footsteps padding behind him, and he whirled—knife raised to strike. A big raccoon waddled boldly past him, its tail dragging on the ground. Micah let out his breath and resumed his crawl. Soon, he was inside the forest, crawling deeper along the trail until he felt it safe to come erect. Then he began trotting easily toward the pond, reaching it in an hour, just as the sky cleared and the stars began to shed a soft light upon the water.

Micah gave three sharp whistles, and a voice called, "I am over here, my brother."

Micah saw the Indian step into view from behind a clump of foxtails. He ran up to him and seized his hand. "You've saved my life!" he exclaimed in gratitude; and then, puzzled: "But, why?"

"Because you are my brother," the man said, adding: "Come, we cannot stand here and waste time. We must run. They will try to run us down once they find you gone." He started off along the trail, and Micah ran alongside him. "How far to your camp?" the Indian asked, and Micah said: "About ten miles."

"Good. They will never catch us in ten miles. We have too much of a head start. Did you kill the guards?"

"Yes."

"That is even better. We will be almost at your camp before they find out. Can you run ten miles?"

"I . . . I think so. We went on a lot of training hikes at Canso, and I think I can."

The Indian nodded, and the two men ran side by side in silence. Micah was bursting with curiosity. He wanted to know why the man kept calling him brother, what his name was, why he helped him to escape, why he ran away himself—but each time he thought he would ask, he decided it would be wiser to save his breath until they were safely inside the English lines. They reached them at daybreak. A sentry jumped erect and pointed his musket at them. "Halt! Who goes there?"

"Captain Gill of Colonel Vaughn's regiment. I'm returning from patrol."

"Oh, it's you, Captain Gill. Your men came back last night. Said they thought you was captured."

"I was, but I got away."

"Good for you, Sir. The colonel will be pleased as peaches. He was going to send a search party out for you today. Go right ahead, Sir."

Micah nodded and led the Indian past the sentry and the other outposts. He walked on silently for five minutes, until he came to a cluster of sod huts and lean-tos and sailcloth tents. He sat down on a fallen log and motioned the Indian to sit down beside him. "Now, why do you . . . ? By Jesus, I don't even know your name."

"Red Deer."

"Red Deer! We had a ship named Red Deer. Why do you keep calling me your brother, Red Deer?"

"Because you are. My name is Gill, too. And my father is also named Jedediah Gill."

Micah Gill stared at Red Deer in astonishment. "But, how? I don't understand."

Red Deer grinned and pulled a piece of heavy parchment from inside his deerskin shirt. He unfolded it and handed it to Micah. It was a baptismal certificate.

Astounded, Micah began to read: " 'Jedediah Red Deer Gill, baptized by me this date, the Twenty-second of July, Feast of St. Mary Magdalen, in the Year of Our Lord, Seventeen Hundred and Ten, in the church of the Village of Caughnawaga, in New France. Signed, the Reverend Sébastien Rale, S.J.' By Jesus, you *are* my brother, Red Deer!" Micah yelled, jumping up from the log and pulling Red Deer erect to embrace him. "But, how?"

"When our father was a prisoner of the Caughnawagas, he fell in love with my mother, Redbud. He—"

"—Redbud!" Micah interrupted in amazement. "That was the other ship. Why, the old deceiver . . . *friends* of his, eh?" Micah's dark eyes twinkled mischievously. "I can't wait to introduce you to him," he murmured. " 'Pa, you never told us we had an Indian . . .' " Grinning to himself, Micah motioned to Red Deer to continue.

"Our father wanted to marry my mother, but she sent him away. She said he could not be happy as an Indian, and she was happy to bear his child. So I was born and baptized by Father Rale. I grew up as a Caughnawaga, speaking the dialect and learning French from Father Rale. When I was twelve, my uncle, Half Moon, took me and my mother with him to help Father Rale at Norridgewock. My mother and Father Rale were killed there, and our father saved my life. My uncle escaped. Our father was very kind to me. But he said he could not take me to Boston with him because he was afraid it would wreck the new life he had begun with your mother after his escape. He took me to Springfield to my stepfather, who had a tavern there."

"Who was that?" asked Micah, who had been listening intently.

"Daniel Quinn. He was an Irish deserter from the British Army that tried to take Quebec in Seventeen Eleven. Our father helped him get away. Daniel Quinn married the daughter of the Widow Bartlett, who had owned the tavern, and when she died they ran it together. He sent me to school, where I learned to speak English. Then I married his daughter, Kathleen."

"But you're a British subject, then. What are you doing with the French?"

Red Deer's lips tightened and his blue eyes went cold with anger. "They made me. I had heard that my Uncle Half Moon was sick, and I went to visit him in Caughnawaga. While I was there, the war broke out. When the French found out I could read and write both French and English and also spoke Caughnawaga, they made me work for them. They said I was a French subject and if I didn't do as they told me, they'd kill me. Wherever I went, they had two Caughnawaga braves watching me. That's why I couldn't get away. But after you were captured and I heard your name, I saw my chance."

"How so?"

Red Deer shrugged, grinning happily. "The guards they put over you were my old guards. For the first time, I was free." His voice hardened and his eyes went cold again. "I am glad you killed them, my brother. It was the wise thing to do."

"Have you been here in Louisbourg long?"

"About four weeks. They took me to Quebec first. They thought that was where you were going. When they found out it was Louisbourg, they brought me here."

"Did you see much of the city's defenses?"

"Oh, yes. Because of my knowledge of Caughnawaga and French, they took me everywhere."

Captain Gill was delighted. Obviously, Red Deer was of more value than fifty French prisoners. "I must take you to see Colonel Vaughn," he said. "But, first, let's go see Pa."

Red Deer smiled in pleasure to hear Micah say "Pa," and the two arose from the log and walked toward Jedediah's sod hut. They found their father seated outside it, cleaning his mess utensils. "Well, Pa, looks like you got your wish," Micah called out, unable to repress an anticipatory grin. "My big brother got here, after all."

"Malachi's here?" Jedediah asked eagerly, barely noticing the Indian with his son.

"Nope."

"You're not trying to tell me Mordecai isn't minding the counting-room?"

"Nope."

"All right, Micah," Jedediah said irritably, "what's the joke?" He glanced again at Red Deer, puzzled, studying him. His face softened. "Red Deer?" he asked gently.

"Yes, my father."

Jedediah Gill came slowly to his feet, arms outstretched. Red Deer came to him, and they embraced, both averting their faces to conceal the tears in their eyes. "Red Deer, I . . . I'm sorry," Jedediah mumbled.

"For what, my father?"

"I . . . I don't think I've been too good to you."

"But you saved my life and found me a good home. I am a happy man because of you."

Jedediah shook his head, unable to speak, and Micah pushed him gently back onto the stump he had been sitting on. "Red Deer saved my life, Pa. The French were going to hang me for a spy." Speaking quickly, he gave his father an account of what had happened. "I'm going to take him to Colonel Vaughn," he said in conclusion. "He's got a lot of valuable information on Louisbourg."

"Excellent," Jedediah said, seizing Red Deer's hand and squeezing it warmly. The two brothers turned to leave. As they did, Jedediah drew Micah aside for a moment, growling in his ear: "Not a word about this to Parson Lowry. Y' hear?"

Jubilant, Colonel Vaughn took Red Deer to see General Pepperell. The general sat at a field desk inside his tent—the only genuine shelter in the army—questioning Red Deer.

"Do you have any idea of French strength?" he asked. "We've been told they may have as many as three thousand regulars."

Red Deer shook his head gravely. "Not that many, Sir. At

most, they have about six hundred regulars. Some of the companies are Swiss. Then they have about fourteen hundred militia. They got them from the town and the surrounding neighborhood. They're not very dependable, Sir. Neither are the regulars. They mutinied last Christmas over their food. They didn't get paid for extra work on the fortifications, either. That made them madder. Duchambon put down the mutiny, but now he doesn't trust his men, and neither do his officers."

General Pepperell and Colonel Vaughn exchanged glances. "Now we know why Duchambon has let us alone," Pepperell mused. "What do you think, Vaughn—assault the fort?"

Vaughn shook his head. "I'd like nothing better, General, but I think you're right to besiege it."

Nodding, Pepperell turned to Red Deer. "You say you've seen their fortifications. Are they strong?"

"Very strong. They have a fortified line in front of the town from the harbor to the sea. There's a ditch eighty feet wide and about twelve hundred yards long. Behind that is a rampart of dirt faced with masonry. It's sixty feet thick."

General Pepperell frowned heavily. "Impossible, Vaughn. The ditch would be filled with our dead. We've got to stick with the bombardment."

"I agree, Sir," Vaughn said. "But our own guns aren't heavy enough. We've got to have those big French guns in the Grand Battery."

"Grand Battery, Sir?" Red Deer interjected. "It is very strong. I think there are thirty cannon there. Twenty-eight forty-two-pounders and two eighteen-pounders."

"Forty-*two*-pounders," Vaughn murmured wistfully. "What we couldn't do with them."

"No doubt about it, Vaughn," Pepperell said. "The Grand Battery is the key. We've got to have it. D'y think you could take it by storm?"

Vaughn did not answer, glancing inquiringly at Red Deer. "It's very strong, Sir," Red Deer said. "If you came from the sea, I think they'd sink all your boats. The land side is well guarded. They have a permanent garrison there, Sir. Barracks and all." He paused, his blue eyes lighting up. "I just remembered, Sir. Behind the Grand Battery there are magazines for naval stores. They're unprotected. Maybe if you blew them up, it might frighten the garrison."

"Not very likely," General Pepperell said disdainfully. "But I think they should be destroyed. Take your regiment over there tomorrow, Vaughn, and raise a little hell."

"I will, indeed, Sir," Vaughn replied.

On the following day, guided by Red Deer, Colonel Vaughn led four hundred men to the hills behind the Grand Battery where the naval magazines were located. They were unguarded, and it needed but a few minutes to set them afire. Within a quarter-hour the stores of pitch and tar and other combustibles had become a great red-and-yellow, swirling, crackling, spitting holocaust from which a prodigious black cloud climbed thousands of feet into the sky. As the fire grew, so did the heat, forcing Vaughn's cheering soldiers farther and farther away from it. The fire burned through the day into the night, illuminating the camp set up by the English.

In the morning, Vaughn formed most of his men into ranks and sent them marching back to their lines, while he took thirteen men on a scouting party toward the Grand Battery.

"We've got to find a way to get those big guns," he said to Captain Micah Gill, just as Red Deer stopped short to seize the colonel's arm and point toward the battery. "Look, Sir— no flags flying and no smoke from the barracks' chimneys."

"By God, they've pulled foot!" Vaughn exclaimed. "Here, Red Deer," he said, taking a flask of brandy from his coat pocket, "take a swig of this and pretend to be drunk. Just stagger up to the fort and see if its empty."

Red Deer nodded, throwing his head back to take a long pull at the flask. He choked, and tears came to his eyes. "My stomach's on fire," he mumbled with a rueful grin. Then he sprinkled a little of the liquid on his hair and staggered off. Vaughn and Micah watched his swaying progress anxiously. They smiled when they saw him disappear through an embrasure, and they cheered wildly when he poked his head out and shouted: "It's deserted!"

Still cheering, Vaughn and his men rushed inside the cavernous but empty fort. They rushed from cannon to cannon and found them intact. Only their touchholes had been spiked. Vaughn quickly sent Adam Jenkins up the flagpole, gripping his red jacket in his teeth. He fastened it to the top and slid down. Almost immediately, Louisbourg's batteries opened fire on the Grand Battery. Most of the balls passed wildly overhead.

"Some shooting," Vaughn sneered, sitting down at a table and drawing a sheet of paper toward him. "May it please Your Honor," he began to write to General Pepperell, "to be informed that by the Grace of God and the courage of thirteen men, I entered the Grand Battery about nine o'clock, and am waiting for a reinforcement and a flag." He gave it to Micah, who entrusted it to Private Jenkins. Vaughn glanced up from the table with a broad smile. "By Jesus, I can't believe it!" he exulted. "Twenty-eight forty-two-pounders! They didn't even knock off the trunnions or burn the carriages. Goddammit, Gill, we can drill those touchholes out in a few hours. And they even left us plenty of cannon cartridges and what looks like almost three hundred big bombshells. By Jesus, Gill, what d'y think made them pull foot like this?"

"Maybe the fire yesterday frightened them off," Micah mused, stooping to pick up a French soldier's diary lying beneath the table and hand it to Red Deer.

He leafed through it until he came to the last entry, dated May 2, 1745, the day before. "No, it wasn't even the fire, Colonel," Red Deer said. "Listen to this: 'A detachment of the enemy advanced to the neighborhood of the Grand Battery today. At once we were all seized with fright, and on the instant it was proposed to abandon this magnificent battery, which would have been our best defense, if one had known how to use it. Various councils were held, in a tumultuous way. It would be hard to tell the reasons for such a strange proceeding. Not one shot had yet been fired at the battery, which the enemy could not take, except by making regular approaches, as if against the town itself, and by besieging it, so to speak, in form. Some persons remonstrated, but in vain; and so a battery of thirty cannon, which had cost the King immense sums, was abandoned before it was attacked.' "

"Well, I'll be damned," Vaughn exclaimed. "Nothing but the white feather, eh? Well, we've got them now, Gill—just like a pudding in a bag."

Shouts came from outside the fort, and Vaughn and Micah rushed out to the open beach to see four boats loaded with French soldiers approaching. They drew their pistols and fired. Red Deer opened his powder bag to prime his musket before he knelt to take aim and pull the trigger. A French soldier arose in the stern of the closest boat, clutching his stomach before he toppled backward into the water. Still, the boats came on, their occupants kneeling to return the English fire. Suddenly, from the land side of the fort there came a squeal of fifes and rattle of drums. About twenty or thirty militiamen rushed onto the beach, shooting from the hip. More followed. At once, the French veered off and pulled vigorously for the safety of the town. The English burst into cheers again. Vaughn and Micah joined them.

"It's only a matter of time now, Gill," Vaughn said, turning to survey the captured fort with shining eyes. "Tomorrow, we start saluting the frog-eaters with their own guns. No doubt about it, now—we've got the bastards licked!"

It was, indeed, a matter of time—much more than the impetuous Colonel William Vaughn had supposed. Although the ensuing weeks saw a total of five new batteries added to the fire issuing from the captured Grand Battery, and although it seemed that the English cannonade must surely level Louisbourg, the French resistance continued. French cannon answered English cannon, and French musketry briskly returned the fire of the besiegers. Still, the Chevalier Duchambon made no effort to send out sallies to destroy the guns that were destroying him.

"I think it's like Red Deer said," Colonel Vaughn said to General Pepperell. "The French don't trust their men. They're afraid they'll mutiny."

"Perhaps," General Pepperell said slowly. "But Duchambon might also be aware of our own predicament."

"But I thought we were winning!" Vaughn protested in dismay.

"At the moment, yes," Pepperell said grimly. "But time favors the French. Our food supplies are low and our ammunition is running out. Many of the men are without shoes or clothing. We've lost quite a few men to French gunfire, but nothing in comparison to dysentery and fever. Right now, Vaughn," Pepperell said gravely, "there are only twenty-one hundred men fit for duty out of four thousand. We need reinforcements badly."

"But what of the Committee for War? Can't they help?"

"As often as I appeal for aid, Chairman Osborne writes me

courteous letters explaining why it can't be sent." A note of despair crept into the general's normally patient voice. "I tell you, Vaughn, this has been a trying time." He gestured irritably toward the pile of letters on his field desk. "Petitions and petitions and petitions. Sometimes I think a democratic army is not really fit to fight a war. Don't misunderstand me. The men have been magnificent. But these letters from wives and fathers entreating me to send their husbands and sons home. Here's a captain afraid his wife and family may be massacred by Indians. Two whole companies want to go home for the same reason. One corps complains that it's doing too much work, and another insists that it's doing all the fighting. Here, I've got a man from Cambridge named Morris asking me to return his runaway slave who joined the army. And the parsons!" General Pepperell rolled his eyes and pointed to piles of printed papers in a corner. "They're bombarding me with copies of their sermons, which they want me to distribute among the men. A heavenly shower, Vaughn—which I could well do without."

The door opened and a subaltern entered. "Bad news from the advanced battery, Sir. One of the French forty-two-pounders blew up, and another was dismounted. Powder barrel went up, too. Two men killed and two wounded."

Colonel Vaughn swore fiercely. "God *damn* those idiot amateurs! Will they never stop double-shotting the guns? They're destroying our siege train. And they won't listen. Only yesterday, I told a militia captain to order his men to stop chasing French cannonballs until after they're spent—and today I received a report one of them had his head taken off. We need some professional gunners, Sir."

"Yes, indeed," Pepperell replied wearily. "Fortunately, Commander Warren has kindly consented to lend us some of his. He has also sent me some distressing news. A French ship named the *Vigilant* is approaching Louisbourg with reinforcements."

"But surely Warren has the strength to stop them."

"If he can see them, yes. But in these fogs . . ."

"By God, General, I think we ought to storm the town!"

"Nonsense, my dear Vaughn. It would be the utmost folly to make such an attempt, now. The walls haven't been breached yet. Not even the best-trained and best-led troops could do it."

"But, General—if the *Vigilant* gets into the harbor, we're doomed."

"Not exactly doomed," Pepperell said wryly. "But at the very least embarrassed. Trust Warren, my dear Vaughn—he won't let us down."

Colonel Vaughn shook his head stubbornly. His eyes were still blazing. "The least we can do, General, is capture the Island Battery. It's the key to Louisbourg. While the French hold it, they keep the harbor open for their ships and keep ours out. If we hold it, Warren's ships and men can attack the town from the harbor while we storm it from the land side."

Lieutenant General William Pepperell pushed his full lower lip out thoughtfully. "Now, that is not such a bad idea," he said musingly. "Perhaps we should put it up to a Council of the Army."

The New England army embraced the plan to capture the Island Battery. Captain Micah Gill was delighted to discover that more than half of his company had volunteered for "this glorious mission," as the proclamation described it. He was, of course, not so naive as to suppose his liberal issue of rum had nothing to do with it.

"You can't beat bottled patriotism," he said to Red Deer with a grin. "It's a lot quicker than the natural kind."

With Red Deer beside him, Micah marched his men to the Grand Battery, where a small fleet of whale boats had been assembled. Hand grenades and scaling ladders were issued to the three hundred men who were to make the assault. On the dark midnight of May 26, 1745, the men silently entered the boats and began paddling softly toward the Island Battery, where another, smaller force from Lighthouse Point was to join them. The boats moved slowly but soundlessly toward the vaguely distinct bulk of the island and fort looming out of the darkness. The men did not withdraw their paddles from the water, but feathered them forward in the water for the return stroke. Captain Micah Gill sniffed about him suspiciously. Rum! Much as he might approve of bottled patriotism for getting men to volunteer, he distrusted its false and sometimes foolhardy courage. But if the men had been drinking, it was too late to stop them.

A steady rumble and a growing but blurry whiteness ahead

indicated the surf lashing the rocks. Soon it became a roaring, frothing white foam. Under cover of the sound, three boats at a time, the New Englanders pushed into the only safe landing place among the rocks. They scrambled ashore. Captain Gill's boat was still afloat, awaiting its turn to land. Micah peered tensely at the still-silent Island Battery. Suddenly:

"Hip-hip . . . hurray!"

"Hip-hip . . . hurray!"

"Hip-hip . . . hurray!"

The Island Battery blazed with light, with the flashes of cannon, gun swivels and musketry pouring a converging fire on the foolish men huddled beneath it.

"Oh, the Goddamned fools!" Micah Gill wailed. "The Goddamned simpleton, rum-drinking jackasses!"

Now the French gunners raised their sights slightly, sending a plunging fire of grapeshot, langrage-shot and musket balls into the waiting boats now dimly visible bobbing in the surf. Micah heard the balls and nails-and-bolt clusters rattling against the side of his boat and threw himself down. He also heard young Adam Jenkins moan softly and pitch on top of him. Putting out a hand, he felt the bolt sticking out of the dying youth's eye and swore again.

"Let's go, Red Deer!" he called, scrambling erect. "They may be fools, but they're English and we've got to help them."

"No, we don't," Red Deer yelled, pulling him down below the gunwales again. "They're lost, my brother—can't you see that? If we go ashore to help them, we'll be lost, too. When daylight comes, they'll all be as naked as flies on a window-pane. All they'll be able to do is surrender."

Micah paused, his resolution waning. Red Deer was right, he knew, and yet, he thought, grinding his teeth helplessly . . . All around him, the militia were shouting "Sheer off! Sheer off!" The paddlers in the boats ahead had reversed course and were furiously back-stroking out of the surf. Above the thunder of the breakers he could hear cries and screams from both the island and the boats. Even if he wanted to, Micah realized, he could not possibly land, and he reluctantly gave the order, "Sheer off!" to his own men.

A few seconds later, his brain blazed with pain and light, before his entire being sank into darkness.

"Micah! Micah! How do you feel?"

It was his father's voice, Micah Gill realized, instantly closing his eyes against the burning brightness of daylight. Opening them again, he saw that he lay on a rough bunk of crossed ropes in a large makeshift tent filled with other bunks and casualties.

"Micah, how do you feel?"

Micah put a hand to his throbbing temple and felt a bandage there. "All right, I guess," he said in a weak voice. "Can I have a drink of water?"

At once, Jedediah pressed a canteen to his son's lips and gently raised his head. "You damn near died," he said. "The surgeon told me you were exactly one millimeter between life and death."

"Wh-what happened?"

"A French ball hit you in the temple. It wasn't a glancing shot, either. In fact, it splintered a lot of bone. But if the angle had been one millimeter sharper, you'd've been killed."

Micah drank the blessed cool liquid gratefully. "Is Red Deer all right?"

"Oh, yes—he went back to his family in Springfield."

"What about the fellows who landed?"

"Those damn fools?—the ones who gave those three frigging foolish cheers?—they surrendered at dawn."

"I think they were drunk."

"Probably. But none of them will admit it."

"Admit it? I thought you said they were captured."

"They were. But they've been freed. Louisbourg surrendered, Micah—it's all over."

Micah Gill felt his temple again and glanced in dismay at his thin sticks of arms. "So I missed being in on the kill," he mused in a voice of disgust.

"You didn't miss much. The Island Battery affair—General Pepperell called it a fiasco—was the only real battle of the campaign. He was so torn up over it—he hardly spoke to Colonel Vaughn afterward—I think he would have pulled foot if Commander Warren hadn't captured the *Vigilant*. That put the shoe on the other foot. Instead of us starving and hurting for ammunition, now we had the French supplies for ourselves and it was Louisbourg that was hungry. The general set up another battery at Lighthouse Point and began pounding the Island Battery so hard the French soldiers took to hiding in the ocean. Still, the French didn't quit. They even began sending out sallies against the batteries, but they never amounted to much. Once, though, their Indians captured some of our men, and instead of letting them live as they promised, they tortured them and killed them. Funny, how a small thing like that could change the whole campaign. The French marquis who commanded the *Vigilant* had refused to tell Duchambon he'd lost the ship. He said the rules of war didn't require him to be a messenger of misfortune. But, then, after Warren told him about the Indians, he wrote Duchambon a letter saying how well he was being treated by the English and he hoped the French would do the same to their prisoners. When Duchambon read that the *Vigilant* had been captured, he realized that that was the last nail in his coffin. He beat a parley two days ago—June 15—just when we were going to hit them all-out from land and sea. So, you see, Micah, you really didn't miss much."

"I suppose so," Micah said wearily, closing his eyes and passing a hand over them. "But I still would have liked to have seen the surrender ceremony."

"They're all alike," Jedediah Gill sniffed. "Let's just hope the king lets us keep Louisbourg. Remember, Micah, to keep Port Royal, we had to take it twice."

The French and Indian War

_____18_____

The Marquis Duquesne, the new governor of Canada, was a descendant of the great French naval commander of that name, and was cast in the same iron military mold. Arriving in the colony in midsummer of 1752, he quickly held a review of French regulars and Canadian militia. To the surprise of the Canadians, who disliked the marquis's lofty bearing, he gave them better marks than the regulars.

"I think you can rely on the militia much more confidently than the troops from France," he told General de Marin, who was to command Duquesne's expedition into the Ohio territory held by the English. "They know how to shoot and fight in the woods, and they are much tougher."

"I agree with you, Monsieur," the aging soldier replied. "I have seen these _coureurs du bois_ march through the woods for days with nothing to go on but a few slices of pemmican. But do not the people of the colony oppose this operation?"

"The people do, but the militia don't. It is a great opportunity, Marin. The Ohio is wide open. If we can seize it, we can pin the English colonies between the Atlantic Ocean and the Allegheny Mountains. All of western America will be ours to explore and exploit. Look," he said, pointing to his wall map of the eastern continent, "we already possess the

288

two great waterways—the St. Lawrence and the Mississippi. We have two great bases of operation, Canada in the north and Louisiana in the south. King Louis claims the continent from the Alleghenies to the Rockies, from Florida and Mexico to the ultimate north. Now it is up to us to occupy all the points controlling the waterways between Montreal and New Orleans. That means the Ohio. Here," he said, pointing to the map again, "here are the vital Forks. Here, the Monongahela and the Allegheny meet to form the Ohio. It is here that the colonial ambitions of France and England must inevitably collide, *mon général*. It is here that we must build a mighty fort to command all of America west of the Alleghenies." He paused dramatically. "Someday, perhaps, as far west as the Western Ocean."

"*C'est un plan magnifique*, Monsieur le Gouverneur," General Marin said in a breathless voice. "A magnificent plan! A daring plan! You are yourself *magnifique*. But what of the treaty?"

"Aix-la-Chapelle?" the marquis asked in a tone of contempt. "It is no better than Ryswick or Utrecht. True, Louisbourg was returned to us. Otherwise, nothing has changed. The boundaries remain undecided. I tell you, *mon général*, it will come to a fight one day."

"I agree. But it is such a long way . . . with only fifteen hundred men . . . and the English, do you think they will stand still?"

"New York did nothing to stop us when we built the stone fort on Lake Champlain," Marquis Duquesne replied, assuming his customary air of superiority. "Why should the Ohio Forks be different from Crown Point? Virginia and Pennsylvania are just as indecisive as New York. None of them help each other. All they do is argue over money. Before Virginia or Pennsylvania can move, the Ohio Valley will be ours." Duquesne smiled grimly. "So will its Indians. If we can bar the English traders from the region, the Indians will be deprived of English guns and knives, of hatchets and blankets—in a word, of English gifts. They will become completely dependent on us. They will also begin to forget Louisbourg. The Indian respects nothing so much as force and daring, and this operation is bound to excite his admiration."

"It will be a master stroke," General Marin said, nodding in assent. "The colonial minister must indeed be excited."

"Not exactly," Duquesne said dryly. "He is not what I would call enthused. Here is his latest letter to me," he said lifting a paper from his desk and beginning to read: " 'Be on your guard against new undertakings; private interests are generally at the bottom of them. It is through these that new posts are established.' "

"True enough," Marin mused. "A young officer no sooner gets command of a fort before he begins to calculate his profits and marries right away. Rotten food, moldy powder, all sold to the post by him at twice their value. Canada, the land of clip-and-cut and rob the king."

"That's exactly what the minister said. Here, listen: 'The expenses of the colony are enormous; and they have doubled since the Peace. Build on the Ohio such forts as are absolutely necessary, but no more. Remember that His Majesty suspects your advisers of interested views.' "

" 'Interested' is hardly the word for it," Marin murmured. "Fortunately, there does not seem to be much opportunity for graft in this operation. By the way, who will be my second in command?"

Duquesne glanced away. "The Chevalier Pean," he replied in a tone of embarrassment.

"Pean! *Ce cocu*? That cuckold? He's the laughing stock of the colony!"

"Perhaps he is. But he is also a fine officer. It cannot be helped. The intendant insisted, and I could not resist him."

"I see. And I understand. Evidently, François Bigot is as enterprising in his pleasure as in his greed. Am I correct in suspecting that the intendant's affair with Pean's wife might have something to do with it? A clever way of getting the fellow out of the way. But who is more clever than the Crown Prince of Clip-and-Cut?"

The marquis smiled a thin smile. "I am aware of the intendant's . . . ah . . . practices—and of those of that pack of rascals around him who are bleeding the colony white. But he is an able and vigorous man, and I need him."

"Who dines with the devil must sup with a long spoon," Marin said sententiously, and Duquesne smiled his thin superior smile once more. "I will take care of François Bigot," he said, "And you, *mon cher général*, you will take care of the Ohio?"

"I will indeed!" the old soldier cried, his enthusiasm returning. "And I tell you, Monsieur le Marquis, that upon my return I will find you a duke!"

In the spring of 1753, the waters from Montreal to Lake Erie were covered with war canoes and bateaux carrying Marin's soldiers toward the Ohio. At Presque Isle they built a fort of squared chestnut logs. Then they cut a road about ten miles long to French Creek, placing at the road's end another outpost called Fort LeBoeuf. They could now follow French Creek to the Allegheny River, descending that turbulent stream to the Forks.

Carrying the supplies and baggage across the portages was heavy work, but the Canadians fell to it cheerfully. General Marin urged them on exuberantly. At first, Marin had been enraged and then discouraged to find that some of his supplies were actually silks and velvets and other useless luxuries sold to the king at enormous profits. But then, the sight of tribe after tribe of Indians coming to the fort to make submission restored his gruff good nature. Some of the Indians brought English scalps. Marin rewarded them, calling upon them to clear the area of the English. Though General Marin was sixty-three, he endured the hard wilderness life with great fortitude—until he fell ill with dysentery and died. To replace him, Governor Duquesne chose another old soldier, Legardeur de Saint-Pierre, who had just returned from a journey of exploration to the Rocky Mountains.

Upon his arrival at Fort LeBoeuf, Saint-Pierre ordered Captain Philippe Joincare and two subalterns forward to Venango, the place where French Creek enters the Allegheny. An English trader named John Frazier had a home there. Joincare evicted him and seized the house.

Venango was now France's farthest outpost. It was but a clearing in the wilderness, caught between the steady roar of merging waters and the eternal silence of the forests. Here, one day in December 1753, Joincare and his officers heard the sound of horses' hoofbeats approaching. Riding out of the woods came a tall young Virginian named George Washington, and with him an equally tall but more strongly built youth from Springfield, Massachusetts, named Daniel Quinn Red Deer Gill.

In the fall of 1753, Daniel Gill set out to see the world. At the door of the tavern in Springfield, he said good-bye to the grandfather for whom he had been named, kissed his mother fondly on the cheek, and shook the hand of his father, Red Deer. Then, as quickly as he could, for fear he might burst into tears, Danny Gill swung aboard the fine gray stallion his grandfather had given him and rode south.

It was a brilliant day, the air full of the golden light of autumn, the forests riotous with color. As he rode, Danny Gill sang in that faint Irish lilt he had acquired from his grandfather:

> She was just the kind of lass, me boys,
>   That nature did intend,
> To walk around the world, me boys,
>   Without a Grecian bend.
>
> Nor did she wear a chignon,
>   And I want you all to know,
> That I met her in the garden
>   Where the praties grow.

Danny finished his song with a shout of delight which went reverberating around the woods. His horse snorted in pleasure, and Danny leaned forward to pat him on the withers. A great sense of peace came over the young man, to be followed by an almost unbearable joy. He was out on his own at last! His youth was behind him, and before him lay adventure and the test of his manhood.

Danny was riding through a wide valley of the Berkshire Hills. It was mostly farmland. The bright green of the crops contrasted with the copses or hills in bright autumnal colors—reds and golds, browns and tans and burgundy mixing in with the green of the pines—rising from the valley floor. Ringing the valley like the inner walls of a cup were the darker hues of the distant mountainsides. Danny could see the black dots of cattle grazing on the pale green patches of the hillsides. Stacks of hay six feet high rose from the reaped meadows like great loaves of brown bread. Above him,

Danny Gill heard a wild crying. Looking up, he saw an immense ragged V perhaps a mile long formed by hundreds of wild geese heading south. He exulted in their high keening call, he loved it. "I'm going south, too," he cried, pulling off his hat and waving it at the geese. "I'm going to Virginia!"

Danny replaced his hat, sobering. Yes, he was going to Virginia. He remembered talking about it to his Great Uncle Half Moon the preceding August. Since he was twelve, Danny's father had sent him to Caughnawaga every summer to study French under the Jesuits and learn the tribal dialects and Indian skills from his great uncle.

"You are lucky, Danny, to be living when you are," Half Moon had said to him. "Look at me, I am in my sixties. I don't look good anymore. The squaws don't look up when I pass like they used to." He smiled a gap-toothed smile. "I don't have many teeth left. I don't know if I will be alive to see the great things that are going to happen. But you will, Danny. You will see the French and the English fight to the death. Which side will you be on?"

"On the side of my father's people, the English."

Half Moon snorted in contempt. "You are foolish, my great nephew. The English are women. They sit forever in council chambers wearing petticoats and quarreling. The French are men. They do not talk, they act. They are building forts everywhere, fortifying the passes and the crossings of the waters of the Ohio."

"The Ohio?"

"Yes, the great river that empties into the Father of Waters. I have seen it many times. Its lands are beautiful and rich. The French want the valley of the Ohio, and so do the English. But the English are asleep in their nightgowns, and by the time they wake up, the Ohio will belong to France."

A dreamy look came into Daniel Gill's dark blue eyes. He gazed thoughtfully at his uncle. "It is time for me to seek my fortune in the world," he said. "Do you think I should try the Ohio country?"

"Why not Boston? Your grandfather," Half Moon said, his lip curling slightly, "is a big man there. He has much of the things that white men value. Money . . . ships . . . forests of timber . . . Your grandfather could help you, Danny."

"That's what my father says. But I don't want to go to

Grandfather Gill on my knees. I want to meet him as a man, on my own two feet."

"Spoken like a true Caughnawaga brave," Half Moon had said approvingly. "Go to the Ohio, then."

And that was where Daniel Gill was going. He would ride to Albany, only a short distance away—deliberately avoiding Boston—and take ship on the Hudson River for New York City, whence he would sail for Norfolk and ride overland to Williamsburg, the capital of Virginia. Travelers stopping in the tavern at Springfield had told him that Williamsburg was the place where frontiersmen and settlers bound for the Ohio organized and equipped themselves.

Robert Dinwiddie sat at his desk in his chambers in the governor's palace in Williamsburg. He was reading a sheaf of reports from the frontier. From time to time he laid a contented hand upon his corpulent middle, belching gently. Governor Dinwiddie was fond of a good meal, and he had never ceased to marvel at the delights of the table he had encountered in Virginia. The woods were actually alive with all manner of game. It was like living in Paradise. To eat, all a man need do was pluck fruit from the trees or point his musket at ducks or turkeys or deer. However, of late, a serpent had insinuated itself into Paradise.

The French.

The reports which Robert Dinwiddie studied, and which caused his normally calm blue-gray eyes to blaze with anger, concerned the encroachment of the French upon the Ohio territory. The last, and most infuriating, was the eviction of the settler John Frazier from his house at Venango. The cheek of them! That was why Governor Dinwiddie had sent for young Major Washington. He called, "Come in," after a knock on the door, and Washington entered.

He was very tall—probably about three inches above six feet—narrow-shouldered, and wide-hipped. Dinwiddie knew that Washington was only twenty-one, yet he seemed much older. Perhaps it was because of the deep pits with which smallpox had scarred his face. Or it could be the quietly determined set of his heavy jaw, or the glint of limitless ambition that even his humorless pale eyes could not conceal. Dinwiddie approved of George Washington's unfailing seriousness. Dour Scot that he was, he considered wit or humor a defect in an officer of the king.

"Sit down, Major Washington," he said, and his visitor took his seat, immediately composing his features in dignity. "I am pleased to have you volunteer for this very important mission," the governor continued. "The French at Venango must be warned that they must leave the Ohio territory." He lifted a heavy document bearing the seal of King George II. "Our gracious majesty has most kindly consented to my proposal to evict the French. He is going to provide military equipment." Dinwiddie scowled. "That should satisfy these penny-pinching burgesses," he muttered. "But the king also does not wish to provoke a war. That is why he has asked me to warn them first. Anything that happens afterward can then be laid at their door. And if they do not move out, I assure you, Major Washington, something will happen."

"When would that be, Sir?"

"Next spring," Dinwiddie said grimly. "I should like to build a fort at the Forks of the Ohio then. That is why it is most important for you to get my warning message to the French before winter sets in. It is very cold out there, Major. You must hurry. And it is also very important to get the French reply back to me as soon as possible. That way, if it is negative—and I expect that it will be—I can begin preparing immediately for my spring campaign." He lifted a sealed envelope from his desk and handed it to Washington. "Here is my message."

George Washington took the envelope and placed it inside his uniform coat of blue trimmed with red. "I will guard it with my life, Sir," he said, saluting crisply. "And I think you, Governor, for the honor of this mission and for your confidence in me."

"Very good, Major," Governor Robert Dinwiddie said, lifting a hand to his lips to suppress a tiny belch."

Major Washington rode hurriedly from the governor's palace to the inn where he was staying. It was dark when he got there. George glanced up anxiously at the sky. He had hoped to set off at once for Alexandria to purchase the supplies he would need for his trip. But it was too late, he thought, and went inside the taproom to eat.

George sat alone at a table lighted by a single candle. The

only other occupant of the taproom was a big strong youth in fringed buckskin. Washington was impressed by the breadth of the young man's shoulders, the good health and cheer seeming to radiate from his bronzed face. His high cheekbones suggested Indian blood.

The taproom door burst open and an Indian in war paint brandishing a tomahawk staggered inside. Seeing Washington, he gave a whoop and came swaying toward him with upraised hatchet. Instantly, the youth in buckskin was on his feet, dashing softly up behind the Indian to seize him in a double armlock, until, gasping and howling hideously, he let the tomahawk fall. The youth put his foot on the weapon and pointed toward the door, shouting at the Indian in dialect. Astonished, the Indian went stumbling out into the night, and the youth closed the door behind him.

"He's drunk," he explained.

"You should have let me send for the constable," Washington said. "He ought to be locked up. People aren't safe with drunken Indians like that roaming the streets."

"He can't do much harm without his hatchet," the youth said, grinning. He stooped to pick up the tomahawk and feel the edge of the blade. "Like a razor," he muttered. He grinned again. "Well, I really let him go because he's a fellow tribesman," he explained.

"You're an Indian?" Major Washington exclaimed in astonishment.

"One-fourth Caughnawaga, Sir. Two-fourths English and one-fourth Irish." He winked cheerfully. "My Grandfather Daniel Quinn always said, sure and bejasus the Irish were used to such odds."

George Washington attempted a thin smile. Then, as though remembering his manners, he exclaimed, "By the great Jehovah, I haven't even thanked you for saving my life. Your name, Sir?"

"Gill. Daniel Gill."

"Thank you, Daniel. You are very quick. You don't sound like a Virginian. Where are you from?"

"Springfield, Massachusetts."

"What brings you to Virginia?" Washington asked, motioning to Danny to sit down with him. Danny did, and replied: "I'm thinking of going out to the Ohio country."

Washington looked at him with interest. "That's odd. So

am I. I noticed you spoke to the Indian in dialect. Can you speak their languages?"

"Most of the eastern ones. French, too."

Major Washington's pale eyes shone. "By God, Daniel, you might be just the man I'm looking for. I am Major George Washington of the Virginia Militia. I am going to the Ohio on a mission for Governor Dinwiddie. What I need most of all is an interpreter. One for the Indians and another for the French." His appraising eye went over Danny in open admiration. "I would certainly like to have you come with me."

Daniel Gill stared thoughtfully at the earnest young officer opposite him. "Fact is, Major, I was thinking of settling out there. My Indian uncle says the lands are beautiful and rich. Would the governor think my services worth a grant of land?"

"Certainly. Governor Dinwiddie has an interest in the Ohio Company. I'm sure something can be worked out, Daniel. Are we agreed?"

"We are," Danny said with a warm grin, and Major George Washington signaled to the barmaid to come to his table.

A few weeks later, Major Washington and Daniel Gill set out on horseback for the Ohio Company's trading station on Will's Creek. There, Washington met the frontiersman, Christopher Gist, who was to act as his guide. Four woodsmen also joined the party as servants. They would care for the immense baggage Washington had purchased for the expedition: guns, ammunition, compass, tents, corn for the horses, provisions, presents for the Indians, medicines, tobacco, some wampum and even Indian dress for Washington to wear should he find it useful. In the middle of November, the party left Will's Creek. They passed through a desolate forest inhabited only by bears and rattlesnakes. As they climbed steadily upward, moving both north and west, they ceased to hear the warning whir of the rattlers, facing, instead, a new and perhaps more deadly enemy: the iron cold of the northwestern winter. Eventually, the ceaseless cold rain that pelted them became interlaced with snow. They plodded on, reaching an elevation of three thousand feet before turning west for the Ohio.

They came to it in a swirling snowstorm, standing breathlessly on the windswept point about twenty-five feet above the water where the Allegheny and Monogahela met to form the mighty river sweeping westward toward the Mississippi. Major Washington gazed around him with his sparkling surveyor's eye.

"This is where we must build our fort," he said to Danny Gill. "See how the point commands all the rivers. The land is flat and well-timbered, very convenient for building. I must tell the governor about it. From here, we would have no trouble controlling the entire valley."

At once, the woodsmen began loading the baggage into a canoe, ferrying it across the Allegheny. Then men followed, while the horses swam the chilly river. Washington then proceeded down the right bank of the Ohio to the village of Logtown fifteen miles downstream. There, he found the friendly Indian chief called Half-King. While Danny interpreted, Half-King told Washington how he had journeyed to Fort LeBoeuf to confront General Marin and order him to leave the Ohio.

"I said to him, 'For be it known to you, Father, that this is our land and not yours,'" Half-King recalled. "'If you had come in a peaceable manner like our brothers, the English, we should not be against your trading with us, as they do. But to come, Father, and build houses upon our land and to take it by force is what we cannot submit to.'" Half-King said he then threw down a belt of wampum as a substitute for the one previously given to him by Marin and told him to withdraw.

"But he said to me, 'Where is my wampum that you took away, with the marks of the towns on it? This wampum I do not know, which you have discharged me off the land with. But you need not put yourself to the trouble of speaking, for I will not hear you. I am not afraid of flies or mosquitoes, for Indians are such as those. I tell you, down that river I will go and will build upon it. Therefore, here is your wampum. I fling it at you!'" Whereupon the French officer threw the belt at Half-King's head.

There were tears of rage in Half-King's eyes when he finished his narrative, and the recollection of his humiliation had much to do with his consenting to accompany Washington's party to Venango. Two other chiefs came with him. On the fourth of December 1753, with winter full upon them,

Washington and his men rode out of the bare and freezing forest into the clearing at Venango. The French fleur-de-lis waved over the log structure that had once belonged to John Frazier. Dismounting with great dignity, followed by Daniel Gill, Washington strode to the open door of the building, where Captain Joincare stood in full uniform, with his two subalterns behind him.

With flawless manners, Captain Joincare invited the two men inside. Major Washington, who had seen at once that the French officer was a half-breed, turned to Danny and said: "Tell him that I have come to deliver a communication from Governor Dinwiddie to the French officer commanding in this area." Danny nodded and spoke to Joincare in dialect. The Frenchman stared in mild surprise, and answered in the same tongue. Then Danny shifted to French, and Joincare was again startled. They spoke for a few more minutes, after which Danny said to Washington: "His name is Captain Joincare. He's the son of a French officer and a Seneca squaw. I've heard of him. He's very popular with the Indians. He says he commands only on the Ohio. You will have to take your message to General Saint-Pierre up at Fort LeBoeuf." Washington frowned. Fifty more miles! Three or four more days with the winter setting deeper and deeper. . . . He bowed, and Danny went on: "But he would like us to dine with him tonight."

Major Washington bowed again and said: "Tell him we accept."

That night at dinner, Washington politely declined repeated offers to refill his wine glass. He sipped the liquid slowly, while his hosts opened bottle after bottle. Suddenly, George heard Indians singing outside. He recognized the voice of Half-King mingling with those of other, stranger Indians. He guessed at once that Joincare had prepared a banquet for Half-King to lure him to the French side, or at least to delay the party's departure to LeBoeuf. He concealed his dismay, listening while Danny Gill translated what Captain Joincare, who had turned voluble with the wine, was saying to him.

"He calls you Vassington," Danny said with a grin. "He says, 'Major Washington, we intend to take possession of the Ohio, and, by God, we're going to do it. The Ohio was discovered by La Salle and belongs to France, not England.' He says he knows that the English outnumber the French by two to one, but he says they will move too slowly to stop them."

George Washington nodded, instructed Danny to ask a few pointed questions relative to the French strength in the area, and then politely withdrew to his camp. In the morning, he awoke to the sound of a cold December rain pounding furiously on his tent canvas. He could not find Half-King. He could not find him the next morning, either, and sent Danny Gill looking for him.

"He's got a hangover," Danny reported. "Joincare's got him mixed up with a bunch of Delawares, and they're trying to get him to change sides. I don't think he wants to, but brandy has a way of changing an Indian's mind."

Another day passed. At length, on December 7, Half-King and the other two chiefs, abashed but sober, rode off with Washington toward LeBoeuf. Four days later, having passed through forests choked with snow, drenched with rain while they floundered through swamps and marshes, the party came to LeBoeuf.

Major Washington dismounted outside the log fort. His careful eye marked the surrounding fields studded with stumps. He did not miss the hundreds of canoes drawn up on the banks of the creek. For use in the spring, he guessed—and then made his presence known to the French general.

Like Captain Joincare, Legardeur de Saint-Pierre was the soul of courtesy. He listened politely while Danny Gill translated Dinwiddie's letter for him: "I must desire you to acquaint me by whose authority and instructions you have lately marched from Canada with an armed force, and invaded the King of Great Britain's territories. It becomes my duty to require your peaceable departure; and that you would forbear prosecuting a purpose so interruptive of the harmony and good understanding which His Majesty is desirous to continue and cultivate with the Most Christian King. I persuade myself that you will receive and entertain Major Washington with the candor and politeness natural to your nation; and it will give me the greatest satisfaction if you return him with an answer suitable to my wishes for a very long and lasting peace between us."

Saint-Pierre did entertain Major Washington with great courtesy, while taking three days to prepare his reply. Each night, George Washington lay in his tent listening to the singing and laughter of the parties honoring Half-King and the two other chiefs.

"Their packs are stuffed with French gifts," Danny Gill told him.

George nodded grimly. "We can't leave them behind. If they join the French, there won't be an Indian in the area still friendly to us. We could even lose the Iroquois. Besides, we need them to steer the canoes. Do what you can with them, Danny. Every day's delay makes our chances of getting back before winter sets in that much less. And our control of the Ohio depends on our getting back."

While Danny Gill set out to find Half-King and his friends, George Washington calmly walked about the fort inspecting the French defenses. He found barracks, stables, a smithy and other buildings full of cannon and other supplies. He now counted 210 canoes, in addition to many others being built. Obviously, the French intended a mighty push in the spring. He returned to his tent, where Danny Gill awaited him.

"They're waiting for the gifts the French promised them," Danny said. "Guns and beads, and, of course, their favorite beverage. They're supposed to get them tomorrow. But if they get drunk again, that means at least another day."

"We can't afford to lose even one more day," Washington said grimly. "Come with me, Danny—I'm going to speak to Saint-Pierre."

The elderly soldier greeted George Washington with grave courtesy, barely raising his eyebrows when the young officer came straight to the point: "General, I must speak to you candidly. I do not believe I am receiving the candor and courtesy requested by Governor Dinwiddie. I have been here for four days, now, and I still am unable to leave. My Indians are being feasted and regaled in a manner which suggests an attempt to detach them from their British allegiance, or at least to detain them to my great discomfort."

Saint-Pierre stared at the impertinent young Virginian for one fleeting cold moment, and then, regaining his suavity, replied: "*Mon cher* Washington, I know of no conspiracy to detach or delay your Indians. I assure you I will do all in my power to speed your departure."

"You are still going to give them those presents tomorrow—the guns and things and the brandy?"

Saint-Pierre gave an urbane shrug. "How can we refuse, *mon cher commandant*? They ask for these guns and trinkets, and we must give them to them, lest they sulk like spoiled children. *Comprenez vous?*"

"I do understand," George Washington said curtly, and with a frigid bow he stormed out of the general's presence, hastening to find Half-King and to wring from him a promise to leave immediately after receiving the presents.

In the morning, before General Saint-Pierre and his officers, the delighted Indians received their gifts. Jugs of brandy were brought out to them. The three chiefs hesitated. They were obviously suffering from the excesses of the previous night's drinking and yearned for the immemorial remedy provided by more of the same. Half-King shot an agonized glance at Washington. His fingers twitched.

"Remember your promise!" Daniel Gill shouted in dialect, and Half-King backed sullenly away from the jugs. He signaled to the other two chiefs to follow him, and they picked up their presents and walked rapidly down to the waiting canoe.

"We've won!" George Washington muttered to Danny Gill, squeezing his arm in jubilation. Turning, with a grace and polish almost the equal of his suave host's, he received Legardeur de Saint-Pierre's reply to Governor Dinwiddie and set out on his return journey.

It had rained fourteen of the first fifteen days of December, but the next two days were dry. The Indians informed Washington that the swollen waters of the creek were falling fast. They paddled hard downstream for three days, watching anxiously while the freezing water thickened. On the fourth, the ice was so thick they were forced to carry the canoe and its contents overland to more open water. On the following day, they reached Venango, where they parted company with the Indians.

Major Washington saw with dismay that his horses had become thin, starved creatures, their bones visible beneath their hides. Still, he pressed on with them and the four woodsmen. Snow began to fall again. The horses stumbled repeatedly on the icy trail. The woodsmen also suffered, bundled up in their Indian matchcoats, or woolen mantles, against the terrible cold. On the morning of December 26, Major Washington found that the horses could go no further. Three of the four men were so severely frostbitten they could not move. Washington decided to leave all four behind and proceed with Gist and Gill on foot.

"I would not advise it, Major," Gist protested. "Danny and I are used to the forest, but I don't think you are. You will get tired or footsore, or both."

George Washington shook his head. "I cannot wait. I must get the French reply to Williamsburg within the next few weeks. If I die trying, it will be no worse than not getting there until spring—and at least I will be trying."

Gist and Danny stared at George in admiration. Wrapping themselves in matchcoats, packs on their backs and muskets in their hands, the three men set out through the snowbound forest. Before nightfall, Washington was trail-weary. Luckily, they found an empty Indian cabin. They spent the night there, rising at two o'clock in the morning to press on through woods half-lighted by the snow.

They came to Murdering Town, where an Indian who knew Gist and spoke English joined them as a guide. He carried Washington's pack. But George soon became footsore as well as weary. The Indian offered to carry his musket. George refused. Gist and Danny eyed the Indian suspiciously. What would he do with two weapons? Now the Indian became churlish. He warned the white men not to tarry in the forest. It was full of Ottawas, he said, who would kill them and scalp them if they found them. Gist came to Washington and confided in a low voice: "I don't trust him. He's leading us too far to the northeast."

Washington nodded, and Gist began to question the Indian about his direction.

"I'm heading for my own cabin about a gunshot sound away," he answered.

"Very well. Lead on."

The Indian trotted forward with the three white men behind him. He entered a meadow. Suddenly, he wheeled, lifted his musket and fired at them.

"Are you shot?" George cried to Gist, and the frontiersman shouted, "No." Together, the two men ran forward and seized the Indian, who had hidden behind a big white oak to reload.

"Let me kill him," Gist pleaded.

"No," said Washington.

"Then, let me send him home. But we'll have to travel all night, just in case he comes back with his friends."

Washington wondered if he could go on. His feet pained him with every step, and they were like lumps of ice. But he realized that their tracks in the snow could be easily followed, and started out in the dark with his two companions for the nearest crossing of the Allegheny. By now, they reasoned, the river would be frozen solid and they could cross on foot. When they came to it, they stared at it in despair. It was frozen indeed, but only about fifty feet to either side. The turbulent Allegheny's wide middle was open, black and angry. Chunks of ice floated swiftly down it.

Refusing to give up hope, they began to build a raft. It would have to be made of standing timber, and there was only one hatchet among them. But they built it, hacking away by turns with frozen hands. It was ready by sundown. Cutting poles, they carried it over the ice and pushed it gingerly out into the forbidding current. Ice chunks struck the frail craft and spun it around. Soon they were drifting helplessly downstream. There was no chance to get to the other side. They poled desperately against the flow. Washington's pole caught a snag and he was dragged into the freezing river. Flinging up a long arm, he caught a log of the raft and pulled himself aboard.

"Pole!" Danny Gill cried, pointing to a little island just ahead. "Pole for that island!"

Poling wildly, driven by the current, they scraped up on the island's icy shore and let their raft bob crazily downstream. Exhausted and shivering, Major Washington already sheathed in ice, they sank down to a dreadful, fitful sleep, snuggling against each other for warmth. They awoke with all three of them coated in ice. But they looked at the river with shining eyes.

It was frozen solid from shore to shore.

Danny Gill went on his knees and crossed himself, bowing his head to pray. Crossing himself again, he jumped to his feet with a shout of joy. "Glory, glory, hallelujah!" he yelled.

Washington looked at him curiously. "You're a Catholic?"

"Yes."

"By God, I don't think I've ever met a Catholic before. That sign you made, is that the sign of the cross?"

"It sure is."

"I know I never saw that before. Why do you do it? Is it superstitious or magic? I'm a Mason, you know, and they say at the lodge that that sort of thing is mumbo jumbo."

Danny grinned impishly, brushing the ice from his match-coat. "Maybe witchcraft, too, Major? But there's nothing wrong with it. It's just something we do before and after prayer. The sign of the cross shows that we're followers of Christ."

"We are, too—but I don't think you need to do that to show it. Or go down on your knees."

Danny Gill grinned again. "No disrespect to you, Major—but wouldn't you kneel to the king? That's something my Irish grandfather made me swear I'd never do." Major Washington's sallow face reddened, and Danny said: "Then why not kneel to the King of Kings?"

"You have a point, there," George Washington said slowly. "But let's not waste time in religious bickering. Let's get across the river."

Walking stiffly and slowly, but faster as their frozen limbs warmed to their movement, the three men crossed the Allegheny. Ten miles later they entered the unaccustomed but welcome warmth of John Frazier's new trading post. Procuring horses there, they rode on to Christopher Gist's settlement, where George and Danny bought horses and sent their other mounts back to Frazier's. They hurried on to Will's Creek . . . to Belvoir . . . to Williamsburg. On January 16, 1754, George and Danny entered the capital of Virginia. Major Washington hastened to the governor's palace.

Robert Dinwiddie was shocked when he saw the emaciated body and gaunt face of the young emissary standing before him. Washington had lost perhaps thirty pounds, and he looked ten years older.

"My God, Major, what you must have endured to get back here! I shall inform his majesty of your devotion to his service."

Dinwiddie took the letter which Major Washington handed him in silence. As he read, the governor's slate-colored eyes became thoughtful. He put the document down and stared fixedly at Washington, saying in a quiet voice:

"Major, this means war."

The next time Governor Robert Dinwiddie sent for George Washington was in the spring of 1754. Washington, now twenty-two and a lieutenant colonel, had recovered his health and weight and was once again the soul of sobriety and confidence when he presented himself to the governor.

"I have received a report from Captain Trent that he has begun construction of the fort at the Forks of the Ohio," the governor said. "He wrote from Will's Creek, where he is now with most of his men. Why he left the Forks, I cannot say. But he left only forty men there under Ensign Ward. That is not nearly enough to complete the fort and defend it. And we cannot afford to let it fall to the French, Colonel Washington. The Forks are vital to the king's interest in the west. So I am sending you with about half the Virginia regiment—say one hundred and fifty men—out there to reinforce it and to help complete it. In the meantime, I will be sending you a company of British regulars from South Carolina under Captain Mackay."

Governor Dinwiddie sighed and passed a hand over his forehead. "As you know, the House of Burgesses has finally voted a most frugal grant to finance this undertaking. I don't mind telling you, it may have come too late. If they'd voted it in November instead of February, the fort would by now be built and garrisoned. But as it stands now . . ." He shook his head wearily. "The Marquis Duquesne is an experienced soldier. He has no assembly to haggle with or withhold his funds. He need not send letter after letter to brother colonies begging for assistance which is almost never forthcoming. At a word from him, all Canada springs to arms. He may already have set his forces in motion. That is why you must hurry, Colonel Washington. The Forks must not fall to France."

Colonel Washington crossed the Alleghenies in April to a point about 110 miles southeast of the Forks. He was preparing for bed when Captain Daniel Gill came hurrying into his tent. "Colonel, Ensign Ward and his men just entered camp. He wants to speak to you."

Washington was thunderstruck. "Ward? What is he doing here?"

"He surrendered the Forks to the French," Gill said quietly, and Washington, now aghast and trembling with anger, turned to confront the young commander who had come into his tent.

"I couldn't help it, Sir," Ward pleaded, seeing Washington's temples begin to throb, fearing the terrible temper with which the Virginia Militia was familiar. "They came down the Allegheny on the seventeenth. The rivers were covered with bateaux and canoes as far as you could see. There must have been a thousand of them." He looked at Washington appealingly.

"Go on," the colonel said grimly, certain the man was exaggerating.

"They ran cannon right up to our stockade and summoned us to surrender. With only forty men . . . no cannon of our own . . ." Ward lifted his shoulders helplessly. "They burnt our fort and began building a bigger one of their own. Fort Duquesne. Then they let us go."

Washington gestured brusquely toward the tent entrance. "Get your men fed and bedded down. Report to Captain Gill in the morning." There was not a word of sympathy. Crushed, Ensign Ward departed. Washington stared gravely at Danny Gill. "We will have to push on farther to the northwest. Establish a forward base and wait for reinforcements and artillery." Gill nodded, and the colonel sat at his field desk to write his report to Governor Dinwiddie: "The Forks have fallen without a shot fired in their defense," he began. "Fort Duquesne now holds the west for France . . ."

In the morning, Washington received a message from his old comrade, Half-King. It warned him that the French were on the march from Fort Duquesne under a young officer named Jumonville and meant to attack him. Colonel Washington immediately changed his marching plans, moving his men to Great Meadows. It was a level field of bushes and tall grass surrounded by wooded hills and traversed by a gully. Washington set his men to work turning the gully into an entrenchment.

At night, a runner from Half-King came to Great Meadows. He said the chief was encamped only a few miles away and that he had found a party of French hidden in a glen. At once, Washington led a group of forty men into the forest. It was a black, rain-swept night. Again and again, the English stumbled from the narrow path and went floundering through the wilderness. Seven men lost their way. At sunrise, Washington reached Half-King's camp. They conferred, and Washinton's soldiers, now joined by Half-King's Indians, marched in single file through the woods to the rocky hollow where Half-King said the French were.

They were there, snatching their muskets the moment they saw a tall young figure rise up above them and shout, "Fire!"

An English volley crashed out. Cries of pain rose from the French. A dozen of them threw down their muskets and ran to their rear. They sprinted back, their hands held high, screaming, *"Indiens! Indiens!"* The French fired again. Half-King took aim at a young Frenchman and pulled the trigger. Joseph Coulon, the Sieur de Jumonville, fell dead.

Suddenly, the skirmish was over. Before Washington could restrain them, Half-King's warriors brained and scalped the wounded, then scalped the dead. There were ten Frenchmen killed and one wounded. Twenty-two were taken prisoner. Washington suffered one man wounded.

The young colonel looked jubilantly around the tiny field—his first battleground—until he saw the Indians moving menacingly toward his cowering captives. He went at once to Half-King and ordered him to leave the prisoners alone.

"They must be killed!" Half-King shouted angrily. "Killed and scalped. They are French, and the French ate my father. I must avenge him!"

Colonel Washington shook his head calmly. "They are my prisoners, Half-King. On my honor and by the rules of war, I am bound to protect them."

The Indian chief stared into the young Englishman's eyes. Tossing his head sullenly, he wheeled and walked away. Within a few more minutes, Lieutenant Colonel George Washington with his men and his prisoners had started the march back to Great Meadows.

The death of the young Jumonville shocked and angered Canada. To avenge him, his brother, Coulon de Villiers, marched from Montreal to Fort Duquesne with four hundred Indians. Reinforced by about another five hundred French troops, Villiers made for Great Meadows.

There, Colonel Washington had built a rough, square enclosure of logs with a trench, which he named Fort Necessity. It was crowded with Washington's militia, Half-King and his followers, about thirty Indian families and an independent company of regulars from South Carolina. Washington found the Indian families, with their helter-skelter wigwams, their scurrying children and their ceaselessly barking dogs an almost unbearable nuisance. The regulars were almost less welcome. Captain Mackay refused to accept orders or even the countersign from Washington.

"I hold my commission from the king," he said. "It supersedes any colonial commission. If you do not place yourself under my command, I shall act independently in this affair."

With difficulty Washington controlled his temper. "I could almost wish the regulars hadn't come," he complained to Captain Gill. "They won't help building the fort unless I pay them an extra shilling a day. So my men have to do it all for eight pence a day, and they don't like it." He frowned. "Any sign of the supply train from Will's Creek?"

"None, Sir. We're still very low on ammunition, and there's almost no bread. Fortunately, we've got the cows and should have fresh beef for some time."

Washington nodded. "Half-King's scouts have found the French. I expect them to attack tomorrow morning."

It rained next day. About eleven o'clock in the morning, the French and their Indians appeared at the edge of two wooded hills above the fort. Hiding behind trees and bushes, they began to rake the English with a steady musket fire. Washington's men in the trenches returned the fire. The rain poured down. Eventually, the English in the trenches were standing knee-deep in water. Suddenly, a weird screaming and roaring and barking rose above the sound of battle.

"My God, what's that?" Colonel Washington called to Captain Gill.

"It's our cattle and our horses! Even our dogs. The French are slaughtering them. They mean to deny us our transport and our meat."

Gradually the hideous cries of the dying animals subsided, but the screams of the dying and the moans of the wounded did not as the battle continued in the pouring rain. At one point, Washington ordered swivel guns to be mounted against the enemy. But the French on the high ground cut down the gunners. Twilight began to fall. The fusillade rose sharply, only to be drowned in a deluge of rain.

It was a disaster for the English. The rain overflowed the

trenches. It wet the men's flintlocks and all but swept away the powder carefully placed in what had been considered a dry place inside the stockade. They were now down to their bayonets.

At about eight o'clock, out of the gathering gloom, came a French voice, shouting: *"Voulez-vous parlementer?"*

"What does that mean?" Washington asked Captain Gill.

"They want to know if you'll parley."

"No," Washington said grimly. "It's a trick. They just want to see the condition of our camp."

The battle sputtered on. Again, the French called out.

"They want to know if you will send a French-speaking officer," said Danny Gill. "They promised he'll be returned unhurt."

George Washington pondered his predicament. One-third of his effectives were dead or wounded. Their muskets were fouled. His powder was wet. His horses and cattle were gone, and to feed his men he had only two bags of flour and a little bacon. Even if a change in weather should dry the powder, there were only two screws with which to remove the wet charges from the fouled muskets. Washington was still wavering when he heard the sound of singing.

"The men have found the rum you brought for the Indians," Captain Gill said in a shocked voice.

"So it seems," Washington said sadly. "Go ahead, Daniel. Take Captain Van Braam with you."

"The Dutchman?"

"Yes. He says he can speak French."

Captain Gill nodded and left, ducking low at the entrance. Colonel Washington sat in the silent darkness, inwardly contemplating what seemed to be the wreckage of a military career that had hardly begun. The drunken singing rose in volume, like a dirge for his ambition. Captain Van Braam came into the tent.

"Where is Captain Gill," Washington asked.

"He fell down in der dark and hurt his head," the Dutchman replied, lighting a candle to study the water-stained document in his hands. "Der Doctor is fixing him up already." Van Braam peered at the text. "Dey say dey iss here to avenge Jumonville," he began. "Ach! Such handwriting!" At length, he translated Villiers's terms, which, after some changes, Colonel George Washington found acceptable.

Next day, the defeated English marched out of the slime of Fort Necessity with drums playing, colors flying, and guns sloped, while the enemy Indians went rushing in to plunder all that had been left behind. Even Washington found it difficult to maintain a proud face. Like his men, he was weary, hungry and dirty. In his ears were the moans and entreaties of the wounded, who, with no horses to pull the hospital wagons, had to be carried on the backs of their comrades. He also heard the whoops and gunfire of the Indians who harried his force all along the sixty miles back to Will's Creek. It was the darkest day of Washington's young life, and he always remembered the date.

It was the fourth of July.

19

As had been his custom for years, Jedediah Gill took his midday meal at Gill's Tavern and Landing. At sixty-five, Jedediah was still an imposing man. His paunch was no larger than it had been at forty, and he still walked briskly with an erect carriage. Only his wife, Rachel, knew of the constant rhematic pain which he suffered in his shoulders and his lower body.

Entering the taproom, he stopped to stare at a familiar figure at one of the harbor-window tables. An expression of delighted disbelief crossed his seamed face, and he sprang forward eagerly. "Benjamin Franklin! What a pleasant surprise! What brings you here, Ben? I thought you were at the Colonial Congress in Albany."

Benjamin Franklin glanced up, his little eyes twinkling behind his spectacles. "I was," he said sourly, "but it turned out to be the useless dogfight I thought it would be."

"That's not good," Jedediah said gravely. "We've got to find some kind of union, or the French will swallow us up one by one."

"That's what I told the delegates," Franklin said, a frown wrinkling his bald, belligerent forehead. "They've got us

312

north, south, and west with the sea at our backs—divided and disorganized."

"But I thought they agreed to your plan for an intercolonial union."

"They did, at least on paper. But before I left Albany, the royal observers told me the crown would turn it down because it gave too much power to the colonies, and the delegates said the colonies would ignore it because it gave too much power to the crown. So I'm sure it'll die a slow death in the dustbin of history," he finished ruefully. Then, looking up, his eyes twinkled again. He said: "But I do say you're looking fine, Jed Gill. Especially for a man your age."

"What d'y mean, my *age*," Jedediah retorted scornfully. "I'm only sixteen years older than you, and I'll wager I can still jump up on that table of yours." They both chuckled, and Jedediah continued: " 'Course, I can't shake the rheumy. My son tells me it'll go away if I quit drinking. 'Goddammit, Malachi,' I told him, 'I never knew a doctor yet who wouldn't tell a sick cow to stop eating grass!' "

Benjamin Franklin laughed aloud, showing his false teeth. "You haven't changed, Jed Gill. I take it your family is well."

"All fine," Jedediah replied proudly. "Rachel is fine, happy as a brood sow with all her grandchildren. All the children are married now, Ben. For a spell, I thought I was the end of the Gill line. But now I've got so many grandchildren I feel like the old woman who lived in a shoe." He flushed slightly, looking cautiously around the rapidly filling taproom. "Got another branch of my family down Virginia way, too, Ben," he muttered. "I think I told you about it last time I was in Philadelphia."

"Indeed you did, Jed—after I don't know how many bottles of my best Madeira." Franklin smiled a faintly leering smile. "Such . . . ah . . . indescretions are not uncommon."

"This boy's a fine strapping young man. Got Irish blood in him besides the Indian and English. Not a bad combination for fighting, eh, Ben? Fact is, he was with young Washington at Fort Necessity."

Benjamin Franklin was impressed. "He *was*?" he said in surprise, removing his spectacles to polish them before replacing them on his long nose. "You can be proud of that, Jed. The Gill family will boast about that long after you and I are gone. I tell you, that young Washington has started something. When he killed Jumonville and fought the French at Necessity, he set Europe on fire again."

"But there's no war on now, Ben."

"There will be," Franklin said grimly. "Both King George and King Louis are talking out loud about peace and friendship, but they're both secretly preparing for war. North America and India are going to be either French or English. Each one wants colonial supremacy. That's what's really behind all the fighting we'vc had since 1690."

Jedediah Gill touched the faint scar on his forehead. "Who knows that better'n me?" he mumbled. "I told you how I was born."

Franklin nodded. "That was the first round, and this is the last. I can tell you in confidence, Jed Gill, the king has already ordered two regiments of regulars to Virginia. And a British major general came over last February. My friends in Paris have informed me that Louis is send—"

The taproom door flew open and Micah Gill burst into the room. His thick black hair was turning iron-gray, making him look more saturnine. "Pa! Pa!" he shouted in excitement. "There's been a big naval battle up around Newfoundland! They say an English fleet tried to stop the French from reinforcing Canada. Most of their ships got away in a fog, but we captured two big transports and two battalions of soldiers."

The two friends at the table exchanged glances. "I guess this is it, Ben," Jedediah Gill said quietly. "What was the name of that general in Virginia?"

"Edward Braddock."

Major General Edward Braddock had indeed landed in Virginia in February 1755 to take command of his majesty's forces in North America. Short, stout and choleric, Braddock was as brave as he was bullheaded. He was a veteran of forty-five years of service, having been trained in the school of warfare developed in Europe since the turn of the century. This was based upon the foot soldier armed with musket and socket bayonet. He was drilled incessantly and subjected to a brutal discipline which made of him a battlefield automaton. He fought in the open against other automatons also taught to wheel and dress ranks amid the very smoke and stress of battle, to load and advance, fire and reload—and to drive home the assault with the bayonet under the smoke of the final volley. General Braddock had the utmost faith in these tactics, and he lost his temper when Colonel George Washington, whom he had selected to serve on his staff in his expedition against Fort Duquesne, brought them into question.

"Stuff and nonsense, Washington!" he sputtered. "Damn poppycock, this bush-fighting business."

"I am sorry, Sir," Washington said calmly, "but I feel in duty bound to insist that European infantry tactics cannot succeed in the forests of America. Here, the premium is on dispersion, cover and accurate gunfire."

"It is, eh? Where's your shock? Where's the final shivering shock that wins the battle and makes the other fellows bugger off? I'll admit cavalry would be useless over here. But we still need shock, young man—and massed infantry will give it to us. Eh, Orme?" he said, turning to Captain Robert Orme, his aide-de-camp. The handsome young officer nodded, fixing Washington with a disdainful stare.

"There is no shock in the forest, General Braddock," Washington said with quiet insistence. "There is no room to mass. Movement is only along the trails or on the rivers. You must cut your own roads."

"I should think we could mass well enough outside Fort Duquesne," Braddock said thoughtfully, stroking his bulldog chin with a pudgy hand.

"But you must pass through the forest to get there, General—and the forest is made for ambush. That is why I have recommended that you train the regulars in American bush-fighting techniques. Like my militia."

"Your blues? Those contemptible fellows? Much as I regret it, Colonel, I must tell you that your blues are quite a sorry lot. Slothful and lazy. They do not seem to me at all fit for military service."

George Washington's sallow face reddened, and he glanced sideways in embarrassment at the amused Captain Orme—just as an orderly entered his tent to announce: "A gentleman from Philadelphia named Benjamin Franklin to see you, Sir."

Washington's eyes lighted up. Even Braddock's good nature returned, and he arose with a smile when the colonies' deputy postmaster general came into the room.

"Indeed a pleasure to meet you, Mr. Franklin," Braddock said. "I must tell you that you are probably the most famous

American on the continent. My aides, Sir—Captain Robert Orme and Colonel George Washington."

Acknowledging the introductions with a nod of his head, Franklin turned to Washington and said: "I have just come from Boston with a message for your intrepid friend, Captain Daniel Gill. His grandfather, Jedediah Gill, wants him to know how proud he is of him—just as we all are of you, Colonel Washington."

"You've a right to be," Braddock grunted grudgingly. "Judging from what Governor Dinwiddie's told me, this young man is the only officer fit to command in all America."

"Oh, come now, General," Franklin said easily. "I think you're inclined to be a little hard on us."

"Hard, eh?" Braddock said grimly. "Not by half. I tell you, Mr. Franklin, I've been a soldier forty-five years and I've never seen the like of these provincials. You'd think we were the enemy. They just don't trust us. They say there's no French encroachment, they say it's just a trick to reduce their liberties. So they won't give up a horse or a bale of hay. Contracts broken! Contracts ignored! Want of horses . . . want of wagons . . . want of food. . . . Delay, delay, delay! Goddammit, Sir, do you know what that scoundrel Horace Walpole is saying about me in London? He says Edward Braddock seems to be in no hurry to get scalped!"

Benjamin Franklin struggled to suppress a smile, fearing that it might cause the panting, red-faced, apoplectic Braddock to burst a blood vessel. Instead, he said calmly: "You need horses and wagons, General?"

"I do indeed! Orme, do you have those wagon returns?"

"Yes, Sir," Captain Orme replied in a languid voice. "Just twenty-five."

"TWENTY-FIVE!" Edward Braddock was on his feet shouting. His hands fumbled at the red sash at his waist as though he would tear it in two. "The expedition is CANCELED! It's OFF! God damn the Ministry! God damn the duke for sending me into this godforsaken country without the barest means of transportation!"

Colonel Washington was appalled. Even the urbane Captain Orme was slightly aghast. But Benjamin Franklin did not lose his composure. "I will get you horses and wagons, General Braddock," he said calmly. "In Pennsylvania, every farmer has his own horse and wagon. In fact, General, if you had landed in Philadelphia rather than Virginia, your march to Fort Duquesne would have been infinitely easier. You could have moved directly west through the richest of the colonies. Supplies would have been no problem. I venture to say, General, you would have saved forty thousand pounds in money and six weeks in time."

Braddock scowled. "The Ministry again," he growled. "A certain Mr. John Hanbury persuaded the duke that Will's Creek was the best route."

"Ah, yes," the Quaker merchant. Strange how these pacifists detest war, but don't mind taking a profit from it. Mr. Hanbury has a large interest in the Ohio Company, which stands to profit in your presence at Will's Creek. To say nothing of the road you will cut. But I promise you, General Braddock, I will get you those horses and wagons. At least one hundred and fifty of them. On my word of honor."

"I am indeed in your debt, Mr. Franklin," said Major General Edward Braddock. "If there were only more men in these provinces like you . . ." Turning to his secretary, William Shirley, son of the governor of Massachuestts, he said, "Put that in my report to the Duke of Newcastle. 'Mr. Benjamin Franklin is almost the only instance of ability and honesty I have known in these provinces.'" And then, to Orme: "We will march from Will's Creek in early June."

Braddock had about 2,200 men: two 700-man regiments of regulars, nine 50-man companies of Virginians and the rest composed of sailors and artillerists. A company of 300 axmen led the way to cut and clear the road. On the tenth of June 1755, to the rattle of drums and squeal of fifes, the army began its march.

General Braddock took the utmost precaution against surprise or ambush. Squads of men were thrown out on the flanks. Scouts roamed the woods, searching for skulking Indians. An advance party under Lieutenant Colonel Thomas Gage covered the front.

The road was only about twelve feet wide, studded with stumps, roots, and stones. Sometimes the marching column was four miles long. It snaked through the forest like a serpent colored red, blue and brown. Its members were soaked in sweat, toiling up the ridges or descending them with braking step; crawling around crags or crossing steeps and chasms bridged by logs cut only an hour or two before their arrival. Occasionally, a faint scream from the forests to either side told them that a flanker had grown careless with his life. Soon, for fear of the lurking tomahawks, the men chose not to go into the woods to relieve themselves, but ran forward beside the column to a point where they might do so in safety and still not be left behind. After nine days of marching, the army came to the Little Meadows, a place only thirty miles from Will's Creek. They had gone scarcely three miles a day, and now fever and dysentery were breaking out.

Colonel Washington was dismayed. He, too, had come down with "the flux," as dysentery was then called. He was once again a gaunt, emaciated figure—a scarecrow in buckskin, riding with a pillow in his saddle, wincing at every jolt. But his indomitable spirit was uncrushed.

"Dammit, Danny," he muttered to Captain Gill, riding by his side. "This can't go on. The column is too cumbersome. We've got to move faster. There are supposed to be five hundred French regulars marching for Fort Duquesne. We've got to get there before they do. I'm doing to speak to General Braddock about it," he said, and turned his horse toward the rear.

General Braddock agreed, and at once called a council of war, at which it was decided to send an advance corps of about twelve hundred soldiers ahead under Sir Peter Halkett, while the remaining forces brought up the rear. Washington was delighted. But the advance corps moved hardly faster than the entire column had.

"Damn these regulars!" Washington said. "Do they have to dress ranks every fifty yards? Do they have to level every mole hill, bridge every brook? Why can't they just push on and let the devil take the rough road? By the great Jehovah, Daniel, it's taken us four days to move twelve miles."

On July 7 Halkett's troops reached Turtle Creek, a stream which entered the Monongahela about eight miles from Duquesne. But Braddock, informed that the road ahead passed through a perilous defile made for ambush, decided to avoid this danger by fording the Monongahela, and then fording it again to recover the road to the fort.

Claude Pierre Pecaudy, the Sieur de Contrecour, the general commanding at Fort Duquesne, had been warned of the approach of the English. Because he considered his numbers insufficient to defend the fort, he was preparing to evacuate it—until Captain Daniel de Beaujeu came to him with a plan to ambush the enemy on the march.

"They are heading for the fords, *mon général*," Beaujeu said. "We can strike them as they cross the second one. It is a great opportunity."

"Very well," said General Contrecour.

That night, at about the same time Braddock decided to try the fords, Captain Beaujeu proposed his plan to the Indians. They rejected it, in the words of one of their chiefs: "Do you want to die, my father, and sacrifice us besides?" In the morning, they again refused to go, and the fiery Beaujeu shouted at them: *"Je suis déterminé de rencontrer les anglais. I am determined to meet the English! Quoi!—laisserez-vous votre père y aller seul?* What!—will you let your father go alone?"

The Indians caught fire. Putting on their war paint, howling hideously, they gathered around the open barrels of gunpowder and bullets placed outside the fort gate, scooping the contents into their pouches and powder horns. Beaujeu watched them with blazing eyes before hurrying to the chapel, where he and the other Frenchmen received the sacraments. Nine hundred strong—about 640 Indians, 150 Canadians, and the rest French regulars—Beaujeu led them toward the Monongahela.

Sir Peter Halkett's advance corps had crossed the first ford. General Braddock rode toward Colonel Gage, a tall, handsome man with sandy hair who commanded the special force that had crossed the ford and covered it from the farther bank.

"Take the second ford, Gage. Be careful. If they're going to be anywhere, that's where they'll be. They'll have the high ground against us. But, mind you, no heroics. If they're too strong, wait for Halkett."

Gage nodded and rode off at the head of two companies of grenadiers and a group of scouts. At the second ford, they surprised about a half-dozen naked Indians, who flung themselves into the river to escape the English bullets. Gage ordered his men into the water and they waded rapidly across, muskets held high. Gage's horse splashed after them, just as Captain Orme rode up with a message from Braddock.

"By God, Orme, the frog-eaters have missed their chance! We'll be in Duquesne tonight, or my name's not Tommy Gage."

Orme smiled his supercilious smile. He was resplendent in dress uniform: scarlet coat and both his small three-cornered hat and his impeccable white waistcoat heavy with gold lace, a silver gorget hanging around his neck. "The general is going to have a parade," he told Gage in his tired voice. "They'll form up once they're over the river and come parading through the meadow here." Orme smiled again at the surprised look on Gage's face. "The general says the men have lost all sense of discipline on the march. He wants to buck them up again. Impress the frog-eaters if they happen to be watching."

Gage chuckled, just as the opening notes of "The Grenadier's March" came squealing and rattling across the meadow. Both men sat their horses in soldierly delight, watching as a party of light horse burst prancing from the thicket, followed by the advance guard, and then, the lengthening red ribbon of the main body. The regulars marched smartly, heads thrown back, arms swinging in unison. Every white-clad thigh and brown-gaitered leg beneath the scarlet coats rose and fell like pistons. A bright sun glinted off the bared bayonets of their sloped rifles. It was a gay, soldierly parade, and even the horses capered and danced in time to the music.

"By God, that's something to see," Colonel Gage said. "I hope the frog-eaters are watching. They'll know they're in for it, now, with British regulars coming against them." He started. "There's General Buckskin," he said contemptuously, pointing to Washington at the end of the column. "He's got his Indian clothes on."

"Where is his bow and arrow?" Captain Orme simpered.

"Under the pillow," Gage sneered.

"Do you know that chap had the effrontery to suggest to the general that all the officers dress like the men?" Orme fingered the silver gorget at his throat fastidiously. "He'd have us dismount, too. He said our uniforms and our horses made us conspicuous targets. We'd all be picked off."

Gage gasped in disbelief. "Is the man a coward?"

"Oh, no—he volunteered to go ahead with his Virginians and the Indians to clear the woods of skulking Indians."

"Until the first shot is fired," Gage sniffed, sneering again. He glanced up as Captain Daniel Gill cantered past him. "See here, Captain, where are you going?"

"Reconnoitering," Danny said. "Colonel Washington and I have been here before. See," he said, pointing to a house beside the road. "That's John Frazier's trading post." Gage nodded disdainfully, and Danny disappeared into the woods.

It was silent in the forest. A bee buzzed by Danny's head, its wings beating a tiny wind into his ears. He ducked instinctively, but raised his head quickly when he heard a twig snap. Bounding toward him along the path came a man dressed like an Indian but with a silver gorget around his neck. Behind him, the woods swarmed with French and savages. Danny ducked back, but the officer saw him. He also saw the head of the long red column stretching beyond Danny's back, and he swung his hat to right and left. With that, the French and Indians vanished. They took cover behind trees, rocks, and bushes and opened fire.

Danny Gill dived for the safety of a rock, watching while Gage's column wheeled deliberately into line. "God save the King!" the scarlet-coated soldiery shouted, and fired a volley. Another . . . another . . . Captain Beaujeu—the man Danny saw—dropped dead, and all but a few Canadians turned and fled. "*Sauve-qui-peut!*" they cried. Every man for himself!" For a moment, the Indians hesitated, but Beaujeu's junior officers rallied them. They poured a withering fire into the close red ranks of the English, their hideous war whooping mingling with the roar of the muskets, seeming to clang and reverberate off the forest dome as though it were an iron vault.

Soon the screams of the stricken English joined the terrible chorus. They fired volley after volley against the unseen force, but their bullets merely splintered the rocks or plunged harmlessly into the trees. Now the Indians slipped through the woods on both flanks of the English. Many of them occupied a small hill above the English right. Together, ceaselessly screeching their war cries, they opened a deadly fire on the helpless English, now huddled desperately together, still firing useless volleys at the unseen enemy, and falling by the score.

Like a mounted bulldog, General Edward Braddock rode

into the melee. When he heard the firing, he had rushed forward with the main body. More scarlet coats became visible to the invisible French and Indians. Gaps also appeared in their ranks. Braddock rode among the broken ranks of Gage's men and beat them with the flat of his sword.

"Form, God damn you!" he roared. "*Form*! Form on the standards and fall back on the ford. Form!"

Sometimes the frenzied general did not use the flat of the sword. Danny Gill shuddered when he saw the point of Braddock's sword enter the throat of a tall soldier who had raised his musket in defense. He saw Braddock's horse rear and sink to the ground and watched the general mount another brought forward by Orme.

"Form!" Braddock bellowed, riding down his men, and they answered piteously:

"We would form, if we knew what to form against."

"How can we fight bushes?"

"How can we fight what we can't see?"

A company of Virginia blues ran forward to take cover behind a fallen tree. Danny Gill joined them. They waited for flashes of a painted face or the movement of a bush before squeezing their triggers. Their sporadic fire brought screams from unseen throats. Other Virginians rushed to join the counterattack. Danny heard Colonel Washington yelling, "Take to the trees! Hold them in check!" But Danny also heard Braddock's now-familiar voice bellowing, "Form! Form, God damn you! Form and fight like soldiers!" as he now rode the Virginians down, striking at them with the edge or the flat of his sword, he seemed to care not which.

"God damn him!" Danny Gill muttered, just as a hail of bullets swept among the blues lying behind the log. It came from the English, who had mistaken the smoke rising above the log for the fire of the enemy. Screams and cries of anguish rose around Danny. He jumped to his feet to flee, but something caught him behind the left shoulder and spun him around and drove him to the ground panting, while the bullets sang above him or soughed into the log. He saw Sir Peter Halkett ride up with the rest of the main body and fall lifeless from his horse. Halkett's son ran to his father and fell dead on top of him. Braddock still rode wildly over the battlefield, and Danny saw that he had still another horse. He caught a glimpse of Colonel Washington mounted on a new horse with his buckskin torn by bullets. British officers were falling like leaves. Gage was down . . . Gates was wounded . . . young William Shirley was killed . . .

The arrival of artillery had produced a momentary hope among the English, but the shells struck only trees and boulders, and soon the decimated gunners abandoned their pieces. Reinforcements became more of a hindrance than a help. Mobs of soldiers, stupefied with fear, stood huddled together on the trail, mechanically loading and firing, loading and firing—sometimes merely shooting into the air, or, worse, into the ranks of their comrades. Friendly fire took a terrible toll among Washington's troops. Again and again, peering through the smoke with sweat dripping from their foreheads into their eyes, the redcoats mistook the crouching, skulking blues for Indians and cut them down. "Hold your fire, you Goddam poltroons!" Washington yelled, riding the English soldiers down on his third horse. "You're murdering my men!"

Soon, it became difficult for the mounted officers to move along the trail. The ground was covered with the dead, dying and wounded. Maddened horses reared and bounded everywhere, their terrified neighing and screaming mixing with the continued clatter of the muskets, the roar of the cannon and the incessant whooping of the savages.

Danny Gill came slowly to his knees. The pain had begun in his shoulder and was becoming excruciating. He tugged at his bullet pouch with his good right hand and shoved a bullet between his teeth, grinding his teeth into the lead to keep from screaming. He saw Braddock again, on his fifth horse, this time, waving his sword toward the hill on the right as though ordering a lieutenant colonel who rode beside him to take it. The colonel clattered off into the smoke, and Braddock's horse reared. His front feet pawed the air. Braddock flew forward in the saddle and then hit the ground.

Captain Orme ran to kneel beside the stricken general. So did Braddock's servant, Bishop. A cry rose among the regulars. "They got the general! The old bugger's down, God rot his friggin' soul!" At once, the ranks broke and a struggling red tide flowed to the rear. Orme and Bishop tried to get the fleeing soldiery to help them move Braddock.

"Here, lend a hand with the general!" Orme shouted, clutching their wrists. But they yanked free and shouted,

"Bugger the fat old toad!" and ran away. Next, Orme tried to bribe them, offering money, but they ran past him cursing.

Danny Gill was propelled toward the fallen general by the flood of soldiers rushing to the rear. Captain Orme saw him, and said: "Here, lend a hand, Captain." Then, seeing Danny clutching his left shoulder with his right hand and the bullet between his teeth, he said: "You'd best get to the rear."

"I'll stay," Danny said, the words ground between his clenched teeth.

Colonel Washington rode up and dismounted, kneeling beside the general. Braddock tried to raise himself. "The ford," he gasped. "Washington . . . rally the men . . . at the ford . . ." He coughed, and a bright blob of blood bubbled from his mouth. He sank back upon the ground.

"Yes, General," Washington said. "But first we must get you out of here." Washington looked around him as Captain Robert Stewart rode up. "We'll have to find means to carry him between us," Washington said.

"What about his sash?" said Stewart.

Gently, Washington unrolled Braddock's sash. It was seven feet long and about two feet wide. They made a sling of it. Each of them—the servant, Bishop, Washington, Stewart, and Orme—took one end of it.

Orme coughed and fell forward.

"He's hit badly," Washington said gravely. He glanced at Danny Gill. "Can you help us, Dan?"

"I'll try," Danny said.

Fighting off waves of pain, Danny stumbled along the trail, helping the other three to drag the general to a small cart. Heaving, the four men got the general aboard it. Next, they lifted up Orme, who had been carried to the cart by medical orderlies.

"You'd better get up there, too, Dan," Colonel Washington said. "You're not so good yourself."

With the colonel's help, Danny clambered aboard, lying down gratefully on the fresh-smelling straw. A wave of pain swept over him, and he lost consciousness.

He awoke to the swaying of the cart. It was dark. Stars shone overhead. He could hear the soft sloughing of many footsteps to either side of the cart, many voices moaning . . . muttering . . . cursing. Behind him, he could see the dark black water of the Monongahela gleaming beneath the stars.

They were across the fords, he thought. Thank God! The cart lurched, and a heavy body rolled over on Danny.

"Who would have thought it?" a cultivated British voice asked the darkness. "Who would have thought it?" There was a prolonged silence, and Captain Daniel Gill again lost consciousness.

Next time he awoke he was in an infirmary at Will's Creek. He could hear the voice of the general gasping weakly. "I cannot bear the sight of a red coat. Colonel Washington, your blues were above praise. I hope to live to reward them." There was a silence, and then, in a fading voice: "We shall better know how to deal with them another time." This time, the silence that claimed Edward Braddock was eternal.

20

It was a cold night in Quebec. Powdery white snowflakes drifted down upon the snow-packed courtyard outside the palace of the intendant. Vapor puffs shot from the mouths of the sentinels there. Sometimes the sentinels laid their muskets against the palace wall to beat their mittened hands together for warmth.

By twos and threes, citizens of the city began to emerge from the palace. They had been dancing in the hall provided for the populace by the bounteous Intendant François Bigot. Although they were never allowed to join Bigot's dinner guests on the floor of his private dance hall, they were allowed to watch them from the gallery. They did not begrudge Bigot this, but rather were grateful to him for giving them their own *plaisance*.

Seeing the snow, the emerging revelers cried out in childish delight. They paused to watch a party of workmen loading sledges with baggage. Other sledges were already loaded with bedding, blankets, table service, cooking utensils, dressed meats, wines and brandy, cheeses, chocolates and other delicacies. Curious, the Canadians walked toward them, their boots making crunching noises on the hard-packed snow.

"Careful, there, good people," shouted a thickset man

named Pierre Venet, the chief steward of the intendant. "Those are the belongings of Monsieur Bigot's guests."

"Aha," one of the Canadians called. "Is the intendant going on another of his famous excursions to Montreal? *Un voyage de plaisir?*"

"Indeed, he is," the steward replied, stamping his feet.

"How many guests this time?"

"Twenty."

"Ah. And is the lovely Madame de Pean among them?"

A shout of laughter rose from the crowd, and Venet shook his cane at them angrily. "Off with you, you *canaille*—you rabble. Monsieur should hear how you reward his generosity."

"Don't forget the cards, Monsieur," someone yelled.

"Or the perfume or the wine," cried another. " 'Oh, Monsieur,' " he murmured, mimicking a fallen woman, " 'it was ze wine. I do not do thees without ze wine.' "

Now the laughter turned ribald, and the first man to have questioned the steward put his hand on the bedding in a sledge, exclaiming in a grave voice: "Surely, this is not enough for our gracious intendant."

Still laughing, jeering at the infuriated steward, the crowd disappeared. Venet called to the working men. "Get those sledges with the food and things harnessed and sent on ahead. And you, lieutenant," he said to a young officer, "Monsieur Bigot desires you to commandeer the inhabitants along the way to clear the snowdrifts and beat the roads smooth with their ox teams."

"And what if they desire payment?"

"They'll be paid," Venet grunted. "Paid so well that the cost of hiring a horse for Montreal will cost the king what he paid for it."

The lieutenant snickered. "Clip-and-cut, and rob the king —it is the way of life in Canada, eh, Monsieur?"

"Never mind that," Venet said coldly. "And be sure the baggage sledges are harnessed in the morning."

In the morning, François Bigot served his guests a sumptuous breakfast. In the highest spirits, they trooped outside the palace and took their places in the sledges, their bodies swathed in furs and blankets to protect them against the biting cold. Behind them were the supply sledges and those of the steward and the servants. They drove at a full trot along St. Vallier Street past an admiring and shouting crowd and headed for Pointe-aux-Trembles, where each took separate lodging. Next morning, they warmed themselves with tea, chocolate or coffee, and drove for two hours to the home of the militia captain to warm themselves again and breakfast. In the afternoon, they reached St. Anne-de-la-Perade, where Bigot entertained them at dinner in the house where he lodged, and they played cards till midnight. The next morning brought them to Three Rivers and the home of Madame de Rigaud, wife of the governor of the place. Being ill, she received them in bed, ordering a delicious dinner be provided them, after which they returned to her chamber for coffee and conversation. As they left, the cannon of the fort saluted them.

Continuing on, they reached Isle-au-Castor, where they were greeted by the governor of Montreal and his chief officers, and treated to another fine dinner. In fact, the food served the intendant and his guests was of such fine quality and abundance that Madame Pean was mildly troubled about what the endless feasting might do to her figure. Marie Pean sat in the foremost sledge, which she shared with the intendant. She patted her stomach ruefully, thinking of the meal at Isle-au-Castor: pâté, a kind of fish soup made with deliciously firm winter fish pulled from the frozen St. Lawrence, sweetbreads in a chestnut sauce, cheese, almond tarts, cognac, chocolates and a different wine with every course. She sighed. François liked to eat and drink almost as much as he liked to gamble and . . .

Marie listened dreamily to the crack of the drivers' whips and the hissing of the sledge runners on the snow. One of the horses discharged a cluster of round turds. They fell smoking into the snow. Marie glanced to her left at the broad, winding, snow-covered river to her left and wondered if Canada were not prettier in winter than in summer. She felt a strong hand grasp her thigh, and she pushed it roughly away—until she realized that Major Pean was home in Quebec. Smiling coquettishly, now squeezing the offending hand, she gazed up into the scrofulous, leering face of François Bigot. His hand advanced toward her crotch, but she held it and shook her head. "No, François," she said, looking at the column of sledges uncoiling behind her. "Not here."

"You did not mind it in the carriage in Quebec."

"No, but there are too many people here."

"*Ce soir*? We shall all sleep in the same house tonight."

Marie nodded. "After cards. I will complain of a headache and go to my room."

Bigot nodded, leering again, and withdrew his hand. Madame Pean glanced quickly away. Sometimes she could not bear to look at the pimples on her lover's face. Yet, she was always able to conceal her disgust. When François undressed or made love to her, she always kept her eyes closed, assuring herself that one could not expect the richest man in Canada to be a veritable Adonis. And he *was* clever! Marie remembered the coup that had led her to the intendant's bed. Her husband had bought a huge quantity of grain with money of the king's lent to him by Bigot. Then François, using the extraordinary powers of his office, had arbitrarily raised the price of grain. Major Pean had made a profit of fifty thousand crowns at a single stroke! No wonder he had smiled and shrugged when she had told him she was moving in with François. "Do not forget your dear husband," he had jested, winking broadly.

Marie had not. Major Pean was now worth up to four million francs. His wife was also rich. Much of the goods stored in the warehouse which the people called La Frippone—or "The Cheat"—belonged to Marie. It was she who had helped to hatch the scheme which had made millions for Bigot. They made a deal with the Bordeaux firm of Gradis and Son to ship goods to the colony. Then François informed the colonial minister that there were enough supplies in Canada to last three years, and that it would be cheaper for the king to buy them there than to take the risk of shipping them from France. When the goods from Gradis and Son arrived in Canada, Bigot had one of his cronies at the custom house declare them to be the king's, thus escaping the import tax. Then they were sold to the king, always at huge profits and under fictitious names.

François *was* clever, Marie thought again: there is an agile brain behind that ugly forehead of his.

That night the party stopped at the largest house they could find. While Marie and the other ladies dressed for dinner, the servants removed the partitions of the rooms to make a single large hall. Here, the intendant and his guests sat down to another seven-course meal. They danced and then returned to the tables for the inevitable gambling.

About an hour later, Marie Pean lifted a hand to her forehead and complained of a headache. She excused herself.

Forty-five minutes later, François Bigot threw down his hand. "My luck, she is running out, Vergor," he said to his closest friend, the Chevalier Duchambon de Vergor. "I think I'll go to bed." He arose amid murmurs of sympathy from the others at his table and left the hall.

Winking, Vergor said: "Cards is evidently not the intendant's only passion." The men chuckled, while the women giggled and blushed charmingly.

Marie Pean had dozed off, and was awakened by the feel of Bigot's thick hand between her thighs. His thick lips pressed down on hers, and she repressed a shudder. Soon his lips were traveling down to her breasts, to her navel and down toward her crotch. She seized his head and restrained him.

"Please, François," she pleaded. "Tonight, let's do it my way."

Louis Joseph, Marquis de Montcalm-Gozon de Saint Véran, was infuriated. He had come from another exasperating interview with Pierre François de Rigaud, Marquis de Vaudreuil. Vaudreuil, son of a former governor of Canada, was himself in 1759 the governor. Montcalm was the military commander.

"We can agree on nothing," Montcalm complained to the Sieur Louis Antoine de Bougainville, one of his most trusted aides. "Vaudreuil has been told again and again by the minister that he must consult with me on military matters. But he keeps interfering. Last night at his home, in the presence of eight of my officers, he reproached me for the twentieth time for not having taken Fort Edward after I burnt Fort William Henry. For the twentieth time, I told him that at the moment it was not feasible. I told him that one is not pleased with his commanders, then one must take the field himself in person."

Bougainville chuckled, shifting his short, plump body in his chair to have a better view of the small, handsome, fiery general whom he so much admired. "What did he say to that?"

"He muttered between his teeth that maybe he would. So I told him I would be delighted to serve under him."

Bougainville laughed aloud. "Vaudreuil in the field? Has he ever been?"

"Yes, once," Montcalm replied with a smile. "He went with a party of Indians that succeeded in catching an old Iroquois and burning him at the stake. *Monsieur le marquis* thought it was outrageously funny. The poor old Iroquois made such droll faces!"

"*Dégoûtant*," Bougainville murmured, making a face. "Disgusting."

"He would never take the field," said Montcalm. "He is too fond of his comforts. Or too busy protecting the thieving Bigot and his crony Vergor. Vergor *le cochon*. The cowardly pig surrendered Beauséjour and all of Acadia with just one shot fired. Before the English could even begin their siege. Anyway, Vaudreuil kept at it and then his wife, *Madame Nigaude*—Mrs. Nincompoop—tried to put in a word. I told her, 'Madame, saving due respect, permit me to have the honor to say that ladies ought not to talk war.' She kept on, and I said: 'Madame, saving due respect, permit me to have the honor to say that if Madame de Montcalm were here and heard me talking war with *Monsieur le marquis*, she would remain silent.' Imagine! All this in front of my officers. A pretty story they will make of it."

Bougainville nodded. "And Vaudreuil will have some more falsehoods for the minister. I tell you, *mon général*, when I was in Versailles it seemed that the entire court was taken in by his lies. He has claimed credit for all your victories. It is he who recaptured Crown Point. Vaudreuil, the savior of Fort Ticonderoga! Vaudreuil, the hero of Oswego! Of Fort William Henry!"

"Yes, I know," Montcalm said grimly. "And then he blames me for the loss of Louisbourg and Fort Duquesne, when he knows very well I was busy defending Ticonderoga. Louisbourg was lost because the English were superior in every detail. Duquesne was abandoned because Vaudreuil gave it to a drunken commander whom the Indians detested. But in Versailles, I suppose," he said sadly "it is all the fault of Montcalm. I tell you, Bougainville, if we do not have peace before the end of this year, Canada is lost. Rapacity, folly, intrigue, falsehood—all these will soon ruin this colony. And what it has cost the king! Think of what that *salaud*— skunk—of an intendant has stolen from him alone. And now he sits up there in Montreal licking his greedy lips and entertaining his sultana."

Bougainville smiled. "Madame Pean? She is most desirable, *mon général.*"

"Yes, my dear Bougainville, and she may very well be Canada's Helen of Troy."

Bougainville's nod was slow in coming. The allusion to Madame Pean had reminded him of Madame de Vienne, equally desirable and willing upon the sieur's visits to Jacques Cartier upriver. Bougainville felt Montcalm's piercing eyes upon him and paid closer attention.

"It is almost too late to save the colony, Monsieur," the marquis said, his eyes hardening. "The English now hold the Forks and Louisbourg. We are flanked east and west. Quebec itself is now open to attack. It cannot be worse. English ships are watching the mouth of the St. Lawrence. Only a few of our ships can slip through. We have had a disastrous harvest. A barrel of flour now costs ten times what it cost three years ago. Most of the cattle and many of the horses have been slaughtered for food. The people are starving on a pittance of salt cod and whatever rations the king can issue." He paused, anger entering his voice and eyes. "My officers look like scarecrows. And yet, thieves like Bigot and Vergor are getting fat. What a country! All the scoundrels grow rich while honest men are ruined. I tell you, my dear Bougainville, I have already requested my recall. But, now, with the colony in such danger, I must remain at my post. But you, my dear Sieur, you must go to Versailles. Our only hope is in a strong appeal to the court. You must make the minister understand how desperate our situation is. Even Vaudreuil agrees on this. He has promised to give you a letter introducing you to the minister with the highest recommendation. You will go, eh, my dear Bougainville?"

"I will sail immediately, *mon général.* Before the river freezes."

The Sieur de Bougainville was well received at court. He was already famous as a navigator in France, and had written a paper on integral calculus which had gained him election to the British Royal Society. Before becoming a soldier, he had been a rising advocate in the parliament of Paris. Even the king and the mistress who controlled his licentious life, Madame de Pompadour, consented to see Bougainville. He was made a colonel and a Chevalier of St. Louis. Bougainville looked forward confidently to his interview with Monsieur Berryer, the colonial minister.

Berryer eyed Bougainville frostily when he sat down opposite him. His manner was cold and unfriendly. Dismayed, Bougainville immediately produced Vaudreuil's letter. "Read it," the minister said curtly, and Bougainville read: " 'M. Bougainville is in all respects better fitted than anybody else to inform you of the state of the colony.' " Glancing up hopefully, Bougainville saw an open sneer on Berryer's face.

"That is strange, Monsieur," the minister said, lifting a letter from his desk. "I have received a quite different communication from *Monsieur le marquis*. It says: 'In order to condescend to the wishes of M. de Montcalm, and leave no means untried to keep in harmony with him, I have given a letter to M. de Bougainville; but I have the honor to inform you, Monseigneur, that he does not understand the colony, and to warn you that he is the creature of M. de Montcalm.' "

An angry flush suffused Bougainville's face. Recovering, he met the minister's accusing eye and said calmly: "It is such duplicity, Monsieur, that is ruining and will destroy Canada. I have come here for no other reason than to beg for the support that will save the king's colony."

"Colony, eh? Do you think the king has no other concern? What about his kingdom? What about Europe? Eh, Monsieur, when the house is on fire, one cannot occupy oneself with the stable."

"At least, monsieur," Bougainville replied, getting to his feet, "nobody will say that you talk like a horse."

With that irreverent remark, he left; and when he returned to Canada, it was only with a pitiful few hundreds of reinforcement, together with enough arms and supplies to sustain the colony for one more campaign. He also brought with him an intercepted enemy letter which revealed the English plan for Canada.

When the Chevalier de Bougainville set foot on the strand of the Lower Town of Quebec, he immediately sent word to the Marquis de Montcalm in Montreal to hasten at once to the capital, where the English intended to strike their major blow. Montcalm, who had anticipated that the chief strokes would come on Lake Champlain and at Fort Niagara, at once joined the chevalier in Quebec.

"I have sad news and good news for you, Sir," Bougainville said when the two met in Montcalm's quarters. "One of your daughters is dead."

A quick tear formed in Montcalm's eye. He brushed it aside, and asked in a grieving voice: "Which one?"

"I do not know, sir. I just heard it before I left Brest."

"It must be Mirete," Montcalm said in a sad voice. "She was very much like me. I loved her very much." He put a finger to his eye again. "I shall ask the bishop to say masses for her soul."

"Here is the good news, *mon général*," Bougainville said softly, laying a gold-edged roll of parchment bearing the king's seal and signature on his desk. Montcalm took it and unrolled it. "So I am now a lieutenant general," he murmured dryly. "I am honored, yes. But methinks my country is too poor to give rewards other than honors. How happy I would be to be free of this proud yoke to which I am bound. When shall I see my family again, my château at Candiac, my plantations, my chestnut grove, my oil mill and my mulberry trees?"

Montcalm fell momentarily silent, grief and sorrow in his eyes. Then they hardened and he straightened. "At least we know where the enemy will strike. That is quite a bit. Vaudreuil has already ordered our ships upriver to be out of danger. That will free about a thousand sailors for duty on the city's guns. We have one hundred and six guns. I would have liked to emplace some of them above Cape Diamond, but Vaudreuil swears there is no way an enemy fleet can get upriver. I hope he's right. Otherwise," he said, smiling grimly, "there is no city in the world with such natural defenses as ours. No one can climb those cliffs. No one!"

He struck his small, fine hands together. "So we will defend at the Beauport shore. See, Bougainville," he said, pointing to a wall map. "Here is our left flank. Where Phips landed almost seventy years ago and tried to get into our rear. I'm sure they'll try it again. So I am going to build a line seven miles long. One end will rest on the gorge and the falls of the Montmorency and the other on the St. Charles. I will block the mouth of the St. Charles with a boom of logs chained together and sink two ships there. To pass the falls of the Montmorency is, of course, impossible. So they must come at the Beauport shore, where I will be waiting for them with fourteen thousand regulars and militia and the Indians. From such a position, Monsieur, I could hold off a hundred thousand men. And the English do not have ten thousand."

Although impressed, Bougainville was still dubious. "You are sure, Sir, the English cannot sail upriver to cut our supply line to Montreal?"

"Vaudreuil says it cannot be done."

"And the Anse du Foulon. The path up the cliffs to the Plains of Abraham?"

"Ah, my young Chevalier of St. Louis, you have the astute mind, as I have always known. You have put your finger on the one chink in my armor. But I have plugged it. There is a special handpicked guard of about one hundred men at the top of the path. Under Captain St. Martin, one of my most capable commanders. I have placed my best regiment—the Guyenne—close by. There is a night patrol with horses to warn the Guyenne should the enemy attempt to force the path. But they cannot fight up it. It is too steep. And the Anse du Foulon is not visible from the other shore. You can take a boat right past it and still not see that cove."

"You have made your preparations well, *mon général*," Bougainville said admiringly.

"Yes," Montcalm said, staring pensively at the plump young officer opposite him. "But for one thing."

"Treachery?"

"Again you have the mind that runs ahead of me. Yes! Treachery! There are many in this colony who desire its destruction, if only to draw a veil over their conduct. Bigot . . . that butcher's boy, Cadet . . . Vergor . . . perhaps even our friend *monsieur le gouvernour*. Who knows?" he asked, shrugging. "To them, he has been the Marquis Look the Other Way."

Bougainville nodded gravely. "At court, I heard a rumor that a commission is to be formed to inquire into the conduct of the colony. It is said the king is very angry."

"It is already too late," Montcalm said simply. "But I shall not betray my trust. I shall meet the English and I shall defeat them."

"When do you expect them, *mon général*?"

"The letter you brought me says in June."

In June 1759, the great English armada sent to capture Quebec sailed up the St. Lawrence flying the French flag.

Canadians to the fleet's right about fifty miles below Quebec saw the golden lilies on the square of white silk and cheered and hugged themselves for joy. Their prayers and supplications had been answered. Relief had come from France, and the colony was saved.

River pilots quickly launched their canoes and paddled toward the ships. A priest in the black soutane rushed down to the riverbank clutching a telescope. Through it, he watched the pilots clambering aboard. Then, suddenly, an expression of intense revulsion came over his face. He could see pistols being pointed at the pilots' heads. He saw the Bourbon lilies come fluttering down the masts and the crisscrossed red-and-blue of the Cross of St. George unfurled. Amid the groans and lamentations rising around him, the priest sank to the ground in a death fit.

Aboard *Neptune*, the flagship of Admiral Charles Saunders, Brigadier General James Wolfe smiled a thin smile at the success of the ruse. "Congratulations," he said to Jedediah Gill, standing beside him. "It was a good idea."

"Thank you, General. I just couldn't forget what happened to Admiral Walker. I can still hear the screams of the drowning."

"Seventeen-eleven," Wolfe mused aloud. "Almost half a century ago. "And you were there?"

"I was twenty-one," Jedediah said proudly. "My family has been in every war since King William's. And, by God, Sir, this may be my last chance to see the French driven out of America."

"They will be, Mr. Gill," Wolfe said with grim confidence, and walked to the rail. Jedediah studied him. His first impression of James Wolfe had been one of disbelief, and he still found it hard to believe that this tall, thin, awkward, nervous, pallid man was not only a regular officer in the service of His Britannic Majesty but also his youngest brigadier general. Wolfe did not even wear the powdered white wig of a professional officer, letting his bright red hair grow loose and long, pinning it together at the base of his head like any jackanapes. His nose was long and pointed, his forehead receded, and so did his chin—and he might have seemed the very epitome of a military fop but for the fire of boundless ambition burning in his pale, protuberant but piercing blue eyes.

"Don't underestimate General Wolfe," Major Micah Gill had said to his father when Jedediah expressed his misgivings to him. "I was with him at Louisbourg. Remember Fresh-Water Cove where we landed in Forty-five? Well, that's where we landed under Amherst. And Wolfe had the assault regiment. He was the first one ashore, Pa, and the men loved him for it. Well, loved him as much as a British regular can ever feel affection for an officer. But they'd follow him anywhere. And if you ask me, Colonel James Wolfe had a lot more to do with the recapture of Louisbourg than General Jeffrey Amherst."

Remembering his son's words, Jedediah watched Wolfe standing at the rail, plucking nervously at his cuffs and coat buttons. Jedediah's eldest son, Dr. Malachi Gill, stood beside him. General Wolfe's private physician had been a victim of a measles epidemic in Halifax, and Dr. Gill had taken his place. Wolfe spoke to him, but suddenly laid a hand on his chest and bent over in a paroxysm of coughing. When he straightened up, there was a froth of blood on his lips. He brushed it delicately away with a lace handkerchief.

"You must be careful, General," Malachi warned. "You should rest more. You're driving yourself too hard."

"It is nothing. I'm used to it, Doctor. I've been sickly since I joined my father's regiment at the age of thirteen. These things come and go."

"Yes, leaving you just a little weaker each time."

Wolfe nodded carelessly. "I've never expected to live long. Alexander died at thirty-two. Jesus Christ was thirty-three. That is my age, Doctor, and my time has also come." His eyes burned brightly as he opened his telescope. "I shall capture half a continent for my king."

Malachi bowed and walked away. He is mad with ambition! he thought. Comparing himself to Jesus Christ! Alexander is bad enough, but the Savior of Mankind?

Wolfe had focused his telescope aft on the long concourse of ships working their way upriver with slowly flapping sails. He wondered if his force was large enough to force the French fortress. Upon arriving at Halifax he had been enraged to find that more than one third of the 14,000 men garrisoned there were down with measles. He would not have the 12,000 soldiers promised him. Undismayed, he scraped together 8,500 men—including a regiment of Royal Americans—and set sail for Quebec. Studying the fleet behind him, Wolfe realized that his naval forces were more than adequate: 150 ships and 18,000 sailors, together with hundreds of cannon, under Admiral Charles Saunders. A good chap, Saunders, Wolfe thought: but, like many admirals, a bit reluctant to risk his ships. What was the loss of a fleet in comparison to the conquest of half a continent!

James Wolfe had been given the most difficult—and, if he succeeded, most glorious—operation in England's three-pronged campaign to conquer Canada. General Amherst was to move against Ticonderoga and General Prideau against Fort Niagara, but the key to Canada was the city on the cliff above the mighty St. Lawrence.

Wolfe swung his telescope upriver toward the first ships entering the treacherous zigzag passage known as the Traverse. He focused anxiously on the bridge and was dismayed to see an English captain directing the men in the sounding boats to either side.

"Has she no pilot?" he called to the captain of the *Neptune.*

The captain shook his head grimly. Lifting his speaking trumpet, he called ahead: "Who's your master?"

"It's old Killick," an ancient sea dog on the bridge called back. "And that's enough!"

Neptune's captain smiled. "It is, indeed, Sir," he said to Wolfe. "Old Killick can sail where a fish is afraid to swim."

Aboard *Goodwill*, Captain Killick shook his trumpet angrily at the French pilot who had refused to guide the leading ship through the Traverse. "We'll be wrecked, you say? You'll hang the walls of Quebec with English scalps? No French ship would ever try the Traverse without a pilot? Aye, aye, me dear," the old man shouted, shaking his trumpet again, "but, damn me, I'll convince you that an Englishman shall go where a Frenchman dare not show his nose!"

Walking forward, the old man leaned over the bow. "Easy, lads," he called to the men in the sounding boats. "Keep an eye peeled for blue water. It'll be shallow. That ripple there in the smooth water," he shouted, pointing ahead. "It's a submerged ridge. Ah, gray water . . . fine."

"Shoals ahead!" one of the sailors called warningly.

"Aye, aye, me dear, I saw it minutes ago. Chalk it down."

Eventually, *Goodwill* emerged from the Traverse into open water. Captain Killick put his trumpet under his arm and called to his men, "Safe water, me dears." Turning, he started at the astonished French pilot. "Well, damn me," he snorted. "Damn me if there aren't a thousand places in the Thames more dangerous. I'm ashamed that Englishmen should make such a rout about it."

One by one, now, the following ships were entering the Traverse. They guided on Killick's sounding boats flying bright-colored flags. Aboard *Neptune*, James Wolfe opened his telescope again and gazed warily at the mountain of Cape Tourmente on his right. He realized that enemy artillery emplaced there could bombard the English fleet at will. He tensed, waiting for the telltale puff of smoke and the following sound of cannon. He saw and heard nothing, and relaxed. Soon, the entire fleet had passed safely into the South Channel.

On the right was the lower tip of the Island of Orleans, a strip of land about twenty miles long and five miles wide in the center of the broadening St. Lawrence. Off the island's upper tip was the huge basin of Quebec, and four miles across the shimmering blue water, high on the cliffs like a Bourbon crown, the white city of Quebec.

There, on the twenty-sixth of June 1759, the English fleet anchored.

21

But for a few Indians, who were quickly driven off after killing and scalping an American ranger, General Wolfe found the Island of Orleans abandoned, and he put his army ashore there. Next day, accompanied by his aide, Major Micah Gill, he climbed a high point of land to study the enemy shore through his telescope.

High, high above him, beautiful and white in the sunlight, was the city. He could see the stone houses, the churches, the palaces, the convents, the hospitals, the forest of spires and steeples and crosses glinting beneath the white flag whipping in the breeze. Everywhere he saw thick square walls and gun batteries, even among the huge stacks of firewood along the strand of the Lower Town straggling out of sight to his left beyond Cape Diamond. To his right as he swung his glass slowly like a swiveling gun, Wolfe perceived the entrenchments of Montcalm. He saw the sealed mouth of the St. Charles and the thundering falls of the Montmorency guarding the French left flank. He saw the little town of Beauport and the mud flats before it beneath the grape and muskets of Montcalm's redoubts. From left to right he saw steep brown cliffs scarred with the raw red earth of fresh entrenchments, the stone houses with windows reduced to firing slits by piles of logs, and behind them the tops of the Indian wigwams and the white tents of the regulars. If Wolfe could have seen beyond Cape Diamond to his left, he would have been appalled by natural obstacles more formidable than Montcalm's fortifications. Here for seven or eight miles west to Cape Rouge rose steep after inaccessible steep, ranges of cliffs atop which a few men might hold off an army, all ending at another river and waterfall like the Montmorency.

James Wolfe held his telescope delicately. Micah Gill noticed the marks of scurvy on the backs of his long, thin hands. The general finally snapped his telescope shut, standing silently for a full minute, his face still toward Quebec. Then he turned to Micah and said: "Major, I have just looked upon the strongest country in the world."

Governor Vaudreuil had been convinced that General Montcalm should not have allowed the English to land on the Island of Orleans unopposed.

"You should have attacked him then," he complained to Montcalm. "You have allowed a great opportunity to slip by."

Montcalm shook his head politely. "*Non, Monsieur*. The English fleet is far too strong. They would have made *la bouillabaisse* of my men in their boats. No, let him amuse himself outside our lines. We are too strong. If he attacks, he will wear himself out."

"I disagree, General," Vaudreuil replied, his voice rising. "We cannot sit here and await our destruction. We must attack!"

"Eh, Monsieur—does the turtle leave its shell? I tell you, if he bangs his head against my lines, he will get a bloody nose."

"I think we should send fireships against their fleet. Without a fleet, they will be helpless."

"So it is your fireships again, *Monsieur le gouverneur*? I tell you they are a military bauble. They have cost us a million, and will be good for nothing at all."

"They will save Quebec!" Vaudreuil cried angrily. "And I shall use them!"

That night, Wolfe called a conference among Admiral Saunders and his three junior brigadiers: James Murray,

Robert Monckton and George Townshend. Major Micah Gill was also present, along with his father, upon whose familiarity with the area General Wolfe depended. They sat around a field desk in Wolfe's tent near the river, the light of candles stuck in empty wine bottles flickering on their faces. Wolfe's visage was grave as he opened the meeting.

"Gentlemen, I am afraid that the plan devised in Halifax will not work. It is impossible to land upriver, and from what I have seen today, equally impossible to force an entry between the St. Charles and the Montmorency as Phips did seventy years ago. However," he said, his pale eyes shining fiercely, "I intend to take Quebec if we have to stay here until November."

"Not November, General," Admiral Saunders said slowly. "The river will be frozen solid by then."

"But it will thaw in the spring," Wolfe retorted. "And we shall have Quebec by then. Come, gentlemen—only positive suggestions."

"I still think we should try upriver," said General Murray. "Do you think you could force the city's guns, Admiral?"

"Possibly," Saunders replied, again without enthusiasm. "But I would have to have much more covering fire from the ground artillery. The end of this island falls too far short of the city."

Wolfe nodded soberly. "What do you say, Mr. Gill?" he asked Jedediah. "Do you know of any soft spot—a ford, a path, a gap—anything we might probe?"

Jedediah pondered for a moment. "Of course, I wasn't here with Phips. But my uncle was." His face brightened. "By Jesus, there *is* a ford! I can remember Uncle Jon talking about it. They tried to force it, but the French drove them back. It's about two or three miles behind the Beauport shore."

"Excellent!" James Wolfe exclaimed, his eyes shining again. "I will send a party of rangers to—"

A huge flash of light outside the tent illuminated the men inside it like a bolt of lightning. It was followed by a monstrous explosion, and the ground beneath their feet shivered. Wolfe came to his feet and ran outside, followed by the rest. Micah Gill stood transfixed.

Sheets of fire shot up from the river, roar after roar shook the camp, while the air was filled with flying pieces of burning wood and whizzing bits of steel. Micah could hear the frightened cries of the English sentries as they turned and ran away from the riverbank. As they did, it seemed as though they were pursued by dragons from hell, belching out columns of suffocating smoke and suffusing the air with the sulphurous reek of their breath.

"Fire ships!" Micah yelled above the uproar. "The French have launched fireships downriver against the fleet."

"It may be a night attack," General Wolfe said calmly. "Murray, Monckton, Townshend—form your brigades on the beaches."

The three generals hurried away, shouting for their colonels, while Wolfe drew his telescope and opened it. Micah opened his. The two men focused on the river where the fire ships were now in full view drifting down on the English ships. Flames ran up their masts and sails like fiery snakes, and then the vessels—soaked in pitch and tar and stuffed to the gunwales with bombs, grenades, old iron, fireworks, rusty cannon swivels and muskets loaded to the muzzle—burst apart like floating volcanoes. The St. Lawrence hissed and roared like a stricken beast while the night was slashed and crisscrossed with cascades of fire and showers of flying sparks. In that unnatural glare, Micah could see crowds of excited French soldiers crowded in front of their white tents on the Beauport shore. They stared across the glittering river to the Orleans beaches, where red-coated English regulars were marching to form squares. Micah swung his telescope to the English ships, all now flying warning lights and firing signal cannon. He saw boats being lowered away and seamen swarming into them carrying grappling hooks.

"Look, General," Micah called, "they're going to try to take the fire ships in tow."

"Aye, Major—and they will. There's no braver or better sailors on earth."

Both men watched anxiously while the boats were rowed boldly toward the drifting fire ships. They saw the grappling irons go arching through the air; heard the faint cheerful calls of the sailors making them fast; and then, sighing with relief, saw them being pulled slowly toward the Orleans shore, where they would burn themselves out. Both men put down their glasses, now able to watch the approach of the Marquis de Vaudreuil's expensive fizzle with the naked eye.

And both of them chuckled to hear one of the sailors shout to another:

"Damn me, Jack, didst thee ever take hell in tow before?"

The French fire-ship attempt against the English ships had impressed James Wolfe with the value of the fleet and the necessity of forcing a passage upriver.

"We need to be closer to Quebec," he told his brigadiers. "If Saunders tries to sail upriver, we've got to be able to cover him as far as Cape Diamond. If he succeeds, we can cut Montcalm's supply lines from Montreal." He pointed to the map on the field table before him. "This tip of land— Point Levi—is just the spot. It's only a mile across the basin from the city. We can cover Saunders from it and also bombard Quebec. Monckton, I desire you to take it and hold it."

On the following day, a party of rangers and light infantrymen from Monckton's brigade scaled Point Levi's unguarded cliffs and advanced inland. Monckton followed with the rest of his troops. Next day the English drove off a force of 650 Canadians and 350 Indians and armed settlers. The French countered on the following day by sending a floating battery to lob shells onto the clifftop occupied by the British. Out in the open, the redcoats began to take casualties. A French warship added to their travail until the British frigate *Trent* sailed upstream with blazing guns and drove off their afflictors.

On rocky soil already reddened with English blood, the soldiers worked desperately to get underground. Now and then, Indians came screeching out of the woods to kill a straggler and take his scalp. Eventually, the invaluable heights opposite Quebec were fortified. And the French made no move to recover them.

Wolfe came over to Point Levi and went to the heights opposite Quebec. Again he studied the city through a glass. Then he chose a position from which to bombard it. Cannon and mortars were brought over from Orleans. Entrenchments were thrown up and batteries planted, even as the French guns hurled ball and shot into the toiling English.

In Quebec frantic citizens saw the batteries growing and appealed to Vaudreuil to dislodge the English. Montcalm, who considered the move at Point Levi as a feint to draw him off, was against the attack. However, he allowed a hundred of his regulars to join a ragtag force of about fifteen hundred armed citizens, some students from the seminary, and a few Indians.

They crossed the St. Lawrence above Point Levi in the dark of night. They had hardly come ashore before they grew nervous. The seminary students fired on each other. Mistaking the warning shouts of the British soldiers for war cries, they panicked and went tumbling down the hillside to their boats, reaching Quebec shamefaced and leaving seventy of their number dead or wounded on the enemy shore.

And the British kept on mounting guns.

On the night of July 12 a rocket exploded above the river between Quebec and Point Levi, and Monckton's cannon roared into life.

Both the first and the second salvos fell into the river, and cries of derision rose from the French. But the English gunners eventually found the range. Shells began bursting among the wharves and the streets of the Lower Town, and some even shook the walls of the Upper Town itself. Soon the French batteries were belching back. A furious artillery duel raged throughout the night, and it would continue to roar intermittently for the next two months.

On the night of July 15 an English shell set fire to a building in the Upper Town. High winds carried the fire to the cathedral, which burned to the ground within an hour. A week later another fierce fire all but demolished the Lower Town. Soon the Lower Town was a shambles and the crowded streets of the Upper Town were not safe for passage. One by one, sometimes in family groups, the residents of the crumbling city began to flee to the sanctuary of the countryside.

General Wolfe had moved the bulk of his forces across the river to the east bank of the Montmorency, across that stream from the French left flank. "I can wait no longer," he had told his brigadiers, twisting his little ceremonial cane in his hands. "I have got to lure Montcalm out of his shell. I have got to meet him in decisive battle."

"But where, Sir?" General Murray asked. "I'm as anxious for battle as you are. But there is no chink in their armor."

Wolfe pointed to Major Gill, seated at the table next to him. "At the ford his father mentioned."

"But that's three miles up the Montmorency through a wilderness full of Indians. There's a guard of a thousand Canadians there as well."

"I shall cross it," Wolfe said. "It's passable at low tide. I want you, Townshend, to take your brigade there, while you, Murray, will boat your brigade and make a feint at the Beauport shore. In the meantime, we will bombard Quebec from Point Levi and our new camp on the Montmorency."

On the morning of July 31 the sixty-four-gun frigate *Centurion* sailed down the St. Lawrence and anchored off Beauport, while a pair of fourteen-gun catamarans worked their way close inshore. *Centurion* and her tiny twins opened up, battering the Beauport redoubts. From Wolfe's camp on the Montmorency and Monckton's cannon to the west at Point Levi came a crossfire aimed at the clifftops. The thunder of the cannonade continued for two hours, and the blue basin of Quebec echoed and reechoed once more to the roar of discharging guns and the crash of exploding shells.

Meanwhile, Murray's troops—grenadiers and Royal Americans—were boated. They were rowed toward Beauport, moving back and forth opposite the tiny town that served as Montcalm's headquarters. General Wolfe stood in an open boat, cane in hand, his pale face flushed. Dr. Malachi Gill, who shared the boat with Wolfe and his brother, Micah, muttered: "I wonder how much of that flush is exultation and how much is fever."

Micah nodded silently, studying the brown edge of the Beauport flats becoming gradually visible with the ebb of the tide. Hearing the sound of musketry from the Montmorency ford, he said: "It's low tide. Townshend must be crossing the ford." General Wolfe lifted his cane in the air and waved it as the signal for the attack.

Shouting "God save the king!" the grenadiers and Royal Americans were rowed toward the Beauport flats. But the ebbing tide swept them downriver.

"Hold off!" Wolfe shouted from his boat. "The tide is not low enough!"

No one heard him in the rattle of the plunging fire the French on the heights poured into the English. Redcoats crumpled in their boats. Others toppled overboard. Three times, James Wolfe put his hand to his face and body where splinters struck him. His cane was shot from his grasp. "Please, Sir," Micah pleaded, "get below the gunwales. You'll be killed up there!" Fixing him with a cold and icy eye, Wolfe replied: "You are perfectly free to take cover, Major Gill." Stooping, the general retrieved his cane and waved it once more in the attack signal. Blushing with shame, Micah came to his feet beside him. Together, they watched the boats beaching on the broad expanse of mud before them.

The French in the redoubts on the beach fled at the English approach. Cheering again, the grenadiers and Royal Americans pursued them, shouting and challenging each other—just as the French on the heights renewed their withering fire.

All was confusion on the beaches. Boats were piling up. More and more units of soldiers leaped ashore, enlarging the mob that milled about beneath the enemy guns. Men screamed and fell. Non-commissioned officers ran wildly about, looking for officers to give orders. Suddenly, the grenadiers took direction of the battle into their own hands. They went storming up the heights to get at their tormentors above them. The heat was oppressive. Thick, scattered raindrops began to fall. The grenadiers swarming up the slopes began to slip and stumble. French fire scourged them. Their breath came in agonizing gasps. Sweat stained their once-immaculate uniforms, now red with blood or black with mud. Straining for handholds, using their muskets as crutches, sometimes falling to roll downhill until they were stopped by a bush or a fallen comrade, they continued their ascent into the terrible flashing muskets of the enemy. It was then that the skies darkened and a torrent of rain fell on the battlefield.

It squelched the battle. Wolfe sounded the retreat, and the surviving English came sliding down the hill to return to the boats. They pulled out onto the river just as the rain stopped. When the clouds lifted, Major Micah Gill could see Montcalm's Indians on the heights draw their scalping knives and go clambering down among the dead and wounded.

The Marquis de Montcalm was jubilant. A deserter from the English camp had provided him with details of the English defeat, and he discussed them at length with the Chevalier de Levis, the commander of his left flank.

"They lost four hundred and fifty men, my dear Levis, most of them killed. And we did not suffer a single scratch." Grinning derisively like a private soldier, he said: "Our only casualty was a corporal in the Queen's Regiment who cut himself shaving."

Levis burst into laughter. "*Excellent, mon général*—but please, now is the time to attack them. While they are in despair. I beg you to allow me the honor . . ."

Montcalm shook his head grimly. "That is exactly what General Wolfe desires."

"But we have them outnumbered."

"Yes, but most of our troops are Canadians. In the woods, one Canadian is worth two regulars. But in open battle, one regular is worth four Canadians. No, let them amuse themselves, my dear Levis. Besides, the deserter has informed me that General Wolfe and his brigadiers are not on good terms. They blame him for the defeat. He has lost the respect of all of his officers, and his army hates him. He issued a General Order putting the blame on his grenadiers. Imagine! A general blaming private soldiers for his own mistakes. Even Admiral Saunders is angry. *Monsieur le général* also managed to blame the English Navy." Montcalm smiled. "He is thorough, is he not, this young hothead? But I do not fear Wolfe's army, my dear Chevalier. No, the army I fear is General Amherst's at Ticonderoga. If he can come up Lake Champlain, he can capture Montreal and threaten my rear. I would then be between Wolfe in the east and Amherst in the west. . . . Eh??" he inquired, lifting his head as an aide came into the room and handed him a message.

"*Sacristi!*" Montcalm exclaimed. "The English fleet has forced its way upriver! A frigate and two smaller ships. This is serious," he said, putting down the message and studying Levis gravely. "They may now be able to threaten the north shore between here and Montreal. Even cut my supply line." He sighed. "I do not like to weaken my position, but you must tell Dumas to take six hundred men to guard the heights between the city and Cape Rouge."

"And the Anse du Foulon?"

"It is safe. The Guyenne and St. Martin are still there."

Nodding, the Chevalier de Levis arose to carry out his general's orders.

General James Wolfe had not only attempted to shift the blame for his defeat onto the shoulders of his soldiers and Admiral Saunders but had also turned in his frustration upon the Canadian civilians occupying the south banks of the St. Lawrence.

"Because of your most unchristian barbarities against my troops on all occasions," he said, dictating a General Order to Major Gill, "I can no longer refrain from chastising you as you deserve."

East and west, parties were sent forth to scourge the Cana-ian *canaille*. One of these under Captain Alexander Montgomery went to the village of St. Joachim. Robineau de Portneuf, the curé there, invited Montgomery and his officers to dinner, but Montgomery declined. Next day, he attacked the priest's house. After Portneuf surrendered, Montgomery had his eighty parishioners shot down in cold blood while the priest was slashed to the ground, scalped, his skull beaten into the earth, and his church and parish burned.

Night after night the residents of Quebec could see the glow of burning villages. Montcalm also watched this savaging of his countrymen, but with no intention of ending it. He would not be drawn into open battle under any circumstances, and thus, the tormented Canadians were caught between two fires. Where Wolfe was wasting the countryside in an effort to starve Quebec and force the militia to desert to defend their homes, Montcalm kept the militia in check by threatening to turn his Indians loose on their families.

Even the armed English soldiery lived in daily dread of Montcalm's savages, especially after a private of the 47th Regiment returned from captivity in an Indian village to tell a horrible story. He had escaped the night before he was to be boiled and eaten. For three days before that, the villagers, women and children as well as men, had amused themselves by sticking splinters of wood under his fingernails and into his penis, exploding little charges of powder packed into cuts in his flesh made with a tomahawk, and smashing his toes to a pulp with small stone hammers. Little girls had torn the hair from his chest and little boys had poked sticks and thorns up his nose. Such details, inevitably exaggerated in the retelling, had the fortunate effect of so terrifying the English that there were fewer and fewer sentries surprised at their posts or stragglers relieved of their scalps. In fact, the English had grown so adept at bush warfare that the Indians began to complain of redcoats who no longer stood still to be shot at.

Meanwhile, Quebec was collapsing under the hammer of Monckton's artillery. Fires in the Lower Town were a daily occurrence, and in the Upper Town 167 houses were destroyed in a single dreadful night. On August 10 a shell crashing into a cellar set a vat of brandy afire and burned down many buildings, including the beautiful Nôtre Dame des Victoires.

Once again, Governor Vaudreuil pleaded with General Montcalm to march against the English. "The city is in ruins," he told him reproachfully. "The Lower Town is all but gone. Can't you do *something*?"

"I will not do what General Wolfe wants me to do," the general replied calmly.

"But we have almost no food left. We can barely feed the soldiers, let alone the people."

"It was you, *Monsieur le gouverneur*, who assured me that the English could never get upriver. Now they are up there in strength. They are intercepting my supply ships from Montreal and crossing the river to strike the villages on the north shore. Why did you not inform me of our weakness? Why did you not give me the opportunity to emplace artillery above Cape Diamond?" Vaudreuil grimaced and opened his hands in a gesture of despair. "Now, I must weaken myself again to contend with the English ships upriver. Today, I have instructed the Chevalier de Bougainville to take fifteen hundred more men to the west."

To Vaudreuil's surprise, Montcalm smiled. "But there is good news nevertheless, Monsieur. Even though we have lost Ticonderoga, Crown Point and Fort Niagara, Montreal is safe. General Amherst has dragged his feet. He is not so impetuous as that young redhead out there," he said, pointing to the Montmorency. "He cannot possibly reach Montreal before winter."

"That is good news," the governor said. "I should be able to release a few thousand militiamen to help in the harvest up there. But I still think you should do something to discourage the English."

Again General Montcalm shook his head. "Two months more, and they will be gone."

"We've only got another month, boys," Jedediah Gill said to his two sons, staring moodily at the black surface of the Montmorency River to his left. The three men were walking toward the falls, which they had not yet seen. They could hear the thunder of the great cataract coming faintly through the forest. The sound reminded Jedediah of the waterfall where he and Redbud used to meet. He thought momentarily of Half Moon, wondering if he were still alive. If he were, would he be among Montcalm's Indians?

"Why do you say that, Pa?" Malachi asked. "It's only the end of August."

"There's no autumn up here, Mal. Hardly even a spring. Just winter and summer, and I can already feel a hint of winter in the air. One more month and the ice floes will be forming in the Gulf of St. Lawrence. We've got to do something before the end of September. I just can't bear thinking that this'll be the third time a member of my family dragged his tail away from Quebec."

"It's all Amherst's fault," Micah said reproachfully. "He should have been attacking Montreal by now. That would have forced the French to defend in two places, instead of just here. I told you, Pa, I never thought much of Amherst."

"I'm beginning to think about the same of your General Wolfe," Jedediah said. "What's wrong with him, anyway? The army's melting away. He's lost eight hundred and fifty killed and wounded since we got here. And the desertions, what are they up to now, Micah?"

"Twenty or thirty a day," Micah said grimly.

"Dysentery is very bad," Malachi put in. "The hospital is full, and I've had to start putting my patients in the empty farmhouses."

The thunder of the waterfall was growing louder. Coming around a bend, they saw it before them, a massive white wall of water cascading into a roaring, boiling froth. "Oh, my Jesus," Jedediah cried. "I've never seen Niagara, but I can't believe it's bigger'n this."

Pinnnng!

The three men threw themselves down. "Let's get out of here!" Micah shouted. "It may be a beautiful sight, but it isn't worth your life." They crawled back around the bend, rising to brush the mud from their clothes.

"Goddam frog-eaters," Jedediah muttered, scowling darkly

in the direction of the sniper. "Oh, how I'd love to get my hands on them. If the general would just—"

"I don't know what's wrong with him," Micah muttered gloomily. "Ever since Beauport he's been like a man in a trance. It's as though he's afraid of another defeat. The only time he talks to Murray or Townshend is to argue with them."

"You can't blame him for hating Townshend," Malachi said. "He knows the things he says about him. Calls him 'General Popeye' and draws pictures of him bombarding Quebec with his behind. Today at mess, he drew a caricature of him fortifying a whorehouse. I have to admit it was funny. All the officers were roaring with laughter when General Wolfe walked in. He turned white when he saw the picture. He crumpled it up and stuck it in his pocket and told Townshend if he lived he'd have him court-martialed."

Jedediah Gill rolled his eyes heavenward and exclaimed: "If he lives, if he lives, if he lives! Almost everything he says comes out with that prefix: 'If I live.' What's wrong with him, anyway, Mal?"

"Consumption. Both physical and spiritual. He's consumed by both fever and a fear of failure. He's a very sick man, Pa. Only this morning, he came to me with a fever and I had to put him to bed in a farmhouse on the river."

"Oh, my Jesus," Jedediah groaned. "What if he dies?"

Neither of his sons gave an answer.

"My dear Marie," François Bigot said to Madame Pean. "I should like you to go to Deschambault tomorrow."

"But why, François?"

"Ostensibly, to see your sister there. Actually, to be captured by the English."

"Please don't be so clever. Sometimes your sense of humor can be tiresome."

"I am not trying to be clever. Vergor has told me of a communication from a friend in Versailles. A commission is being formed to inquire into the conduct of the colony."

Marie Pean's face whitened. *"Mon Dieu,"* she breathed, her fine white hand going to her bosom. "That means . . . ?"

"Yes, it means the Bastille for us all. That is why I want you to go to Deschambault. I have information that the English are going to strike there in a few days. I want you to be there to be captured."

"But, surely, François . . ."

"You will not be harmed. The English treated their captives from Pointe-aux-Trembles very courteously." A leering smile crossed his ugly face. "Especially the women. . . . Once you are in their camp, my dear Marie, you will use all your charms to come into the presence of General Wolfe. You will tell him that you and I are in danger of being sent back to France in irons, and—"

"*Me*?"

"Yes, my lovely one—you. You and me and Vergor and Cadet and your charmingly complaisant husband as well. But it is only with you and me that I am concerned. You will tell him that, in exchange for his protection, I will betray the colony to him." Marie Pean gasped, and Bigot lifted a restraining hand. "Yes, my dear. If the colony is destroyed, it will be difficult for the commission to come here to make inquiries. If General Wolfe agrees to take us back to England with him, it will be impossible. You understand?"

"Yes, François," Marie Pean said, her breasts rising and falling in her distress, her voice still breathless. "But how will you betray Canada?"

"You will show General Wolfe the path up the cliff from the Anse du Foulon."

Captain Alexander Montgomery, the officer who had directed the massacre at St. Joachim, was in command of the expedition to Deschambault. He was accompanied by Major Micah Gill, whom Brigadier Murray, in the continued absence of the bedridden General Wolfe, had asked to explore the possibilities of an invasion at the little upriver village.

Although Bougainville had twice turned back two earlier English sallies against the towns of the northern shore, there was no opposition at Deschambault. Montgomery's men quickly set a large storehouse afire and burned down another building filled with the spare baggage of Montcalm's officers.

"They'll be traveling light from now on," Montgomery said with a laugh, standing alongside Major Gill to watch the second structure collapse in flames.

An orderly rode up and saluted. "We've taken all the villagers prisoner, Captain. But there's one very fine lady who says she will not surrender unless we take her straight to General Wolfe."

"Where is she?"

The orderly pointed up the narrow village street. "In that stone house at the end of the road."

"I think this is a matter for you, Major," Montgomery said, turning to Micah.

"I agree," Micah said, and walked quickly up to the stone house. Finding the door open, he went in. It was deserted inside. But Micah thought he heard a woman humming in what seemed to be a bedroom. He knocked on the door. "Is someone in there?"

"*Oui*," a musical voice called.

"May I come in?"

"*Oui*."

Micah was agreeably surprised by the beauty of the woman who awaited him inside the bedroom. "I am Madame Pean," she said, smiling.

"I am Major Micah Gill, aide to General Wolfe. May I be of service?"

"*Oui*. I would like to speak to General Wolfe."

"For what purpose, may I ask?"

"I cannot tell you. But you may tell the general that I can be of great assistance to him."

"I see." Micah studied Marie Pean intently. "Your request is most unusual. You would not, perhaps, have an ulterior motive?"

Marie lifted her chin haughtily. "I do not understand you."

"You would not, perhaps, intend to kill the general? You do not have a knife or a pistol concealed somewhere beneath that beautiful dress of yours?"

"Ridiculous!"

"May I search you?" Micah said, advancing toward her.

"Do not touch me," Marie replied, putting a hand on her bosom and drawing herself up haughtily.

Micah shrugged, a smile playing about his saturnine features. "How else can I be sure?"

"I will show you," Marie replied, beginning to unbutton her dress. To Micah's amazement, she suddenly stood proudly before him in all her naked beauty. She turned slowly around. "So you see, Monsieur le commandant, I have nothing to conceal from you."

"No, but what you do have to show me is a thousand times more interesting."

Now it was Micah who disrobed. He moved toward her. Her eyes fell upon his erect penis, and she gasped in astonished delight. "Are all your countrymen so abundantly endowed, Monsieur?"

"Most of us," Micah said, coming closer.

"Then, Monsieur," Marie Pean paid, entering his arms, "it is not only a pleasure but a duty to surrender."

Upon his return to the Montmorency headquarters, Major Gill was delighted to discover that General Wolfe was on his feet again. He was not, of course, completely recovered, but he was well enough to walk, and he had immediately called for Dr. Malachi Gill. "I know perfectly well that you cannot cure me, Doctor," he said. "But pray make me up so that I may be without pain for a few days." Malachi obliged with the customary leeching and bleeding, and Wolfe, his eyes and cheeks still bright with fever, immediately plunged into a round of conferences with his brigadiers.

Once again, they recommended that he land upriver from Quebec, to seize a position between Quebec and Montreal. Thus he would cut the French supply line, giving Montcalm a choice between starving or fighting.

"But where, gentlemen?" Wolfe asked, standing near a map. "Pointe-aux-Trembles?"

"Decidedly not," Murray said. "They gave us a bloody nose there."

"Deschambault, then?"

"I think not, General," said Major Gill, who was present. "The cliffs are too steep."

"But, *where*? *Where*?" Wolfe bit his lip petulantly, still studying the map. "We've *got* to land somewhere. By God, I will not go back to England without making another attempt. Gentlemen, we cannot delay. Admiral Saunders has told me that ice has begun to form in the gulf. He is threatening to sail home with the fleet. We have only a few more days. It is my wish that you confer again on a landing place and return to me within the hour with your decision."

Their swords rattling in their sheaths, the three officers

arose and left. Major Gill spoke to the general. "I have a prisoner who wants to speak to you, Sir. She says she can be of great help to you."

"A woman?"

"Yes. She is . . . ah . . . the companion of the intendant Bigot."

Wolfe's eyebrows rose, and his pale eyes gleamed. "Bring her to me, Major—and, pray, leave us alone."

When Marie Pean stood before James Wolfe, she abandoned all thought of charming or seducing him. If ever there was a man who cared nothing for the pleasures of the boudoir, she thought, this was he. Instead, she came straight to the point. "I am the mistress of Intendant Bigot," she said, her bold eyes on Wolfe's. "He sent me to Deschambault on purpose to be captured so that I might speak to you."

"Very clever," Wolfe murmured.

"The intendant begs for your protection. A commission is being formed in Versailles to investigate his conduct in Canada, and he is afraid that he will be sent home to face trial."

"I see," Wolfe said coldly. "He has been robbing his king?"

"You may call it that," Marie said coolly. "But he asks that you take both him and me back to England with you."

"In return for what?"

"Quebec."

There was a pause, during which James Wolfe's bulging blue eyes gleamed again. He drew his ceremonial cane from his belt and tapped it against his fingers. "How?"

"There is an unknown path up the side of the cliffs leading to the Plains of Abraham west of the city."

Now Wolfe's eyes glittered. "Plains, you say? Suitable for maneuver? Between Quebec and Montreal?"

"Yes."

Wolfe pondered. It could be a trap. "The top of the path—it is guarded?"

"Yes. By a picked force under a brave officer. And a crack regiment is nearby."

"But then, madame, you are offering me suicide."

Marie Pean shook her head. "They will be sent away," she said confidently.

"There are others, then, who wish to see the colony destroyed?"

Marie nodded silently.

Wolfe pondered again, his heart beating with suppressed excitement. It could be done! He would not need to risk his army in what might still be a trap. He would send a forlorn hope up the cliff—a hundred and fifty picked men under Major Gill—and if they seized a position on the clifftop, he could lead the rest of his forces up to the Plains of Abraham. Montcalm would *have* to come out and fight!

"You will show me this path?" he asked Marie, his eyes boring into hers.

"Yes, if you will promise in writing to take us back to England with you."

Wolfe's eyes turned cold again. He shook his head firmly. "I can give no such written promises. I can only give you my word of honor that, if you show me this path and Quebec is mine, you shall be separated from my other prisoners and shall return with me to England."

Marie Pean's eyes fell. Her eyelashes fluttered. Then she raised her eyes again and said in a low voice: "Agreed."

22

At two o'clock in the morning of September 13, 1759, the tide on the St. Lawrence River began to ebb. A fleet of English ships carrying 4,800 soldiers, which had earlier drifted upriver on the flood tide, began to slip silently downstream. Aboard the *Sutherland*, a lantern with its light shrouded from the Quebec shore was hoisted to the main topgallant masthead. It was the signal for General Wolfe's forlorn hope—150 picked volunteers under Major Micah Gill—to cast off. Soon the boats began to drift with the current toward the Anse du Foulon.

James Wolfe stood in one of them. Beside him stood Jedediah Gill. To Jedediah's surprise, he heard the general begin to recite poetry in a low voice. " 'There is a time in the affairs of men,' " the general began, and then paused as though puzzled. " 'Time?' Is that the right word?"

"It isn't, Sir," Jedediah murmured. "It's 'tide.' 'There is a tide in the affairs of men, which, taken at the flood, leads on to fortune. . . .' "

"Egad, you are right, Mr. Gill. And that is exactly what we are doing on this night that shall go down in eternal history. True, the tide is ebbing, but we are on the flood to victory."

358

Wolfe paused. "So you know Shakespeare, Mr. Gill. I'm surprised. Are you fond of poetry?"

"Very much, Sir."

"While I was recovering, I memorized Gray's *Elegy Written in a Country Churchyard*." He began to recite it.

The curfew tolls the knell of parting day,
The lowing herd wind slowly o'er the lea . . .

Wolfe's voice intoned slowly on, barely audible above the sound of water lapping gently against the side of the boat. Finishing, he turned to his aides and said: "Gentlemen, I would rather have written those lines than take Quebec."

An embarrassed silence ensued. Someone coughed. Jedediah Gill sensed that no one believed him. Neither did he, as he silently reflected on one of the lines:

The paths of glory lead but to the grave.

François Bigot's guests had only just departed. Some of them were in high spirits, for they had won handily.

"What luck!" Bigot moaned, staring despondently at the cards scattered over the table in his private dancing hall.

"How much did you lose tonight?" Marie Pean asked anxiously.

"Ten thousand."

"François! You must stop. There will be nothing left to live on when we get to England."

Bigot eyed her warily. "You are sure General Wolfe will keep his word?"

"He promised me, and I believed him."

Bigot sighed. "I have never trusted a man in my life. And now, I trust my life with a man I never saw."

"There is no other way, François. Please, what did the governor say today?"

The intendant winked. "It has been arranged, my dear. Vaudreuil ordered the Guyenne Regiment away from the Plains today."

"Does Montcalm know?"

"Not yet. And *Monsieur le marquis* has also obligingly removed Captain St. Martin from command of the cliff guard." He winked again. "Vergor is in command, now."

Marie Pean gave a scornful laugh. "Ah, yes, Vergor—he is good at surrender, that one. He will not like going home in irons."

Bigot shrugged. "It cannot be helped. We cannot all presume upon the generosity of General Wolfe. It would sink the ship. So all is in readiness. And as a final precaution, my dear, I have arranged that the horses of the cliff patrol will be stolen tonight."

"You are thorough, François," Marie said admiringly.

"Thank you, my dear. Come, let us go to bed. I fear we shall be awakened early by the sound of cannon."

Although James Wolfe had delayed until it was almost too late, once he had seen the narrow path leading up to the Plains of Abraham, he rapidly devised a masterly plan for battle.

First he began the difficult withdrawal from the Montmorency. As he disengaged, Montcalm sent a strong force to fall on his rear. Monckton saw this movement from Point Levi and quickly embarked two battalions to make a feint at Beauport, and Montcalm withdrew.

Next Wolfe made a feint at Cape Rouge, held by Bougainville, and during the next few days he drove Bougainville and his men into weary distraction by having the ships above the city drift upriver with the flood tide and drift downriver on the ebb, forcing the French to march and countermarch to remain abreast of the English fleet. To delude Montcalm into believing that the movement above the town was a diversion for another attack against his fortifications east of Quebec, Wolfe asked Admiral Saunders to deploy his main fleet in a demonstration off Beauport. Finally, two deserters told Wolfe that Bougainville was sending a convoy of provisions down to Montcalm on the ebb tide on the night of September 12. Wolfe immediately saw the possibility of sending his own boats down ahead of the convoy so as to deceive the French sentinels. Wolfe did not know that Bougainville had postponed the provision convoy, but neither did Bougainville inform the sentries below that the familiar store ships were not coming.

On the night of September 12, all was in readiness. The stars were visible, but there was no moon as perhaps 4,800 English began drifting upriver. Bougainville, wearied by the promenade of the past few days, was confident that they would only drift downriver again. In fact, the chevalier was going to spend the night farther west at Jacques Cartier. The desirable and accommodating Madame de Vienne was at Jacques Cartier. Below Quebec, Saunders was lowering boats filled with sailors and Marines, his guns were thundering, and the Marquis de Montcalm was massing troops at the wrong point ten miles below the Anse du Foulon.

The English boats had been drifting downstream for two full hours, unchallenged and unseen. Now the tide was bearing the leading craft with Wolfe's spearhead—twenty-four volunteers under Major Micah Gill—toward the towering shore. Above them, there came a shout.

"*Qui vive?*"

No one spoke, and then Major Micah Gill shouted back, "*France! Et vive le roi!*"

"*A quel régiment?*" the sentry persisted.

"*De la Reine,*" Micah shot back, aware that part of this unit was with Bougainville.

The sentry was satisfied, and the boats drifted on, one of the men giggling aloud in relief. Again the challenge. A sentry had come scrambling down the cliff face to stand at the water's edge and demand the password.

"Provision boats!" Micah hissed, deliberately disguising his accent with a hoarse whisper. "Don't make such a bloody noise! The *maudit* English will hear!"

The sentry waved them on. Micah could see the gray of his cuff against the black of the cliff behind him.

On the boats drifted, and now the current was running strong and they had rounded the headland of the Anse du Foulon. The sailors broke out their oars and rowed desperately against the tide. But the spearhead boats were swept too far downstream. Undaunted, Micah and his men leaped out. He led the party softly up the cliff face. The figure of a sentry materialized out of the gloom above them. He shouted down at them. Still hissing his hoarse whisper, Micah told him that he had come to relieve the post. "I'll take care to give a good account of the *maudit* English if they land!"

On the shore of the cove below, General James Wolfe and Jedediah crouched helplessly in the dark—their ears straining for the sound of firing. It came, and Wolfe despaired.

Above, the sentry had hesitated for too long. There were twenty-four shadowy figures around him before he could reply, and then the English charged with blazing muskets. Captain Vergor came dashing out of his tent barefooted in a nightshirt. He fired two pistols wildly into the air before he turned and sprinted for Quebec at the head of his departing troops. A musket shot pierced his heel, and he fell screaming.

It was then that Wolfe's despondency changed to a fierce wild joy, for he had heard the huzzahs of his triumphant volunteers. Quickly he gave the order for the second wave to land. In came the boats, and soon the cliff face was crawling with British soldiers. Among them was James Wolfe. Diseased, weakened by bloodletting, never strong, he was climbing on his magnificent will alone; and as he got to the top, the empty boats of the first wave were returning to the packed transports for the rest of his troops.

Now the guns at Point Levi and the Island of Orleans had joined those of Saunders firing on Beauport. Soon Beauport's batteries were thundering back, followed by those at Quebec and at Samos to the west of the Anse du Foulon. Wolfe immediately sent Colonel William Howe's light infantry against that battery menacing his rear, and the British silenced it.

By dawn, the last of Wolfe's sweating soldiers had struggled up to the undefended Plains of Abraham. Some 4,-800 soldiers began to form and to march into a north-south line parallel to and about three-quarters of a mile distant from the western walls of Quebec.

That was how the Marquis de Montcalm saw them as he rode up in a drizzling rain.

Montcalm had been completely deceived by Saunders's feint. Nevertheless, he rode over to Quebec that morning with the Chevalier Johnstone, a Scots Jacobite who had been given a commission in the French Army. En route, a messenger informed him of the British landing. Montcalm set his horse on the path to Vaudreuil's house. From there he could see clearly to those plains which had once been owned by a French pilot named Abraham Martin. He could see the thin red lines of British soldiers stretching from the St. Foye Road on their left—and his right—to the cliffs of the St. Lawrence. Faintly, skirling on the wind, came the wail of the Highlanders' pipes. The enemy array stood motionless, as though awaiting inspection, their regimental colors drooping in the gentle rain.

"*C'est très sérieux*," Montcalm said in a grave voice. "This is very serious. Please ride to the city for the field pieces. Send a courier for the troops at Beauport."

Johnstone clattered off, just as Governor Vaudreuil came out of his house.

"Ah, Monsieur le Marquis Look the Other Way," Montcalm said sarcastically.

"What? What's that?" Vaudreuil spluttered, obviously shaken.

"By what authority and for what reason did you order the Guyenne away from the Plains to the St. Charles? Why did you relieve St. Martin and replace him with that cowardly traitor, Vergor? Who arranged to lame and steal the horses of the cliff patrol last night?"

Vaudreuil drew himself up. "I am the governor of Canada. I need not answer to my military commander for my actions."

"You are the governor of a Canada that is about to vanish. To disappear by reason of your treachery."

Vaudreuil's face reddened. "You shall answer for those words," he cried in a trembling voice.

"I will do so gladly, Monsieur. And if I live, you shall answer to the king."

The Chevalier Johnstone rode up. "The governor of the city refuses to give up his cannon. He will release only three." Johnstone stared boldly at the trembling Vaudreuil. "And the governor of Canada has ordered that the troops at Beauport must stay there."

Montcalm wheeled on Vaudreuil with a face full of wrath, but before he could open his mouth, the governor hurried back inside his house. One by one, Montcalm's officers rode up. They sat their horses in a circle around their chief.

"The question is, shall we attack now?" Montcalm said to them. "Or shall we wait until Bougainville can move on the English rear? If we wait for that, the English can improve their position. If we attack now, we will have to do it without Bougainville and with only the troops in Quebec. But we can also strike the enemy before he can dig in. What say you, *mes officers*?"

"Attack!" they cried with one voice.

"Attack before *le traitre* Vaudreuil can pull down the flag."

"*Oui,*" Montcalm said with a sad little smile. "*J'attaque!*" And he ordered his troops out to the Plains of Abraham.

Out they marched to the last battle of New France. All that was French, all that Samuel de Champlain had planted 150 years before on the cliff above the river, was to be defended here this day. Golden lily and gilded cross, dream of an empire stretching to the Rockies, fervor and faith and feudalism, all that had nourished or corrupted the martial and colorful little colony along the great river was at stake on the plains beyond. Through the narrow streets they thronged, white-coated regulars in black hats and gaiters, with glittering bayonets, troops of Canadians and bands of Indians in scalp locks and war paint; out of the Palace Gate they poured, the battalions of Old France and the irregulars of the New, the victors of Fort Necessity, the Monongahela, Oswego, Ticonderoga and Fort William Henry, tramping to the tap of the drum and the call of the bugle for the final fight in the long war for a continent.

With them rode their general. He had never seemed more noble to his officers and men. The Canadians might have been more careful, they might have let New France live yet a little longer—but he gave no murmur of complaint. Mounted on a dark bay horse, he was a splendid figure in his green-and-gold uniform, the Cross of St. Louis gleaming above his cuirass. "Are you tired, my soldiers?" he cried. "Are you ready, my children?" They answered him with shouts, and as he swung his sword to encourage them, the cuffs of his wide sleeves fell back to reveal the white linen of his wrist bands.

Montcalm's eyes fell on an old Indian whom he recognized as Half Moon, the aging chief of the Caughnawagas. With his left hand, Half Moon held a musket over his shoulder, and in his right he grasped a tomahawk.

"Hold it, mine old," the general called. "Where do you think you are going?"

"*A bataille,*" Half Moon shouted back. "Today I will kill many English, and I will die happy."

"You hate them?"

"With all my heart."

"You have seen many winters, mine old," Montcalm said dubiously, calming his horse, frightened by the passage of an enemy cannonball overhead.

Half Moon grinned, revealing his toothless gums. "My teeth are gone, but my heart beats strong and my eye is clear." He shook his tomahawk toward the ranks of the English and said: "My mortal enemy is out there, and today I will find him and kill him."

"Go with God," Montcalm replied, and rode off to form his troops in line of battle.

In splendid composure, the English watched the French form. Since dawn, when the high ground less than a mile away had become suddenly thronged with the white coats of the tardily arriving Guyenne, the redcoats had been raked by Canadian and Indian sharpshooters. After Johnstone's three cannon had begun to punish them, Wolfe had ordered them to lie in the grass.

James Wolfe had put on a new uniform: scarlet coat over impeccable white breeches, gold-edged tricorne on his head. He walked gaily among his reclining men, making certain that they had loaded their muskets with an extra ball for the first volley, pausing to chat with his officers. Wolfe ignored the enemy sharpshooters and exploding shells. A captain near him fell, shot in the lung. Wolfe knelt and gently took the man's head in his arms. He thanked him for his services and told him he would be promoted when he was well again, immediately sending off an aide to Monckton to make sure that his promise was carried out should he be killed that day.

The desired battle had arrived, and James Wolfe was exalted. All his black moods and indecision had vanished. His step was light, his voice was steady and his pale face shone with confidence. Although he did outnumber Montcalm 4,800 to 4,000, it was the quality rather than the number of his troops which gave the English general his assurance. He had trained them personally and he had taught them to stand in awesome silence until their enemy was close enough to be broken by a single volley.

Toward ten o'clock the French began coming down the hill, regulars in the center, regulars and Canadians to the right and left, and Wolfe ordered his men to arise and form ranks. On came the French, shouting loudly, firing the moment they came within range, two columns inclining toward the English left, one to the right.

The English stood still.

Gradually the French lines became disordered by Canadians throwing themselves prone to reload, but they still came on, shouting and pouring a musket fire into the silent English.

"Fire!"

A single volley as loud as a cannon shot struck the French, not forty yards away. Again a volley, and then a clattering roll of muskets, and then, in the lifting smoke, the English saw the field before them littered with crumpled white coats, and the French, massed in fright, turning to flee.

"Charge!"

The British cheer and the fierce wild yell of the Highlanders rose into the air, the pursuit was begun. Redcoats with outthrust bayonets bounded after the fleeing enemy. Highlanders in kilts swinging broadswords overhead leaped forward to decapitate terrified fugitives with a single stroke.

Half Moon did not flee. He lay prone and squeezed off shot after shot, grunting in satisfaction each time a Highlander fell. At intervals, he searched the moving, smoking, yelling, screaming battlefield for a glimpse of Yellow Head. He saw him walking behind the English general. Whooping, Half Moon arose with brandished tomahawk—just as a Highlander's sword went thrusting up beneath his armpit into his lung. Half Moon sank back onto the ground. Blood gushed from his mouth. He felt a scalping knife cutting a ring around his skull. Fingers fumbled at his skin. "Leave the old buzzard be," a voice above him growled. "There's fatter pickings up ahead." A black, bottomless dark engulfed Half Moon.

James Wolfe was leading the charge. He had already taken a ball in the wrist and had wrapped a handkerchief around it. Now, at the head of the Louisbourg grenadiers, with Micah Gill beside him, he was wounded again. He pressed on, but a third shot pierced his breast. He swayed, and Micah caught him, lowering him gently to the ground. Malachi Gill rushed up.

"There's no need," Wolfe gasped. "It's all over with me. Attend to someone you can save."

He began to lose consciousness, while a group of sorrowing officers gathered around him. Suddenly, Micah Gill shouted: "They're running! See how they run!"

"Who runs?" Wolfe cried, rousing himself.

"The enemy, Sir. They're giving way everywhere."

"Go, one of you, to Colonel Burton," Wolfe gasped to his

aides, "and tell him to march Webb's regiment down to Charles River, to cut off their retreat from the bridge." Turning on his side, he murmured: "Now, God be praised, I will die in peace." A few minutes later he was dead.

The Marquis de Montcalm was also stricken. His horse had been borne toward the town by the tide of fleeing French, and as he neared the walls, a shot passed through his body. He slumped but kept his seat rather than let his soldiers see him fall. Two regulars bore him up on either side. He entered the city streaming blood, in full view of two horrified women.

"Oh, mon Dieu! Oh, mon Dieu!" one of them shrieked. "The marquis is killed."

"It is nothing, it is nothing," Montcalm gasped in reply. "Don't be troubled for me, my good friends."

He rode on into the city, slumping lower and lower in the saddle.

Jedediah Gill and his two sons walked sorrowfully behind the cart bearing James Wolfe's body from the battlefield. They passed beside a fallen old Indian, moaning in his death throes.

"Half Moon!" Jedediah exclaimed in a voice full of grief. He knelt beside him. "Half Moon, it's me. Your brother, Yellow Head."

Half Moon's hand groped for the tomahawk lying beside him. Jedediah covered the hand with his own. "Don't . . ." he murmured softly. "Don't hate me, anymore. Can't you forgive me, Half Moon?"

Half Moon snarled, baring his gums. "I am . . . sorry . . . I will not live . . . to kill you."

"Please forgive me, Half Moon. You are dying, and I know that I have not long to live. You killed my parents, Half Moon—and I forgive you. The men I killed—Beartooth and Howling Wolf—they hated you. Please. . . . You know it wouldn't work. I was too old to become an Indian. I always wanted to go back to my people. I love you, Half Moon, my brother. I still do. Please, if you cannot talk, press my hand with your fingers and say that you love your brother again."

Tears came into Half Moon's eyes. Jedediah Gill sobbed aloud when he felt the weak but unmistakable tightening of

Half Moon's fingers on his own. He glanced up to see a
French priest moving quietly among the dead. He had a stole
around his neck.

"Come quickly, Father," he called in French. "My brother
is dying. He wants absolution."

The priest hurried over and knelt beside Half Moon. "Are
you sorry for your sins?" he whispered into his ear. Half
Moon moved his head slightly, and the priest raised his hand
above him in the sign of the cross, beginning to murmur the
Latin formula: *"absolvo peccata te* . . . I absolve you of your
sins." Half Moon shuddered and lay still. The priest glanced
up at Jedediah and asked in a puzzled voice: "You said he
was your brother?"

"Yes. I was adopted by the Caughnawagas for almost five
years. We were brothers there—and now he has gone to meet
the father of us all."

Arising, the priest peered into their faces anxiously.
"Would you be kind enough to direct me to a physician?"

"I am a surgeon, Father," Malachi said. "Can I be of
help?"

"Oh, yes," the priest replied eagerly. "General Montcalm is
badly wounded. I think he may be dying."

"I will go to him immediately," Malachi said, and the four
men hurried to the palace. One glance at Montcalm's wound
sufficed for Malachi.

"Am I dying?" the marquis gasped.

"Yes, Sir."

"I am glad of it. How much longer will I live?"

"About twelve hours."

"So much the better. I am happy that I shall not live to see
the surrender of Quebec." Montcalm's fading eyes strayed to
the priest standing quietly by his bedside. He motioned to
him, and the priest, replacing the stole around his neck, knelt
beside him. Jedediah and his two sons walked softly from the
room, in their ears the low gasping voice of the last great
captain of New France making his last confession.

Outside, Micah's eyes fell on the familiar figure of a
woman hurrying toward the palace of the intendant. Micah
started. It was Marie Pean. He could see that she was crying,
and he hastened to her side. She pushed him away and
rushed on. Inside the palace, she hurried to Bigot's quarters.
He was at his safe, transferring money into a portmanteau.

"The general is dead, François," Marie sobbed. "All is lost!"

"Lost?" Bigot repeated with a bewildered air. "I do not understand. General Montcalm is no friend of—"

"No, no! Not Montcalm! He is dying, I know. But General Wolfe is already dead!"

Stark horror looked out of François Bigot's piggish little eyes. The color drained from his coarse face, making the pimples stand out in red blotches. "And you, my dear Marie," he said with sinister softness, "you did not get the general's assurances in writing."

"He would not give them to me!" she wailed. "François! François . . . don't—"

In a stride, Bigot came around his desk and struck her full in the mouth.

"*Saligaude!*" he snarled, as the blood broke from her lips. "You slut!"

Stepping over her prostrate body, Intendant François Bigot ran out of his chambers and through the rubble of the ruined city, making straight for the home of Governor Vaudreuil.

Jedediah Gill and his two sons also moved through the blackened wreckage of Quebec, walking slowly toward the cliffs above the Lower Town overlooking the broad blue basin of the St. Lawrence. Jedediah stood there for a time, his sons to either side of him, his hands in theirs.

"Quebec . . ." he breathed in a low, exulting voice, "Canada . . . Ours. . . . No more French north of the river. Our borders safe at last. If only my Uncle Jon were here."

Micah and Malachi studied their father anxiously. Both had felt his grasp growing weaker in theirs.

"What's wrong, Pa?" Malachi asked, placing his thumb and forefinger on his father's pulse.

"I'm going, boys. This was all I ever wanted to see. Tell your ma I went with her name on my lips . . . Rachel . . . Redbud . . . Tell Red Deer . . ."

"Pa, Pa, lie down for a minute!" Malachi pleaded, alarmed that he had lost his father's pulse.

Jedediah Gill shook his head slowly. "One last look," he said, staring out over the great basin. His hands were growing cold in theirs. His voice was barely audible. "You know, I never saw them," he whispered, touching a finger to the faint scar on his forehead.

"Who, Pa, who?" Micah cried.

"My parents. My ma and pa." Both bent their ears closer to his mouth to hear him gasp, "But I think . . . I'm going to see them . . . soon. . . ."

Actual Historical Characters

Beaujeau, Capt. Daniel de; French officer who ambushed British in 1755

Bigot, François; intendant of Canada in French and Indian War

Bougainville, Louis Antoine de; trusted aide of Montcalm in French and Indian War

Braddock, Maj. Gen. Edward; British commander in North America in 1755

Bradstreet, Simon; governor of Massachusetts in 1690

Dinwiddie, Robert; governor of Virginia in French and Indian War

Duchambon, Chevalier; French commander at Louisbourg in 1710

Dummer, William; lieutenant governor of Massachusetts in 1723

Duquesne, Marquis de; govenor of Canada in 1752

Franklin, Benjamin; deputy postmaster general of colonies in 1755

Frazier, John; English trader in the Ohio country 1752–55

Frontenac, Count de; governor of Canada in 1690

Gage, Lt. Col. Thomas; British infantry commander in 1775

Gist, Christopher; English frontiersman in Pennsylvania in 1753

Half-King; Indian chief of the Ohio friendly to English 1752–53

Halkett, Sir Peter; commander of British advance corps 1755

Hanbury, John; Quaker merchant who misinformed British government in 1755

Hill, General Jack; chief of British ground forces at Quebec in 1711

Howe, Col. William; commander of British light infantry at Quebec in 1759

Johnstone, Chevalier; Scots Jacobite with French at Quebec in 1759

Joincare, Capt. Philippe; French commander at Venango in 1753

Jumonville, Coulon de; French officer killed by Washington in 1754

Levis Chevalier de; French officer at Quebec in 1759

Mackay, Capt.; commander of company of British regulars in 1754

Marin, Gen. de; French commander in Ohio territory in 1752

Mather, Rev. Increase; famous parson at Boston in 1690

Mather, Rev. Cotton; son of above, famous minister

Meneval, Chevalier de; governor of Port Royal in 1690

Monckton, Brig. Gen. Robert; brigade commander at Quebec in 1759

Montcalm, Marquis de; military commander at Quebec in 1759

Montgomery, Capt. Alexander; British officer at Quebec in 1759

Murray, Brig. Gen. James; British brigade commander at Quebec in 1759

Moulton, Capt.; Massachusetts officer in Abnaki War

Nicholson, Francis; conquerer of Port Royal in 1710

Orme, Capt. Robert; British officer and aide to Braddock in 1755

Paddon, Capt.; master of the *Edgar* at Quebec in 1711

Pean, Chevalier de; French officer during French and Indian War

Pean, Madam Marie; wife of above, mistress of Intendant Bigot, same period

Pecaudy, Gen. Claude; commander of Fort Duquesne in 1755

Pepperell, William; English commander at Louisbourg in 1745

Phips, Sir William; Massachusetts commander at Port Royal and Quebec in 1690

Portneuf, Rev. Robin de; French priest massacred with his flock in 1759

Rale, Rev. Sébastien; French Jesuit priest 1704–24

Sainte-Helene, Jacques de; French-Canadian officer in 1690

Sainte-Pierre, Gen. Legardeur de; second French commander at the Ohio

Saunders, Adm. Charles; British naval commander at Quebec in 1759

Shirley, William; governor of Massachusetts in 1745

Shirley, William; son of above, secretary to Braddock in 1755

Stewart, Capt. Robert; British officer with Braddock in 1755

Subercase, Chevalier de; governor of Port Royal in 1710

Shute, Samuel; govenor of Massachusetts in 1723

Townshend, Brig. Gen. George; British brigade commander at Quebec in 1759

Vaudreuil, Marquis de; governor of Canada in Queen Anne's and Abnaki Wars

Van Braam, Capt.; Washington's French interpreter in 1754

Vaudreuil, Marques de; son of above, governor of Canada in French and Indian War

Vaughn, William; regimental commander at Louisbourg in 1745

Vergor, Chevalier Duchambon de; French officer and crony of Bigot in French and Indian War

Vetch, Samuel; English second in command at Port Royal in 1710

Villiers, Coulon de; brother of Jumonville, opponent of Washington in 1754

Walley, John; commander of ground troops at Quebec in 1690

Walker, Adm. Hovenden; British naval commander at Quebec in 1711

Warren, Cmdr.; British naval commander at Louisbourg in 1745

Ward, Ensign; Virginia militia officer at Ohio Forks in 1754

Washington, George; Virginia militia officer 1753–1755

Westbrook, Col.; Massachusetts officer in Abnaki War
Whitefield, Rev. George; preacher of Great Awakening circa 1745
Wolfe, Brig. Gen. James; British commander at Quebec in 1759

About the Author

Born in 1920, Robert Leckie grew up in Rutherford, N.J., where at sixteen he began working as a sportswriter for *The Record* of Bergen County. Mr. Leckie joined the Marines on Pearl Harbor Day, 1941, and served nearly three years in the Pacific as a machine gunner and scout for the First Marine Division, being both wounded and decorated. From that experience came *Helmet for My Pillow,* a personal narrative of the war which he wrote while pursuing his postwar career as a newspaperman and newsreel editor. With its publication in 1957, Mr. Leckie devoted himself full time to writing and has since had more than thirty books published, most of them on military history, as well as short stories and articles.

Mr. Leckie, who attended New York University and Fordham, is married to the former Vera Keller. They have three grown children and live in Byram Township, New Jersey, where Mr. Leckie is now at work on the second novel in the Americans at War Series.

SIGNET Books You'll Enjoy